WAR CHILD

Russ Elliott

All flesh is not the same flesh:
but there is one kind of flesh of men,
another flesh of beasts,
another of fishes, and another of birds.

I Corinthians 15:39

INTRODUCTION

In 2003, a team of scientists in Shanghai developed the first successful human-animal hybrid in a laboratory dish. Fusing human cells in rabbit eggs, they created the embryos of a new creature that was half rabbit and half human.

Eleven years later, a team of researchers injected mouse pups with human brain cells. Within a year, the human cells had multiplied to the point where the mice's brains were considered to be half human. As a result, the memories of the humanized mice were four times greater than those of a common mouse.

On March 27, 2019, researchers from Kunming Institute of Zoology in China made an unnerving leap forward. They successfully inserted the human brain gene MCPH1 into rhesus monkeys. The MCPH1 gene allows the human brain to develop more slowly and, accompanied by a process called neural plasticity, allows the human brain to continue to grow beyond infancy and into adulthood. It is this longer growth process that accounts for our higher level of intelligence, whereas the brain development in primates ends after birth.

This changed on March 27. As a result of receiving the human brain gene, the altered monkeys exhibited longer "human-like brain development" and showed marked increases in short-term memory. Some researchers involved with the experiment admitted that the study was morally wrong. However, despite the controversy, the experiments were scheduled to continue.

Presently, researchers at the University of California are attempting to create human-animal hybrid embryos known as chimeras, which they believe could be studied to help us learn more about the progression of certain diseases.

"We're not trying to make a chimera just because we want to see some kind of monstrous creature. We're doing this for a biomedical purpose."

Pablo J. Ross, reproductive biologist at UC Davis

"The road to hell is paved with good intentions."

Henry G. Bohn's *A Book of Proverbs*, 1855

WAR CHILD

CHAPTER 1

INSPIRATION

Under the cover of night, the hunter moved swiftly across the Afghanistan desert, taking strides far greater than any creature known to man. The dry desert air whistled between the deep, bark-like ridges in its gnarled back. The passing clusters of locoweed and sagebrush were just a blur. Now, every sensory device tingled, assuring the beast that each stride brought it closer to its reward.

A sole mountain of rock reached up from a dark horizon like an ancient pyramid, barely discernible in the pitch. A light flickered at its base, offering the only hint of life on the desolate landscape. Pressing on with its cheetah-like gait, the distant light slowly took on the form of a tent.

Closing to within fifty feet of the tent, the beast paused behind a rock and crouched low on all fours. Clouds of dust settled around its clawed feet and hands as its lantern-like eyes locked on the target.

A woman's shrill scream escaped from the tent.

The beast crept out from behind the rock, every sense heightened. Like a sprinter getting set, its hind quarters crouched lower, its rear claws pressed deeper into the sand.

A single guard was visible, an AK-47 assault rifle dangling from a strap over his shoulder, his black beard arcing in the wind. He lit a cigarette, dark, weathered cheeks and the folds in his turban glowing briefly in the flair of the lighter.

The creature leapt forward, and in a single bound crossed thirty feet of desert and landed, crouching low.

Tossing his cigarette, the guard squinted into the pitch, thinking his eyes were deceiving him. Before he could aim the rifle, there was a hiss of torn flesh. A swath of blood crossed the tent, and the rifle hit the sand.

The hunter rose onto its hind legs in front of the vertical gap in the tent, lifting higher until its glowing eyes towered seven feet above the sand. The muffled screams from inside grew louder. Slipping its clawed fingers into the gap, the creature ripped open the entryway, its eyes adjusted to the glaring light.

Inside, three men in veiled headwraps and black sweatsuits stood lined before a camera. The first man to the left held a bound woman horizontally across his waist, while the second man pressed a machete to her throat. The third man's fingers were deeply entwined in her long, auburn hair, pulling it taut as if ready to raise her severed head to the camera.

Flanking the cameraman were four men with their backs to the entryway flap, cheering and waving their weapons in revelry of the woman's terrified screams. It was a scene straight from hell.

And the devil had just arrived.

Simultaneously, the veiled figures froze before the camera. Although their faces were covered, their eyes professed their terror. The man holding the woman dropped her to the sand. The man with the machete reeled backward from the intruder, while the third man yanked his fingers from the woman's hair.

However, those with their backs to the entry carried on with the celebration, oblivious to the intrusion.

The beast unleashed a guttural roar.

The cheering ceased as the men with their backs to the

creature turned around. Eyes bugged out. Jaws dropped. Machine guns whirled with the men cocking them.

Whap! A clawed hand hit the camera, knocking it from the tripod and sending it spiraling through the side of the tent.

At first there was stunned silence, save the bound woman screaming and squirming in the sand. Then, seeing the postures of those around her, she too looked up and went stiff in further shock.

A man directly in front of the creature was the first to open fire. Dipping its left shoulder, the beast deflected the bullets with its gnarled back, sending two of the rounds into the face of a nearby soldier while the rest riddled holes through the top of the tent. The beast then thrust upward with its right arm and severed the gunman's hand at the wrist. The MAC-10 machine gun with the hand still gripping the handle twirled through the air, spraying rounds until the rogue weapon hit the ground, kicking up pelts of sand.

A high-pitched wail, and the man wielding the machete leapt over the woman and charged the creature. He was abruptly met by a gnarled backhand that sent his turban unfolding through the air as his headless body stumbled to the sand.

Flames leapt from gun barrels, and spent shells tumbled through the air as the tent erupted in gunfire. The veiled figures surrounded the intruder, but at such close range, the outnumbered creature still held the advantage. Another weapon hit the sand—then two more. For a brief moment, all machine gun fire ceased, and rapid Arabic prayers filled the tent.

But their prayers went unanswered that night.

The beast belted out a raspy war cry, a sound not out of rage, but rather sheer elation. And as naturally as an eagle soars on high, a fish swims or a nightingale sings her beautiful song, the abomination of nature unleashed a torrent of violence on those unfortunate enough to still be alive until only one man remained.

The final figure squared off with the creature. He pulled his scarf away to reveal the wide grin that was sitting atop his long, black beard. He ripped open his shirt to expose a tangle of dynamite and wires. A hideous wail, and he rushed the beast—detonator in hand and a crazed look in his eye.

Snatching him by the neck, the beast turned and flung him through the entryway. A beat later, a plume of sand erupted outside as flames leapt through the torn opening in the tent, igniting the fabric.

The creature closed its eyes. And like a heroin addict getting a fix, the animal shuddered in ecstasy as an intense rush of pleasure flooded its being. A euphoric growl rose above the crackling flames. Turning away from the burning entry, the beast scanned the sand floor to confirm all hostiles had been neutralized.

Stepping over the carnage, the creature reached down to the trembling woman and raised her to her feet. A swoosh from a clawed finger, and her rope bound wrists were freed.

She looked up at the creature, her tear-streaked and bruised face a mixture of terror and confusion. "How . . . who?" was all she could muster.

The beast reached behind her, and with a blood-streaked saber protruding from its forearm, slashed an opening in the rear of the tent. The loose fabric flapped in the downdraft from a helicopter's thumping rotors as a glaring spotlight pierced the opening.

The woman stepped through the torn fabric, out of a burning hell and into freedom as the bright light enveloped her form. Her auburn hair flailed in the wind until it, too, was overcome by the light. . . .

The sound of the thundering rotors faded into the low

hum of a ceiling fan as research geneticist Jim Randle awakened on his couch. *A dream for now, but soon to be a reality*, he thought, staring blankly at the fan's slow-moving blades.

He was sprawled in the small office of his laboratory, which was located in a vast, wooded area south of Orlando, Florida. It was an ideal spot, chosen for its proximity to MacDill Air Force Base and Orlando, a cornucopia of the exotic animal species whose DNA formed the backbone of his work.

"Well, daylight's burning," he muttered with a grunt.

Rising from the worn green couch, his gaze met a copy of the *Orlando Sentinel* lying on an end table. Its cover displayed a familiar face surrounded with long, auburn hair. The block letters above the photo read, "Terrorists Post Video of US Reporter's Beheading."

"If only I'd finished sooner," he whispered as his eyes studied the contours of the young face that now haunted his dreams. Although the paper was three months old, he left it there. Not to torture himself, but as a constant reminder of the urgency and necessity of his work.

Stretching out the kinks in his sixty-one-year-old neck, he noted the time on a digital clock beside the newspaper. "Fifteen minutes already," he gasped.

He was eight days into what he called a "da Vinci"—sleeping fifteen minutes every four hours while working around the clock. Practiced by the original renaissance man, Leonardo da Vinci, the bizarre sleep cycle required only 1.5 hours of sleep per day. This allowed the Italian master an extra six hours of productivity daily, which he claimed helped him produce such works as the *Mona Lisa* and *The Last Supper*.

Opening the door to his office, Jim's gaze drifted down a long hallway, past doors with tall windows that peered into his various laboratories. *Yes, but I'm soon to unveil a masterpiece of my own*, he thought as his gaze stopped on the thick steel door at the end of the hall. The only door without a window.

~ ~ ~

At 10:30 AM, the Oak Ridge High School hallway was alive with the clatter and chatter of students as Frank Wheeler closed his locker and eased back against it. The wiry seventeen-year-old wore weathered jeans, a sleeveless Rolling Stones T-shirt, and his jet-black hair combed straight back. He had crystal-blue eyes, a misleading facade to the disturbing thoughts that lingered behind them.

He looked down from an *Oak Ridge Pioneers* banner stretched above the lockers, and into the passing river of students. Frank ignored the guys and only made eye contact with the girls, who almost always responded with a flirtatious smile.

Everywhere it's the same. Students were like clones from one of five different molds: the jocks, the geeks, the stoners, the popular girls, and most pathetic of all, the invisible.

Orlando, though, was a lot different from the Bronx, where his fellow gang members had deemed him "Frankie the Wheel," for his ability to break into a car, hot-wire it, and be burning rubber in under a minute.

And oh how Frank loved being at a new school where no one knew him. He could assume any identity he wanted. "A fresh start for the both of us," his mother would always say with renewed zeal. But to Frank, it was like all of his sins were forgiven, and he could start anew.

A jovial, freckle-faced boy with bushy red hair and lugging a huge backpack stepped up to Frank. "Hey, aren't you in my fourth period science class with Mr. Wellerby?" He extended a hand. "I'm William Sanders. I hear that you're from New York."

Beyond William's backpack, Frank spotted a blond ponytail bobbing through the crowd. "Nice to meet you. Now hit the bricks, Willie. I've got business to tend to." He turned the boy around and shoved him back into the passing current of students.

"The new guy at a new school. Now I just need the right girl to make the right impression," Frank muttered, his eyes plucking the pretty blonde from the crowd. *Michelle Winters from second period biology class. Yep, it looks like you're the one*, he thought as she and a nerdy kid she was talking with came nearer.

Frank had to act fast.

Without the slightest hesitation, he grabbed a passing boy by the shirt, picked him up, and slammed him back against the lockers, his sneakers dangling high above the floor.

"Michelle Winters is not a slut!" Frank barked at the boy's face at point-blank range. "Say it again and I'll break every—" Frank paused when he saw Michelle frozen in the crowd, her eyes and mouth agape. *Wham!* He slammed the boy back against the lockers again, then released his shirt, letting him fall to the ground.

"I-I didn't say nothing," the terrified young man stuttered as he scurried away, bumping into students like a pinball until he disappeared into the crowd. "I didn't say nothing!" The boy's voice rang through the hall.

"Yeah, sure you didn't, you little liar," Frank hollered.

A final sneer in the fleeing boy's direction, and Frank turned to Michelle, who still seemed to be trying to comprehend the situation.

Frank's menacing snarl transformed into a gentle smile. "Sorry. I didn't mean to embarrass you. But where I come from, a guy doesn't say something like that and get away with it." He winked a piercing blue eye. "Especially about a girl like you."

Michelle blushed and returned the smile. She seemed to be at a loss for words. "It's just that nobody's ever . . . I mean, no one has—"

"What?" Frank broke in. "Stood up for you before? Come on, that's hard to believe. Especially for someone like you."

Michelle glanced at her geeky companion, who didn't seem much impressed with the barbaric act of chivalry. She extended a delicate hand to Frank. "Michelle Winters, and this is Daren Freeman. Nice to meet you." She squinted. "Aren't you in my second period biology class?"

"Oh, am I?" Frank faked, gently taking her hand. "Frank Wheeler. The pleasure is all mine."

The fifth period bell rang, breaking the magic moment.

"Well, I'd better get to class." Michelle started to back away without breaking eye contact. She paused and shyly looked down. "After school, a few of us are getting together at Legends Diner." She raised her gaze, coy. "You're welcome to join us . . . if you like."

Frank thought on it for a long moment, her hazel eyes beaming up at him. "Yeah, I know the place." He shrugged. "Sure, why not?"

"Cool, see ya there," she said with another warm smile. However, Daren didn't seem to share her enthusiasm for the invitation as the pair filed in behind the passing students.

Worked like a charm. Frank watched her ponytail fade into the myriad of criss-crossing students. *Then again, why wouldn't it? Why should Orlando be any different than the last two schools?*

CHAPTER 2

THE BAD SEED

Peering through a large magnifying glass, Jim Randle studied the small GPS receiver in his hand. He was in his main laboratory, filled with stainless steel tables supporting DNA scanners, microscopes, gel electrophoresis machines, and a plethora of other equipment vital to his work.

The south wall was lined with large stainless steel coolers, while the far wall held a more ominous sight. Stretching from floor to ceiling was a photograph of New York's twin towers. Taken at the moment the second airliner had struck, the photo captured the first building billowing black smoke while a swath of fire penetrated the second building. Above the burning towers was his mantra: *Never Forget.*

Similar items were placed throughout the lab, such as newspaper articles relating to the 2,977 victims. "Inspirations," he called them, used to keep his motivation high. It was a tactic that his coach had suggested he use decades ago during his college basketball days. And sure enough, it still worked.

"Yes, the final brush stroke on the masterpiece," Jim muttered, affixing the third electrode to the receiver in his hand. Once installed, the GPS receiver would pick up a remote signal, and via the electrodes, deliver it to the creature's nervous system.

A doorbell chimed through the laboratory, making Jim

jump and yank one of the electrodes from the receiver. "How am I supposed to get anything done with these interruptions?" he grumbled, placing the component into a steel tray.

Exiting the lab, he headed along the well-worn, tan linoleum floor that led to the front door.

On the opposite side of the hallway, across from the various laboratories, were the rooms that housed the more docile test subjects. A pig, mice, snakes, iguanas, armadillos, and various species of small primates peered out from cages behind the glass doors. Another room held fish, eels, and other forms of marine life as the blue hue from the aquariums danced along the glass. Outside were the kennels for the dogs, five more pigs, a reinforced steel cage that temporarily housed a grizzly bear, and a twenty-foot pit that contained two juvenile alligators.

Jim mis-stepped. He took a moment to bend his left knee that was locking up on him again. The doorbell again echoed along the hallway. *It's probably Wendy with Arnold's antibiotic.*

Whoever it was resorted to pounding on the door. "I'm coming," he hollered, increasing his stride. *That doesn't sound like Wendy. She's not so impatient.*

Reaching the foyer, Jim pressed the button on a wall monitor. It showed a man in his fifties banging on the steel door as the dreadful sound echoed inside. "Marty," Jim muttered. "Like I really have the time for this." He contemplated ignoring the guy completely and returning to his work.

"Open up, Jim. I know you're in there," said a muffled voice from the other side of the steel door. "Your truck's out here."

Jim pressed a button, and a massive lock clanked. The thick door cracked open. "Oh, Marty, what a pleasant surprise." Jim's words were dripping with sarcasm.

Marty didn't wait for an invite, but rather forced his way inside.

"Oh . . . well, come right in, my dear brother."

Marty was the spitting image of his older sibling as far as his receding gray hairline, green eyes, and tall stature, only he was much more fit. Standing side by side, they could have passed for the before and after photos of the same person in a diet commercial. Marty was also sporting a Magic Kingdom T-shirt and bad case of sunburn.

"I know you don't like for me to barge in on you like this, but Linda and I are worried about you."

"I thought your flight left yesterday," Jim said, not hiding his disappointment.

"We decided to stay an extra day so Tommy could do the Jurassic Park ride at Universal. A shame you couldn't have at least joined us for lunch." Marty sighed. "Tommy's eight, and I can count on one hand the times you've seen him."

"Sorry, Marty, but I'm on a tight schedule, so . . ."

Marty leaned closer to Jim and squinted. "My God, your eyes. Don't tell me you're still following that crazy sleeping schedule?"

"Takes a little getting used to, but one can't deny its efficiency."

"Oh yes, the great Leonardo da Vinci used it," Marty bellowed dramatically. "Well, are you aware, my dear brother, that Nikola Tesla also tried to mimic da Vinci's sleep cycle. Many believe that it drove him to his nervous breakdown at the age of twenty-five." He then added, "You might try Albert Einstein's sleep schedule: ten hours of sleep per night, plus frequent naps. That one I could get onboard with."

"Perhaps you should. Then you would most likely be sleeping this very minute instead of interrupting my work," Jim scoffed as he turned back toward his lab.

Trailing his brother, Marty looked at the various species of animals inside the windows they passed. "Every time I come here, there are more animals." They ambled by a room stacked with aquariums containing numerous species of snakes. In one aquarium, a king cobra lifted from the sand and flared its back, darting its tongue at them. In the containment beside the cobra lay the thick, brownish-green trunk of an anaconda. "I wish you would let me bring Tommy in here to see all this."

"I've told you this is not a safe place for children. Other than the veterinarian, you're the only one I allow in here."

Nearing the main lab, Jim's left knee locked again, making him catch himself on the door handle.

"Come on. Jim," Marty blurted. "That knee's still giving you trouble because you won't take the time for rehab. ACL surgery shouldn't leave you with such a limp. You're still a young man. You don't have to walk like that."

Jim's patience was nearing its end. "I'm confused, dear brother. Did you come here for an intervention or to give me a physical examination?"

"All right, all right." Marty threw his hands up. "I'll lighten up. It's just that I worry . . . the physician in me."

The duo headed further along the hallway, passing more stacked cages and aquariums behind the windows of the doors. Marty looked through another window where a pair of rhesus monkeys were swinging in a large cage. "So, all these animals are hybrids, sharing genes from other animals?"

"Most of them, but not all."

"But they don't look like it," Marty said. "Most of them appear quite normal."

"On the outside, yes," Jim said. "But many of them have blood and internal organs composed of genes from other species. Take for example the rhesus monkeys you're looking at. In one of them, I replaced almost every glial cell in its brain with human cells, leaving only the monkey neurons intact. The human cells multiplied at an incredible rate. Within a year, their glial cells had been completely replaced by human brain cells. When tested, the memory of the altered monkey scored four times higher than its counterpart. But when you look at the two, you can't tell them apart."

"My God, Jim. Do the ethics of your work ever bother you?"

"I'm hardly the first to do this." Jim snickered. "Back in 2014, a group of researchers did the exact same thing with mice. But as far as ethics go, my dear brother, I might ask you how ethical is Parkinson's disease?"

"Yes, all in the name of finding a cure for Parkinson's disease?" Marty questioned.

"That's right."

"Parkinson's you say?" Marty muttered coyly. "Yes, I recall reading something about inserting human stem cells into the brains of rats infected with the disease. If your work is similar in nature, why do you need so many different species to test?"

Before opening the door to the main lab, Jim looked back to find Marty staring through a window where a large pig was rooting around a dirt floor. For a long moment, Marty looked up and down the hallway as if taking in the sheer number of animals in containment. "Jim," he said in a dull voice, "I think I know what you're really up to here." He gave a slow nod. "I've had my suspicions all along."

Jim's hand froze on the door handle. *I knew I should have never brought him in here.*

Marty then turned to face him with a big wide grin. "You're building a huge ark out back, aren't you?"

Jim gave a chuckle of relief. "We get enough rainfall around here to consider it," he said, opening the door to the main lab.

Once inside, Jim noted Marty staring beyond the tables filled with equipment, to the image of the burning towers on the back wall. But rather than pointing out the elephant in the room, Marty seemed content to turn his attention to the framed pictures on a wall to their left. They were from happier times that they both knew so well.

They paused before a picture of a young, strapping blond basketball player poised at the free-throw line. "Remember that guy, the Thumper?" Marty said. "You were a brute. Remember how if anyone gave you a cheap shot, you would thump your chest and point them out." Marty grinned with the pride of a younger brother. "They never made it to the end of the game. The Thumper took them out. What happened to that guy, huh? Do you even take the time to shoot a few hoops, check out the playoffs on TV?"

"Life happened to that guy." Jim was staring at a younger version of himself with an attractive woman with curly, blond hair and a little boy whose features mirrored them both. A captured moment from his life prior to September 11, 2001.

Marty rested a hand on his brother's shoulder. "Look, Jim, you can't bring them back by burying yourself in a lab like this. I know it's hard, but it's been over two decades. You have to let it go."

"You don't know hard," Jim snapped.

His brother gestured at the various newspaper clippings and the massive image of the twin towers on the back wall. "I know all of this isn't healthy. You can't keep doing this to yourself!" Marty took in a deep breath, as if trying to regain control of his emotions. "Whatever it is you're working on will be here when you get back."

"Get back?" Jim's brow furrowed.

"Come with Linda and me, back to Colorado for a week. Just one week. We'll go fishing, cycling, get that knee of yours back in shape. We might even take in a Denver Nuggets game like old times." He looked through the window, toward the animals contained on the other side of the hallway. "As far as your friends here, you could have that gorgeous veterinarian feed them for a week. What do you say?"

As Marty rambled on about Colorado like a desperate tour guide, Jim returned his attention to the GPS receiver. Studying the electrodes beneath the magnifying glass, he said, "You can stop the pitch, Marty. The answer is no. Same as last month, and the month before."

"As I would have guessed." Marty sighed. "Suppose I just like hearing the sound of my own voice." He leaned over the table where Jim was working. "What's that? It looks like some sort of receiver?"

"It is."

"And what does a receiver have to do with finding a cure for Parkinson's?"

"I believe that question exceeds the amount of allowable questions for one visit." Jim replied.

The chime of the doorbell echoed through the lab.

"Saved by the bell," Marty said. "Suppose I should be on my way. We have a flight to catch."

Leaving the magnifying glass, Jim headed for the door. "That must be Wendy, the vet. Hopefully she has the antibiotic for Arnold, one of the pigs."

Matching pace with his brother along the hallway, Marty grinned. "Wendy, huh? If you were ever going to spend some time with your own species, I would start with her."

A click and a clank of the metal lock, and Jim opened the door to find an attractive, petite woman in her mid-forties. She wore khaki shorts and a beige button-down shirt, and her honey-blond hair was pulled back in a ponytail. She had a satchel in one hand and a surprised look in her eye.

She glanced toward the white Mustang parked in the

driveway. "When I first pulled up, I thought I was at the wrong address when I saw an occupied vehicle in the driveway." She snickered. "Then I assumed that someone was lost."

Marty stepped outside of the door. "Afraid I'm not here for directions. I'm his brother, Marty."

"He has a flight to catch," Jim interjected and waved to the brunette and young boy awaiting Marty in the rented Mustang.

Stepping past Wendy, Marty glanced back at Jim. "Remember your own species," he said with a wink, pointing at Wendy's back. Nearly tripping over his feet as he turned around, Marty proceeded to jog toward the car. He and Linda would go on to discuss every detail of his strange visit with Jim for weeks. But before the door had even closed, Jim had expelled it to the furthest reaches of his mind.

Wendy stepped inside the foyer. "Well, the bloodwork showed that you were right, a bacterial infection." Following Jim down the hallway, she reached into her satchel. "I'll start him off with a shot of antibiotics." Withdrawing a bottle of pills, she tossed them to Jim. "Then it's one of these every twelve hours until they're gone."

Jim felt his knee tighten again, which caused him to misstep.

"You know a little physical therapy would probably get rid of that limp," Wendy suggested.

"So I've heard," muttered Jim. He opened the door to reveal an exceptionally large pig rooting around in the dirt floor near a trough.

"Wow, Arnold looks bigger every time I see him," she said. "I guess he must be your favorite, the way you keep him inside and not out back with the others."

"Oh, he's my special boy indeed," Jim said as he stroked the huge animal behind one ear.

"Isn't he also the culprit behind your torn ACL?" Wendy extracted a syringe from her satchel.

"That was more my fault. I should have known better than to get between Arnold and his trough at feeding time."

She knelt down onto one knee and injected the enormous swine, which didn't as much as flinch—just continued chewing on a corn cob. "So how's the research coming along? Making any progress?"

"Oh, yes," Jim said, fighting the insatiable urge to return to his work.

"After losing my dad to complications related to Parkinson's, I'll do anything I can to help." She glanced up at him. "Like the time I risked my job, not to mention my butt, to get you DNA samples from the gorilla and other exotic species I treat at Central Florida Zoo." Capping the empty syringe, she nodded with pride. "But if it helps to put an end to such a horrible disease, it was well worth the risk."

Oh, it'll help cure a disease, Jim thought. *Not Parkinson's, but rather the disease that laid claim to nearly three thousand lives on September 11, 2001.*

Jim had often wondered if Wendy would be so helpful if she knew the truth behind his work. Or for that matter, how she might feel to know that thumping inside the chest of the pig that she had just injected was a hybrid replacement heart for the greatest killing machine the world had ever known.

~~~

Det. Scott Pine sat alone in a corner booth of Legends Diner polishing off a burger and fries. He wore a gray suit and his short, brown hair combed to one side. Legends, as the locals called it, was a throwback to the golden era of Hollywood, complete with celebrity lookalike food servers, retro dining tables, and countless pictures of vintage movie stars adorning the walls. Outside, more celebrity imposters on roller skates affixed food trays to car doors like drive-ins of old.

Scott could live without the Hollywood motif. What retained his patronage was the Brando Burger: a half-pound of Angus beef for $6.95. Not a bad price for this neighborhood.

The diner's close proximity to the police station made it a favorite with members of the OPD, as the row of dark blue shirts at the bar would attest. The reasonable prices and drive-in atmosphere also made it a hot spot for local students who flooded the place after school.

The detective glanced at his watch. *Well, it's about that time.*

A transplant from Miami, the forty-two-year-old had only been in Orlando for one week. And thus far, the reception from his fellow members of law enforcement had been anything but warm. Being the son of a renowned Miami judge, Scott suspected his mother might have pulled a string or two to help expedite his switch. To make matters worse, word had it that one of the locals was next in line to make detective until Scott's relocation bumped him from the spot. And every smug glance back from the blue shirts along the barstools was an pointed reminder. *Gaining their trust is going to be an uphill climb.*

His gaze drifted into the parking lot that was now crawling with students. Groups of teenagers conversed by their cars, listening to music while James Dean and Marilyn Monroe lookalikes wheeled and weaved around them, toting food-laden trays.

In a strange way, Scott felt he could more easily identify with the teens than his peers. At five seven and with his youthful good-looks still intact, he could have easily passed for one of them. That had been another hurdle in itself. In spite of being a seasoned detective, he looked like he'd just stepped out of the academy.

His eyes stopped on a dirt bike affixed to the bed of an old pickup truck. A Honda CR250, to be exact. The sight of the bike transported him to another time and place.

Could I still even ride one of those things?

The five deputies rose from their barstools and ambled past him without as much as a nod his way. "And a good day to you gentlemen too," Scott muttered.

A minute or so later, one of the officers came back into the diner and made a beeline toward the detective's table.

Scott silently groaned.

Grabbing a chair from another table, the officer turned it around backward and pushed it to the end of Scott's booth. Plopping down onto it, the thirty-year-old stared at Scott with a big goofy grin. "You're him, aren't you?"

"Could you be more specific?"

"I saw the way you were looking at that bike. You're Scott Pine, the motocross star."

Scott nodded with relief. It could have been worse. He took a sip of his water. "That was a while ago."

"Monty Cline." The young officer eagerly extended a hand. "And I was there," he blurted, "at Carlsbad Motocross Park the year you were mixing it up with the top pros. You were flying. Even Ricky Carmichael could barely keep up with you. You had the lead, and on the last lap, something happened. Your bike broke."

Scott could remember it like it was yesterday. "I ran out of gas."

"That's right." Monty drew a hand to his forehead. "That was a heartbreaker. But after the speed you showed that day, I thought you would have picked up a factory ride, like with Kawasaki or Honda. But I don't recall seeing much more of you."

"The next weekend at Millville, I broke my wrist during qualifiers," Scott said. "I came back the next season. But the travel and bike repairs . . . it just got to expensive."

There was a loud knocking on the window of the front door. Looking back in that direction, Scott saw an officer glaring at Monty and pointing at his watch.

Monty shot up from his chair. "I've got to go. But it was a pleasure to meet you, Scott. A real pleasure."

"Likewise." Scott nodded, and the young man was off. *Guess I'm not completely invisible*, he thought, watching the officer bolt through the door and catch up to the other men in blue along the sidewalk. Draining his glass of water, the detective slapped a generous tip on the table and headed for the door. His waiter, Charlie Chaplin, tipped his hat to him in passing.

Reaching the door, Scott held it open for three teens who were coming in. A cute blonde gave him a polite thank-you as did the second young man. But the third guy with black hair just gave him a long look and then winked. "Thanks, copper." His smirk was unsettling.

Once outside the diner, the detective looked back through the glass door to the lanky teen inside. *That guy looks like trouble.* And Scott had a keen sense of detecting trouble. His mother claimed it was a survival instinct that he'd developed at an early age to avoid bullies. But that guy in the Rolling Stones t-shirt didn't belong with the other two. The trio reminded him of a wolf trailing two sheep.

~~~

"What made you think that dude was a cop?" Darren asked Frank as they searched for an open table.

"I can smell 'em from a mile away," Frank said, taking a look back at the door. He saw the man in the suit still looking in his direction and mimicked firing a shot at him with his finger.

Finding an empty table, Frank allowed Michelle to slide

into the booth first and motioned for Darren to sit beside her. Frank then eased in across from them until he was face to face with Michelle.

The Hollywood theme is full-tilt around here, Frank thought, noting the Elvis impersonator with tacky, paste-on sideburns flipping burgers behind bar. Whenever someone paid their bill at the register, he belted out from the grill, "Thank you. Thank you very much."

"Cool place." Frank nodded to Michelle.

More like cheesy, he thought. But Michelle seemed to like it, and that was all that mattered. He withdrew a menu from a plastic jukebox that served as a menu holder and handed it to Michelle. He made Darren reach across and get his own.

As Michelle read the menu, he studied the highlights in her blond hair that she was now wearing loose, the silky strands falling just below her shoulders. She was different, a step up from the hardened, streetwise girls from the Bronx.

Frank knew he wasn't Michelle's type. She was most likely used to dating football players or other jocks. Frank could have easily fit into that mold if he so chose. He had the size and the aggression for football. The only problem was this: no coach, or anyone else for that matter, was about to tell him what to do.

A plump Marilyn Monroe rolled up to their table. She took a pen from behind one ear and flipped open a notepad. "Are you guys ready to order?"

Frank looked up at her with a sexy smile. "You know, you really make a great Marilyn."

"Thanks." The waitress's eyes lit up. "You really think so?"

"Yeah, postmortem," Frank blurted. He slapped the table and laughed aloud as the young Marilyn rolled away from the table, clearly upset. Michelle and Darren merely chuckled, which disappointed Frank.

"Hey, man, that was a little harsh, don't you think?" Darren said.

"Nah," Frank said. "She looked stuck-up . . . had it coming." Frank was a master at justifying his actions, a craft that he had perfected on his enabling mother. He turned his gaze to Michelle. "I like a girl who is really beautiful, but isn't always trying to prove it to everyone. You know . . . because she doesn't have to."

Michelle blushed and lowered her gaze to the menu, then looked back up at him with a guarded smile.

You have her now, Frank congratulated himself. He knew that deep inside all girls wanted a bad boy, and he was the genuine article. Now if he could just find a way to impress her, a way to seal the deal.

Darren dropped his menu onto the table with a sigh. "It's not like we need these anymore . . . I don't think Marilyn's coming back." Turning his attention to Michelle, he asked, "How's Tuffy doing now?"

"Oh, he's good now," Michelle said.

"Tuffy?" Frank squinted at her.

"One of her cats that fell from a tree," Darren said. "One of her *seven* cats."

"You have seven cats?"

"And four dogs," Michelle added with pride.

"Where do you live, a friggin zoo?"

She then pulled up an image on her phone and turned it to Frank. "And one of these."

Frank studied the long, furry rodent. "That looks like a long New York rat."

"It's Miley, my ferret."

"Well, as far as your dogs go, I wouldn't let them venture too close to Belle Street," Darren warned.

"Yeah? Why not?" Frank drummed his fingers on the

table.

"They found a dead German shepherd near there. Its paws were swollen, and the fur was stripped from its tail. It escaped from a so-called animal shelter near there." Darren said. "Didn't you hear about it? It was on the news last night."

"*So-called* animal shelter," Frank repeated.

Darren placed his elbows on the table. "I know a guy in school whose dad works for FedEx. He once caught a glimpse inside the place. He said there are all kinds of animals in there, also heard lots of barking out back. But the lab equipment that he saw . . . whoa. Lots of big, high-tech stuff."

Michelle's lips twisted in disgust. "Who knows what they're doing to the animals in there?"

Frank shook his head with his best look of concern. He couldn't have cared less about the fate of any dog, but he was listening.

Darren leaned in closer to Frank. "The guy who runs the lab comes into the grocery store where I work. He drives a blue F-150 and always has a few dogs in the back." He glanced over his shoulder and lowered his voice. "Now that I know what he's doing with them, next time he shows up, I have half a mind to let them out of his truck."

Michelle's eyes lit up. "You should do it!"

And just like that, the opportunity that Frank had awaited presented itself. "No." Frank grinned. "Why not let them *all* go?"

"What?" Michelle stared at him as if he were insane. "We can't just march up to the lab and let all of the dogs loose."

"Why not?" Frank smirked. "Chances are, what he's doing up there isn't legal. He's the one breaking the law. So if you look at it from the right perspective, we would be on the side of justice." Frank was amazed by the lie that had just rolled off of his tongue. It sounded so convincing that he almost believed it himself.

Darren leaned back from the table. "Okay, so we let the animals loose. Then what . . . they'll just get more?"

Frank laced his fingers. "Not if we get rid of the root cause of the problem."

Michelle's pretty eyes went wide. "What are you saying?"

Frank released a wicked grin. "You guys ever hear of a Molotov cocktail?"

CHAPTER 3

THE AWAKENING

Jim Randle stood in the bed of his F-150, parked in the ten-acre field behind his lab. He looked up from the remote control in his hands to the small, plane-like drone soaring above the treetops beyond the property line. A twelve-foot chain-link fence skirted the vast field. Jim thought how his creation could have ripped through the fence as if it were rice paper if not for the electrical current coursing through it. An electrical frequency that triggered a receiver in the creature's back to deliver a disabling shock to its nervous system if it drew within ten feet of the fence. But for the moment, his master work remained at rest in its lair while Jim tested the drone.

He pressed a button on the control unit that read "Perimeter." The red button flashed three times, confirming that the mode had been changed from "ID."

"It all seems to be in working order." Jim said, unable to hear himself above the symphony of barks echoing from the kennels behind him. Beside the dog kennels was a pig pen. And butting up against the back of the lab, was a large, barred containment for a Kodiak brown bear that seemed to do little more than sleep.

Turning the joystick on the remote control, he watched the military drone arc into a turn and soar silently over the containment.

"Well, General, we may make the September eleventh

deadline just yet," he muttered. Still two months out, it was the date that he had chosen to unveil his masterpiece to the military. Just one call would put everything into play. A call to his investor, a retired Air Force general who would arrange for the top brass at MacDill to show up at this very field for the presentation of their lives.

General Willham, as Jim referred to him, came from a family who'd acquired their wealth through Texas oil. Not only was he the sole investor in the project, he was the only person other than Jim who knew of its existence. Secrecy was imperative. Jim knew that if the media got wind of what he was up to, angry hordes would likely be showing up at his door with pitchforks and torches.

The project hadn't been without its setbacks. Having lost two months recovering from his torn ACL, Jim was still dealing with the German shepherd escape. Had his damage control worked, or were they finally onto him? He was absolutely petrified when he'd realized the story had made the news.

Still, it could have been worse. Fortunately, he was able to retrieve the carcass before the SPCA ran any bloodwork on it. Otherwise, they could have discovered that its feet weren't really swollen from hours of running on the hot pavement, or that its tail wasn't void of hair due to mange, but rather to the simple fact that the animal possessed more armadillo DNA than it did German shepherd. Not only did the creature have the feet and tail of an armadillo, a closer examination would have revealed an elongated snout and scales growing along its underbelly.

"No wonder the bugger could dig three feet beneath the fence to escape," Jim muttered with some admiration.

He contemplated relocating the entire project to a new state. To keep the project under the radar, he had done so four times during the last decade. But another move could push the project back a full year.

No way, he thought, watching the drone again cross the containment and soar out across the treetops. "This time I'm too close."

~~~

The silver Honda Accord headed along Belle Street as it meandered through the dense Florida woods. The evening sun glittered between the trees, sending long shadows of tree trunks reaching across their path. Michelle was driving while Frank rode shotgun. Darren was in the back seat nervously holding a crate full of Molotov cocktails.

Frank studied Michelle's shapely form through her jeans and black hoodie that contained all but a few wayward strands of her blond hair. Darren wore the same get-up. Frank found it amusing how they both wore black hoodies as if it were the gold standard of attire for criminal activity.

Frank looked into the back seat, at the crate containing eight Coke bottles filled with gasoline, a white rag protruding from the mouth of each bottle. He glanced into Darren's terrified eyes and grinned. "Hey, no smoking back there, huh?"

"Yeah right." Darren said, staring at the bottles in his lap as if they could ignite at any second.

Frank returned his attention to the passenger-side window as an old brick building finally appeared between the trees.

"I think this is it," Michelle said.

"Yeah, that's the place." Darren craned his neck toward the window. "There's nothing else out here. And I don't see his blue pickup."

"I don't see any vehicles at all," Frank said. "Looks like we're clear."

Michelle slowed down like she was going to pull into the

driveway.

"No, no. What, are you nuts?" Frank barked. "Keep straight . You can't stop here."

"Why not?" Darren said. "No one's here."

"Surveillance cameras. Go about thirty yards ahead and pull over," Frank said.

Michelle did as told, then turned off the car. In the back seat, Darren's knees were shaking so badly the bottles clanked inside the crate.

"Darren, lighten up back there before you give yourself a heart attack." Frank said, looking back at him. "You've got this right?"

Darren nodded, but the clanking continued.

Frank turned back to Michelle. "The kid surprised me. I didn't think he had the stones to tag along."

He then picked up a plastic bag from between his feet, from which he pulled out a piece of cardboard that had "Outta gas – back soon" scribbled on it in marker. He placed it on the dashboard. "This is in case a cop or someone stops to check out the car before we get back."

"Good thinking," Michelle said with a smile.

Reaching back into the bag, Frank withdrew a clown mask with red hair and a can of black paint.

Michelle pointed, her smile now a frown. "What's that for?"

"The black paint is to block out the lenses of the surveillance cameras, and the mask is so they don't see me doing it."

"How do you know this stuff?" Darren asked.

"I watch a lot of movies." Frank squeezed the red ball of the clown nose, making it honk twice, and exited the car. Holding the can of paint in one hand, he stuck his elbows out to the sides and, taking long goofy steps, marched like a clown toward the lab.

~~~

Ten minutes later, the trio met up at the front door of the building. From the front, the nondescript structure could have been mistaken for a modest home, with its redbrick facade, old wooden door, and single window. But from the side, the unpainted block walls revealed the structure's impressive depth.

Frank had already painted the lenses of the surveillance cameras above the door and on each front corner of the building. He now examined the front door, the clown mask pulled up to the top of his head. He took a step back and then thrust forward. *Wham!* He kicked the door, but it didn't budge. "What the hell," he gasped, limping back from the door. "That's more than just wood; there's friggin metal behind it."

Rubbing his right knee, he glanced around. "You guys stay here. I'll find another way in."

With the clown mask covering his face and a Molotov cocktail in one hand, Frank crept around the west corner of the building. A glance along the roofline for cameras—none—and he continued to follow the long driveway toward where it terminated against a tall fence out back. Towering branches of cypress and pine trees swept gracefully above him.

When he heard the distant barks and yelps coming from behind the fence, he knew this was the place. He noted that every window he passed was painted gray. "He definitely likes his privacy," Frank muttered.

With every step, the barking grew louder. Nearing the tall chain-link fence, Frank froze when he saw the back of a blue truck on the other side. Another step closer revealed someone standing in the bed of the truck. It appeared as if he were flying a remote-control plane.

"Just a little wrinkle in the plan," Frank muttered, noting the gate to the fence was cracked open. He lowered his mask and stepped inside.

Off to his right was the kennel. As if on command, every dog rushed to the west side of the fence, pressing their front paws against it, tongues wagging and saliva flying as they frantically barked at him. But the man in the truck didn't turn around.

Beside the kennel was what looked like a pigpen. Behind the pigpen was a large steel cage that appeared to be empty. A look across the back of the building showed that there were no cameras, so Frank slipped off the mask to improve his vision.

His heart was racing now, giving him a surge of adrenaline that he hadn't felt since he'd left the Bronx. Creeping closer to the truck, Frank poured some of the gasoline from the Molotov cocktail until the weight of the bottle felt right. Gripping the bottle by the neck, he then drew it back.

"Hey, sicko!" Frank hollered.

The instant the man turned around, Frank let it fly. The bottle spun through the air, spitting gasoline until . . . *crash!* It hit the man square in the forehead, sending him backward, over the side of the truck, and onto the ground.

"Bull's-eye!" Frank snapped his fingers and ran toward the fallen man. Meanwhile, the abandoned drone arced over the treetops and disappeared into the woods.

Rounding the open tailgate of the truck, Frank found the man lying flat on his back with his left ankle twisted up behind him. A blood-red circle marked the center of his forehead. His face and shirt reeked of gasoline.

Patting him lightly on the cheek, Frank muttered, "You're out cold. Think you're still breathing though." He extracted a keychain from the man's hip pocket and jingled it with a grin. "This is going to be easier than I thought."

Frank pulled out a lighter and flicked it on.

He studied the flame, savoring the moment—the feeling

of power in holding a life in his hand. The thought of doing the unthinkable brough a gleam to his eye.

Turning his attention from the flame to the man's gas-soaked shirt, he noticed a black lanyard around his neck that was attached to a credit card type of key. He clicked off the lighter. "May as well hang on to this." Slipping the lanyard over the man's head, Frank stuffed it into his pocket and set his sights on the building.

~~~

Waiting at the front door, Darren was growing more anxious. "A cardboard note for the dashboard, a mask, and paint to block out the surveillance cameras." Darren said. "Who knows to do that?"

Michelle shrugged. "It's just common sense, really."

"Yeah, for a career criminal. I'm telling you, this guy's bad news."

"If you felt that way," Michell scoffed, "why did you come along?"

"For you." Darren lowered his voice. "I didn't want to see anything happen to you."

Michelle seemed taken aback and didn't respond.

They turned to a distant yelping. The barking grew louder until a golden retriever and a German shepherd darted out from behind the west corner of the building, crossed the street, and disappeared into the woods. Five more dogs of mixed breeds followed suit, bounding across the street and fading into the shadows of the trees. Bringing up the rear, a pig trotted across the pavement, snorting and grunting as it followed the yelping pack.

"He did it," Michelle gasped.

There was a loud clank from behind. She and Darren turned around to find Frank standing in the open doorway, donning the clown mask with his arms spread wide.

"Welcome to the party, boys and girls."

"You already let the dogs loose." Michelle thrust her arms around him.

Frank picked her up and twirled her around before setting her down just inside the foyer."Only the beginning, my dear. You won't believe this place. It's like a friggin zoo."

Frank propped a chair under the handle to keep the front door open. He then glanced at Darren and nodded toward the crate of Molotov cocktails on the sidewalk. "Get the party favors, will ya?"

Once everyone was inside, Frank tossed each of them an old, rusty golf club.

"Where'd you get these?" Darren asked him, feeling more nervous as the seconds ticked by.

"Lying with a bunch of junk in the back." Frank then looked down the long hallway. "Ahhh, so much to destroy . . . so little time. Where to begin?"

"We've got to let all of the animals out first," Michelle insisted, dropping the golf club.

Darren felt like he was about to pass out as he stared at all of the cages behind the windows. "Guys, I thought we were just gonna set some dogs loose . . . but this. Look at all of them."

Frank slapped a hand on Darren's shoulder. "Lighten up, bud. You've got this. Why don't you and Michelle go let the animals loose?" He honked his clown nose and raised the golf club. "And I'll go do a little lab work."

Darren swallowed hard as he followed Michelle deeper inside the building.

~~~

Still sporting the clown mask, Frank opened the third door on his left and entered the main laboratory. *Wham.* He hit the first monitor that he came to with the club, sending it spiraling to the floor. Skipping and twirling with glee, he smashed his club into another large screen. He paused, noting all the 9/11 images and newspaper clippings along the walls, and raised the mask. "Obsess much?" He then laid eyes on the burning twin towers filling the back wall. "How ironic," he snickered. "That's what this dump is gonna look like when I'm done."

With that, he toppled a steel table, sending the equipment crashing onto the floor. He swung the club across a table filled with beakers, spewing glass across the room. Overturning another steel table, he came to a series of framed pictures along the left wall. He looked at one of a basketball player. "Nice mullet. Must be the fool lying out back," he said with a wicked grin.

His eyes lowered to the picture beneath it. He studied the face of the same man now only older, and the beautiful woman beside him. Frank's eyes stopped on the little boy, and he felt something stir deep inside. The picture reminded him of his family, before his father left. Before he disregarded them like trash. Before Frank started holding the divorce over his mother's head to get whatever he wanted. And long before he lost all respect for her for letting him do so.

The rage swelling inside him reached the surface. He squeezed the handle with both hands and swung with everything he had, shattering the picture. He smashed the picture above it, the one beside it, and didn't stop until not one remained.

He proceeded to topple every table in the room like a man possessed. Even the tall refrigerators didn't escape his wrath as he pushed them over onto steel tables, spewing their contents across the floor. With every table in the room upended, Frank turned his attention to the only item that still stood, a plastic table supporting what appeared to be a high-end scanner. He pushed it over, watching with satisfaction as the scanner toppled onto a stack of newspapers and magazines.

Frank's heart pounded as the insatiable rage continued to course through him like an electrical current. He looked across his wake of destruction, noting the toppled tables and the shattered glass and equipment littering the floor. A nod of approval, and he turned toward the door. Looking into the window across the hallway, he saw a giant pig and grinned. He opened the door and lowered his mask.

~~~

Just inside the lobby, Michelle and Darren had their hands full trying to usher a pair of rhesus monkeys through the front door. Clanking their clubs onto the floor, they tried to coax the primates forward. One had a calm demeanor and simply scooted to the front door and left on its own. The second monkey, however, appeared more erratic, jumping onto a windowsill and landing back into the hallway behind them, squealing and flailing its arms.

The monkey paused, peering down the hallway. A loud squeal, and the primate turned tail and darted through the front door. Michelle and Darren looked in the same direction only to find Frank, with the clown mask still on, barreling down the hallway on the back of a giant pig.

Snorting and grunting, the enormous swine charged in their direction as if it intended to run them over. All the while, Frank waved one hand over his head like a rodeo star. "Get out of the way," he howled. "Go piggy, piggy, piggy, piggy."

Michelle and Darren jumped back into a doorway as Frank and the enormous pig flashed by, just missing them.

Reaching the foyer, Frank leapt from the animal's back, slid across the floor, and caught onto the door frame as the pig shot out of the doorway. He then fell back against the wall, laughing hysterically. "Wooooh, that was one wild ride!"

Darren ran up to him. "Something tells me we need to get out of here. We've been here too long." He looked nervously at the front door. "I mean, that guy could come back at any time."

Frank rested a hand on Darren's shoulder and turned him back to face the hallway. "Don't sweat it." He winked. "Something tells me he's going to be out for a while."

Michelle was growing anxious too. "There's a lot of animals left in here." Her eyes grew wide. "And the reptile room with a cobra and a python . . . heck no. Neither of us are setting foot in there."

Frank placed an arm around her shoulders and pulled up his mask. "Just do what you can while I take care of the other labs. And then I'll handle the reptiles. Deal?"

She nodded, and Frank gave her a playful swat on the backside that made her yelp in surprise. She pointed at him as he backed away from her with a wide grin. "You are a bad boy," she said with a flirtatious smile.

"You better believe it." Frank gave her a wink and lowered his mask. He picked up a golf club, completed a pirouette, and entered another lab.

"Michelle we really need to get out of here. We could be in big trouble," Darren insisted.

Michelle knew that Darren was right. *But is he really as nervous as he appears? Or does he just want me to leave because he's jealous of Frank?*

"Just a few more cages," she said.

~~~

After making short work of the last two labs, Frank's reign of destruction brought him to the end of the long hallway. Only two rooms remained unexplored. The door to the right led to the large cage that he'd seen outside. The door to his left was constructed of steel and had no window.

Peering through the window on the door to his right, Frank saw little more than straw strewn about the cage floor. Turning the handle, he clicked open the door and crept inside. On the second step, Frank nearly soiled himself. What appeared to be a pile of discard carpet was, in fact, a brown bear sleeping in a corner of the cage.

"No . . . way."

In the blink of an eye, Frank was back in the hallway with the door closed behind him. "This fool has a friggin bear," he whispered. He looked toward the opposite end of the hallway where Darren and Michelle were emptying cages of mice and other small rodents. *I'd better keep this to myself,* he thought. *If I tell them there's a bear in here, there's no way they'll stay. They'll freak.*

Frank then realized he'd missed a golden opportunity. "Should have released the pig into that cage. Would have been one hell of a show."

~ ~ ~

Ushering several unruly guinea pigs out the front door, Darren could take no more. He looked back at the smashed laboratory windows and the scattered glass strewn into the hallway. His gaze lowered to the crate of Molotov cocktails sitting in the foyer. *No way am I sticking around for this.* He liked Michelle, but no girl was worth going to jail for. *Besides, she has Frank now.*

"I'm out," he shouted to Michelle, who was tapping her golf club behind a cluster of mice. "Sorry, but I didn't sign up for this."

"What, you're leaving?" Michelle said. "How can you when I have the keys?"

"I'll walk," Darren said firmly.

Michelle turned away from him in a huff. Darren exited the building and didn't look back.

~ ~ ~

Frank turned his attention to the last room to be explored. He was intrigued by the steel door's sturdy construction and that, in lieu of a window, it had a wall monitor beside it. "What's in here? Fort Knox?" He pressed down on the handle of the thick, steel lock.

No dice; it was locked.

He then noticed the slit for a key card on the lock. Reaching into his pocket, he extracted the plastic card that he'd taken from the unconscious scientist. *Bingo.*

"Hey, where did you get that?" Michelle yelled from farther down the hallway.

"Found it." With a swipe of the card, Frank pushed down on the handle.

"Voila." The door clicked open.

Entering the large room, Frank was dumbfounded by what lay inside. The entire room was a vast circle. To his right was a cascading waterfall, while the rest of the walls contained large tropical leaves and thick tree trunks with winding branches. Exotic bird calls echoed above the soothing sounds of cascading water. It was as if he were standing in the middle of a tropical rainforest.

Other than the door that he'd entered through, there were no other doors or windows. Overhead was a domed, starlit sky. *How is he doing this?* It was as if the surrounding walls were a video screen or projecting some type of 3D hologram.

In the center of the room was what resembled a massive Jacuzzi. It was about ten feet in diameter with four-foot-tall Lexan walls. Projecting up from the water were a series of tubes that lead to the sole piece of equipment in the room. It resembled something one might find in the ICU of a hospital. On its console were various gauges and readings including a red light that beeped like a heart monitor. An accordion-like pump rose and dropped like a massive ventilator. Beside the piece of equipment, a steel ramp reached up to the side of the aquarium.

Frank looked around the room and inhaled the oxygen-enriched air. "Wow, you could really chill out in this place."

He eased closer to the aquarium. Staring through its Lexan wall, he saw little more than bubbles swirling in a misty haze. *What's in there?*

Creeping closer, he saw something reaching out from the mist. Frank froze, staring at some type of clawed hand. It had four fingers, one of which was an opposable thumb. The skin was gray and pebbled. On top of the knuckles, the skin was thicker and gnarled like a knotted club. "What . . . the . . . hell?"

He stepped back to the control monitor beside the door. He slammed his palm against a large black button. Instantly, the tropical rainforest and waterfall disappeared—replaced by a circular steel wall.

There was another door in the back of the room. But what demanded his attention were the myriad of deep dents and claw marks in the steel wall. Claw marks that had four fingers.

The tropical bird calls and the cascading water sounds ceased, replaced by the hissing click of the ventilator and the beep of the heart monitor.

"I gotta get the hell out of here!" He tried the handle on the door, but it was locked.

"The key. The key." He pulled it from his pocket but dropped it. Then he looked at the door—there was no slot for a key card. His eyes then rose back to the wall console, darting between several buttons. "One of these has to be for the door."

He pressed a red button, and the clank of the ventilator stopped. He turned around to find the console on the machine beside the aquarium had gone dark. A large belch of bubbles rose inside the aquarium and dissipated at the water's surface.

Frantically, he turned back to the wall monitor, pressing buttons. Another red one, a green one. He heard a splash of water and turned to see what looked like a huge sleep-apnea mask, along with a tangle of tubes, rocket from the aquarium and slam against the wall.

Frantically, Frank pounded more buttons. "Let me out!"

There was a loud explosion of water, followed by a deep thud of something landing on the floor behind him. He could hear water splattering onto the floor as if draining from something large. He pressed another button fighting a wave of dread. Frank realized that he had finally stepped into something that his mother couldn't get him out of.

And then there was another sound—the click of the door. It cracked open.

~~~

Michelle turned and looked down the hallway when the steel door had flown open. Frank stumbled out of the doorway until his back stopped against a door on the opposite side of the hallway. His left hand held his stomach as blood streamed through his fingers. When he turned toward her, she saw a deep slash across his abdomen. His right arm was nearly severed, dangling by a piece of skin.

Holding his stomach, Frank looked at her not in horror, but something akin to awe. He then fell face forward, and slumped onto the floor as blood pooled swiftly beneath him.

A god-awful roar erupted from the room and echoed through the hallway. Then, right before the steel door closed, four clawed fingers curled over the door frame and stopped it.

~~~

Darren was jogging alongside the road when he heard a bloodcurdling scream echo through the trees behind him. "Michelle." He stopped cold and turned around. But rather than following the road back to the driveway, he cut straight through the woods. The frantic teen raced between the trees, bursting through small branches and grazing tree trunks until he finally reached the old sidewalk in front of the building.

He darted through the open doorway. "Michelle," he called out, his chest heaving as he gasped to catch his breath. An iguana scuttled past his feet, followed by a green snake. At the end of the hallway, he caught sight of Frank lying face down in a large pool of blood.

"Michelle," he shouted again, but there remained no answer.

A glance through the door to his right showed only empty cages and a few mice scurrying around the floor. Again he called for Michelle. Again, no response.

Then he saw the bloody footprints trailing from Frank's body. Bizarre, clawed footprints that faded as they grew closer to where Darren stood.

He ran to the next door on his right to find it hanging from a single hinge against the wall. When Darren looked inside, he nearly fainted. Behind several smashed aquariums, he saw Michelle lying upside down in a corner like a discarded rag doll. Her body was contorted horribly. Her blond hair hung down onto the floor as her head lay flat against her shoulder. Blood seeped from the side of her mouth and onto the concrete where a coral snake squirmed through.

Snakes were strewn everywhere, twisting and winding beneath her mangled form. The undulating serpents grew blurry, and Darren stumbled back against the doorframe.

"No. This can't be real."

Glass crackled in the hallway behind him. Darren turned around and . . . *Whoosh!* A blur of gray, pebbled flesh was the last thing he saw. Ever.

CHAPTER 4

THE SIGNAL

In a vast wooded area south of Orlando, Blake Wilson peddled his Mongoose mountain bike swiftly along a winding dirt trail. The twelve-year-old was running late for dinner, again. He had spent the last hour watching the older boys ride their ATVs and dirt bikes at a small track that the local riders had built in the woods. And as always, he'd lost track of time. Being late for dinner again would mean no phone or devices for three days. So little Blake peddled with everything that he had.

Rounding another corner, he passed a cluster of saw palmetto bushes and his eyes flared. He squeezed the hand brakes, and the locked tires bounced across the dirt until he stopped.

"Wow. What is that?"

Through a maze of winding branches, he saw a small plane lying in the woods. Letting his bike drop to the ground, he raced to the downed aircraft and picked it up. "Cool." It was unlike any remote control airplane he'd ever seen. It was gray and about three feet long. There were no decals, logos, or markings of any kind. The plane's only prominent features were the antenna protruding from its top and a small orange ball affixed to its underside.

"Kinda weird."

Blake peered through the woods in every direction, but didn't see or hear anyone. Only the faint rumble of the dirt bikes echoed in the distance.

"Finders keepers." He grinned and carried the plane back to his bicycle. His new acquisition tucked under his left arm, and his right hand on the handlebars, he proceeded cautiously along the trail.

I'm definitely gonna lose my phone, he thought, steering with one hand. *But this is so worth it.*

~ ~ ~

Cruising through Hidden Lakes, an upscale, gated community south of Orlando, Blake kept the plane tucked tightly under his arm. So far, he'd gone unnoticed . . . until he spotted a classmate, Randy Freeman, playing basketball in his driveway.

"Hey, Blake. Whatcha got there?" hollered the chubby, redhaired boy as Blake whisked by.

Coasting for one more block, Blake turned into the driveway of a single-story, Mediterranean-style home and entered the open garage. After resting the plane on the hood of his mother's black Lexus SUV, he leaned his bike against the wall beside the garbage cans.

He snatched up his new acquisition and crept into the laundry room to find his German shepherd, Rexy, waiting for him, tongue dangling and tail wagging.

"I can't play now, Rexy. I have to go to my room first." He stepped around the dog and into the kitchen. The moment Blake exited the kitchen and turned down the hallway, his mother's voice rang from the dining room. "You're ten minutes late. . . you know what that means?"

"Yeah, Mom. Be right with ya." Entering his bedroom, Blake sat on his bed, and Rexy jumped up beside him and sniffed the plane.

"Pretty cool, huh?" Blake said, turning the plane in his hands.

Hanging from the ceiling via strings were twenty or so model airplanes, ranging from WWII bombers to an F-22 Raptor fighter jet. Although his dad, a pilot for Delta Airlines, had helped him build them, Blake knew the technical stats on every last one of them.

He looked up at the miniature aircraft seemingly gliding beneath the ceiling. "Always room for one more." *But until I can put it up there, I'd better hide it,* he thought. *Otherwise, she might think I stole it and try to find out who it belongs to.*

The boy opened the door to his closet. Before placing the plane inside, he noted the orange, tangerine-size ball attached to the crafts underbelly.

"Look, Rexy, there's even something for you." With a grunt, he separated the ball from the plane. But as he went to throw it, the ball flashed three times as if there were a light pulsing inside.

"Wow, that's cool." He tossed the ball onto the floor, and Rexy snatched it from the air on the first bounce. The ball in its mouth, the playful dog dropped down on its front paws at Blake's feet then darted through the door.

~ ~ ~

Nathen and Grayson Cummings were sprawled on chaise lounge chairs on the back deck of the two-story, contemporary-style home. Situated on the northwest corner of the gated community, Nathen admired his view of the nature reserve. Beyond his wrought-iron fence, there was nothing but a lush landscape of towering pines and oaks—and not another roof in sight. That's part of what had sold him on the 1,500-home community of Hidden Lakes. That and the fact that it was less than a twenty-minute commute to his work in Orlando, where he was a regional manager for Hertz Car Rental.

"Close enough to the city, yet far enough away from the

hustle and bustle of it all," a cliché line the realtor had used to sell him. And she was right. *This is the life,* he thought, pouring another glass of lemonade.

Taking a long sip, Nathen returned the glass to the small table between him and his ten-year-old, who was already sporting his favorite Captain America pajamas.

They were ten minutes into Men's Quiet Time, as Nathen called it. A nightly ritual that followed dinner and an hour of working out the ten-year-old's math problems. *The complexity of the math they dish out to a fourth-grader is ridiculous,* Nathen thought, letting his eyes drift over the pool and into the tangle of tall trunks and sweeping branches beyond.

He closed his eyes, listening to the wind rustling the trees. *What beautiful music, a sound every bit as calming as waves breaking on a shoreline.*

A moment later, little Grayson interrupted his respite. "Hey, Dad?"

"Yes, Grayson."

"Does the Boogeyman live in the trees?"

Nathen snickered. "Why would you ask such a thing?"

"Look."

Opening his eyes, Nathen peered in the direction the child was pointing. When he did, a towering oak tree jerked dramatically, as if something of significant size had just leapt from it. The tree beside it then jolted and swayed, sending a shower of pine needles and leaves fluttering onto the deck.

His eyes fixed on the trees, Nathen snatched Grayson by the wrist and rose from his chair. "I think I heard your mother calling you for bed."

~~~

Det. Scott Pine entered the Orlando Police Department to find only a half-dozen officers still working at their desks. No one looked up as he walked by, seemingly unnoticed. Were they engrossed in their reports or simply ignoring him? *Tough call,* he thought.

Reaching a small desk that temporarily served as his office, he was met by a familiar sight. *Another token of appreciation from one of my adoring fans.* He approached the small gift box perched on his desk.

Opening it he found a pair of thick insoles. The heading atop the package read, "Guaranteed to Increase Your Height by One Full Inch."

None of the officers looked up from their reports, but snickers echoed throughout the room.

Scott pulled out a desk drawer to add the risers to the collection. His eyes wandered across a book on overcoming Napoleon syndrome, another on the pros and cons of surgical leg lengthening, and a long grabber device used to pick up items beyond your reach.

Being a decent-looking guy and well-built for his stature, Scott had no problem with his height. Besides, five seven wasn't really that short. Just look at Tom Cruise, Sylvester Stallone, and other leading men in Hollywood. At least that's what girlfriends would often tell him. The bottom line was the officers had nothing else on him, so their simple minds went with the obvious.

Closing the drawer, he thumbed through several reports on his desk. A short, heavyset African-American woman seated at the next desk looked up at him. She lowered the mike on her headset. "I'll tell you who did it if you want."

"That's all right," Scott said. "It doesn't really matter."

That was Izabella Jones, the reception operator, or Izzy as everyone called her. Since Scott's first day at the precinct, Izzy had taken him under her wing like a mother hen in a proverbial rainstorm of BS. She was the only one who seemed to give him the time of day and was willing to show him the ropes.

Unlike the flurries of officers darting in and out of the station, Izzy seemed perfectly content perched at her desk observing it all. And as far as Scott could tell, no one messed with Izzy. She had a sharp tongue and the wit to wield it.

She nodded toward a wide back two desks up. "That's GJ, the little elf who left your gift. He's the belle of the ball around here.

"He played half a season with the Tampa Bay Buccaneers before a broken ankle took him out of the game." She lowered her voice. "But according to my husband, he was too slow and too dumb to make it even before the ankle thing." She waved a hand and wrinkled her nose. "He's all about football, but I never watch it. I tell him I get enough testosterone and fools butting heads around this place."

The detective nodded toward the huge guy. "A football star, huh?"

"Yep." Izzy smirked. "The great Larry Webber, a legend in his own mind. You know most of the crew here are good folks. It's just Larry and his minions you have to watch out for."

"But you call him GJ. How do you get GJ from Larry Webber?"

Izzy leaned closer to him. "Oh, that's just my pet name for him," she said in a hushed tone. "It stands for giant jackass. That boy doesn't have the sense God gave a mule." She winked. "But he doesn't know what it stands for. It's been driving him nuts trying to figure it out."

The detective snickered and returned to his papers.

The hulking officer then rose from behind his desk. "Time to unleash the Kraken," he bellowed as his voice echoed through the precinct. Tucking a magazine under one arm, he headed toward the hallway.

Scott turned toward Izzy. "Unleash the Kraken?"

Izzy just rolled her big brown eyes. "That's his subtle way of informing the world he's going to evacuate his bowels. You know, take a dump." She then gave a slow nod. "Giant . . . jackass."

"Gotcha," muttered the detective as big Larry lumbered down the hallway, whistling along the way.

The phone rang, and Izzy raised the mike on her headset. "OPD. How can I help you?" Her brow furrowed as she listened. "How high up? You think that's what it was, but you didn't actually see it?"

She listened for a moment, nodding. "Okay, just stay inside, and we'll send someone out to have a look. I need your full address."

Punching the keypad, Izzy swung her chair around to face the officers still collected in the room. "I just received a call from a Mr. Nathen Cummings, who claims to have seen a large bear in a tree behind his house. He's located in Hidden Lakes, a community south of Orlando."

"I know the place," a tall officer with a black moustache called out. "Probably just another Florida black bear looking for food. Early in the season though. They don't usually start nosing around for extra food until closer to their hibernation time . . . around November."

Florida black bears, Scott thought. *These calls are certainly different than Miami.*

The phone rang again, and Izzy swung back around to her desk. Taking the call, her eyes lit up. She opened a notepad and started scribbling. "At least two that you saw?" She jotted down more notes, nodding. "Okay, got it. Just stay out of the building and remain in your vehicle until the officers arrive."

When Izzy swung back around to face the group, her eyes were wide. "Forget the bear. I'll relay that to wildlife control. We've got a one-eight-seven." At the mention of the number, everyone looked her way, including Scott.

A homicide.

"A FedEx driver just went to deliver a package at a building off of Belle Street. He found the front door propped open. When he stepped inside, he discovered at least two bodies. It was some type of lab that had apparently been vandalized."

Izzy glanced at her notes and cringed. "He couldn't stay in there long because there were all sorts of empty cages and snakes crawling all over the place."

"Now that sounds more like a Miami call," Scott said and headed for the door.

~~~

Ashley Hanes stood in the dark family room of her two bedroom home, staring through the back sliding glass doors. Stripped down to her bra and panties, the twenty-six-year-old's gaze drifted from the silhouetted tree trunks to the glittering waters beyond. Technically, the small lake backed up to her neighbor's yard, but to Ashley's delight, she had a clear view of it from the entire left side of her house.

Being a first-time homeowner, the young nurse still couldn't believe all of this was hers. *Finally . . . no roommates, no parents. Just me.* She spun, completing a joyful pirouette on her large throw rug. When she stopped, she caught sight of her reflection in the glass doors. She stepped back and forth before the glass, watching her distorted reflection turn narrow and then stretch wide like in a funhouse mirror. "Looks like someone needs to hit the gym," she snickered. She did a double take on her bulbous image. "My God, if I ever got that big, Brad would . . ."

Normally, Ashley wouldn't dare to stand before an open window at night. But every light in the house was off, making her invisible from outside.

Or so she thought.

Slipping out of her bra and panties, she let them drop onto the rug. "Couldn't do this before, *and* no one's here to tell me to pick them up," she said. Adorned in only her engagement ring, she scampered down the dark hallway, the cool ceramic tile nipping at her bare feet.

Using the moonlight peering in through the tall windows as a guide, Ashley rounded the corner and stepped into the guest bathroom. The tender soles of her feet welcomed the soft warmth of the floor mat. Switching on the light, she saw her true form in the mirror above the sink. "Ah, now that's more like it."

Turning sideways, Ashley admired her curvaceous reflection and the way her long raven hair draped down her naked back. Extracting the two-carat diamond ring from her finger, she placed it on the counter with a wink. "Well, Mr. Brad Hensley, you're about to become the luckiest man in Orange County."

Leaning forward, Ashley threw her long hair down toward the floor, fashioned it into a bun, and stood back up. Her pre-shower ritual complete, she turned on the water and allowed it time to warm. After that double shift at the hospital, the hotter the better.

It wasn't long before steam billowed over the top of the plastic curtain and fogged up the mirror. Reaching behind the curtain, she tested the water with her hand. *Perfect.* Ashley then swooshed back the curtain and stepped inside. Closing her eyes, she felt the warm water flow down her back, cascade onto her hamstrings, across her calves, and pool around her sore feet.

"Ahhhh. I am so overdue for this."

Opening her eyes, she peered through the two-foot-tall window, which was situated to her left inside the shower stall. Although the glass was frosted, she could still see the tranquil glimmer of the lake outside.

Reaching for her body wash, she noticed that the light reflecting from the lake had disappeared. She wiped the steam from the glass with her hand, but the dark window remained. "The moon must have gone behind the clouds," she muttered, but thought little of it.

A gust of steam reappeared on the window. Ashley wiped it with her hand, but it was apparently on the outside. As quickly as it appeared, the mist was gone. Then once again, a mist filled the window and faded. When it happened yet again, she noticed an unnerving rhythm to it.

Something was breathing against the glass.

A pair of red eyes appeared just in front of her.

She screamed, reeling back from the window, when all of the sudden, a clawed hand burst through the glass, collecting the shower curtain and Ashley in one sweep.

Screaming and wailing, she twisted and turned in the crinkling curtain, trying to escape the grip of her unknown assailant. Placing her left foot on the edge of the tub, she thrust her body upward, toward the ceiling. Her shrill screams echoed from the tile.

She felt the cold, coarse skin slip around her waist.

Wham!

The creature jerked Ashley sideways, slamming her head into the tile above the window and knocking the bun loose from her hair. Disoriented, and peering through her tangled locks, she saw a red smear on the tile as warm water sprayed her kicking thighs.

Again, her face rushed toward the wall—and *bam!* Fire shot through her nose and forehead as a gushing warmth flowed down her neck. Her vision was obscured by the blood.

The gnarled arm again pulled against her back. Her palms slapped against the bloody tile above the window, and she fought against the pull with everything that she had.

"God, no!" she howled.

But only her scream escaped the powerful grasp.

A final jolt on her waist produced a loud snap. Her torso seemed to fall backward, and the backs of her feet came up to meet her head as her spinal column folded.

The pain was gone, and nothing seemed real. All Ashley could see was steam collecting at the ceiling, the empty curtain rod, the blood-smeared tile. Then the broken glass at the top of the window frame scraped across her face, and for a fleeting moment, she caught a glimpse of the night sky.

~ ~ ~

Seventy-one-year-old Bill Hailey tossed an aspirin into his gullet and chased it with a tall glass of water. It was a new addition to his list of pre-bedtime rituals that his cardiologist had ordered.

Right before doing so, he thought he heard a muffled scream from outside. "At this hour, it better not be those Wilson children again," he grumbled. Setting the glass into the sink, he scuttled across the kitchen and turned off the light. Stepping to the window, he separated the vertical blinds with his fingers.

Peering through the darkness toward his neighbor's house, he saw a single illuminated window with a piece of shower curtain dangling from it. "What's that all about?"

Affixing the belt around his blue, terrycloth robe, he entered the laundry room and slipped into a pair of sandals waiting by the door to the garage.

Entering the dark garage, he took a flashlight from a shelf and proceeded toward the side door. With a squeak of wood, Bill stepped from the doorway and into the damp night air. He switched on the flashlight and eased toward the glaring window, the circle of light searching the grass before him.

Drawing closer, he could hear the steady hiss of a shower spraying inside the window as it continued to belch steam. A few steps further, and he heard another sound. A sound not unlike what he had recently heard on a lion documentary. The gruesome sound of tearing flesh and jaws slapping together.

And then he noticed the large lump beneath the window.

Raising the light toward the object, Bill saw the tousled hair of a woman with her upper body protruding from a bundled shower curtain. Turning his light to the opposite side of the blood-soaked curtain, he saw her legs and feet a good distance away. A distance too great for them to be adjoined to her upper half.

The light rose above the crimson curtain to reveal a clawed hand streaming with blood. Lifting the light higher, Bill knew there had to be a Heaven and Hell, because he was staring at the face of the Devil.

Above the hand was a horrible display of interlocked teeth, four of which had to be seven inches long as they protruded out over green, pebbled, reptilian skin, blood draining down from between them. Between the pair of upward-bearing fangs was a large gorilla-like snout. Crowning the monstrosity was a mane of long, tentacle-like projections that seemed to move on their own.

The horrible head tilted upward, and a pair of lantern eyes locked on him. The creature then rose from all fours, growing taller and taller until its red eyes towered into the night. All the while, the slitted pupils remained fixed on him.

Like a deer transfixed by oncoming light, Bill stared at the creature's full silhouette against the light from the window. Most notable was the wavering mane and the broad, gnarled shoulders. What he saw beneath them was a blur of primate and human mixed with something else. Something horrible. Something ungodly.

Silently and majestically, the creature stepped over the

body, heading in Bill's direction. Its movement was every bit as fluid as a premier danseur. The jittering light flashed across a pebbled chest that was slick with blood.

Bill raised the light to its face. The vertical pupils dilated. The horrible teeth separated, and the jaws stretched wide.

Like a bolt of lightning, a searing pain shot through Bill's chest and radiated down his left arm. He dropped the flashlight as his buckling knees hit the ground. Clutching his chest, Bill caught a glimpse of a clawed foot until his face came to rest in the damp grass.

CHAPTER 5

THE MARK

Wheeling a brown, unmarked Crown Victoria, Detective Pine followed the patrol unit along Mill Creek Road. The red and blue lights from the police cruiser reflected from the tall tree trunks as they passed. The odometer on the old Crown Vic read 89,000 miles. Scott figured it had to have been rolled over at least once. No doubt it was the most antiquated heap in their fleet—so, naturally, it was assigned to him.

Tires squealing, Scott came out of another corner, pushing the old Ford for all it was worth. He could tell the officer driving the patrol unit ahead of him was trying to leave him behind. And driving a new Dodge Charger, he should have been able to do so. But it would take more than a few extra ponies under the hood. Scott's years of racing experience easily trumped any emergency vehicle operation training that the other officer had taken.

~~~

"Come on, Tiny. I thought you could drive," barked Ofc. Leon Jones, a large, well-built African American, from the passenger's seat. "This thing's got a Hemi in it, for God's sake. You should be able to gap that runt."

"I know," grunted the portly officer gripping the wheel. "I'm pushing it, but the kid's pretty good." Ofc. Tim Bell glanced in the mirror to find the headlights still on his bumper.

When he looked back down, he realized that he'd carried too much speed into the corner. He whipped the car sideways, just missing the tree line. Winding branches glazed the windshield as billowing dust clouds glowed in their headlights.

~~~

The detective snickered, watching the police cruiser bounce from the dirt and back onto the pavement. *I'd better back off before they end up in the woods. Besides, we should be getting close.*

Moments after the FedEx driver had called the station with his first report, he'd placed a second call. He reported finding an older man lying unconscious in a field behind the building. Presumably, an ambulance was already at the scene.

Rounding yet another winding corner, Scott saw the ambulance lights pulsing between the trees. The patrol unit pulled into the driveway and stopped beside the emergency vehicle while Scott parked the Crown Vic just off the road.

He vaulted from the old Ford and jogged along the driveway, the ambient light from the emergency vehicles playing off the trees and the brick face of the building. Reaching the ambulance, Scott peered inside to find a man in his sixties sprawled on a stretcher with a paramedic hovering over him. Scott proceeded to the back of the vehicle where another paramedic stood beside the open door.

"What's his condition? Did he say anything?" the detective asked the young man who appeared to be in his early thirties.

"No, he's out cold," replied the paramedic with a hand on the door. "He suffered a blow to the forehead. From the wound mark and the glass scattered around him, it appears he was hit by a thrown bottle. His pulse is weak, but stable."

Scott glanced at the open door to the building that the

pair of officers had disappeared into. "Did you go inside?"

"Nah. We were ordered to stay outside until you guys showed up. Should we head out, or wait to see if there's anyone else inside?"

Officer Jones appeared in the doorway and looked their way. He motioned at the paramedics, saying,"You guys can take off. There's nothing in here for you." The officer's expression, though, seemed more ominous than his words.

The paramedic leapt into the back of the ambulance, and Scott closed the door behind him.

~~~

With overturned and smashed lab equipment, glass, and open cages strewn about, the damage inside the building was staggering. But Detective Pine's sole focus was the male corpse slumped in the hallway. The positioning of the body was gruesome. The way the side of his face and his left arm lay in the pool of blood reminded him of a rat caught in a glue trap. But even more disturbing were the large tracks that trailed from the blood and led down the hallway.

Peering through the eye of his camera, Scott knelt down to get a close shot of the massive wound. The right arm was practically severed. The position of the body didn't allow him to see how far it extended into the victim's torso. But the size of the pool of blood suggested it was deep enough to have severed the abdominal aorta.

On the opposite side of the blood pool stood Officer Jones with his hands on his hips. "Something sure laid that boy open. What in this place do you imagine could do such a thing?"

The detective stood and lowered his camera. "It doesn't appear to have come from an animal. The wound looks more consistent with a sword or a machete. It's so clean, the way it severed the humerus and biceps of the right arm."

"Well, if it was a sword fight, he definitely placed second," Officer Jones said. "What do you make of these . . . all of these tracks?"

Careful to avoid the pooled blood, Scott stepped around the body and started photographing the tracks. Most of them were smeared, but one of the tracks showed the distinct outline of four clawed toes.

Jones knelt in the hallway, studying one of the bloody prints. "I don't know, but they look like bear tracks to me."

"I'm not so sure," said the detective, taking another photograph. "When I get back, I'll do a comparison."

"Do you always take your own photos? You know, in Orlando we have people for that. They're called forensic photographers, and one of them is on the way."

Taking one final snapshot, Scott pocketed his camera. "Sometimes when evidence is logged in, things get lost. I prefer to have my own set of backups."

"Oh, I see," Jones said. He then motioned for the detective to follow him. "The next victim is . . ."

Bam. Bam. Bam. Three gunshots echoed down the hallway.

The detective followed Officer Jones into the next doorway to find a large snake writhing wildly in the middle of the floor. Several yards away, Officer Bell stood with his back against the wall, his sidearm still trained on the squirming reptile.

"Nice shooting, Tiny," Jones blurted. "Looks like you just took out a king cobra. Watch your step, gentlemen. This place is still hot."

Stepping back into the hallway, Jones motioned for the detective to follow him farther along the hallway, toward the foyer. "The second body is over here. Wait until you see this."

They stopped where a white sneaker was lying among shattered glass. Above the shoe, was a four-foot hole in the window of a laboratory. The officer pointed inside the jagged opening. "That's the owner of the shoe over there."

Peering inside, the detective saw a boy in a black hoodie lying beside a toppled lab table about twenty feet away.

Officer Jones shook his head. "Something sure knocked the hell out of him."

~~~

Studying the body of the young teen donning one shoe, Detective Pine almost had to look away. The only thing he could liken the injury to was something he'd seen in an auto accident. The nose had been completely demolished and caved into the face. Beyond recognition.

"Incredible," Scott muttered. "The body wasn't dragged to this spot. It clearly had landed here. Something in the hallway knocked him out of his shoe, through the window, and twenty-five feet across the lab."

"Bizarre." Officer Jones was looking over the detective's shoulder. "Other than the impact wound, the rest of the body appears unmarked. You ever seen anything like this?"

Looking up from the body, the detective saw the image of the twin towers on the far wall. His eyes were then drawn to other related articles along the walls.

Jones was studying them too. "I'd say the guy who runs this place has a strange fascination with 9/11."

"Hello? Is anyone in here? What happened?" a female voice called out from the hallway. "Can anyone hear me?"

Exiting the laboratory, Scott saw a petite blonde standing in the foyer.

"What happened?" she gasped, gazing around at the destruction.

"Ma'am, you can't be in here!" Jones hollered. "This is a crime scene. Besides, there's all kinds of creepy crawlies still running around."

"I'll take care of this," Detective Pine said. Approaching the young woman, he could see she was terribly upset. Ushering her toward the front door, she looked down the hallway toward the body slumped in the pool of blood.

"No!" she gasped with tears streaming down her cheeks. "Is that Jim?"

"Who's Jim?" asked the detective as they paused just outside the doorway.

The woman wouldn't break her gaze from the hallway. "He's the man who runs the facility. He's a research geneticist."

"No. I don't think that's Jim. This is someone younger, probably a high school student."

"Well, where is he? Where's Jim?" she demanded, craning her neck to look inside the doorway.

Maintaining a good grip on her arm, Scott said, "Could you tell me about your relationship to Jim?"

"Oh, I'm so sorry." She seemed to calm herself. "I'm Wendy Marshall, a local veterinarian. I help him with the animals here."

Great, Scott thought. *Maybe now we can get some answers.* "I believe the Jim you're referring to was just loaded up on an ambulance and taken to the hospital. He was found here unconscious."

"Thank God he's alive," Wendy said, "but how's . . ."

Scott nodded in understanding. "He's still unconscious, but to the best of my knowledge, he's stable." He loosened his grip on her arm. "Now just relax. He's in good hands."

Scott took a long breath, more so to calm himself. "Now think . . . as far as the animals go here, did Jim have any large primates in captivity, such as gorillas?"

Wendy shook her head. "No gorillas, but there was Sleepy, an adult male Kodiak bear."

Bingo. "But that's it? Just the bear?"

"There were some primates, but nothing larger than a chimpanzee. He also had a few large snakes."

"You're sure that's all?"

"Yes, I'm certain." Wendy raked back a strand of honey-blond hair. "I'm well acquainted with all the animals. But what happened? Where are they?"

"Apparently, there was a break-in involving vandalism." Scott withdrew his notepad. "But can you tell me more about the bear? Like where its cage is located, inside, outside?"

"It's out back and butts up to the building. There's a cage door around back of the building as well as one inside. The inside door is the last door at the end of the hallway."

That's it. That lines up with the footprints. Coming from the end of the hallway, the bear would have tracked the blood in this direction.

He returned his attention to the young woman, whose hazel eyes seemed to be studying him. He jotted down a few notes. "The area's still not clear. Please wait in your vehicle until the area is secured. I'll have a few more questions for you."

"Yes sir." She turned and headed toward the parking lot, calling over her shoulder, "I'm in a Jeep."

Pocketing the notepad, Scott stepped back through the doorway. Although he was in the middle of a homicide investigation with his mind spinning a hundred miles a minute, he couldn't get over how cute she was.

~~~

Back inside the lab, Scott met up with Officer Jones in the hallway. They were standing beside the large hole in the glass that the second male victim had been ejected through.

"So did the little cutie outside have any insight on this mess?"

"She's a veterinarian, familiar with the animals that were

here. Including Sleepy, an adult Kodiak bear." Scott nodded past the body toward the end of the hallway. "His habitat is the last door down there. Those are most likely his tracks that we're seeing here." The detective gazed around the wreckage. "Looks like a few kids broke in for whatever reason and got more than they bargained for."

"Sleepy, huh?" Officer Jones said. "Well, it looks like he woke up . . . and was pissed."

"So have we secured every room now?"

"All but the one at the end of the hall on the left. The door is stainless steel with a heavy duty lock. It has a keycard slot with a wall monitor beside it. I fiddled with the buttons on the console but couldn't get it to come on. We'll have one of the geeks check it out."

"There was one more body?" Pine asked.

The life seemed to fade from Officer Jones's eyes. "It's just to your right." He sighed. "Female. A pretty little thing. It's just so wrong to see her all twisted up like that."

Ushering Scott to a door hanging from one hinge, the big officer paused in the doorway. "I'll give you two a moment alone while I take another crack at the console to the steel door."

Scott sensed Jones was reluctant to come inside the room again. Stepping through the doorway, he discovered why. Just when he thought he had mastered severing every emotion from his work, along came a crime scene like this. It was unnerving, the way the young woman was lying inverted in the corner with her head pressed against her shoulder. Not one of her appendages was situated in a natural way. Blood from the internal trauma of her broken neck had seeped from her mouth and pooled onto the floor.

The concrete beneath her looked like an abstract painting. Snakes had slithered through the pooled blood leaving red squiggly lines in every direction.

Careful not to step in the blood, Scott eased closer. Studying her tousled blond hair, he felt a sense of familiarity. He recalled the Rolling Stones T-shirt on the first victim, and realization crept over him. *These are the same three kids I saw at Legends Diner today.* He muttered, "I knew that one guy was trouble—"

Wham!

Something slammed him from behind, knocking him forward and into the cages and aquariums. Rolling across the cages, he saw the thick, greenish-brown trunk winding around his right leg and torso. *The trunk of an anaconda.*

The giant snake continued to wind around its prey when Scott heard a raspy hiss. He saw the huge head draw back from his face with its jaws hyperextended, the forked tongue curling.

With his hands still free, the detective grabbed the serpent by the throat just below its head. More cages crashed and shattered around him. And then the creature started to constrict. He tried to call out for help, but he had no voice.

Scott held his breath. He knew that the giant reptile was waiting for him to exhale so that it could constrict and keep him from breathing in again.

A horrible hiss escaped his mouth as a precious breath slipped from his lungs. And 9,000 pounds of pressure per square inch tightened around his torso. A warmth flowed down his left leg from the tension on his bladder.

Scott knew he didn't have long.

He noticed the broken window in the door leaning against the wall and stumbled toward it with his free leg. The giant head writhed and swayed wildly to escape his grip. The strength of the animal was incredible.

On the verge of blacking out, Scott forced the head of the serpent through the broken window and pressed its neck down onto the jagged glass.

With his last ounce of energy, he worked the snake's neck back and forth across the glass, sawing through the scaled flesh. Two hundred fifty pounds of muscle constricted and spasmed against his body, but he did not stop.

Finally, the head came off in his hands. Blood from the severed trunk painted a crimson streak across the wall and splattered onto his throat. But the decapitated reptile still held its grip.

Officer Jones appeared in the doorway, a look of horror sweeping across his face. Unholstering his side arm, he aimed it at the swaying creature until *splat*. A swath of blood slapped the officer in the face. Wiping his eyes with his sleeve, he emptied his clip into the coiling serpent as blood still spewed from its neck.

Wham. The detective hit the floor, still entwined in the massive reptile as it writhed and squirmed in the blood.

A horrible scream echoed through the room, and he glimpsed Wendy in the doorway. She rushed toward him and tried to help the officer unwind the huge snake from his body. Gripping the scaled trunk, they stumbled, sliding in the blood.

With the serpent's mighty grip finally broken, Scott gasped for a breath as he felt Wendy and Officer Jones dragging him into the hallway. It was as if a truck had been lifted off of him. His chest heaving, Scott felt the life slowly creeping back into his body. His head was pounding.

Officer Jones stepped back into the room and fired twelve more rounds into the headless creature. "I don't believe it, but that thing's still moving," he said, backing into the hallway with his eyes locked on the snake.

"It's just nerves at this point." Wendy was hovering over Scott with a look of concern.

"Well, that thing's got a hell of a lot of nerves."

"How do you feel?" Wendy asked Scott.

"Like I've had the piss squeezed out of me," Scott hissed,

"literally."

Tiny came thundering down the hallway with his 9mm drawn. His wide eyes darted between the detective and the bloody serpent still writhing inside the doorway. The portly officer gasped. "Woah, what did I miss?"

Scott peered up at the two officers. "I thought you said all the rooms had been cleared?"

"I did," Tiny countered."I went in there and looked around, and nothing happened."

Officer Jones patted the officer's rotund stomach. "That's all right." He then winked down at Scott. "It was probably hiding . . . and waiting for smaller prey."

Scott eased his head back onto the floor. "Please don't make me laugh."

~~~

Detective Pine awakened to a rhythmic beep that kept pace with his heartbeat. The single-bed hospital room was dark, save the illuminated screens on the equipment at his bedside and light from the hallway that streamed in through the partially open door. His ribs were sore. Raising a hand to his side, he could feel they had been taped.

It wasn't until then that he noticed the small, female silhouette in a chair beside the bed. She looked up at him, the faint light playing off her blond hair.

"Oh, you're awake." Wendy stood and leaned over the bedrail.

Scott looked up at her. "Earlier, when you said a few large snakes . . . *that was your way of saying 'anaconda'?*"

"I suppose I could have been more descriptive." She snickered and pulled nervously at her beige blouse, which was crusted with dried blood.

Scott glanced at the dark walls but didn't see a clock. "How long have I been here? What time is it?"

She glanced at her watch. "It's quarter past twelve."

He felt his heart flutter as the heart monitor revealed his emotion. "You've been here the entire time?"

Wendy lowered her gaze briefly as if thrown by the question, or perhaps a little embarrassed. "Well, after returning home, I decided to see how Jim was doing. Then I poked my head in to check on you."

The detective in him called BS. If she had gone home, she would have certainly changed out of her bloody clothes. Either way, Scott was quick to notice that none of her fingers curled around the bedrail bore a wedding ring.

"Is Jim awake? I need to get in there and question him." Scott strained to sit up. When he did, a thousand bee stings shot through his ribs.

Gently placing a hand on his shoulder, Wendy eased him back against the bed. "No, he's still out. And you need to stay put. According to your chart, you have a few bruised ribs." She grinned. "Besides, I don't think you'll be questioning anyone without your pants."

Scott's eyes darted around the dark room. He couldn't just sit there; he had to get back to the station. Wendy seemed to detect his restlessness. "Hey, just relax. Officer Jones just left. I overheard him say that Animal Control is clearing the lab as we speak, and there are a couple dozen officers combing the woods for the bear. "So relax, everything is being taken care of."

A gray-haired nurse in her sixties ambled into the room carrying a pitcher of water. Filling his cup, she glanced at Wendy. "Honey, you should go home and get some rest. You've been sitting there for hours. He's fine, just a few bruised ribs. He's scheduled for release in the morning."

Before exiting the room, the nurse paused and winked at Scott. "You're one lucky young fella. That's a devoted girlfriend you've got there."

Wendy's mouth dropped. But before she could correct her, the nurse was gone.

Even in the dark, Scott could tell that Wendy was blushing. She quickly spoke up as if to change the subject. "Back at the lab . . . that poor girl and the others. Do you think it was the bear that did that to them?"

"That's what we're trying to find out," Scott said, then shrugged. "For the moment, that appears to be the case." But deep inside, the detective in him remained troubled. He recalled the bloody footprint that showed four distinctly clawed toes. To the best of his knowledge, bears had five.

CHAPTER 6

CLOSE ENCOUNTER

"I've got another set of markings over here." Thirty-seven-year-old Marlin Wells pointed his tranquilizer rifle up to where two patches of bark were missing from a towering oak. "They look to be about thirty feet up."

"Yep, they line up with the others," confirmed Sean Barnes, his younger cohort from Orange County Animal Control.

Armed with a pair of tranquilizer rifles, and a thorough knowledge of black bears and other animals native to Florida, the duo had tracked the escaped animal from the woods behind the lab to about a mile and a half northeast.

It wasn't until around 4:00 a.m. that they discovered the first set of strange claw marks high up in the trees. And they had been following them ever since.

"At least they're easier to follow in the daylight," Sean said as the early sun twinkled between the branches.

Marlin squinted his eyes up at another tall oak. "Another set," he hollered to Sean. *But I don't know of what*, he thought. His fifteen years with Animal Control provided no answers for what he was looking at.

Sean approached him, holding a rifle over his shoulder. "All the way over here, huh?"

"Yeah," Marlin muttered, studying the gap between the trees bearing the sets of claw marks. "It's weird though."

"What—how high up the markings are and that there are

no tracks on the ground?"

"Not just that." Marlin was still peering upward. "It's the distance between them. Those trees have to be at least twenty-five feet apart, the biggest gap yet. Quite an impressive leap for a bear."

Taking a swig from his canteen, Sean replaced the cap. "And the landing marks," he added. "They are almost at the same height as the markings on the tree that it leapt from. Almost as if it sprang straight across from one tree to the next without descending in the slightest. What animal has a jumping force capable of doing that?"

Peering through his binoculars, Marlin noted more of the strange markings on the trees leading deeper into the forest. Lowering the binoculars, he slipped the strap of his rifle over his shoulder. "I guess we'll find out."

~~~

Bob Reno, or Rango, as his military buddies called him, was sprawled on a leather couch in his den watching TV. A sculpted US Marine Corps logo filled the wall behind him. Adorned in camo sweatpants, the well-built thirty-year-old punched a button on the remote. The sixty-inch TV screen flashed past a deodorant commercial and went back to the pre-recorded Tampa Bay Buccaneers game.

"Can't believe it's still friggin tied." He raked a hand across his blond crew cut. "Come on, pass the ball for once. I've got fifty bucks riding on this."

In walked his pride and joy. As usual, the six-year-old was geared up for battle—full fatigues, helmet, boots, two belts of plastic bullets crossing his chest, and a plastic AK-47 squirt gun.

Billy crouched behind the hassock and gave his father two squirts to the chest.

"Hey," Rango blurted. "That's friendly fire. I'm one of the

good guys."

The tow-haired boy lowered his weapon and saluted. "Just a training mission, sir. No harm intended."

"Training mission, huh?" The father laughed.

The mother zipped by donning large hair curlers and carrying a loaded clothes basket. "Do you think it's a good idea for him to always be playing with that gun? It's a different world today, not like when we were kids."

"Come on, hon, do you always have to be so politically correct?"

One eye on the poor excuse for a football game, he said to the boy, "So, little Rambo, what's the mission for today?"

Billy held up a pair of children's binoculars. "Thought I'd start by securing the perimeter. Checking the trees in the back yard for snipers."

"A noble mission indeed," barked the father with a salute. "Carry on, soldier."

Rango then returned his full attention to the TV and squeezed his eyes shut. "Come on . . . can't make a thirty-yard field goal. I swear they're trying to throw the game."

~~~

Following the strange claw marks in the tree trunks farther northeast and around a small lake, towering gable rooftops bearing clay shingles began to appear between the trees.

"Interesting that the marks are getting lower on the trees as we near the housing community," Marlin said.

"It is interesting, indeed," Sean agreed. "Deeper in the woods they ranged between thirty to forty feet up. These are lower, only about twenty-five feet."

They neared the wrought-iron fence that separated the community from the nature reserve. Marlin continued to head along the edge of the reserve, his gaze fixed upward, studying the markings that went from tree trunk to tree trunk. He paused, peering up a towering pine where the strange gouges in the bark apparently stopped.

"That's weird. Looks like this is the last tree . . . like it just disappeared."

"It didn't. Look."

Marlin glanced down to find a pair of clawed footprints sunk deep into the soil.

"You've got to be kidding me," Sean gasped. "The markings in the last tree are still about twenty-five feet high. What kind of bear can jump from that height to the ground?"

"And land on its back feet," Marlin added, "with its front paws barely touching the ground." He indicated a second pair of paw prints in front of the others that weren't nearly as deep. "This is where its front paws came down. By the depth of the impression, you can tell that the front paws bore hardly any of the animal's weight. It's almost as if they just touched the ground to assist in balance."

Sean scratched his scalp beneath his baseball cap. "And what kind of bear does that?"

"Who said we're still looking for a bear?" Marlin knelt to study the prints more closely. "Too bad the soil is so soft here. Can't take a toe count. But the proportions are off. They're too long and narrow for a bear."

"Look, there's another track," Sean said, pointing. The two made their way through a chest-deep cluster of saw palmettos to where a single clawed foot had left an imprint in the Florida sand.

"That's at least ten feet from the other prints," Marlin said. "What kind of animal has a stride like . . ." He paused at the sight of another track near the wrought-iron fence that surrounded the silent community.

Peering between the black iron bars, he searched for other tracks in the sprawling back yard. That's when he noticed a sliver of shower curtain dangling from a window on the west side of the home. The rising sun allowed him to see the shape of a woman's body just beneath the window. Even at this distance and in the low light, he could see that she was not in one piece. He then discovered a second body not far away from hers.

There was a rustling in the brush behind them. Marlin turned around to face the forest, and his eyes flared. A brown blur erupted from the saw palmettos and landed on top of Sean, pinning him against the ground. Ripping out Sean's throat with its massive teeth, the Kodiak bear raised its head and looked at Marlin, blood dripping from its muzzle.

Before Marlin could sling the rifle from his shoulder, the bear lunged toward him and, with a swipe of a powerful paw, knocked him back against the wrought-iron fence.

~~~

His elbows perched on the roof of the doghouse, little Billy peered through his binoculars, scouring the trees for the enemy. Beside him, his cocker spaniel, Sammy, was sitting back on his haunches, gazing in the same direction. Just to their right, the early morning sun danced across the water of the pool.

"Nice and quiet, Sammy. Let me know if you see something," the boy whispered without breaking his gaze from the trees.

He heard a rustling deeper in the forest. Billy lowered his binoculars, and sure enough, the brush was moving. Someone or something large was making its way through the woods. "Sammy, we've got something," he whispered, slipping the plastic AK-47 from his shoulder and laying it on top of the doghouse, well within reach.

The dog was growling and baring its teeth now.

"You see it too, don't you, boy?" But when he glanced at the dog, he noted that Sammy was peering almost straight up into the trees.

Billy raised his binoculars toward where the dog was looking. Sammy, however, turned tail and took off along the fence, rounded the far corner of the pool, and shot through the doggie door and into the house.

"Hey, that's desertion, Sammy," Billy scolded. "You can get court-martialed for that."

And then his binoculars discovered the spot where the dog had been looking. His jaw dropped. The binoculars fell as well, bouncing from the roof of the doghouse and tumbling into the grass as he stared at the thing about thirty feet up. Just visible behind a large cluster of oak leaves, the creature remained perfectly still.

With his left hand, Billy slowly picked up his plastic rifle from the roof of the doghouse and trained it on his adversary.

Immediately, the gruesome head cocked downward, and its red eyes locked on the boy. The thing stood taller on the branch. An explosion of leaves, and the monster sprang forward from its perch, plummeting thirty feet and landing with a deep thud just behind the wrought-iron fence.

The creature then recoiled from its four-footed landing stance, rising on its hind legs until its chest was well above the five-foot fence. Up close, the thing appeared to wear a gray mask. And then the gray covering appeared to ripple, and like interlaced fingers, the long tentacle-like mane protecting its face separated to reveal the true horror beneath. Billy gasped at the long, spiked teeth, wrinkled gorilla snout, green pebbled flesh, and the red, glowing eyes.

The child stared up at the creature's full form—its broad, knotted shoulders that supported long, thickly muscled arms terminating into gnarled knuckles and claws. Its pebbled chest was also heavily armored which tapered down into a cheetah-like waist and powerful quadriceps. At the knees, the brawny legs arced back like a canine and tapered down into clawed feet.

As horrible as the thing's features were, they were barely noted compared to those eyes. Eyes as hypnotic as they were hideous. Eyes with vertical, cat-like pupils that refused to release him from their gaze.

The long, interlocked teeth parted, and a guttural growl reverberated from deep within the beast. There was no mistaking it for a warning growl that it was—much like a dog would make before launching an attack.

Billy peered down the barrel of his plastic weapon and awaited the kill shot.

Its red eyes locked on the boy, the beast slipped its clawed fingers between two of the vertical bars of the wrought-iron fence. The creature pushed its hands outward and, to a series of snapping clanks, shoved the metal bars back from its path. Then with another snap of metal, it broke the horizontal support bar at the top of the fence and separated it to the width of its shoulders.

Before the beast could take a step, Billy opened fire. A thick stream of water arced over the doghouse and splattered the gnarled chest. The beast threw its arms out wide, and a long, shaft-like saber protruded from the back of each wrist.

The monster then looked down at the liquid draining from its pebbled skin. The beast curiously touched the water with its fingers and looked at the child as if saying, *"What the hell?"*

Billy raised his aim toward the creature's face, ready to take another shot. But he paused. His first rounds to the chest had been ineffective. This foe was clearly too much for his weaponry. *Too bad I don't have dad's AK-47.*

Realizing he was outgunned for the time being, Billy reluctantly lowered his weapon to the ground behind the doghouse. He inched his fingers toward the plastic knife on his belt and again paused, peering up at the towering beast.

Its horrible eyes remained fixed on him.

Billy studied the sabers protruding from the creature's forearms. *Maybe hand-to-hand combat wouldn't be such a good idea either. Yes, this is a reconnaissance mission. Gather intel and report back to base. Let the boys take care of this one with an air strike.*

A click of its wrists and the long sabers retracted into the backs of its forearms. The beast then nodded into the distance behind Billy and made a shooing gesture with its clawed hand.

Billy immediately understood. It was like when he and his dad were fishing. He'd hooked a small grouper, but his dad said it wasn't big enough to keep and tossed it back into the water. *Maybe I'm not a big enough catch either.*

The creature gave a low, guttural growl and again gestured for Billy to take a hike.

Billy gave a slow nod. "Okay, I get it." Before he could turn around, there was another growl, this time from the woods.

Just behind the beast, the trees shook. Another loud roar, and the brush parted to reveal a Kodiak bear rearing up on its hind legs. The creature turned away from Billy, threw its arms out, extracting its sabers, as it faced off with the bear.

Not wanting to see how things turned out, Billy raced back toward the house.

~~~

Frustrated with a missed call by the referee, Rango jumped to the edge of the couch. "Come on, ref, couldn't you see that was pass interference? Mr. Magoo would have called that one."

His wife shouted from the kitchen that was attached to the family room, "Football gets you so worked up. Let's turn it to a movie. Bet I could find us a good one on the Women's Channel."

Rango sank back into the couch. "Sorry, babe. But even a

bad football game has got a chick flick beat by a long shot."

His wife snickered and turned back to the sink, where a large window offered a picturesque view of the pool area and the nature reserve beyond.

"But nice try," Rango added.

He turned to Billy, who had just burst through the door huffing and puffing. "Dad, I think we need to call in an air strike," the boy blurted, his wide eyes glaring at his father from beneath his helmet.

"Why?" replied Rango, half watching the game. "Run across something out there that the squirt gun . . . I mean the AK couldn't handle?"

"Yeah," the boy said between gasps of breath. "A shot to the chest didn't faze it." Another breath. "It's an alien, and it's back there fighting a bear right now."

"That's pretty good." Rango snickered and patted the couch. "Have a seat, soldier, and watch the rest of the game with me. If you can call it that."

"No, Dad. You have to take a look. I'm not making it up. It's right behind the doghouse. I swear!"

The mother leaned over the sink counter and peered out the window, as if humoring the child. But she grew rigid and her eyes wide as she surveyed the yard. "Rango, the trees are shaking. Something *is* going on out there."

Rango rolled from the couch and raced through the doorway, adorned in only his sweatpants and a look of perplexity. Striding across the yard, he stopped and turned to his son, who was hot on his heels. "No, Billy, you have to stay back and protect your mother. Return to base, soldier."

A quick salute, and little Billy obeyed the order.

Crossing the yard in bare feet, Rango paused as he neared the doghouse. "The fence . . . what happened to the fence?" He studied how the vertical bars had been shoved away and separated from the horizontal support bar which was now split and curled upward toward the trees.

The force of a grenade could barely do that, he thought. And he hadn't heard an explosion. Only one thing troubled him now—that he hadn't taken the time to grab his assault rifle.

Stepping over Billy's abandoned squirt gun, he crept around the doghouse and stood before the mangled opening in the fence. When Rango first bolted from the house, he'd half expected to find a coyote attacking a dog or a deer. The last thing he'd expected to find was what lay before him.

A severed bear paw.

About twenty feet from the paw was a bear, or what was left of one, lying between two trees. In addition to its left paw, the animal's right arm and head were severed. In the center of its chest, a massive section of tissue was missing, as if the result of a large shark bite.

A few slow steps closer to the carnage revealed more claw-like marks near the bears shoulders. A single deep slash went horizontally across the abdomen, revealing knotted bulges of intestine. The fact that blood was still pooling beneath the severed appendages unnerved him immensely.

This is a fresh kill.

Rango's military instincts had him looking in every direction, even straight up into the trees. Nothing. Not a sound. The only thing moving were the crimson streams still running down the bark on a tree beside the carcass.

Now only one thing was for certain. Rango wasn't about to take another step without his gun.

CHAPTER 7

CONFLICTING EVIDENCE

Fresh out of the hospital, Detective Pine felt like he'd crawled out of a grave as he ambled through the nearly empty precinct. His taped ribs were sore, but not as painful as one would have imagined. Fortunately, his only other injury was a bloodshot left eye, where several capillaries had burst from the tremendous pressure he'd sustained. A condition that he had remedied with a pair of Oakley sunglasses.

Izabella was either away from her desk or not in yet. Neither was Officer Jones. There were only five officers in the room, all of which happened to be Larry's minions. It felt like walking into a classroom full of bullies when the teacher wasn't around.

"Nice shades, Hollywood," muttered one of the guys.

"No, man, that's Ray Charles," blurted someone else.

"No, no, Crocket. You know from that '80s show, *Miami Vice*." Tiny threw his hands out. "He's from Miami, a detective . . . it works."

Drawing closer to his desk, Scott noticed another presumed gift awaiting him. This time it was a book. Picking it up, he noted the cobra on its cover. The title read, *A Guide to Handling Large Snakes and Reptiles*.

Squeezed to within an inch of his life, and these fools thought it was a joke.

Tossing the book into the drawer with the other stupid gifts, he plopped down in his chair. He was in no mood for anyone's "wit," if you could call it that. *This is not the day,* he thought, peering through his Oakleys at the other officers perched smugly at their desks. His mind was on the destroyed lab. With the geneticist Jim Randle still unconscious, it was up to Scott to piece it all together. Everyone considered it a cut-and-dry case, with the evidence pointing to the bear. But Scott remained troubled. He ached to see what was on the other side of that locked steel door.

Izzy appeared in the hallway carrying a cup of coffee. Reaching his desk, she slipped her free arm around his neck and gave him a motherly hug. "Glad to hear that that snake didn't get the best of you, honey." Looking up, she added, "Speaking of snakes, here comes another one."

"Sorry I'm late." A deep voice echoed through the room. "I didn't get to see your expression when you opened your present, Pine. Hope you liked it." In walked big Larry and three more of his crew. "Nice shades."

Tiny spoke up. "We were just trying to think of a name for him. I said Crocket. You know like in *Miami Vice.*"

"Nah." Larry waved off the suggestion. "That's not demeaning enough for this pip-squeak." He then grandly extended a hand toward Scott. "Ladies and gentlemen, behold the Snake Whisperer!"

As laughter erupted through the room, Scott's mind's eye drifted back to the fourth grade. Darrel Henry, the official school bully, had pushed him down, making him drop his books for the third time in a row. Everyone was laughing as Scott felt the burn of humiliation, anger. He'd had enough. He turned to Darrel and kicked him square in the crotch. When the big boy dropped to his knees, Scott followed through with a knee to his nose that sent blood spewing into the hall.

"There's only so many times you can pick up your books," he muttered, staring at the hulking officer bearing an arrogant grin. As big Larry turned and lumbered back to his desk, Scott called to him, "So I hear you played in the NFL."

Larry turned to face him with a wink. "You bet."

"What does that stand for?" the detective asked.

Larry looked around at his fellow officers and pointed at Scott. "This little dingleberry doesn't know what the NFL stands for." He placed his hands on his knees, leaned forward, and pronounced it nice and slow. " National. Football. League."

The detective shook his head.

Larry laughed aloud and looked around at the guys. "You believe this little runt?"

"That's not what it stands for," Scott said. "*Not for you.*"

Larry cupped his beefy hands beside his ears. "Well, tell me what it stands for, then."

Scott grinned. "For you, it stands for *not . . . for . . . long.*"

There was a moment of stunned silence as if no one could believe their ears, especially Larry. And then the officers howled and slapped their desks, but no one laughed louder than Izzy.

Enraged, the big man stepped toward the detective. "I'll rip you in half, little man." And then he noticed the detective's sidearm trained on his crotch.

Scott squinted down the barrel of his 9mm. "I'm sorry, Larry, but my tolerance level for your BS is at an all-time low this morning. One more step, and you'll be singing soprano."

Big Larry squinted in confusion. "Singing what?"

"He's going to blow your balls off," Izzy belted out from her desk.

Larry looked at her with his hands out. "What? You're taking his side?"

"No," Izzy said. "I just don't want to see you separated from your family jewels."

Then all around the room, chairs squeaked on the tile as

officers came to their feet, their service sidearms trained on the detective.

One hand on the pistol, Scott pulled a prescription bottle from a desk drawer and held it up. He squinted at the label. "Don't drive or operate heavy equipment . . . no, here it is. Can impair your thought process . . . especially decision making." He looked at the other officers. "According to this, I'm not responsible for my own actions."

"All right, men," one officer spoke to the others. "Let's just holster our weapons. This has gone far enough."

After all of the officers had complied, Scott laid his 9mm on the desk and blew Larry a kiss.

"This isn't over," Larry grumbled as he headed back toward his desk.

After the tension had lifted and everyone had returned to their work, Izzy looked at Scott with a grin. "That was pretty good, though you're a little crazy." She eyed the prescription bottle. "What is that they've got you on?"

The detective tossed her the bottle. Catching it, she studied the label.

"I'm not taking anything," Scott said. "That empty bottle was already in the desk when I came here. It's paroxetine, an antidepressant drug used by menopausal women to treat hot flashes."

Izzy tossed the bottle back to him with a wide grin. "I knew there was something I liked about you."

Her console lit up, and she turned toward her desk. Jotting down a few notes, she spoke into her headset. "No, you don't have to warn your neighbors. We'll take care of that. Just keep your family indoors. We're on the way."

Punching a button on the console, she turned to face the crew. "All right, gentlemen. There has been another bear attack. Four people dead. Two of the victims were believed to have been from Animal Control." She looked at her notes.

"The attacks took place in Hidden Lakes, a residential community about two miles northeast of the lab where the initial attacks occurred."

Rising from his chair, Scott Pine looked at Izzy. "Do they *think* the attacks were from the bear, or did someone actually see the bear?"

"According to the witness, he saw a large bear leave one of the bodies and disappear into the woods."

Scott gave her a quick nod and filed in behind the officers as they headed for the door. As a precautionary measure, he let big Larry leave the building well ahead of him.

~~~

"My word, she's worse than the victims at the lab." Officer Jones cringed as Detective Pine raised the corner of the blood-crusted shower curtain to reveal the remains beneath it. Bisected at the waist, the young woman lay nude on her back with deep lacerations across her face and breasts. Below her left breast was an apparent bite mark that had dissected a large amount of tissue, ribs and all.

Trailing from beneath her severed waist and backbone was a four-foot swath of bloody grass that led to where her lower half lay beneath a sheet. Raising his gaze from the sheet, Scott studied a torn section of shower curtain dangling from a broken bathroom window. Like perfectly painted pinstripes, several lines of dried blood reached down from the windowsill to the shrubs below.

Officer Jones was looking there as well. "What took place in there must have made the shower scene in *Psycho* seem like a Disney movie." He shook his head. "The sheer force of how it slammed her into the wall, breaking the tile. And then to snap her spine while pulling her through the window . . . That bear must have tremendous strength."

Officer Jones proceeded to walk along a black tarp that

was strung between the two homes to shield the view of the crime scene from the road. He knelt beside the second body while Detective Pine had another look at the female victim.

Scott's eyes were drawn to four parallel shadows near the curtain's torn edge. Lifting it up with a gloved hand, he saw four long claw marks that ran to the torn edge. "There you are again," he muttered. With his free hand, he slipped out his camera and took a few shots.

"Hey, Detective," Jones called to him. "Take a look at this."

Taking a final shot of the remains, the detective headed to where Officer Jones was knelt beside the second victim. It was a man in a robe lying on one side with his upper body partially covered by a sheet.

The detective eased down on his haunches beside the officer.

"Not much to see here, no wounds," Officer Jones said. "Only this." He pulled back the sheet to reveal that the man's face was frozen in a state of horror. His mouth was stretched open wide as his bulging eyes seemed to stare up at them.

"He definitely saw something." The officer lowered the sheet. "My guess is that the sight of it gave him a heart attack."

"And no wounds," the detective added. "Maybe there's something to the rule of playing dead to ward off a bear attack."

"Only he wasn't playing."

"You said there was a witness who saw the bear at the scene?"

"A Mr. Aleck Stein," Jones replied. "He lives on the other side of the cul-de-sac. At approximately 6:00 a.m., he was taking in his trash cans when he noticed the female victim on the lawn. When he came closer to investigate, that's when he saw a large bear on the other side of the fence. It was hovering over one of the last two victims. He said the bear locked eyes with him and then trotted off into the woods. That was the last he saw of it."

Detective Pine peered across the misty lawn to where a pair of covered bodies lay on the opposite side of a wrought-iron fence. In the woods behind the bodies, several officers wound yellow tape from tree trunk to tree trunk, marking off the crime scene.

"So, Mr. Stein only saw the bear on the opposite side of the fence, never on this side?"

"Correct," Officer Jones said. "And that's the strange part. There isn't a single track on the property to suggest the bear had been on this side of the fence."

"Let's have a look," Pine said, and they headed toward the fence.

~~~

"For the last time, Darlene, where did you hide my guns?" Rango shouted at his wife. After searching every room in the house, he teetered on the verge of rage. He lifted the pillows from the couch in the family room and reached beneath them. "Come on," he demanded. "I'm wasting time."

"Stop screaming," Darlene pleaded. "You're scarring Billy."

"No, you're upsetting Billy by hiding my AK-47."

"But you can't go out there! Not after what you saw." Darlene was standing in the entry to the kitchen beside Billy. "Besides, this is not your job. You're on leave. This is a job for the police."

"The police." Rango laughed. "This is a fresh kill. Whatever took down that bear couldn't have gone far just yet. But by the time the police show up, it'll be long gone."

Darlene was on the verge of tears. "I go through enough of this every time you're deployed," she sniffled. "Don't I at least deserve a break from the stress when you're on leave?"

Before he could think of a response, Darlene darted into the bathroom and *click*. She locked the door behind her.

Rango then turned to little Billy, who was still donning his plastic helmet. "Soldier, did you see where she hid the AK?"

~~~

Kneeling beside the body of the male victim with his shoulder leaning against the bottom of the iron fence, Detective Pine studied the long wound across the man's chest. He was quick to note the five distinct claw marks that tore through the khaki shirt and deep into the flesh. "One, two, three, four . . . five." He counted them again to be certain.

A similar wound went across the victim's throat and had severed his jugular vein. It was clearly the death wound, as the large pool of blood collected on the sand beneath his neck would attest.

The wounds on the younger male victim from Animal Control were more severe, including a single bite to the neck that had nearly decapitated him.

Rising from the body, the detective turned his attention to the myriad of paw marks left in the sand. Although they were slightly obscured due to a brief Florida rain, every track possessed five distinct toes.

"So, what do you surmise, Detective?" asked Officer Jones, crouched over the younger male victim.

"From the positioning of the bodies and the placement of the tracks, I would say the younger victim was attacked first." The detective turned to the remains lying at the foot of the fence. "Then it knocked the second victim into the fence and disabled him. But before it could complete its meal, the bear locked eyes with Mr. Stein and got spooked, then hightailed it back into the woods."

"Finish its meal," the big officer said. "It was probably half full after the chunk it took out of the poor girl."

"I don't think so." The detective was staring beyond the fence toward the remains lying beneath the shower curtain about thirty yards away. "These attacks didn't occur at the same time. Not even close."

"Come again?" blurted the officer.

"These attacks occurred only a couple of hours ago. Mr. Stein saw the bear at 6:00 a.m., practically when it occurred, interrupting its meal. The blood is still pooled, barely coagulated. The blood on the wall beneath the windowsill and on the shower curtain is crusted. You could see where some parts of it had flaked off during the rain. I would say that she was pulled from the window sometime during the night. Forensics will tell us for certain though."

"That seems to make sense," Officer Jones said. " One of the neighbors said she was a nurse and works mostly the day shift. Guess she would probably shower after a long shift."

The officer looked at the bodies of the men from Animal Control, their green pants and khaki shirts strewn with blood. "But what are you saying? That the bear killed the woman last night, and then hung around or came back and killed these two at 6:00 a.m.?"

"Not saying that at all." Detective Pine was studying the pristine grass on the other side of the fence. "There's not a single bear track on the other side of the fence in the yard. The fence itself is completely intact. And there are no large tree trunks or branches overhanging the fence where it could have dropped down from. The witness saw the bear on *this* side of the fence."

"Okay," Officer Jones said. "I see where you're going. There's no evidence that the bear had ever entered the yard over there. So, enlighten me already. How did the bear get over the fence and attack the girl?"

"It didn't," said the detective.

"It didn't what?"

"It didn't go over the fence or attack the girl."

The officer was taken back. "Then what the hell did?"

The detective's phone rang, and he answered it. "Where . . . the address again? Okay, got it. We're on the way." Pocketing his cell phone, Scott looked at Officer Jones. "Well, the good news is they found the bear."

~~~

Escorted by a young Marine on leave who went by the name of Rango, Detective Pine and Officer Jones stepped through a mangled section of wrought-iron fence and into another blood-soaked crime scene. They were only one block west of the last attack site.

At least this victim isn't human, the detective thought. But if the remains did prove to be that of the Kodiak Bear they'd been searching for, that was another issue in itself.

Rango pointed out a severed bear paw lying near the mangled fence. When the detective saw the size of the mutilated carcass lying twenty feet away from the severed limb, a chill crept up his spine. Although the head and some of the limbs were missing, he immediately knew these weren't the remains of a Florida black bear native to the area, but was indeed the animal they'd been looking for.

Studying the scattered remains, everyone remained silent. Even Officer Jones seemed to be at a loss for words. But his wit couldn't be stifled for long. "It doesn't look like Sleepy will be waking up from this one. It looks like he had a run-in with a shredder."

Stepping away from the severed paw lying near the fence, the detective followed the splatters of blood to a thick oak that was near the carcass. He studied where scattered chunks of bark were missing; claw marks that led up the tree to about fifteen feet, where the trunk was slick with blood. Crimson streams had run down from the spot and pooled onto the branches.

"Looks like you tangled with something near the fence, lost a paw, and tried to make your escape up this tree," Scott concluded. "Until something stopped you."

Then about twenty feet away, he spotted the bear's head lying at the base of a pine tree. "What could do this?" he muttered.

Rango was beside himself. "I'm sorry. But if it hadn't been for my wife hiding my AK-47, I could have caught up with it by now."

The big officer chuckled. "So, did you find it, or did she finally fess up?"

"After you guys arrived, she finally told me. It was behind the washing machine—in a room she said I wasn't familiar with."

"Can't say that I would have found it either." Officer Jones said.

"Too bad though." Rango sighed. "If it weren't for the thirty minutes I lost looking for the gun, I probably could have caught up with it. Whatever it was."

Detective Pine was studying the deep bite mark in the chest of the headless remains. "Be sure to get her something nice for Christmas."

"Why?" Rango said.

"For saving your life."

Staring at the huge carcass, Officer Jones's demeanor turned more ominous as he seemed to ponder the obvious question. "Do you think there's a possibility that the lab had two bears in containment?"

"Not according to Wendy, the veterinarian," Scott said.

"Then what in these woods could do that to a Kodiak bear?"

"No. What in *this world* could do that to a Kodiak bear?" said the detective as he knelt down to a four-clawed foot print in the bloody soil. Holding his hand over the massive print for scale, he added, "The steel door back at the lab . . . I think it's about time we cut the lock off."

CHAPTER 8

BREAKING AND ENTERING

Sparks flew from the lock, bouncing from the steel door and up toward the ceiling as the shrill sound of metal grinding against metal filled the laboratory hallway.

Detective Pine and Officer Jones waited anxiously until there was a loud clank of metal and the shower of sparks ceased. Lowering the circular saw with a carbide-toothed blade, the rescue worker flipped up the shield on his helmet and stepped away from the door.

"We're in, sir," he said to Officer Jones.

Jones graciously extended a hand toward the door. "Be my guest, detective."

Pushing open the vault-like door, Scott stepped inside a circular steel-walled room. A keycard with a lanyard lay on the floor not far from the doorway. Trailing from the card was a speckled line of blood that led back to where he stood.

Easing deeper into the vast room, he studied the glass, Jacuzzi-like container that still emitted bubbles and the toppled equipment lying beside it. His gaze then rose to the numerous imperfections in the steel walls. Imperfections that he realized in horror were countless deep dents and four-fingered claw marks.

"Incredible," he whispered, noting that some of the claw marks reached up to the twenty-foot domed ceiling.

Officer Jones followed his gaze. "What did they have in here?" He shook his head. "No bear, that's for sure."

Detective Pine lowered his gaze to the console beside the door. Near the console, a bloody claw print was curled around the doorframe.

Taking out his cell phone, the detective punched in a number. "Wendy, this is Scott. Would you mind meeting me at the lab ASAP?"

~~~

Just beyond the tree line on the northwest side of Hidden Lakes, Officers Larry Webber and Tiny were combing the woods. Each carried a pair of binoculars and an assault rifle.

"Wow, what's that stench?" Larry peered through the trees through his binoculars. "Smells like we might be coming up on a carcass."

"No, I think that's me." Tiny squinted anxiously at his surroundings. "Sometimes I get a little flatulent when I'm nervous."

"Well, you must be friggin terrified," muttered Big Larry, completing another sweep of the trees ahead. "It's a shame they already offed the bear though." Larry sighed. "I wanted to take it out myself. Imagine the headlines, 'Former NFL Star Turned Cop Kills Rampaging Kodiak Bear.' Would have been awesome."

"So, since the bear is dead," Tiny said, "why do they still have us out here beating the bushes?"

"They think there's something else out here."

"Like what? What kind of animal?"

"Didn't say. Just said to be on the lookout for anything unusual. Dead animals, whatever." Larry adjusted his binoculars. "Wow. I think I've got something."

"What?" Tiny slung the rifle from his shoulder.

"It's about five foot seven, brunette, and wearing a red bikini," Larry replied with his binoculars trained on a screened pool enclosure beyond the trees. "Word is they might be calling us in soon to warn the residents to remain indoors. If that's the case, I'm definitely starting at her house."

"Give me a break," Tiny said. "You already have all the women you can handle."

Big Larry lowered the binoculars and winked. "There's always room for one more on the roster. Besides, you never know when one might leave the game."

Listen," Tiny said. "What's—"

The pine tree above them swayed and shook to the sound of snapping branches. The tree next to it jostled, and they heard something large rocket through the treetops. By the time Larry slipped the rifle strap from his thick shoulder, whatever it was had disappeared.

Tiny reached for his shoulder radio mike, but Larry stopped him.

"No. Don't call it in just yet." Larry raised his binoculars and scanned the treetops along the edge of the reserve. "Let's see if we can find it ourselves."

~~~

"No. None of the animals Jim had in containment could have done this." Wendy stared upward in astonishment at the array of deep dents and claw marks that marred the steel walls in the large, cylindrical room.

Detective Pine and Officer Jones shared a look. The news was no surprise to them.

"And a bear couldn't have done this?" the detective asked. The question was posed out of formality; he already knew the answer.

The attractive blonde snickered as if he were joking. "There are claw marks in the ceiling. That has to be twenty feet up." She bit her lip, perplexed. "I'm not aware of any animal capable of this."

She turned her attention to one of the deep impressions

in the wall. "And to dent the steel like that. I don't think even a four-hundred-pound silverback gorilla could exert that kind of force."

Detective Pine stepped over the toppled equipment and the various tubes that connected to a bizarre mask lying near the wall. Beside him, the large Jacuzzi-like bath continued to emit bubbles as its contents cast shimmering shades of blue along the steel walls. "A heart monitor, respirator, and an oversized sleep apnea mask. He was definitely keeping something alive in here. And it's not here anymore."

Officer Jones grunted, then said,"What was in here . . . that's what you think killed the girl at Hidden Lakes?"

Scott was staring blankly at the swirling bubbles inside the large water tank, the blue water radiating on his face. "The blood tells us she was killed much earlier than the two male victims. The bear most likely caught the scent of the girl's blood, and that's what drew it to the area where it encountered the two men from Animal Control. My guess would be the bear then tracked the other creature, hoping to scavenge off of its next kill."

"But Sleepy followed it a little too close and ended up *becoming* the next kill," Officer Jones suggested. He glanced around the room with revelation in his eyes. "Whatever was in here is probably still in the vicinity of that neighborhood."

"Exactly," said the detective.

"I've got to call the chief." Officer Jones's voice now reflected a deeper sense of urgency. "We've got to evacuate the neighborhood, or at least get it on lockdown."

~~~

Fifty-eight-year-old Chief O'Hern stood at a large picture window in his office, staring blankly across the Orlando skyline while listening on his phone. His stomach seemed to tighten with every word.

"And Detective Pine is certain the victims weren't killed by the same animal?" he asked, then listened for a beat. "Yes, obviously. The fact that the bear was killed in such a manner confirms there's another dangerous animal on the prowl. Yes, I did see the photographs of the remains."

He thought for a moment, staring across the rooftops of the city to the woods beyond: *to evacuate the area would be chaos.* "Okay, I want the entire community on lockdown. No one goes in or out for the next twenty-four hours. No trips to the store, soccer practice . . . nothing.

"I want six units patrolling the area to make sure everyone remains indoors. The rest of our men should be combing the woods. With any luck, we can have this buttoned up and end the quarantine by morning."

He slammed the phone receiver onto its base and prayed the plan would be that easy.

~~~

The noon sun glared through the sliding glass doors as Rhines Smoothies store owner, Bret Rhines, was sprawled on his favorite recliner in his den. Adorned in black sweatpants and a tank top that showcased his full-sleeve tattoos, the thirty-five-year-old sipped a Blue Blast. It was a blueberry-flavored amino acid concoction that he'd created to aid in muscle recovery.

Exhausted from his 11:00 CrossFit session, Bret would shower soon enough. For the moment, he just wanted to relax and catch his breath in his sanctuary. Before him, an eighty-inch TV formed the centerpiece in a lavish cherry wood entertainment center. Around the huge screen, a plethora of small nooks held family photos and mementos from his and Sandy's various ski trips and hiking adventures.

Above the sprawling entertainment center was a deep nook that ran the width of the wall and shelved exotic plants that reached up toward the eighteen-foot cathedral ceiling. To his left were four sliding glass doors that could retract into the walls and open up the room to the lavish pool enclosure. And above it all was the sun, which was becoming a nuisance. Bret knew it was affecting the picture quality on the TV, but he didn't feel like getting up and closing the blinds.

Flipping the channel from a dog show, he landed on a fight scene where a pair of brutes were going toe-to-toe in a caged, octagon-shaped ring. "Now that's what I'm talking about," Bret howled and turned up the volume.

"Hey, hon, how about a couple of turkey sandwiches?" he called out to an open doorway that adjoined the den. But there was no answer. *Must still be in the shower.* He another sip from his mixer cup.

Lowering the drink, he cringed at the TV. "Oooh, I felt that one. That boy can throw a punch."

A little white terrier padded into the room from the hallway and proceeded to bark at the sliding glass doors. The dog looked at Bret and gave him another loud yelp.

"All right, Whisky. Just shut up, and I'll take you out after this round."

But the dog didn't comply.

The dog's coat grew dark as a shadow stretched across the wood floor. The glaring sun to Bret's left was gone. A slow look in that direction, and he saw a horrific form silhouetted by the sunlight.

No way. That can't be there, he thought until the thing lowered its gruesome head and slowly stepped through the hurricane-proof slider as if it weren't even there. Chunks of glass rolled and bounced down gnarled skin and rained onto the floor.

Bret sprang from the chair and landed in his practiced MMA stance. His last move. Ever.

~ ~ ~

Finished drying off with a towel, Sandy tossed it over a corner of the tub and slipped on a Boys Lie t-shirt that was lying on the counter. Looking in the mirror, she unfastened her wavy black hair and let it fall down below her shoulders.

Exiting the bathroom, she knelt in the sprawling bedroom to pick up a dirty pair of leggings, slid into them, then continued toward the den. She heard Whisky barking and shook her head. "Is Daddy too lazy to take you out again?"

Sandy stepped through the doorway. "Don't worry, Sugar. Mommy's com—" The words died in her mouth when she saw the glass strewn across the floor, the busted slider.

Turning around, beside the blaring fight on the TV, she saw a red line running down the wall. Following it upward, her eyes locked on her husband's lifeless gaze as he seemingly looked down from the edge of the nook with one arm dangling toward her.

Her scream echoed through the vast home as her vision blurred and she grew dizzy. Everything was moving. The next thing Sandy knew, she was wailing and racing down the hallway toward the front door. Her bare feet slid to a stop and *wham!* Her shoulder thudded against the door.

She frantically fiddled with the lever on the lock until it clicked and the door cracked open. When it did, a clawed hand came from out of nowhere, blocking her exit, and violently hurled her back. Sandy flew backward until she landed hard and slid another ten feet farther down the hallway.

Scrambling to her feet next to the kitchen area, she saw a blurry gray mass until *whap!* A gnarled backhand turned her world black as she felt her body careening across the kitchen counter, knocking plates and pans onto the floor. Sailing from the end of the counter, she finally rolled to a stop in a corner, spilling the dog's water bowl.

~~~

Sixty-one-year-old, Cal Harrison sat on a stool in his garage with the love of his life. Squirting another dab of polish onto a buffing pad, he proceeded to apply it in perfect circular motions to the driver's-side door of his green 1971 Plymouth Barracuda.

Guns 'N' Roses' *Paradise City* blared from an old radio perched on a shelf behind him. No earbuds for Cal. He liked to feel the beat thumping through the garage and beyond so that the neighbors could hear it too. When Cal was detailing the Hemi Cuda, everyone knew it.

Bobbing his head and swirling the buffer pad in rhythm to the beat, he heard something yelp just above the music. He turned to find the neighbor's little white terrier standing at his feet and barking at him.

Killing the radio, he knelt down to the dog. "Whisky, you little escape artist. How did you get out this time?"

Tossing the buffer pad onto the hood of the car, he scooped up Whisky with one arm and headed for the Rhines's house. Trotting up the driveway and onto the walkway of the sprawling home, he noticed that the front door was cracked open. "No wonder you got out."

Knocking on the door, Cal hollered inside, "Bret, Sandy . . . anyone home?"

Not hearing an answer, he opened the door further and stepped inside, cradling Whisky in his right arm. "Hello," he hollered again, his voice echoing down the hallway. The only sound to be heard came from a big-screen TV playing in a room beyond the far end of the hallway.

Heading deeper into the presumed empty home, Whisky began to growl and fidget in his arm. "Okay, boy, you go find them," muttered Cal as he sat the dog down in the hallway. But the moment the dog's paws hit the floor, he turned tail and bolted through the front door.

A crackling noise came from an office to his left. "Hey,

Bret, is that you?"

~~~

Sgt. Chris Hayes wheeled his patrol car west along Weeping Elm Drive. His young partner, Ofc. William Stevens, was perched beside him, scouring every residence they passed.

In the distance, a motorcycle patrol unit pulled onto the road from a side street and headed in their direction.

"Looks like they're calling everyone in," muttered the sergeant.

"So what exactly are we supposed to be looking for?" asked Officer Stevens.

"Signs of a break-in, like forced entry. Anything that looks out of the norm."

Just then, a man flew through the front window of a house and landed in the yard.

"Like that?"

"That definitely fits the bill," replied the sergeant as he pulled the cruiser up onto the sidewalk in front of the large home. The motorcycle officer had seen it too, and rolled into the driveway. Leaning the bike onto its kickstand, the female officer with a ponytail dangling from the back of her helmet headed for the front door.

Exiting the cruiser, Sergeant Hayes motioned Officer Stevens. "Check the victim and then meet me inside." After a nod from the young officer, Sergeant Hayes jogged through the grass. Leaping over a row of hedges, he landed on the paver walkway and raced to the elaborate wooden front door.

Easing the door open, he stepped inside and stopped cold. At the far end of the long hallway, he found the motorcycle cop standing frozen with her gaze fixed upward on the monstrosity before her.

Towering above the officer's helmet, the thing too stood perfectly still, its clawed hands held slightly out to the sides, red eyes glaring down at her. The only thing that moved at all were the tentacle-like hairs writhing on top of its head.

The blazing eyes raised in Sergeant Hayes's direction as if welcoming him to the party. The thing then lowered on its hind legs until it was nearly eye level with the female officer, who still seemed to be held captive by its hideous gaze.

It's using her as a shield so I can't fire, Sergeant Hayes thought. He ran toward her, unholstering his sidearm.

The creature snatched her by the throat. Lifting her from the floor with its left hand, it wrapped its clawed right hand around her helmet, and *crack*. It snapped her head off. Her dangling feet kicked and fluttered.

Sergeant Hayes raised his weapon in disbelief. "You son of a—"

But before he could fire, the creature spun around and hurled the decapitation his way. Still bearing the helmet, the head spiraled down the hallway like a cannonball, ponytail twirling, until *wham!* It caught Sergeant Hayes square in the chin, lifting him from his feet and sending him sprawling across the floor.

~~~

Finding no pulse on the middle-aged male in the middle of the lawn, Officer Stevens hurried along the walkway toward the front door to assist Sergeant Hayes.

Turning the handle, he realized something was blocking the door. He shoved it open to find a police motorcycle helmet rolling away, a brown ponytail flopping in its wake. The helmet finally stopped to reveal a female face inside.

Near the helmet was Sergeant Hayes, lying in the hallway.

His sidearm drawn, Officer Stevens crept toward his motionless partner. The sergeant's nose and lips were smashed, with blood draining down his chin and into the collar of his shirt.

Keeping his eyes on the empty hallway, the young officer knelt down and placed two fingers across the man's carotid artery. *No pulse.* In addition, the angle of the sergeant's head as it leaned against the crown molding suggested his neck was broken.

At the far end of the hallway was the headless body of the female officer. In the room behind the corpse, a soccer game was playing on a big screen. Someone scored a goal and ran across the field with their arms thrust over head as the roars of the crowd echoed down the hallway.

Stevens's heart pounded, and his mind reeled. Two officers were dead, and he hadn't heard a single shot fired. *What the hell is going on?* Again his gaze lowered to the head lying in the hallway, then to his lifeless partner.

Wham! A crashing sound echoed from the other end of the hallway. Raising his sidearm, he looked up to find that the TV had been smashed. Sparks leapt from the broken screen and twinkled on the floor as an eerie silence filled the vast home.

Fresh out of the academy, the final words of one of his instructors rang clearly in his mind: *"Heroes don't last long."*

He slowly walked backward, out the front door, which he closed. Then he ran to the patrol car and cued his shoulder radio to call for backup.

~~~

Back at the circular steel room at the lab, Detective Pine studied the Jacuzzi-like tub with growing frustration. That room held a deadly secret, and with all of the computers and equipment in shambles, it was not likely to be divulged.

Wendy was in the hallway on her cell phone while Officer Jones scoured the other laboratory rooms for any computer that might still work.

Pocketing her phone, Wendy entered the room and shook her head. "I just tried the hospital again. Jim is still unconscious."

Officer Jones barreled into the doorway, nearly knocking her down. "There's been another attack at Hidden Lakes," he blurted. "Two officers are down, and they think whatever's doing the attacking might still be in the home!"

CHAPTER 9

CONFRONTATION

Trailing Officer Jones's cruiser along Weeping Elm Drive, Detective Pine's heart rate increased in tempo at the thought of the creature still being in the residence. *Finally I get to see what we're dealing with,* he thought. Through the windshield, he saw a line of patrol cars parked along the sidewalk in front of a sprawling Mediterranean-style home. A single officer stood in the front yard. Behind him, a body covered by a sheet was sprawled in the grass not far from a shattered bay window.

"Looks like this is the place," Scott muttered, parking the old Crown Vic on the sidewalk across the street from the chaos. More patrol units were sprinkled up and down the road as officers on foot m sure civilians remained in their homes.

Slamming the car door closed, his heart seemed to keep pace with the pulsing lights reflecting in the windows. Never has a case unnerved him like this.

He saw Wendy's Jeep pull onto the curb behind his vehicle. Scott pointed at her as she peered through the windshield. "Stay there, and *do not* get out of the vehicle," he ordered. Once he saw Wendy give the thumbs-up sign, he jogged across the street and approached the covered body in the lawn.

Scott exposed the badge on his belt to a young officer who greeted him. His badge read *Stevens.* "Officer Stevens, is it still in the home?" Scott asked with an anxious eye on the front door.

"No. Looks like whatever it was is long gone," the officer replied. "We've searched the entire residence. It's clear."

Immediately, his heart lowered its tempo. It wasn't the answer that Scott wanted to hear, yet he couldn't deny it brought a sense of relief. He couldn't help noticing Stevens's troubled look. "Are you okay, Officer?"

"I'm the one who called for backup." He lowered his gaze. "My partner is one of the casualties inside. Sergeant Hayes."

"I'm sorry to hear that."

"He was my field training officer. I'd only known him for three weeks."

That's some luck of the draw, the detective thought. *Fresh out of the academy and thrown into a nightmare like this.*

Turning his attention to the body, Scott knelt down to have a quick look before entering the home. Raising the sheet, he already knew what he would find. *Yep. There you are again, blunt-force trauma.* He studied the middle-aged man's collapsed face and couldn't help but wince.

Lowering the sheet, Scott rose and turned toward the home. *God only knows what I'll find in there.*

~~~

A gentle breeze swept through shattered sliding glass door and into the spacious den as Detective Pine peered up at the dent in the eighteen-foot ceiling. His gaze then shifted to the male body sprawled on a long nook just beneath it. Eerily the corpse seemed to peer over the ledge as a tattooed right arm reached down toward him.

Officer Jones was in front of the smashed TV screen, studying the ceiling. "It knocked him all the way up to the ceiling, hard enough to dent it. What are we dealing with—an oversized Rock 'Em Sock 'Em Robot?"

A good question. Pine took note of how the blood spilled over the ledge and down the wall, seeming to have originated from the victim's chest. *An upward blow to the thoracic region that lifted him eighteen feet from the ground.* All the recent victims had similar wounds, except for Sergeant Hayes.

As four other officers, toting assault rifles explored the home, Officer Jones made his way to the corpse of the female officer splayed between the den and the hallway. Looking down at her decapitated remains, he sighed. "I'm really getting tired of seeing this . . . and now two of our own."

Scott could tell the other officers felt the same. There was a new intensity in every eye, every gesture. With two cops dead, it was personal now.

"They've got things covered in here," Jones said. "I'm going to help the others check the woods out back, see if I can find an exit path."

As he made his way to the back slider, Pine turned his attention to Sergeant Hayes lying in the hallway. He studied the broken nose, teeth and, split lips, noting that the trauma wasn't nearly as severe as in the other victims. On the others, such as the head cradled in the helmet a few feet away, the faces were completely caved in. *As if they were hit by a high-speed battering ram,* he thought. *But not this one.*

A Sergeant Ramirez paused beside the detective. He was only slightly taller than Scott, but more stout. His coarse face seemed to fit his stern demeanor. "So, what do you make of this one, Detective?"

Scott followed a splattered blood trail to the helmet containing the female officer's severed head. He stooped down beside it. Tilting the helmet so that the frozen eyes looked away from him, he studied an arced indentation in the back of the helmet.

"Unbelievable," he muttered, rising to his feet.

Ramirez repeated his question. "So, what do you make of this one?" He added, "It's like he wasn't hit as hard."

"More like he was hit by something else," Scott replied. "He was hit by something blunter, rounded." He paused, looking at the helmet. "I know it sounds preposterous, but it appears that he was struck by the helmet."

"The helmet with the head in it?" Ramirez laughed. He looked toward the decapitated body lying near the den and back to the corpse sprawled at their feet. "That body is twenty feet away." He snickered again. "You're telling me that something threw her head into this officer's face with enough force to snap his neck? You're out of your mind."

"Well, perhaps you can explain the tooth marks in the back of the helmet, and why there's a broken-off tooth still occupying one of them?"

The sergeant's smirk faded as his eyes drifted to the helmet.

"Were there any witnesses?" the detective asked him.

"None that are still alive," Sergeant Ramirez muttered, gazing back and forth between the officer's bloodied mouth and the helmet lying in the hallway.

"So, have you seen anything that might suggest an exit path?" Scott asked, peering down the hallway toward the den.

"Probably left the same way that it came in. Through a large hole in the screened enclosure out back."

An affirmative nod, and Detective Pine headed down the hallway toward the rear of the home. Stepping around the blood pool surrounding the decapitated officer at the end of the hall, he passed below the male victim lying in the nook and paused before four, large sliding glass doors that stretched across the rear of the den. The second door to his left was completely shattered with the majority of the glass strewn inside the room. A light breeze drifted in through the jagged opening, accompanied by the tranquil sound of cascading water.

Opening the slider to his right, the detective stepped into a tropical sanctuary that contrasted sharply with the horrors inside the home. On the opposite side of the spacious pool, streams of water sprayed upward from a stone water feature and cascaded down onto the glittering liquid surface. Framing the blue oasis was an array of tropical flowers and sprawling robellini palms that reached up the vast screen enclosure.

Looking straight up from just outside the shattered door, he saw a large hole in the enclosure where sections of the screen hung down toward the pool. Above the torn opening, a thick branch from a massive oak reached over the entire enclosure.

"You definitely came in that way," muttered the detective. *But I'm not so sure that's how you left.* He eyeballed the branch that had to be twenty feet above the deck. *Why would it jump all the way back up to that branch? Certainly it could have found an easier way out.*

A quick look around the birdcage-like enclosure showed no other holes or large sections of the screen missing. Pine concluded that the killer hadn't left the way it had come in. *Unless it was courteous enough to use the screen door.*

He continued around the perimeter of the pool, past a bar area, looking for tracks or anything out of order that might suggest the assailant had passed this way.

The detective now stood on the opposite side of the pool, away from the home, and peered out through the screen. There were no disruptions in the row of hedges behind the enclosure. Not a single footprint in the grass. The wrought-iron fence, too, was completely intact without a bar out of place.

Stepping past an inflatable chair, a quick survey of the right-side lawn yielded the same result. Nothing. Perplexed, he looked across the pool to the sliders in the back of the home and saw the silhouettes of the officers milling about inside.

He looked straight down, and his heart leapt to his throat.

There was something lying on the bottom of the pool. His first thought was that he was looking at an officer's body sprawled on the speckled concrete below. But even in the twinkling light and the distortion from the water feature, he could tell that the gray form was far from human.

A cloud of bubbles rose to the surface. But the thing just continued to lie there, looking up at him, its features obscured by the movement of the water. All Scott could see clearly were the red eyes that seemed to be locked on him.

In a split second, the face of every victim–every horrific wound he'd examined— flooded Scott's mind. He knew what this thing was capable of.

Daring not to holler, he waved his right arm just enough to gain the attention of Ramirez, who was standing just inside the shattered slider. The sergeant paused and stared in his direction.

Scott then pointed down at the pool.

Ramirez went rigid, then motioned the others. A beat later, he and three officers filed into the screened enclosure, looking down into the pool, gasping and drawing their weapons.

The creature rolled and turned upright, squatting on the bottom of the pool. Its head darted and looked around the coping. It had clearly seen them too.

The tranquility of the cascading water feature gave way to erupting gunfire as the men unloaded their assault rifles and 9mm pistols at will. Pelts of water shot up in the screened enclosure as streamers of bubbles invaded the blue water below. Dozens of more rounds pierced the glimmering surface and streaked through the water only to lose their force after five or so feet, dropping harmlessly around the beast.

"Cease fire!" Ramirez ordered. "You're just wasting rounds. It's too deep."

"It can't hold its breath forever. It's got to come up sooner or later," said one of the officers as they all reloaded their weapons and spread out along the pool's coping.

All the detective could see was the waving gray mane on its head and the knotted arms stretched out to the sides as it inched its way up toward the shallow end of the pool.

Every weapon trained on it, the creature continued to ascend toward the shallow area. Its gnarled shadow covered the pebbled concrete below, but the water revealed no more of the animal's form than its four appendages and writhing mane.

It appeared as if they had the thing trapped, but something in Pine's gut suggested it was the other way around.

The surface of the water was now no more than three feet above the creature's head.

"Like shooting fish in a barrel," hollered an officer, and fire flashed from rifle barrels as spent shells bounced from the deck and pelts of water reached for the sky.

More rounds streamed around the creature, but this time with greater velocity. The beast crouched lower, ducking its head and letting its back face the line of fire.

Through the waves of water, the detective saw the beast press itself against a bottom corner of the pool. Spent rounds bounced harmlessly from the gray back and rolled down toward the deep end of the pool.

It knows what it's doing, the detective thought. It was as if the creature were intentionally using the water to shield itself.

"Cease fire, men!" Ramirez hollered again. "It's still too dee—"

Before he could finish the sentence, the creature erupted from the water with its arms spread wide, catching the sergeant around the chest. It then crashed through a sliding glass door, holding Ramirez's body, and disappeared inside the home.

Shaking off their disbelief, the three officers raced through the shattered door in pursuit of the sergeant, their right elbows pointing outward, rifle barrels oscillating forward.

Once inside, everyone opened fire.

Being on the far corner of the pool, Scott raced around the coping, his 9mm leading the way. Leaping over a lounge chair, he almost fell as he stumbled toward what sounded like a war zone. Catching himself, he stood in time to see a swath of blood wash across the inside of one of the sliders. He could hear only two rifles firing now.

By the time Scott reached the opposite side of the deck, the melee had been reduced to a single shotgun. A loud thud caused a slider to shake, and then all gunfire ceased. Save for the cascading water behind him, there was a chilling silence as smoke from the spent rounds filled the air.

However, there was still movement on the other side of the slider in front of him. A large obscured shadow, and it was coming at him fast. Raising the 9mm, Scott stepped back. When he did, his right heel caught the coping and sent him tumbling backward into the pool.

The instant he hit the water, a massive gray blur flashed over his face to the sound of erupting glass.

Shards sprinkled across the water.

Surfacing, Scott threw an arm over the coping, gasping. Looking back across the water, all he saw was a gaping hole in the screen. There was not a trace of it. Not even a footprint on the deck. The creature had gone straight through the sliding glass door, over the deck and swimming pool, and through the back of the screened enclosure—in a single bound, it would seem.

Rolling onto the deck, the detective slowly came to his feet and holstered his wet sidearm. He gasped heavily as his heart pounded in his throat. Not from his time spent underwater, but rather from the thought of the gray blur that had just passed over him like a freight train. *It only missed by inches*, he thought. If not for his own clumsiness of tripping on the coping, he most certainly would not be alive.

Stepping through a shattered slider and into the den, it was clear the others weren't as fortunate as he. Beneath the lingering smoke of gunfire, he saw Ramirez's dead form against a wall near the entertainment center. A deep incision ran upward through his chest and exited through his throat, leaving him filleted open, displaying ribs and all.

One of the officers was lying beneath the shattered TV.

Another man was folded over like a marionette in a corner beside the couch. Just above the body was a bloody face imprint in the wall.

Still there was one more, he thought, slogging further into the den as water drained from his heavy clothes. And then he caught sight of a severed arm lying where the den met the hallway. Beyond the limb, a swath of blood ran across a wall in the hall. Where it arced down to the floor, he saw the young Officer Stevens lying facedown in his own blood.

Not one of them made it out.

In a daze, the detective continued to plod through the warzone, doing his best to step over the bodies and around the crimson pools. It was reminiscent of a house of horrors at a carnival that he'd visited as a child. Only this time, the mutilated and bleeding figures weren't hewn from wax, but were horribly real.

Stepping around the helmet with a ponytail trailing from it, the exhausted detective reached for the front door.

Swinging it open, he was met by a blur of red and blue flashing lights. Before them, Big Larry, Tiny, and a host of other officers were crowding onto the walkway with the barrels of their rifles trained in his direction.

"Is it still in the home?" Larry barked.

The detective shook his head, and they all darted past him and flooded into the doorway. Making it past a barrage of bumping elbows and shoulders, Scott stumbled through a row of hedges and collapsed onto his knees in the grass.

A car door slammed, and he saw Wendy run across the street and onto the lawn. Reaching him, she dropped onto her knees and threw her arms around him.

"Thank God," she whispered, her forehead pressed against his shoulder. "When I heard the gunfire and no one came out, I thought you . . ."

When she raised her head, he saw her tear-streaked cheeks. Her puffy eyes darted all over him as if to confirm that he was still in one piece.

"What happened in there? Did they kill it?"

Detective Pine stared blankly into the blur of flashing lights and patrol cars parked haphazardly on the lawn. "Four more officers were butchered, and it wasn't even challenged."

CHAPTER 10

OPEN DOOR

Tiny wheeled the patrol car slowly along Armenia Drive while Big Larry belted from the passenger's side window with a loudspeaker, "This area is under mandatory quarantine. Remain in your homes. Anyone seen outside will be arrested. No exceptions!"

Beyond the rooftops and towering trees, a swath of brilliant blue and purple hues faded as night settled over the community of Hidden Lakes.

Tiny swung the spotlight to a middle-aged man standing in his front lawn beside a golden retriever. He gripped the leash in one hand, a plastic bag in the other.

Popping the door open, Big Larry leapt outside the cruiser. "Sir, return to your home immediately!" he hollered, not bothering to use the loudspeaker.

"But I have to take my dog out," the man insisted.

Larry pointed at him. "Now get back in that house before I put you in there. Or would you rather I take you down to the station?"

"But what about my dog?"

"Let him use the garage. That's what we're advising everyone else to do."

The sound of a helicopter thundered overhead, and a spotlight flooded the lawn.

The man shook his head at Big Larry and begrudgingly pulled the dog back toward the home.

~~~

"They definitely have their hands full down there," Pilot Clark Weise said into his headset as he guided the Bell 407 helicopter over the mayhem below.

"Do people ever listen?" Sgt. Jerry Hill said from the passenger's seat.

"If they did, it would be a first." That was Ofc. Craig Riley from the cargo bay, where he was tethered beside the open doorway, clutching an assault rifle. "But you can hardly blame the guy. I wouldn't want my dog pissing up the garage either."

"Better that than you and the animal getting your lungs ripped out," Hill said.

Beneath the aircraft, the maze of winding streets and rooftops grew dim as beams of light strewn from police cruisers glared between the homes.

Like a wandering eye, the powerful spotlight shone down into a screened pool enclosure which proved to be clear. Further, beyond the northwest end of neighborhood, sprinkles of light peered through the trees as officers on foot scoured the woods.

Nearing the west entrance of Hidden Lakes, the sergeant sighed. "Looks like the vultures have picked up the scent already."

Below, just outside of the closed gate and barricade of police cruisers, were two news vans. Several cameramen and reporters were collected around a pair of officers guarding the gate. One of the cameramen raised his camera toward the helicopter.

"Smile, boys," the sergeant said. "It looks like we just made the news."

"So, what do you want to do, sir? Make another pass over the area?" the pilot asked.

"No. It looks like no one is out on their decks or enclosures. Let's make a low pass over the tree line along the west side of the community . . . give the boys searching the woods a little more light."

"Yes sir."

~ ~ ~

Other than the blip of a heart monitor, the small hospital room was quiet as Jim Randle remained unconscious. Seated beside the bed, Wendy held Jim's left hand while Detective Pine conversed with Officer Jones near the open doorway. A large officer guarding the room was perched in a chair just outside the doorway, fidgeting with his phone.

"They don't have any idea when he could come out of it," Scott said in a hushed tone. His frustration was growing. Every fresh homicide came with a ticking clock, but he'd never faced anything like this.

"Every answer that we need is lying in that bed," he continued. "Where it goes, where it hides. Does it have any weaknesses, vulnerabilities? What does it take to stop it?"

"Not to mention, what the hell it is," Jones added.

"Until he wakes and can give us the answers, these investigations are useless. All we're doing is counting bodies," Scott said.

"*Until* he wakes," Jones blurted. "What if he *never* wakes? What do we do then?"

"Shhhh," Wendy said in a sharp whisper. "Be careful what you say. He can still hear you."

As a series of footsteps neared the room, the guard seated outside pocketed his cell phone and shot to his feet.

Chief O'Hern entered the doorway. He promptly nodded toward the bed. "Still no change?"

"Afraid not, sir," Jones replied.

The chief's stern demeanor professed that he was fed up with the situation. He looked away from the bed, eyes smoldering. "That's all right. The next time it shows up, we'll be ready. I have two SWAT teams already in the community. The next time that thing puts in an appearance will be its last."

A firm nod to the detective and Officer Jones, and he curtly turned for the door.

As the chief's footsteps trailed away from the room, Wendy rose from beside the bed to stretch her back.

A glance at the bed, and Jones said, "The doctor said he'll notify us the moment that he wakes." He gave Scott the once-over. "And considering you still look like a half-drowned rat, you may as well take off. Get some rest for when that thing shows up again, and you know that it will."

Wendy's eyes playfully looked up to Scott. "You look like you could use a good home-cooked meal."

Jones rubbed his stomach. "Oh, Lord knows that I could. I advise you take the lady up on her offer, Detective."

"You're welcome to join us," Wendy said. "I have enough for three."

"As hungry as I am, you'd need enough for five." The officer grinned. "I'm good though. My lady has something waiting for me at home."

The officer turned Scott around toward the door. Ushering them into the hallway, Jones said to Wendy, "Do me a favor, and make sure he gets some shut-eye." He winked. "That's an order."

~~~

"Fried chicken and twice-baked potatoes. It doesn't get better than that," Scott said as he plopped down onto a fluffy pit-group couch in Wendy's apartment. He hadn't felt so stuffed since his last dinner at his mother's house in Miami.

"I would offer you some wine, but I know you're on duty." She stepped away from the kitchen with two glasses of lime Gatorade and handed one to him.

"Well, bottoms up." He raised the glass in a toast, then gulped down a generous dose.

Setting her glass on the teak coffee table before them, Wendy eased down onto the opposite end of the couch. She scooted sideways and leaned back against the arm rest so that she was facing him, then pulled her bare feet up onto the soft cushion.

She had a playful, child-like demeanor that Scott found refreshing. And so did her home, he thought, gazing at the surroundings. The wall to his left had a mountain bike affixed to it, along with pictures of her blazing the trails. On the wall to the right of a big-screen TV was a stylish iron cross. And the wall to his right, behind Wendy, was filled with framed pictures of her with various exotic animals that she had presumably treated. But best of all, he noted that none of the pictures portrayed her with another guy.

And the general décor, the colors, everything seemed so warm and inviting. It had the one thing that his apartment lacked: a woman's touch.

I could get comfortable in a place like this, he thought. He then scolded himself. *Getting a little ahead of yourself, aren't you, buddy? You just met her yesterday.*

"So," he said, "I guess you've always had a thing for animals."

"Not always," she replied. "One day when I was twelve, I heard our Siberian husky, Apollo yelping horribly in our back yard. No one else was home so I went out back to have a look. Mind you, he was huge, and I was terrified of him. He was running around frantically, wouldn't let me go near him. Then I noticed that his jaw wouldn't close.

"Eventually I gathered my courage, cornered him in the fence, and shoved my hand right into his mouth. There was a bone wedged in the corner of his jaw. I took it out, and the way the dog just looked at me afterward . . . it was indescribable, the gratitude. From that day on, he never left my side. That was when I knew what I wanted to do. Now, every time I help an animal, I still see Apollo's gratefulness in their eyes."

Scott nodded contently.

Placing his empty glass on the coffee table, he shifted his eyes to the animal photos filling the wall behind Wendy. From peacocks to panthers, giraffes to gorillas, practically any animal that one could think of was represented.

In one photo, she was perched on the back of a large alligator. Another image showed Wendy with her arms around the neck of a silverback gorilla, while yet another had her arms buried in the thick mane of a lion.

"Who on earth insures you?" he blurted. "I hope some of these animals are sedated, or stuffed."

"I assure you that none of them are stuffed," she boasted, rising from the couch. "But many of them are as gentle as a lamb." She pointed to the gorilla. "This is Bongo at the Primate Preserve. He was raised from birth at the preserve by humans." She indicated the lion. "And this is Samson, just a big kitty nursed and trained by humans. He's appeared in a number of movies."

"Okay, what about the gator you're sitting on. Is he someone's pet too?"

"No. He's from the wild. I don't know what I was thinking that day." She burst out laughing. "I must have been out of my mind."

Still snickering, she indicated a picture beneath it where she was inside a cage with a Kodiak bear that was sound asleep.

The animal definitely looked familiar to Scott, and his laughter faded. Presumably from his expression, Wendy did a double take on the photo and drew her hand to her mouth.

Scott pointed at the picture. "Is that . . ."

"Yes." Her reply was somber. "That's Sleepy. It was taken two months ago at the lab."

Without a word, she stepped away from the pictures and eased down quietly on the couch. And just that quickly, the full weight of the day's events came crashing down on both of them.

To fill the ominous silence, Scott picked up the remote and flipped on the TV. But the station that the set was on did little to ease their nerves. It showed a Channel 9 News van at the entrance to Hidden Lakes, where a female reporter was doing her best to interview a stone-faced officer. Behind him, a pair of patrol cars with lights blaring were parked nose-to-nose in front of the gate.

Her white shirt pulsing in red and blue hues, she shoved a mike at the officer. "Sources say that at least two residents have been killed by a wild animal believed to be a bear. But according to texts that have come from the community, many claim the escaped bear is dead and that authorities are on the hunt for something else. Officer, can you confirm the type of animal you're looking for? A bear, gorilla, lion, gator . . .?"

"I'll answer that one," Scott muttered. "D . . . all of the above."

Flipping off the TV, he returned his attention to Wendy. He studied her as she sat on the opposite end of the couch with her legs crossed, peering warmly in his direction. He discreetly gazed over her petite but perfect body, honey-blond hair, gentle green eyes, and plump heart-shaped lips.

Time to address the elephant in the room, he thought. *Okay, here it goes.*

"You have a great job. You're beautiful, have a kind heart, and can cook. How in the world are you still single?"

A half-hearted smile, and her gaze dropped. "Just over a year ago, I was engaged to be married. Donald Hastings was everything I'd ever wanted—the outdoorsy type, athletic, good-looking, and a veterinarian. In fact, that's how we met, three years prior at a VMX in Orlando. That stands for Veterinarian Meetings and Expo, by the way. After the wedding, we had planned on opening a clinic specializing in exotic animal rescue."

She paused, gazing blankly at the TV screen, their reflections staring back at them. "Back in college, Donald had developed a need for speed—an infatuation for sport bikes."

Oh hell, I don't like where this is headed.

"One rainy evening, he was on his way over on his Ducati. Ironically, he wasn't even speeding, just cruising slowly through an intersection, helmet on. He had the green light. Teenage girl was texting, ran a red light, and that was it. The love of my life was gone."

Scott felt horrible, like a complete idiot for bringing it up. "I'm so sorry. I didn't to mean to—"

Wendy stopped him. "It's okay. I eventually got through it."

"How? I can't imagine how . . ."

"My faith," she said simply. "Prayer got me through it. Not just mine but the prayers of others, the church. I could feel them. Just when I thought that I couldn't make it another day, things started to get easier. There was a sense of peacefulness that didn't make sense, but yet it was there."

She paused and looked away shyly. "Waiting outside that house in my Jeep today, that's what I was doing. When I heard that horrible gunfire, I started praying. Begging God that you would come back out."

Wendy's last statement made his heart flutter. Not because of her unbridled kindness, but rather the fact that had he not clumsily, or perhaps miraculously, tripped and fallen into the pool, he would not be alive.

He looked up at her. "Could you do me a favor?"

"What?"

"Keep ''em coming. The prayers."

Whap! She playfully tossed a pillow at him and came to her feet. "Will do, Detective. Why don't you stretch out here for a while?" A cute wink, and she headed back toward the kitchen. "I have a police order to see to it that you get some shut-eye."

~~~

At 10:45 p.m., Jimmy Davis's mouth felt like it was stuck together as he stirred in his sleep. No matter how much water he drank, the sixty-eight-year-old's new blood pressure medicine made his mouth feel like the Mojave Desert. For a minute or two, he tried to ignore it, but the annoying dryness was unrelenting.

"All right, I'll get a glass of water," he grunted. " I need to take a leak anyway."

Mindful not to disturb his wife, or the little chihuahua curled up between them, Jimmy slid from beneath the covers and put his feet to the cool tile. Working his toes into a pair of slippers in front of his nightstand, he shuffled across the large bedroom.

Opening the door, he crept into the dark den. On the far wall, above the couch, a four-hundred-gallon saltwater aquarium housed his beloveds, his collection of exotic fish. A retired charter boat captain, Jimmy loved all things aquatic. And these were his prized possessions. Big Ben, Little Blue, he had names for them all. Even Stanley, a moray eel that he'd named after an unsavory deck hand.

It seemed he could never pass the aquarium at night without pausing for a look. He found it captivating how the lighting at the top of the unit made the fish seem to glow while floating in the darkness.

"If only you looked at me the way you look at those fish," his wife often said to him.

"And if only you were as quiet as they," he would reply.

Moving on through the den, he entered the hallway where he was met by a stiff breeze. "My word, what does she have the AC set on?" he grumbled. "Her hot flashes will be the death of me."

Venturing further along the hallway in his boxers and slippers, he discovered the breeze wasn't coming from the AC, but rather from the end of the hall where the front door was wide open. Glaring light from a streetlight glittered along the tile as another stiff breeze chilled his bare skin.

"I must have forgotten to close the door all the way when I took the dog out," he concluded. But oddly, he recalled locking it.

Bathed in the ambient light, Jimmy reached for a light switch, when he noticed a dark spot on the wall. He slipped his fingers over it, only to discover it was a hole. There was another hole a few feet above it. And then another.

He looked straight up along a trail of holes that lead into the darkness of the twenty-foot ceiling.

A pair of red orbs appeared in the pitch.

A click of the light switch revealed he'd awakened to a living nightmare. A monstrosity was stretched above him with its clawed hands and feet dug into the walls. Before his heart could skip a beat, the beast released its grip and was upon him.

~ ~ ~

Sixty-five-year-old Margaret Davis rolled over on her pillow, and her eyes fluttered open. She squinted at the stream of light spilling across the wall through the partially open bedroom door.

"Probably forgot to take his blood pressure medicine again," she huffed. "He should at least have the decency to close the door behind him." She started to holler for him to close the door but didn't want to wake the dog.

"I'll do it myself," she grumbled, "like everything else around here."

Careful not to awaken Sweet Pea, Margaret slid out of bed and crossed the bedroom. Reaching the door, she paused, hearing a strange sound. It was like a slurping sound, a moist slapping.

She frowned. *What is he doing out there?*

She shuffled through the den in her hair curlers and long, black nightgown. When she reached the hallway leading to the front door, she froze.

In the glaring light, she saw a gnarled back of a large creature knelt over a puddle of blood. Protruding out from beneath the creature's left knee was a human hand.

Her husband's hand.

She started to scream in terror, but for some reason, the sound did not leave her throat.

The thing with its horrible back to her paused from its snorting and slurping as if to listen. The tentacle-like mane on its head seemed to awaken and wavered about.

Easing one bare foot behind the other, Margaret silently crept back into the bedroom. Carefully, she closed the door behind her, then darted to a window beside the bed and slid it open. Before Sweet Pea could yelp, she scooped him from the bed with one hand around his tiny muzzle.

She dove through the window until *whap!* The window snared her curlers, unwinding several of them as she tumbled hard onto the bushes below. But somehow she managed to keep a firm grip on the dog.

Rolling onto her feet, Margaret heard the hiss of sprinklers as she stumbled through the streamers of water and into the night.

~~~

Tiny guided the police cruiser slowly along Coral Berry Drive while Big Larry rode shotgun, literally, with an assault rifle sprawled across his lap. Right hand on the steering wheel, Tiny shone the spotlight between the homes on their left, while Larry used a flashlight to search between the residences to their right.

After the massacre that had transpired in one of the homes earlier that day, everyone in the department was tense, and these two were no exception. They were like a pair of coiled springs waiting to be triggered.

"How in the hell could they not know what this thing is?" grunted Larry, playing his light across another empty lawn.

"I don't know," Tiny nervously replied. "But it could be anywhere. Pretty freaky though, the way it's taken out four of our own, and no one's really seen it."

The duo continued east along Coral Berry Drive, the beams of their lights discovering little more than dark, silent homes and empty lawns.

Whap! Something slapped against the trunk of the cruiser. Instinctively, Tiny punched the gas pedal, and the patrol car leapt forward, spinning the tires.

"No, stop!" Larry ordered, clutching his firearm.

Tiny slammed on the brakes, and the vehicle nose-dove to a stop. Vaulting from the side door, Big Larry plopped an elbow on the roof of the cruiser and trained the rifle on the dark road behind them.

Squinting down the barrel, he saw a middle-aged woman standing in the road. Her black nightgown was soaking wet, with her hair strung down into her face as she cradled a little dog in her right arm.

~ ~ ~

Scott Pine awakened abruptly with someone shaking his left arm. Peering through his slitted eyes, he saw Wendy's gorgeous face, the couch, the dark apartment. It took him a moment to place himself.

He noted the somber demeanor on her face as she held out his phone. "It's Officer Jones. They have the creature trapped in another home, and the SWAT team is ready to go in."

CHAPTER 11

THE TRAP

A pale circle of light played over the single story home as Detective Pine stood behind a police cruiser parked on the dark sidewalk. He was flanked by Officer Jones and Chief O'Hern. To their left stood Big Larry, Tiny, and a K-9 unit consisting of two trainers and a pair of black German shepherds.

To the right of the cruiser, Scott saw the armored rescue vehicle where the SWAT team was collected. The only man yet to adorn a helmet was the team commander, Bruce Hodges. With a shaved head and a scar running down the left side of his face, the commander had the look of someone you wouldn't want to cross. In addition to the Hodges, there were two team leaders, six team operators, and a SWAT medic. Save the medic, all of them sported full body armor, a tactical radio, either a HK submachine gun or a Benelli tactical shotgun, a ballistics shield, and an air of superiority.

In addition to the SWAT team, numerous police units were parked along the surrounding streets with lights blaring to ensure all civilians stayed clear of the area.

This was war, Scott thought, studying how Chief O'Hern stared intently at the home. After what had transpired at the last residence, the chief was itching for payback. And tonight, he'd taken every measure to get it.

"According to the homeowner, when she fled the residence, the lights were on and the front door was wide open," Officer Jones said. "Now the lights are off, and the door is closed. What do you make of that, Detective?"

The chief responded before Scott could. "If a window is open, the cross ventilation could have closed the door."

"Cross ventilation didn't turn off the lights," Scott said.

"It could have inadvertently bumped the switch."

"What if it didn't?" Jones asked in a somber tone. His eyes darted to the detective. "Do you think this thing's smart enough to turn out the lights?"

That's a good question, Scott thought. A question that only one man could answer. But according to the call that he'd made while en route, a.k.a. Dr. Frankenstein had yet to wake.

A thumping echoed overhead, and a large circle of light crossed the driveway, swept up the front of the house, and into the woods beyond as a police Bell 407 helicopter made another pass over the residence.

Meanwhile, behind the armored rescue vehicle, SWAT Team Commander Hodges started distributing flyers to his men. One of the team operators handed additional copies to Detective Pine and the other officers.

Scott studied what appeared to be a sales flyer of the home. Above a floor plan, it read, *The Bayvista - 3 Bedroom 2 Bath – 2,100 sqft*. A red arrow pointed through the front door and into the foyer. Three more red arrows pointed through the sliders in the back of the house. A red X marked the den.

"Listen up, men," Commander Hodges addressed the group. "This is a basic floor plan of the home. Team One will go in through the front door. The second team will come through the sliding glass doors in back, where we plan to surround and trap the target in the den, cutting off every escape route. Study the plans, men. You go in in five minutes, after the K-9 units."

"K-9 units. What good are they supposed to do?" Scott muttered, glancing at the pair of German shepherds perched like statues at their trainers' feet.

"Confirm the beast is still in the home," the chief replied.

"That's just plain cruel."

"No doubt," Jones put in.

Wham! The front door of the home shot from its hinges, bounced off of the lawn, and twirled through the air until it landed on the hood of the armored vehicle.

The SWAT team members and everyone else shared looks of bewilderment.

The chief gasped. "What the hell was that?"

The searchlight turned to the empty doorway, glittering off of the tile inside.

"I take that as an open invitation," Scott said. *Although I'm not so sure I'd accept,* he thought.

"I guess it's safe to assume it's still in the home," Jones said. "Lucky break for the dogs."

The chief nodded toward the K-9 handlers.

The K-9 handlers looked at the chief, their eyes filled with grave misgivings.

He gave the nod anyway.

"Oh come on," Pine said. "There's no need to . . ."

"Thor." "Max." The handlers each gave the order, and the dogs were off. Bounding across the lawn and up the walkway, the pair of shepherds disappeared inside the doorway. Their barks echoed farther down the hallway, then terminated with a pair of yelps.

Max shot from the doorway, spinning and sliding across the walkway on his side, and tumbled into the grass. Rolling to a stop, the animal hopped up and ran in the opposite direction of the home.

A beat later, Thor burst from the bay window, somersaulting through the air until he thudded onto the lawn. Finding his feet, the animal darted past his handler and bounded across the street.

The K-9 officers called out after them to heel, but the dogs were having none of it. They continued across the street and disappeared behind another home.

"All right, Team One, Team Two, get in position," Commander Hodges barked, and two groups of four men moved in on the home. Team Two proceeded around the west side of the residence at a military trot while Team One approached from the front.

Reaching the walkway, the members of SWAT Team One raised their shields, their HK submachine guns and tactical shotguns readied. They breached the doorway, the lights streaming from their helmets and ballistics shields illuminating the walls of the hallway.

Commander Hodges looked on from beside the armored vehicle. "Team One is in the home," he said into his shoulder mike. "Team Two, wait for my signal."

~~~

Peering over the edge of his assault shield, Cpt. Erick Saunders, leader of Team One, eased along the hallway, the barrel of his submachine gun trained on whatever may be lurking beyond the reach of their lights. Although a veteran with over two decades of field experience, his heart had never pounded like this. Thirty-eight-year-old Aron Wells was to his left, while two more team operators brought up the rear. Each pair of eyes scanned in every direction.

Another step, and the beam of light from Saunders's shield revealed a swath of bloody remains strewn across the tile. To the right of the remains was the kitchen, the dining room off to their left.

Reaching for the light switch he noticed a curious hole in the wall. Looking up, his helmet light discovered what could only be a series of claw marks running all the way to the ceiling. He noted that they ended directly above the remains, and he started to piece it all together.

But not soon enough.

Wham! Something heavy thudded onto the tile behind them.

Captain Saunders whirled around to see the creature rising in front of the doorway, its horrible form silhouetted in the searchlight peering in from outside.

"Light it up," he hollered, and flames flickered from gun barrels, reflecting in the tile below.

The creature dropped down onto all fours. A few rounds sparked off of its armored back, but most of them sailed over head, missing the beast completely.

~~~

Outside, the SWAT team and every member of law enforcement hit the deck as stray rounds flying from the home thudded into the side of the armored vehicle.

Detective Pine winced as two bullets penetrated the cruiser in front of him.

"Hold your fire," Commander Hodges shouted into his mike while ducking. "Are you trying to hit us or the animal?"

~~~

Back inside the hallway, Saunders gave the order to cease fire. The men complied, watching from behind their smoking gun barrels as the lights from their gear illuminated the strange sight before them. Still on all fours, the creature remained perfectly still with its head tucked downward and armored back rounded upward.

"It must be a defensive posture," Saunders muttered. "Like when an armadillo rolls itself . . ."

Without warning, the beast sprang up from the floor. Soaring high over the men's' helmets, the creature glazed the wall with a clawed hand, turning around in mid-air, then thudded down onto the tile behind them.

Captain Saunders was the first man to turn around and face the giant teeth, writhing mane, and blazing eyes. His mind struggled to take it all in—to focus.

The creature backed away from the dumbfounded team, their lighting gear illuminating its gray, pebbled hide in the pitch. The serpentine mane waved furiously on its head. They closed in on the beast, peering from behind their shields. The captain felt his boots slogging through the bloody remains, but didn't dare move his eyes from their strange adversary.

The creature crept back behind a large marble column that separated the dining room from the den. Before anyone could get off a shot, the beast thrust its right forearm through the column, sending out a spray of marble at the team.

Most of the projectiles bounced harmlessly from their shields. But several chunks of spiraling stone caught Captain Saunders in the face mask, causing him to slip on the bloody tile and tumble backward with two other men.

Still clutching his submachine gun, Saunders struggled to get off of the bloody remains. However, Aron Wells was quick to find his feet and lunged toward the creature, firing his weapon. Only two rounds left the barrel before a clawed left hand swatted the assault rifle away, sending it twirling over a marble dining table and into a wall.

A disgruntled snarl, and the creature buried its clubbed fist in the man's shield, knocking him backward and into a wall.

Gasping to catch his breath, Wells regained his footing and stood before the beast. Tossing the folded shield from its arm, the monster glared at Wells as if enraged that he could possibly stand after taking such a blow.

"Get out of there!" Saunders shouted.

The beast spun around, and with a powerful backhand to the helmet, sent Wells's head spiraling across the dining room and crashing through a window.

~~~

Outside, Detective Pine saw a spinning light shoot from a window, thud into the neighboring house, and drop onto the lawn between the homes. His suspicion as to the identity of the object was confirmed when the helmet rolled to a stop. Beneath the helmet's light beaming up onto the neighboring wall, the missing face shield revealed that the helmet was still occupied.

While all of the men shared somber looks, the chief turned back toward the doorway as if he'd seen nothing.

~~~

Back inside, the moment the headless body dropped before the creature, the remaining three men opened fire. Rounds thudding off of its gnarled hide, the beast latched on to the marble table top and hoisted it up. A hideous snarl, and the monster hurled it at the team.

Trying to block it with their shields, the men fell back under the tremendous weight of the slab as it broke in half, knocking them to the floor. Rolling out from beneath the crumbling slab, Captain Saunders continued to fire from the ground until he came to his feet. The two other men recovered as well, one of them limping as they laid down enough gunfire to keep the creature at bay.

Like protective tentacles, the creature's waving mane swept down to shield its face, leaving only a slit for its blazing eyes to see through. Dipping its shoulder toward the team to deflect the rounds, the monster backed deeper into the den. Bullets reflecting from or missing its gray hide riddled the home. The big-screen TV shattered beside the creature as framed pictures exploded and leapt from the walls. A stray round struck a paddle on the ceiling fan, causing it to twirl above the madness. But miraculously, a huge aquarium along the left wall remained unscathed.

The beast eased farther back into the den.

"It's in the den," Captain Saunders said into his shoulder mike.

A beat later, the rear sliding glass doors shattered as Team Two burst into the home and proceeded to fire on the creature.

Red dots from laser scopes swirled around the jagged back.

For a brief moment, the silver mane shielding the monster's face separated as the creature spread its menacing jaws and roared in rage. The beast then threw its arms back, and a saber protruded from the end of each forearm.

Now it was pissed.

Peering through his shield, Captain Saunders closed on the creature, firing his submachine gun. But the rounds merely reflected from the silver mane. The beast lunged at him, and with a swipe of its left saber, the top of Saunders's assault shield dropped from view.

A man from Team Two ventured too close to the creature. Slicing his assault rifle in half with its saber, the beast snatched him up by the neck and waved him before the torrent of bullets. The body jerked and jolted grotesquely in the clawed hand until the creature flung the bullet-riddled corpse at another man, knocking him to the ground.

The beast was nearly surrounded, and it twisted and turned to keep its armored back to the gunfire. The creature paused as if studying something behind the men, then turned away. Snatching a marble vase from beside the TV, it whirled back around and hurled the vase at the huge aquarium.

Boom! An eruption of glass and water shot over the couch, splashing onto the backs of the men, sending them stumbling forward. Some men hit the floor while others wavered to maintain their footing in the gushing water.

Catching his balance, Saunders saw a large eel slither between his boots as multicolored fish fluttered across the flooded tile.

But the creature's break from the onslaught was brief. The team quickly recovered and proceeded to fire at will.

Keeping its back to the gunfire, the monster bound through the bedroom door, knocking it from its hinges. Splashing into the vast bedroom behind it, the team turned their lights on the creature, casting its gruesome shadow across the far wall.

Now they had it trapped.

Captain Saunders noted the open window to the left of the bed. "Block the window. Don't let it escape," he ordered, and two of his men complied.

Ducking low with its back to the team, the creature seemed to be looking for another way out. Save the doorway to the master bathroom, there were no other exits.

Hooking a hand beneath the bed, the beast threw it at the team, bed frame and all. The bedspread whirled through the air, jerking and swirling from the striking rounds as the mattress and frame landed on several of the men. Climbing over and around the unruly mattress, the men continued to fire.

Snatching up a nightstand, the monster hurled it at the men. The piece of furniture tumbled through the air, jolting and fragmenting as the hungry bullets seemed to devour it.

No matter what the creature did, the barrage of bullets continued. Some rounds reflected from the armored back and pelted their shields, but the men didn't let up. Bullets shattered the mirror on a bureau and riddled the walls as smoke from the blazing weapons drifted toward the ceiling. Spent shells danced across the tile and littered the wet floor.

Seemingly out of options, the creature scurried into the

master bathroom. The rain of bullets followed its gray hide, shattering a glass shower enclosure and the long mirror above the his-and-hers sinks.

Its clawed feet sliding on the tile, the creature disappeared around a corner in the spacious bathroom.

"Oh, you better run," one of the men hollered, and he and several others pumped their weapons overhead in victory.

As the gunfire momentarily ceased, Captain Saunders whipped out the floor-plan sheet from a hip pocket. Studying the layout of the home in his helmet light, he clicked his shoulder mike. "There's nothing in there except a toilet enclosure and the master closet. A dead end. It's trapped."

The voice of Commander Hodges echoed in his headset. "Finish it." Saunders relayed the order, which roused more cheers from the team. They were having a time of it now.

Saunders raised a hand, and the men grew silent.

"It isn't over just yet," he said.

Flipping on a wall switch, the bathroom illuminated, and the men cautiously filed inside, the captain leading the way. Instinctively, the first place that he looked was straight up. The ceiling was clear. He passed the bullet-riddled mirror, the lights from their helmets and shields glaring back at them in the broken glass.

Wham! Saunders kicked open the door to the toilet enclosure. Peering inside from behind the barrel of his submachine gun, it too proved to be clear.

There was only one room left.

It had to be in the master closet.

CHAPTER 12

MONSTER IN THE CLOSET

His heart pounding in his ears, Captain Saunders eased toward the dark doorway to the closet. Rows of shirts and other articles of clothing came to life in vivid color as the darkness fled from the approaching light.

Heart thundering, he paused at the doorway, an arsenal of gun barrels aimed over his shoulder. The closet appeared to be about ten-by-ten . . . and empty.

Until he looked up.

There it was, above the shelves with its clawed hands and feet dug into the wall where it met the twenty-foot ceiling. The tooth-studded jaws separated in the glare from his helmet light. The moment Saunders raised his weapon and fired, the men rushed in behind him, knocking him into a row of hanging shirts as his missed rounds tore through the wall beside the creature.

A deafening roar shook the tight confinement.

Swarming into the closet, the team unleashed hell.

Turning its back to the blazing weapons, the beast barreled its clubbed fist into the ceiling, then ripped it open and climbed inside. Bullets rent the ceiling around the fleeing animal, sparking off of its armored back. A few final chunks of drywall rained down onto the men, and the hole went dark.

"Who's the boss now?" one of the men hollered as they all fist-pumped their weapons overhead in celebration of the creature's retreat.

"No one messes with Team Hawk," shouted another.

"Oh hell yeah, you better keep running," someone else belted out.

~~~

Detective Pine looked on as SWAT Team Commander Hodges glanced at the chief with an arrogant nod. The cheers inside the home were so loud they echoed from the doorway and out into the streets.

And then the creature tore through the top of the roof.

"There it is," Tiny said as the beast pulled itself from the shingles and stood upright. Bathed in the spotlight, the animal walked along the ridge of the roof for about twenty feet, then dropped down onto all fours.

Commander Hodges and the surrounding officers fired at the creature to no avail as it proceeded to rip out the shingles and tear into the roof.

The detective raced over to the armored vehicle and grabbed the commander by the shoulder. "Get your men out of there now," he pleaded. "Don't you see what it's doing?"

Commander Hodges just glared at Scott as if he were nuts and shoved his hand away.

~~~

His severed shield in one hand and smoking submachine gun in the other, Captain Saunders made his way out of the crowded closet. Spirits were sky high as men talked smack and fist-bumped while filing out behind him. A few men lingered behind, taking selfies beneath the large hole that was the creature's escape route.

"Let's find that thing and finish the job," someone said.

"Hell yes," barked several others.

The moment the captain passed the door to the toilet, there was a deep thud in the bedroom. And then, in the broken mirror above the sinks, he saw the distorted image of the beast.

Standing on its hind legs, the creature ducked its horrible head below the top of the door frame and stepped into the bathroom.

Click. The overhead lights went out.

All boastful chatter ceased as the men trailing the captain saw the jagged image growing closer in the broken mirrors.

"It's back," one man said in a low voice.

"What the hell? Did that thing turn off the lights?" someone else asked as they once again raised their weapons and backed toward the closet.

The creature stepped around the corner in front of the tub and now faced them, its horrible face shielded by the silver mane.

Gunfire roared around the Saunders's helmet as the men fired while scrambling back into the closet.

The beast dropped down onto all fours as bullets bounced harmlessly from its back and struck the walls. Nowhere to go, Saunders could only watch as the creature planted its clawed feet back against the tub, as if taking a runner's stance. And then like burning coals, the monster's eyes looked up at him.

The captain futilely held up his half-shield. "Incredible," he muttered in awe. "All this time we thought we were trapping you . . . now we're right where you wanted us."

The beast lurched forward and, with the force of a locomotive, slammed into Saunders's chest, driving everyone back into the closet.

~~~

Detective Pine stood behind the cruiser listening to the war raging inside the home. And then all gunfire ceased. And there it was again, the horrible silence. An empty silence like he had heard earlier that day while standing by the pool and staring blankly into the sliding glass doors.

Hodges looked at Chief O'Hern. "It stopped . . . They've killed it."

"No," the detective's voice was somber. "That's not what it means."

"There, look!" Tiny hollered as the spotlight turned toward the roof. And then the creature crawled out of the same hole that it had emerged from only moments ago. Only now its gray hide was slick with blood.

Scott stared blankly and said, "No one's coming out."

"No. It couldn't have . . ." All hope drained from the commander's eyes.

Enraged, Big Larry aimed his assault rifle at the roof. "Why don't you come down here and try that?" he howled, then fired at the creature.

After the round glazed its back, the beast turned toward the men collected behind the vehicles below. A guttural growl, and the monster thumped its chest then pointed a clawed finger at Big Larry.

"This is definitely not good," the detective muttered.

In the blink of an eye, the creature leapt from the ridge of the roof, bounded off from the gutter, sailed over the yard, and landed on the hood of the cruiser—right in front of Big Larry. Its clawed feet burying the hood deep into the engine, the beast roared down at the big man from point-blank range.

Backstepping, Big Larry tripped and fell onto his backside, his assault rifle clanking onto the street. Frozen in terror, he looked up from the pavement as the front of his trousers grew dark from a surge of urine.

The sky erupted to the sound of a thumping rotor as the police helicopter lifted from behind the southern treetops. Looking upward, the creature flushed pale in the circle of light glaring down from the night.

A roar up at the closing aircraft, and the beast leapt from the cruiser, darted across the lawn and bounded back onto the roof. Dislodged shingles tumbling in its wake, the monster scurried across the roof and leapt onto the neighboring home.

~~~

Sgt. Jerry Hill and Pilot Clark Weise stared down from the cockpit of the Bell 407, dumbfounded as the creature crossed the rooftops below. Shingles spraying up from behind its rear claws, the creature amazingly bounded from the crest of one rooftop to the next on a single stride.

No sooner had the spotlight lit up its gray hide than the beast darted from beneath it.

"Do you believe the speed of this thing?" the pilot said into his headset. "It's impossible to keep it in the light."

"Incredible," Sergeant Hill said. "In spite of its size, it runs like a cheetah."

~~~

Harnessed at the edge of the open doorway in the cargo bay, Ofc. Craig Riley tried to steady the sights of his assault rifle on the speeding target. Again, he fired off several rounds that spat up shingles in the creatures wake.

"It's too fast to get a good shot!" he hollered.

~~~

Back in the cockpit, Sergeant Hill barked into his headset, " Riley, you're not in the Afghan desert—be careful. Those are occupied homes down there."

"Yes sir," replied the deep voice in his headset. "But it's not stopping, even when I hit it. I think we're gonna need a bigger gun."

"If you can't kill it, we can try to chase it into the woods away from the homes," Hill said.

Just then, the pilot slowed the aircraft to nearly a hover.

"Why are we slowing?"

"I lost visual," Weiss replied, scanning the windscreen and side window. "It disappeared."

"Could it have reached the tree line?"

"Not yet." Weiss's gaze followed the circle of light playing off of the rooftops below. "It's around here somewhere."

~~~

Peering out from behind a brick chimney of a two-story home, the beast kept a watchful eye on the aircraft. Staying low, the monster anchored its clawed feet deeper into the warm shingles. As the green and white helicopter arced back around, the beast raised its head for better look.

~~~

The sergeant glimpsed the silver mane as it dropped behind a chimney. "Got it," he blurted, then pointed. "It's hiding behind that chimney."

"Roger that," the pilot chirped. The moment the spotlight illuminated the chimney, the structure erupted into a spray of bricks that spiraled toward the craft.

"What the—" Weiss tilted the chopper to avoid the stone projectiles.

Wham! A brick crashed through the top of the windscreen above the pilot. Hill ducked when another brick breached the Lexan and bounced off of his backrest. Below, the rooftops grew dim as another brick took out the spotlight.

More of the stone projectiles thudded off of the fuselage, but one pinged against the tail rotor, throwing the aircraft into a spin.

A blur of rooftops and night sky flashed before the windscreen until the pilot gained control of the cyclic and pedals, steadying the craft. The treetops dropped away from the windscreen, and the helicopter increased altitude.

"Hell of a job, Clark!" howled the sergeant, righting himself in the passenger seat.

But a glance across the rooftops showed no sign of the creature. "Don't worry, men," Hill said into his mike. "We'll find it. It couldn't have reached the woods just yet."

~~~

Six-year-old Mickey Dalton stared through a back sliding glass door to the monstrosity towering beside his swing set. "Whoa . . . a real alien."

His parents were in the hallway behind him, peering up through a transom above the front doors toward the whirling sound of a helicopter.

Little Mickey watched the creature curl its clawed fingers around the chains above the swing and rip both chains and the seat from his swing set.

"Hey!" The boy slammed his palms against the glass. "What do you think you're doing?"

A pair of red eyes glared at the window briefly, then the creature went about its business.

The child hollered back toward his parents, "Mom, there's an alien in the back yard, and he's messing up my swing set!"

Gripping the chains in its right hand, the creature bounded upward and out of the child's view.

~~~

Back in the cockpit of the Bell 407, Sergeant Hill peered across the dim rooftops. "With the spotlight out, I can't see squat down there."

He then noted movement in the shadows on the crest of an upcoming roof. The creature was whirling something overhead like a slingshot.

The pilot squinted, leaned forward. "What's it trying . . .?"

"Pull the hell up!" Hill hollered. But before the pilot could respond, the beast released the object, which twirled through the air, past the passenger-side window and latched on to the tail rotor with a horrible ping.

The pilot fought the cyclic control and pedals. But this time there was no controlling the helicopter as the rooftops spinning before the windscreen turned to asphalt and the aircraft erupted in flames.

~~~

Sixty-five-year-old Frances Hernando peered out from a front window as a ball of fire rose in her cul-de-sac. Flames from the eruption swept up a neighbor's driveway and engulfed their garage door.

She ducked when a spinning piece of rotor blade skipped off of her front lawn, crashed through the window, and embedded itself in the wall behind her.

~~~

Detective Pine, the chief, and others still collected in front of the home of the most recent blood bath looked up as a plume of fire lifted beyond the rooftops several blocks away. No one said a word. The best they could muster was to share glassy-eyed looks as the ambient light from the blaze danced off of the treetops and painted the evening sky in a pulsing orange hue.

Staring toward the blaze, the detective realized that his phone was ringing.

He answered it.

"Detective Pine, it's Izzy." Her voice seemed rushed. "Jim, the scientist at the hospital . . . he's awake."

CHAPTER 13

BLINDED BY SCIENCE

He's going to give himself an aneurysm, thought the detective as he watched Chief O'Hern grill a young nurse in the small hospital room. Behind them, Wendy was seated beside Jim Randle, who, to everyone's dismay, remained unconscious.

"You said he was awake," the chief barked at the nurse. "But from where I'm standing, he looks no different than the last time I saw him. What happened?"

Scott felt the O'Hern's frustration, but there was no point in taking it out on her.

Clearly shaken by the outburst, the nurse in her mid-twenties struggled for words. "When I called you, he was conscious." She glanced down at the patient's chart that she held. "He has an intracranial hematoma, a collection of blood inside his skull that's putting pressure on his brain. He's been deeply sedated to help keep the cerebral blood volume low. He could be awake one minute and out the next."

She nervously glanced between the detective and the chief as if searching for something more to tell them.

"Thank you." Scott gave a gentle nod. "We appreciate your time."

After the nurse returned the clipboard to the holder on the wall and exited the room, O'Hern released a breath. "Still no answers."

"I know." Scott was peering blankly through the

doorway. "Like why this abomination was ever created."

"Turning big rocks into small rocks," uttered a weak voice from behind.

Scott and the chief turned around to find that the scientist's eyes were now open.

Wendy excitedly grabbed his hand. "Jim, you're awake. It's me . . . Wendy. You've—"

Approaching the bed, the chief gave Wendy a stern look and motioned for her to be silent. "Mr. Randle"—he rested his palms on the bed rail—"I'm Chief O'Hern, and this is Detective Pine."

"What do you mean by making small rocks?" Scott asked him.

"That's how it all started," Jim muttered, clearly disoriented. Trying to sit up, he raised a hand and felt the bandage around his head.

Wendy eased Jim's head back onto the pillow. "Take it easy; you've been in an accident."

Jim's eyes darted around the room as he seemed to struggle to take in his environment. "What . . . how?"

"What the hell did you create in that lab?" O'Hern barked, clutching the bedrail.

Easing the chief back from the bed, Detective Pine spoke up. "Your lab has been destroyed, vandalized. During the event, you sustained a blow to the head, apparently from a thrown bottle."

"What happened?" the geneticist still seemed confused.

"As a result, all of the animals escaped, or were set loose."

The scientist's eyes flared as he again tried to sit up. "You mean . . ."

"Yes. All of them," the chief growled. "Including your special project in the back room—that's killed six of my men, two SWAT teams, and God only knows how many others."

The heart monitor increased in tempo, and Wendy rose from her chair. "We need to get a doctor, let them know he's awake."

O'Hern pointed at her. "No one's going anywhere until I get some answers."

Jim looked up from his pillow at Wendy and motioned for her to return to her seat. "It's okay. It's imperative that I speak with them."

Wendy reluctantly eased back down to her chair. She glanced at the heart monitor. "Just remember, he has a hematoma, so be mindful of his blood pressure."

"What you just mentioned about making small rocks. That's how it started," the detective said. "What were you getting at?"

"During the Gulf War, I was part of a team researching genetic engineering and animal behavior for the military. One day during a briefing after a missile strike on a series of tunnels, a frustrated Col. Randolf Blake said, 'All we're doing is turning big rocks into small rocks.' And he was right. There was no way to determine if the tunnels we were bombing were even occupied. It was a guessing game at best . . ." Jim's voice grew scratchy, and he coughed.

Wendy rose from her chair and handed him a cup of water that was on his bed tray. "Here, try some of this."

Taking a long swig from the straw, he nodded to her. "Thank you." Returning the cup to the tray, he continued.

"This led to the Chameleon Project. Through genetic engineering, we created a small, armadillo-like creature that could crawl into the tunnels. Covering its shell were guanine crystals like in a chameleon's skin. These crystals have the ability to separate and adjust the light reflecting from them to match the terrain. This allowed the little creature to sneak into the tunnels virtually undetected."

Scott and the chief shared a look, then turned back to the

injured man, who continued his lesson. They listened intently.

"Once inside, everything the animal saw was transmitted back to the base. If the tunnels were occupied, they would lock in the animal's coordinates via satellite and launch the missiles."

Wendy's mouth fell open. "They launched the missiles after the animal was clear of the caves, right?"

"Of course," Jim replied.

Scott held up a hand. "Wait, back it up a little. You said that what the animal saw was relayed back to the base. How is that possible? Or do you mean by way of lipstick cameras in its shell or something?"

"No lipstick cameras needed." The geneticist snickered. "We connected electrodes to the thalamus region of the animal's brain. This is the region that receives signals through the optic nerve. We then used what is referred to as a Linear Decoding Technique to convert the signals from the stimulated brain cells into a visual image. In other words, as information of what the animal sees is relayed through the optic nerve, it is reconstructed and displayed on a computer monitor."

"My word." Wendy gasped. "That sounds like something Orson Wells might have concocted."

"Not Orson Wells," Jim said, "but rather Garret Stanley and a group of gentlemen from the Department of Molecular and Cell Biology at the University of California back in 1999. They initially used a cat. Over the years, the military has perfected the process."

The chief squinted, his brow furrowed. "Wait—how did you get the animal to go into the cave? How would you guide it?"

"By stimulating the animal's reward center." Jim coughed and cleared his throat. "Beneath the animal's shell is a small electronic backpack consisting of a mainboard and a transmitter/receiver. Then three electrodes were implanted—two in the thalamus region, and a third in the medial forebrain bundle. This third electrode gives a reward stimulus to the brain when the animal completes a specific task. In this case, when it goes in the direction of the coordinates of the cave sent through its backpack."

"And to get the animal out of the cave?" the chief asked.

"To get it out, we simply change the coordinates to the abstraction point."

Scott swiped a hand down his face. "Wow. I never knew that you could control animals like that."

"Oh yes," Jim said. "The technology has been around for some time. It's similar in nature to how we once placed electrodes in a shark's brain, on the neurons controlling its sense of smell. Through remote electronic stimulus we were able to make the animal's left nostril think it smelled blood and lure the shark in that direction, or wherever we wanted."

"How unnerving." Wendy winced. "You could literally select someone swimming off shore and have a shark zero in on them."

"If we so chose," the geneticist replied. "But not just sharks. The technology has been used on mice, moths, beetles, cockroaches, rats, pigeons, you name it. The military's initial intent was to use small animals to clear minefields."

"We're getting a little off subject here," the chief interjected."Let's move on to the subject at hand . . . Your new *killing machine.*"

The comment evoked a rise in the heart monitor, which everyone noticed, including Jim. He let his head drop back to the pillow. A few deep breaths, and the blips grew farther apart. "The Chameleon Project was used successfully up until '08 when the defense budget was cut. But all that time, I had an idea on how to take it to the next level. A way to clear the caves and tunnels without the need for a missile strike or leaving a single US military fingerprint."

Jim paused for a long moment. "The technology was there, but I left it at a thought for years . . . until September 11, 2001. The day that my wife and son were killed when the second tower fell. That's the day that Project War Child was born." He looked up at Scott, eyes smoldering. "The day I created a cure for the disease."

The heart monitor started singing again until Wendy placed a hand on his shoulder. When Jim noticed the tears in her red eyes, he seemed to calm himself.

When you hear it like that, Scott thought, *you almost can't blame the fool.*

The chief let out a long breath. "Okay, well, let's . . ."

But Scott's curiosity was getting the best of him. "But how in the hell did you create such a thing? I had no idea the technology had come this far."

"This far," the scientist scoffed. "In 2003, a team of scientists in Shanghai fused human cells in rabbit eggs, creating a concoction that was half human and half rabbit. The cells took together splendidly and formed an embryo in a laboratory dish. The creature could have easily gone full term had they not destroyed it a few days later."

Wendy gasped. "Oh my God, that's horrible."

The geneticist just looked at them and shook his head. "You have no idea what is really going on behind laboratory doors around the world. Oh, you hear of the pigs with human blood flowing through their veins to help grow vital human organs such as hearts, to potentially be harvested. Or fitting monkeys with human neural stem cells in the name of fighting Parkinson's disease. That's just what they admit to the public." He smirked. "The proverbial tip of the iceberg to what's really going on."

"But what about you? Where did you start?" Scott asked.

"I got a head start from a bit of research conducted in the

1920s. This experiment was highly controversial, especially for the time period."

"Who would have guessed?" the detective muttered.

"For nearly a century, the experiment was thought to have been a mere rumor, but it turned out to be true. One of the first primate research centers was established in Orange Park, Florida, near Jacksonville. It was there that they inseminated a female chimpanzee with human semen from an undisclosed donor. Not only did pregnancy occur, but it went full term and resulted in a live birth."

With these words, Wendy drew a hand to her mouth.

"But within a few weeks, the moral and ethical weight of their decision became too much to bear, and the infant was euthanized. Apparently the military then got wind of the experiment and confiscated the remains. This was initially passed on to me by an old professor of mine who actually knew someone that had worked at the center during the 1920s."

"Incredible," the chief said, obviously hanging on Jim's every word.

"Years later when I started working with the military, I asked them about the specimen from Orange Park. And there it was, the infant remains frozen in a fetal position for nearly a century."

"What did it look like?" Wendy blurted. She quickly waved a hand in front of her face. "No, I don't want to know."

"No, you don't," the scientist assured her. "It was this creature's DNA that helped form the first building block of Project War Child. When combining cells, rejection is always an issue. Success can take years. But when the hybrid cells were fused into a gorilla embryo, it took everything that I threw at it—reptilian DNA, pig, cheetah, everything took seemingly without question.

"Then, using CRISPR technology, I dialed in the genome

until it was exactly what I wanted."

"Wait," Scott said, "what do you mean by *dialed in*?"

The scientist continued. "CRISPR, or Clustered Regularly Interspaced Short Palindromic Repeats technology, is simply a way to locate a specific DNA sequence. When the target DNA is found, Cas9, one of the enzymes produced by the CRISPR system, binds to the DNA strand and cuts it. Then you can make any edit that you like."

He paused for a moment. "It's kind of like locating a single word in the entire Encyclopedia Britannica and then being able to change it. For example, back in 2016, Chinese scientists used this technology to remove the HIV receptor gene from the DNA in a human embryo. Thus, creating a child that was immune to AIDS."

"That's mind boggling," Wendy said.

"Oh, but that was just the beginning." Jim smirked. "Now, a company in China is modifying human embryos before they're transferred into the woman's uterus. They're not only altering genes that eliminate disease, but enhancing the ability to build muscle mass, increase intelligence, choosing eye and hair color . . . almost anything that you like. They're literally creating *designer babies*."

"Just like you did," Scott said in a hushed tone.

"Yes," Jim said. "Once the perfect embryo was formed, I placed it in the uterus of a female gorilla."

"So, the use of hybrid DNA makes the thing part human."

"Minutely," the scientist replied. "The amount of animal DNA that has been combined with the initial hybrid cells has diluted the human element immensely. It's ninety-nine percent animal."

"My God," O'Hern said, shaking his head. "You've taken one abomination from the 1920s and used it to create a new one. And all in the name of fighting terrorism."

"No. Not just to fight it. But to eradicate the contents of every terrorist cave, tunnel, or camp without the use of missiles or firing a single round," Jim said. "The aftermath would appear as if they were killed with swords or clubs, the calling card of a primitive vigilante group. In other words, the terrorist cells would be eliminated without leaving a trace of US military involvement. No political mess left to tidy up or justify to the UN."

"And you would control the large creature's behavior the same way as the smaller, armadillo-like animal?" O'Hern asked.

"Project War Child uses a similar system, but it's much more intensified."

"Intensified," Scott said.

"Like the armadillo, there are two electrodes implanted in the thalamus region and a third electrode in the medial forebrain bundle which controls the beast's reward process, Jim said. "But that is where the similarities end.

"This creature was engineered to produce much higher levels of oxytocin and dopamine, a hormone and neurotransmitter responsible for pleasure. When it moves in the correct direction of a specified target, a small amount of these chemicals are released." The scientist paused for a moment as if reluctant to continue. He blew out a sigh, then, "But when it kills a specified target, a large dose of these pleasure hormones floods its system to where the animal feels nothing less than a sexual gratification."

"Like a shot of heroin," the chief put in. "A single dose can cause the dopamine level in the brain's reward center to increase by two hundred percent."

"Precisely."

"In other words, it literally gets off on killing," Scott added.

The scientist raised his chin. "On accomplishing it's

mission."

The chief jolted the bedrail. "Well, right now its *mission* is butchering innocent people!"

The detective threw his hands out. "Why didn't you engineer some type of kill switch into it . . . a way to abort?"

"Actually, the device has been created," Jim said. "Once implanted, it would have put the animal in a state of paralysis with the push of a button. But before I had a chance to implant it, some fool christened me with a bottle. That's why the beast was on lockdown and sedated. It wasn't scheduled to be tested in the field for another month." He sighed, rubbed his eyes. "The fool that broke in had to do more than unlatch the door. He must have turned off the equipment inside, cut off its breathing to wake it from sedation."

"Hold on a minute," Wendy said. "If it's vision shows up on a monitor like the smaller animal, can't we—"

Jim was already shaking his head, cutting her off. "No, no. The electronics to relay its eyesight were going to be implanted during the same surgical procedure as the so-called *kill switch*."

"What about following its droppings?" Scott asked. "Many animals can be tracked that way."

"It doesn't leave droppings."

"How is that possible?"

"The animal has a specific enzyme as well as a high acid content in its urine. When it urinates on its feces, a reaction is created which dissolves the fecal matter."

"You did think of everything," Scott muttered.

"Enough with the nuts and bolts of this thing." The chief was clearly frustrated. "Can you tell us why it would target a specific place or community?"

Jim locked eyes with O'Hern. "Why do you ask that? What do you mean by *community*?"

"With the exception of the lab, all of the slayings have

taken place in a residential community called Hidden Lakes. It's roughly four miles northeast of your lab," Scott said.

"Is the community gated?"

"What the hell good would a gate do?" O'Hern scoffed.

"Tell me . . . is it gated?"

Scott nodded. "Yes."

"Have there been any killings outside of the community?"

"Only two men from Animal Control," Scott said. "But they were allegedly killed by the bear."

The scientist's face grew pale as the rhythmic blip of his heart monitor increased. "Perimeter . . . that's what happened," he whispered.

The chief crossed his arms. "Would you care to enlighten us?"

"Perimeter," Jim repeated. "It's set on Perimeter Mode."

Scott had no idea what this meant, but it didn't sound good. "Please elaborate."

The scientist rubbed his temples below his bandage as if trying to summon his memory. "Oftentimes, we don't have the coordinates to a given cave or tunnel. With Project War Child, we remedy this by using a drone to drop a small ball containing a homing device into the cave. Once activated by hitting the ground, the transmitter in the ball relays the coordinates to a satellite, which then guides the creature into the cave."

Scott's heart leapt and nearly kept pace with the heart monitor. He didn't like where this was going.

The scientist stroked his stubbly chin. "The last thing I remember was standing in the bed of my truck behind the lab, testing the drone. After I was knocked unconscious, it must have landed somewhere in the woods." He nodded, deep in thought. "The drone resembles a remote control airplane. I hear dirt bikes riding the trails back there. My best guess is that someone found the drone and took it into the community."

His face grew pale. "Somehow they must have dropped the transmitter ball . . . with it set on Perimeter."

"But what does Perimeter have to do with this?" the Chief demanded.

"Perimeter is one of the attack modes." Jim was staring blankly into the distance as he spoke. "It's used for terrorist camps. The creature starts by neutralizing everyone along the perimeter of the camp, usually the lookout guards, and then works its way inside until it finds the transmitter ball."

Jim slowly returned his gaze to each of them in turn. "The creature sees the community as a terrorist camp that has been targeted for annihilation."

"That's why it hasn't killed outside the community," Scott said.

Wendy buried her face in her hands.

O'Hern just eased back against the wall as if his knees had failed him. "But where do we find the thing?" His voice no longer held a demanding tone but resembled more of a plea.

"Most likely the water, small lakes or ponds," Jim said. "The creature finds it calming, helps lower its metabolism and aids in its recovery. I suppose it's my fault for using too much reptilian DNA."

"The water." Scott gasped. "The community is called Hidden Lakes."

"But you don't need to find it—and God help you if you do. Remember, the creature will likely not attack until nightfall, unless it is discovered. But if you can remove the transmitter from the community, the animal will go into a defensive mode and not attack unless threatened. " Jim struggled to sit up. "You have to locate the ball and get it out of the community, somewhere remote—"His words were interrupted by a coughing jag, and his heart monitor let out a series of rapid chirps.

Jim reeled back onto his pillow with a hand on his bandaged head.

The nurse burst into the room, eyeing the monitor. Jim was moaning, on the verge of consciousness.

"You're awake. Why didn't someone call me?" She hastily guided everyone away from the bed. "We have to get his blood pressure down. You all must leave."

As the nurse ushered everyone out of the room, Jim hollered above the heart monitor, "*Just find the ball!*"

Exiting the room, Chief O'Hern's brow had practically caved in over his eyes. The frustration and irritation there was clearly evident. "There's so much more we needed to get out of him, like the animal's full capabilities . . . does it have any weaknesses . . ."

"I know," Scott said as the trio headed swiftly down the hallway. "But at least he filled us in on the vital part, to find that transmitter ball."

"But what a piece of work, that guy," the chief grumbled.

Scott couldn't argue that. "He's a piece of something. He makes Dr. Moreau seem like a humanitarian."

Wendy shot each of them a glare. "At least he was cooperative, told you what you needed to know. You need to take it easy on him; he's been through a lot."

Passing the restrooms, the chief paused and said, "I need to hit the head." Backing into the door, he rolled his eyes at Wendy. "*He's been through a lot* . . . are you for real?"

Noticing how upset she still was, Scott slipped an arm around her and gave her a long, warm hug. He couldn't believe how natural it felt to do so. It was practically an involuntary reaction. Not to mention how wonderful it felt to have her little body pressed up against his. When he released her, Wendy looked up at him, blushing. "What was that for?"

"To see if you were for real." He smiled. "Are you?"

She smiled back sweetly. "I think so. But you guys are wrong about Jim. He's not the monster you think he is."

"Yeah, I'm sure he's a wonderful guy."

"No. You don't think that."

"No, I don't." He swung his gaze farther down the hallway toward the elevators. "Come on, we'd better get moving."

~~~

The electric hospital doors swung closed behind them, and the duo headed into the dark parking lot. Navigating a myriad of glittering puddles from a fresh Florida rain, Scott glanced at her. "Can I borrow your Jeep?"

"Sure, but why?"

"If you'd found something that didn't belong to you, what would you do when a patrol car stops in front of your house and a deputy comes strolling up the driveway?"

"Ah, I see. That's why you're the detective." She tossed him the keys. "But do you really think that someone is going to mistake that piece of crap you drive for a cop car?"

"Probably not," he admitted. "But if I'm the one that locates the ball, I don't need that heap breaking down on me with that thing on my tail." He added, "And no."

"No what?"

"No way are you going with me back to Hidden Lakes."

CHAPTER 14

RUDE AWAKENING

Behind the wheel of the borrowed Jeep, Detective Pine cruised slowly along Pepper Pine Road located in the Hidden Lakes community. The picturesque neighborhood held an eerie silence that seemed out of place. No spandex-clad mothers jogging swiftly behind strollers. No owners trailing their dogs, plastic bags bulging from the pockets. Not a single child playing outside. It was as if death had laid claim to the neighborhood, and its presence lingered in the warm July air.

Passing another residence, the detective searched for chalk games drawn on sidewalks, disregarded balls lying in the lawn, or any other signs of a child-occupied home. Because in his gut, he felt it had been a kid who'd found the drone and kept that fact quiet. Of course, he would keep an open mind—but that was where his instincts were leading him.

It was a quarter past noon, and after searching since sunrise, it felt much later. He'd rung so many doorbells that the knuckles in his index finger were swollen. Although no one had seen the likes of a small gray plane, that didn't stop the barrage of questions:

"What are you really looking for?"

"Did it really kill all those people?"

"When can we leave our home?"

Those were the top three, and in that order.

Although they hadn't had any luck just yet, Scott was

confident. A local food company had donated 4,000 meals to the residents under quarantine. After gridding off the community, they had assigned twenty patrol units to deliver the meals. While doing so, the officers were to question each resident about the drone. It was a clever plan the chief had concocted. The only drawback was the bombardment of questions that each household had for the officers. Covering the entire community was taking hours longer than expected.

As long as we can find the transmitter and get it out of here by nightfall, Scott thought, recalling Jim Randle's warning: "The beast will likely not attack until nightfall, unless it is discovered." For that reason, all efforts from law enforcement had changed focus—locate the drone rather than the creature.

Cruising deeper into what Scott guessed was the center of the community, he noticed an open garage door where a young boy was shooting hoops in the driveway. Braking to a stop at the end of the driveway, Scott called out to the chubby redhead, "Hey, you're supposed to be inside."

The boy tossed the ball again, and the hoop rattled tauntingly from another miss. "Why? You a cop?" the boy asked, catching up with the ball as it bounced near the Jeep.

Scott motioned the boy closer. "Hey, you haven't seen anyone around here with a gray remote-control plane, have you?"

Tucking the ball under a beefy arm, the boy nodded.

Scott removed his foot from the brake. "Okay, thanks anyw—" He slammed the brake and glared at the boy. "What, you did?"

"Yeah, a day or so ago, saw him carrying an airplane on his bike. You are a cop, aren't you? I knew he stole it." His chubby cheeks widened with his grin. "Is he in trouble?"

Yanking the Jeep out of gear, Scott whipped out a notepad and pen. "Do you know his name?"

"Sure," the boy said. "Blake Wilson." He curled his lips. "He's so stuck up, he rode right past me with it. Wouldn't even let me see it."

"Do you know his address?"

The boy shrugged his beefy shoulders. "But you can see his house from here. It's the next block down, second house on the right. The one with the black Lexus in the driveway."

"And your name?"

"Randy Freeman."

Jotting down the boy's name, the detective put the Jeep back into gear. "Thanks, Randy."

"Hey," Randy blurted, "can I watch you bust him? Are you gonna use the cuffs?"

"No. Now get in your house and don't come out. This area is dangerous."

A frustrated huff, and the boy dribbled the basketball back toward his garage.

~~~

Nineteen-year-old Tray Williams was scrolling through images on his phone at his parent's kitchen table. Before him, a picture window offered a gorgeous view of a small pond lined with tall pines and oaks with moss-draped branches. Upon his mother's insistence, he'd popped in for a visit from his freshman year at USF. Tray had only planned on staying for the weekend, but the mandatory quarantine had decimated his schedule. "I knew I shouldn't have come here," he muttered. Not only was he missing out on his classes, and partying, but even more importantly, he was missing out on his gorgeous girlfriend, Marissa. She had a wandering eye and shouldn't be left unattended for too long.

Tired of thumbing through images of his friends partying, Tray decided to do something he hadn't done in some time.

Fishing.

Last night, the mention of the endeavor made his mother laugh out loud. "All you'll catch in that pond is a cold child," she declared. "But keep an eye out for Old Crusty. Four months ago, he snatched a neighbor's chihuahua right off of the bank. He's about seven feet long now. I advise that you stay on the dock."

But Tray knew she was dead wrong about the fish. He was aware that all of the smaller ponds were connected to the larger stocked lakes. Besides, two days ago, he'd seen a good-size bass in there with his own eyes. He grabbed his father's fishing rod from the garage, a pocket full of shrimp from the fridge, and off he went.

He crept out the back sliding glass door and into the glaring sun. Being in a cul-de-sac, he knew that the officers patrolling the streets would be less likely to see him this far out back, especially through all of the trees. Besides, he'd seen neighbors three houses down throwing a football and others playing corn hole. He wasn't the only one ignoring the quarantine.

~~~

Detective Pine backed the Jeep into the driveway beside the black Lexus SUV. Stepping from the vehicle, he left the keys in the ignition and the parking brake off. If this home indeed had what he was looking for, Scott wanted to be ready for a quick exit.

Heading up the walkway to the single-story, Mediterranean-style home, his stomach started to tingle. As far as his nerves were concerned, this was the place.

Ringing the doorbell, an attractive brunette in her fifties, wearing a sweatshirt and jeans, cracked open the door. "Can I help you?"

The detective pulled back his jacket to expose the badge

on his belt. "I'm Detective Pine. I'm—"

She interrupted with, "But no one in this house has stepped outside. We've obeyed the quarantine."

"No. No." Scott raised a hand. "This isn't about the quarantine. Is this the residence of Blake Wilson?"

The woman's jaw dropped. "Is he in trouble?"

"No. He's not in trouble. I just need to ask him about a remote-control plane that he might have found in the woods near here."

The father appeared in a bathrobe with a towel draped over his shoulders. "What's the meaning of this?"

The mother was visibly upset. "He thinks Blake stole a toy plane!"

The father's face twisted in anger. "Blake, get your butt in here pronto."

A beat later, a boy appeared in the hallway. He eased toward the foyer and sheepishly looked up at the detective.

"Blake," the father grumbled, "this gentleman would like to have a word with you."

Scott knelt down until he was eye level with the child. "I'm Detective Pine."

At those words, the boy's eyes flared.

Scott raised his hands gently, but there was an urgency in his voice. "Don't worry; you're not in any trouble. I'm looking for a small gray plane that went down in the woods near here. It's extremely important that we find it. Randy Freeman, a neighbor of yours, said he saw you carrying it on your bike."

The father's brow wrinkled. "That little . . ."

Whap! The mother swatted the father. "Shhhh! Blake, tell him the truth."

Blake seemed to be milling over his options. A stern glance from his father, and the boy quickly nodded. "But it was just lying there in the woods. No one was around. I didn't steal—"

"That's okay," Scott said. "There was a ball attached to it. I need to know where that is."

"I gave it to my dog, Rexy."

"You need to take me to Rexy now."

"Okay. But he loves that ball," Blake said. "The way it vibrates. Good luck getting it from him."

~~~

The blazing Florida sun had slipped behind the clouds, giving Tray a moment of relief from the heat as he crept onto the dock. Toting a fishing rod and a folded lounge chair, he eased out onto the planks and over the small pond. Like peering across a mirror, treetops and shifting clouds reflected from the still water.

With a squeak of rusty hinges, he opened the lounge chair and placed it at the end of the dock. "Wait until I hook one of those big bass. We'll see what mom's got to say then," he snickered.

He snatched a pair of shrimp from his left pocket and dropped one into his gullet. *Can't believe I'm already hungry.* Reaching down to grab the rod, he noticed something barely discernible in the dark water. Just a few feet down from the shoreline was a stretch of jagged skin lying perfectly still.

"Crusty, is that you?" He squinted to get a better look. "I can see your tail, old buddy. I heard you took out one of the neighbor's dogs. Guess you get hungry too, huh?"

Tray quickly whipped out his phone from his right pocket. "I've got to video this and send it to Marissa. She'll freak. She's terrified of gators."

But peering through the phone, he could see little more than murky water. And then came a stroke of brilliance. He'd poke its tail with the rod and then video it as it scurried off. "I'll put it on YouTube, and it'll go viral."

Impressed with his cleverness, Tray knelt at the edge of the dock, phone in one hand, fishing rod in the other.

Peering through the phone's eye, he reached forward with the rod until its tip appeared in the frame. The wavering image of the rod sank deeper into the water toward the dark, jagged shape.

He thrust the rod forward into the object.

But nothing happened.

He jabbed it again. "Crusty, are you even alive?"

The back of his neck grew warm as the sun broke free of the clouds. A wave of light crept down the bank and into the water to reveal that he wasn't looking at a gator tail at all, but rather some kind of pebbled arm that rose into a gnarled shoulder. Above the shoulder, silver tentacle-like projections wavered in the haze.

A pair of blazing eyes flew open.

~ ~ ~

Peering out from between two homes, Deputy Thomas Maloney spotted a teenage boy kneeling at the edge of a dock and peering into a pond. *I knew I saw someone.* The deputy called out, "Hey, you're not supposed to be—"

Splash! Something yanked the teen into the water.

Mahoney stared at the empty dock. "Did I really just see that?"

He cued his shoulder mike as the splash faded into mere ripples on the pond. "Mack, get back here. There's something weird going on with this pond."

A car door slammed from behind Mahoney, and his partner was at his side in no time flat. "What do you mean by weird?" asked his partner, clutching an assault rifle.

"Something in the pond just pulled a kid into the water."

"Gator."

"No. Definitely not a gator."

They crept toward the pond with their weapons drawn.

A knotted back broke the waterline and moved across the smooth surface.

"Looks like a gator to me."

Maloney just shook his head.

The officers reached the water's edge, watching as the strange form paused at the bank on the far side of the pond. Moving closer to the shoreline, the thing rose higher until three feet of its knobby, gray shell arced up from the water.

And there it remained perfectly still.

"You're right. That's definitely not a . . ."

The animal sprang up from the water and latched on to the trunk of an oak tree. The men fired, and the creature bounded onto another tree, landing higher.

Hearing shots fired, another pair of officers appeared from out of nowhere and closed on the pond, assault rifles drawn. The animal moved to about fifty feet up.

A barrage of bullets ripped through the leaves and branches around the beast as it jumped up to another tree, shaking it upon landing. The rain of bullets followed the monster's path. Severed branches twirled toward the bank below.

The beast vaulted to the next tree, but instead of retreating deeper into the woods to make an escape, it swung around the trunk with the finesse of a gymnast and let go, plummeting sixty feet and splashing back into the pond.

The four officers along the bank ran out onto the dock, firing at any sign of movement in the water.

"There . . . at two o'clock. I see bubbles," Deputy Maloney hollered. And the bullets followed, spraying up water. He then raised a hand, and the firing ceased, every eye scanning the rippling water.

Crash. A clawed hand reached up through the dock, latched on to an officer's ankle, and before he could so much as yelp, it jerked him through the planks and into the pond. The three remaining officers scurried around the dock. "It's beneath the dock," chorused two of them.

Again, the beast's hand jutted up through the planks and dragged another officer to a quick, watery death. Simultaneously, the two remaining men fired down through the dock and into the water beneath them.

A stray round from Deputy Mahoney's rifle caught his partner in the ankle, making him stumble onto his knees. Then in an eruption of wood, the creature thrust it's clawed hands through the remainder of the dock, disintegrating the structure beneath them. The echo of gunfire terminated as the men hit the water, flailing.

A swath of blood, a cloud of bubbles, but not a soul returned to the surface.

~~~

A downward stroke of its four-digit hands, and the creature rose through the bloody haze of sinking corpses. For a brief moment, a man locked eyes with the animal, staring through the blood billowing up from his mouth and lacerated neck until he slowly rolled and faded into the muck.

Lifting its lantern eyes above the waterline, the beast searched its surroundings. No activity was detected in the silent homes or trees.

Crawling onto the bank on all fours, the animal rose swiftly onto its hind legs, water coursing down through the channels in its bark-like back. Immediately, its head jerked to the right as if guided by an unseen hand.

The creature leapt onto the trunk of an oak tree and sprang to a rooftop. Cresting the gable roof, the animal stood upright. With a quiver of anticipation, the beast peered west across a valley of rooftops as the chemicals released tauntingly from its brain had commanded.

CHAPTER 15

EYE ON THE BALL

Detective Pine knelt in the Wilson's back yard trying to coax the transmitter ball from the playful shepherd. Blake and his parents fanned out on either side of him to help corner the dog. Carrying the ball in its mouth, Rexy eased closer.

Scott extended a hand, displaying a treat. "That's it, boy . . . How about a trade?"

Meeting Scott's gaze, the shepherd eagerly stepped closer.

"Good booooy," the detective cooed.

The dog dropped the ball from its mouth, took a step back, and knelt on its forepaws, tail wagging. The moment the detective reached for the ball, Rexy snatched it up and took off running.

"I told you it wasn't going to be easy." Blake said. "He thinks you want to play chase. It's his favorite game."

Like I have time for this, Scott thought, recalling the shots that had just rung through the neighborhood. A melee of gunfire that couldn't have been more than six blocks away.

They followed Rexy around the corner of the house and again closed in on him. Running between Blake and his father, the cagey canine paused before the detective and knelt down on its front paws.

There was a scratching noise from above.

Scott looked up and there it was—the creature glaring down at him from the edge of the neighboring roof. The dog had seen it too.

"Everyone, move slowly back toward the house," Scott ordered.

The beast roared down at them. Rexy dropped the ball and took off toward his doghouse. Except for the detective, everyone else scattered as well.

Like a professional center fielder, Scott snatched up the transmitter ball on the run. Shoving it into a coat pocket, he turned for the Jeep.

Thud!

The creature hit the ground, separating him from the Jeep, his escape plan. *Time for Plan B*. The only problem was . . . there was no Plan B. Scott took off on foot along the side of the house and through a neighboring back yard until he came to a six-foot wooden fence.

Placing two hands on top of the fence, the detective vaulted over it. But the moment that his feet hit the grass, the fence erupted behind him to a horrible roar. Fragments of wood rained down onto the lawn around him.

Racing forward, Scott scurried between the bars of a large jungle gym like a mouse fleeing from a hungry cat.

The monster pursued him, twisting its massive form between the labyrinth of bars and slides until it became entangled. A disgruntled growl, a few snaps of aluminum, and the animal threw the troublesome contraption over the back fence. But the diversion was just enough to get Scott around the corner of the house and out of the creature's view.

Passing the side door of the garage, he noticed the glare of yellow paint through the window—the back fenders of an old Yamaha ATV. Swinging open the side door, he pressed the button to open the main garage door. As the noisy electric door proceeded to open at a horribly slow pace, Scott straddled the four-wheeler. He pressed the start button, and the roar of the engine echoed throughout the space.

A man in a pair of boxers rushed into the garage. "Hey, what do you think you're—"

Scott twisted the throttle. No sooner had the four wheeler cleared the rising garage door than the beast landed in the driveway, cutting him off from the street.

How smart is this thing? Instead of entering the side door behind me, it thought ahead, knew where to cut off my path.

Scott leaned his body into a turn and guided the ATV around the side of the home and through the neighboring back yard. He raced across two more back lawns, dodging swimming pools and swing sets, doing his best to hang on to the bulky vehicle. He felt more acclimated to two wheels rather than four. In addition to its awkwardness to him, the old ATV was skipping and bogging down.

It's not even running right.

A glance back showed only his tracks zigzagging across empty lawns, so he kept racing forward. But the path ahead was coming to an end—the next lawn was filled with a huge screened enclosure.

Time to cut between the homes and head back to the street, Scott thought, easing off the gas.

On the other side of the screen, he saw something that made him do a double take. Beside the pool, a teenage boy with long, blond hair was working on a Kawasaki KX 250 motocross bike.

Scott twisted the throttle and aimed the ATV dead ahead. Barreling through the screened enclosure, he leapt off of the back of the four-wheeler and launched it into the swimming pool. With a tremendous splash, the craft plunged deep beneath the water until its four bulbous tires brought it bouncing back up to the surface.

The boy rose from behind his bike and threw his arms wide as the ATV floated sideways in his pool. "What the hell, man!"

Approaching the boy, Scott said, "I never could control those things." He indicated the Kawasaki. "That thing run?"

The teen was still dumbfounded. "What the hell, man!"

"Does. It. Run?"

The boy drew back a wrench. "Touch this bike, and I'll mess you up, bro."

"Don't worry." Scott glanced backward. "He'll explain everything."

"Who?"

Thump. The beast landed just outside of the torn-out screen, stretched its horrible jaws wide, and unleashed a deafening roar.

When the detective turned back around, the boy was gone and the bike was his for the taking. Saddling the cycle, he gave it a single kick and the four-stroke engine thundered to life. Throwing the bike into gear with his left foot, he popped the clutch, spun around on the wet deck, and launched the KX 250 through the screen enclosure, on the opposite side from where the creature stood.

Banking into a turn off the wall of a neighboring home, Scott raced between the houses. *Wham!* His left knee hit a plastic trash can, sending it spinning across the lawn as he shot down the driveway and turned onto the street.

Finally, he was on the road.

~ ~ ~

Losing sight of its noisy prey, the beast charged through the back lawns, leaping over fences or crashing through them . . . it made little difference. Soaring over a swimming pool and landing in another lawn, its quarry was still nowhere to be seen. The animal cut through a side yard to the front of the homes and continued along the main street.

Still nothing in its line of sight. However, its keen sense

of hearing could still detect the revving engine in the distance. Leaping up from the pavement, the animal sprang off of a white Honda minivan, leaving a set of footprints in its collapsed roof, and landed atop the home.

Racing up the shingles, the creature latched its front claws over the ridge of the roof and hurled its body through the air until it caught the ridge of the next roof with its rear paws, propelling itself forward again. Taking tremendous cheetah-like strides, the animal bounded from rooftop to rooftop with blinding speed.

~~~

Tiny rolled the police cruiser toward Leather Leaf Drive while Big Larry sat in the passenger seat, nursing a vanilla latte. Tiny slowed when he heard the sound of a distant motorcycle, and the two officers eyeballed each other. The revving engine grew louder until a man in a business suit riding a dirt bike flashed before them.

"Hey," Larry said, "wasn't that—"

Wham! Something dark slammed onto the hood of the cruiser, bringing the vehicle to a dead stop while compressing the suspension. The latte painted Larry's face as the cruiser rebounded, springing upward with a pair of clawed imprints in the hood.

A glance through the right side window showed a rear view of the creature as it landed on another rooftop and kept going. "Wow, I almost pissed myself," Tiny gasped as he flipped on the lights and turned the cruiser in the same direction.

~~~

From its higher vantage, the speeding beast could now see the motorcycle below, racing along the street. Crossing four more rooftops, its target grew closer.

Louder.

The animal was closing fast.

~~~

Coattail flapping in the wind, the detective proceeded west along Leather Leaf Drive at little more than half throttle. Unfamiliar with the lay of the roads, he feared getting trapped in a cul-de-sac. *This street has to connect to the main road somewhere*, he thought, glancing at another side street.

Something told him to look to the right. When he did, his eyes bugged out and his heart leapt. The creature was barreling across the rooftops—and was only about three houses behind him.

No idea where he was headed, Scott twisted the throttle. The KX 250 rocketed forward with its front wheel lifting from the pavement. Despite the direness of the situation, Scott found himself impressed with the power of the new-model bike.

Passing a side street, through the corner of his eye, Scott noticed an empty lot at the end of a cul-de-sac. On the far side of the lot was a dirt trail that led into the woods.

Tapping the rear brake pedal, the back wheel locked up, sending the bike skidding sideways. Scott slid around the corner without putting a foot down. *Hell yeah, the kid's still got it*, he thought. He twisted the throttle and aimed for the trail.

~~~

Hurtling across the rooftops, the beast saw its prey turn sharply and change direction. Landing onto the next roof, the monster tried to change course as well, but the clay shingles collapsed beneath its claws, sending the animal sliding sideways. Tumbling onto its back, the beast slid over the ridge of the roof and into the open air, accompanied by a shower of broken shingles.

~~~

Eighteen-year-old Tabitha Lee was sprawled on a pink float in her parent's backyard pool while texting away. Still under mandatory quarantine, she figured the rules didn't apply while her mother was in the shower. Besides, their pool had a screened enclosure, so technically she was still indoors.

Still alive after being outside for ten minutes, she texted. Raising her phone for a selfie, the sunlight disappeared.

The sound of twisting aluminum rent the silence as the framework of the screened enclosure bent and snapped before a large thrashing object. Tabitha stared upward, frozen in the object's shadow until it crashed into the water at her feet, catapulting her up from the raft and then splashing back into the pool.

Tumbling to a stop beneath the water, Tabitha turned around to find a pair of burning eyes less than two feet from her face. Silver balls of air swirled through the wavering mane framing its horrible head and giant, interlocked teeth.

She screamed into its face, but the monster didn't bat a blazing eye. It merely looked away from her, latched its claws onto the edge of the pool, and pulled its gruesome form from the water.

Tabitha broke the surface, gasping not just for her breath but out of horror. Lifting just her trembling face from the water, she paddled backward to the corner of the pool and stayed there.

Water draining down from its gray hide, the creature stood upright on the opposite side of the pool with its gnarled back to her. Its gruesome head slowly turned as if following something in the woods. The animal squatted down onto its haunches, then sprang forward through the screen and over the back fence.

And it was gone.

~~~

Bursting from the brush, the monster landed on the dirt trail in pursuit of the distant sound. Like a huge cheetah reaching thirty-foot strides, the animal's forepaws pushed the ground backward until the rear paws reached ahead of them and hurled the world behind it.

The tree trunks and palmetto bushes passing by were just a blur.

Thundering farther along the trail, the animal entered a dust cloud generated from its fleeing target. It proceeded into the haze, encountering one winding turn after another. In spite of the beast's incredible agility, the series of frustrating hairpin turns and berms were slowing its pace.

Bounding up from the trail, the creature soared into the trees, the strands of its silver mane sweeping forward and interlocking to protect its face. With the agility of a primate and the speed of a gazelle, the monster hurtled through the trees. Branches bursting and snapping against its gray hide went unnoticed.

Then from the vantage of the treetops, the animal caught sight of its quarry speeding through the woods below. It's sensory devices tingled as another surge of chemicals released from its medial forebrain bundle offered a tantalizing taste of what would soon come.

~~~

Clinging to the bouncing handlebars, Scott ripped through the winding trail, giving it everything he had. His adrenaline pumped as fast as the revving engine. He was in a race for his life, and second place was not an option.

Flying into the next corner, he simultaneously cut throttle, tapped the rear brake, dropped into a lower gear, and leaned the bike into a berm without putting a foot down. Bouncing out of the corner, he twisted the throttle wide open and rocketed toward the next turn.

Racing down a long, straight section of the path, Scott glanced back to receive a jolt to his senses. The beast was charging through the brush on all fours. Branches and small trees folded before its gnarled shoulders as every stride brought it closer to Scott's dusty wake. The creature was not following the trail, but rather cutting straight through the woods to get him.

Looking straight ahead, another hairpin turn was coming up fast. But slowing down was not an option. Scott shot straight through the corner, jumped over the sand berm, and landed off of the trail.

Clicking into third gear, a rooster tail of dirt spat up behind the rear wheel as Scott sped through a gauntlet of tree trunks and winding branches. *Whoa!* He had to tap the rear brake and swerve to avoid a cluster of pine trees. Then, as if in slow motion, he glimpsed a clawed hand rip through the branches, just missing him.

It's still there!

Clicking fourth gear, he twisted the throttle all the way. And the KX 250 lunged forward with such veracity, it felt as if the bike was trying to push him from the seat.

He flashed between the trees, missing them by inches. Small branches swatted his hands as if trying to knock them from the bars.

Fifth gear. And the Kawasaki shot through the woods like a lime-green bullet.

The trees were just a blur now. Scott ducked low behind the handlebars as branches flashed overhead like wielded swords.

He saw more daylight beaming through the trees in the distance. The woods were beginning to thin out.

The bike was approaching maximum RPM and in top gear, which meant he was blazing through unfamiliar woods at eighty miles per hour. *This is insane.* Scott knew he had to slow down. But he couldn't convince his right hand to ease up on the throttle.

It's not still be behind me. It can't be!

Bursting through a cluster of palmetto bushes, the forest floor disappeared, replaced by a raging river some forty feet below. The engine screamed as the rear wheel spun in the open air.

"What the—"

He sailed off the cliff and out over the water. The river appeared to be about sixty feet wide. Did he have the trajectory to make it to the other side? He would soon find out.

Soaring high above the water, the front wheel started to rise. But an instinctive tap of the rear brake pedal stopped the rear wheel from spinning, creating a gyroscopic effect that eased the front of the bike back down.

But the bank was coming up fast.

Scott braced for impact. *This is going to hurt.*

He was not wrong.

Just clearing the water, the bike slammed down hard onto the bank, the force of the impact fully compressing the suspension.

He'd landed the jump, but the recoiling of the rear suspension had a pogo stick effect, causing the rear wheel to buck high from the ground. Scott tried to ride it out as the bike barreled across the bank on its front wheel. But the front tire caught a rut, sending him over the handlebars and tumbling across the sand.

Slightly disoriented, he lifted his head and spat out a mouth full of sand. Apparently his years of motocross racing had paid off as he still had a left hand on the handlebar with the clutch lever engaged—a racer's instinct to keep the engine running.

Scott lifted the bike with a groan. He'd slammed down onto the seat so hard it felt like his stomach had tried to escape through his rectum.

Throwing a leg over the Kawasaki and clicking it out of gear, he looked back at the gap he'd just cleared. From the ledge of the towering cliff to the bank on this side of the river had to be seventy feet. That was nearly twice as far as he'd ever jumped a bike. Never mind doing so without a helmet and in a torn-up business suit.

And then on the opposite side of the river, he saw the ungodly form lift its head and shoulders from the brush. Lowering onto all fours, the creature crept to the ledge of the cliff, and its red eyes looked down toward the river.

A frustrated growl, and the creature withdrew from the ledge.

Good, Scott thought. *Looks like someone can't swim.*

In the blink of an eye, the creature reappeared, running at full speed, and sprang from the ledge.

Or not.

Arms and claws extended, Medusa mane flailing, the monster sailed through the air with a bellowing roar—until it terminated with a loud splash as the beast plunged into the middle of the river.

A click of the gear lever, and the KX 250 rocketed toward the woods, throwing a rooster tail of dirt across the water. Reaching the tree line, Scott darted between tall oaks and pines, searching for a bike path, anything to help increase his speed. But there was nothing except a maze of tree trunks, branches, and palmetto bushes. He ducked as moss strung from low branches brushed his face, obscuring his vision.

Scott had no idea how long the water would detain his pursuer. He only knew that he needed to keep his lead. *Good luck with that,* he thought. The woods were so dense he could barely get the bike out of second gear.

Moments ago, he'd thought how terrifying it was to race through the forest at top speed. But being forced to slow down was even more unnerving.

For now, all he could do was navigate the myriad of trees as swiftly as possible, ducking branches and twisting the handlebars. His heart pounded, and his breathing grew more rapid. *This is a race that you cannot loose,* he told himself.

Focus!

Scott's forearms tightened, and he started to lose the feeling of the handlebars. He tried to loosen his grip and breathe to ward off a racer's worst enemy: arm pump. It was a condition in which blood becomes trapped in the forearms, usually caused by gripping the bars too tight, nerves, or both. And once arm pump set in, it made a 250-pound bike steer like a semi. In a race, it meant a one-way ticket to the back of the pack.

Come on. Relax and flow, he told himself. *Work with the bike, not against it.*

And then he felt something more unnerving than his blood-engorged forearms.

The bike sputtered.

It choked again as if losing power.

Scott immediately recognized the sound. Oh how he knew that sound. The heart-breaking sound that he had heard over a decade ago at the famed Carlsbad Motocross Park in California. It was as if he had been hurled back in time. He felt the same sinking feeling that he had on the last lap after going toe-to-toe with the top motocross racers in the world.

The bike was running out of fuel.

Only this time, it wasn't just a race or a sponsorship on the line.

Through the trees, Scott saw a ravine just ahead. Rapidly

losing speed, he slipped off of the back of the bike and let the unmanned cycle sail over the ledge. The KX 250 bounced and spiraled down the embankment until it came to rest on the rocks some thirty feet below.

Wasting no time, he pulled the ball from his pocket and hurled it in the same direction, watching it bounce until it vanished in the trees somewhere beyond the smoking bike.

Scott stood at the ledge of the ravine, contemplating how he'd run out of fuel—again. But this time he'd won. There were no cheering crowds. Only the soft rustling of leaves and crackling palmetto bushes applauded him. And it was enough. Because this time he had finished the race. He had safely lured the creature away from humanity, and he was still alive.

At least for the moment.

CHAPTER 16

DEPLOYMENT

After blindly winding along the streets of Hidden Lakes for an hour in Detective Pine's old clunker, Wendy was finally getting somewhere. She spotted her Jeep parked backward in the driveway of a single-story home. On the sidewalk, a couple with a young boy and a German shepherd were being questioned by a pair of officers. The father nodded and pointed westward. But other than the Jeep, there was no sign of Scott. Wendy proceeded in the direction the man had indicated.

Making the next right, onto Leather Leaf Drive, she noticed that the neighborhood had suddenly come to life. *The quarantine must have been lifted.* Residents once held up in their homes were now collected in lawns, driveways, and along the sidewalks while conversing and pointing down the street. A teenage boy mimicked someone riding a motorcycle, then pointed up along the rooftops. Something big had happened here, and they had all seen it.

Wendy passed a driveway where people were gathered around a white Honda minivan. Holding their phones high, they snapped selfies alongside the collapsed roof. Farther down the street, she saw the flashing lights. Several patrol units were collected along one of the side streets.

Her heart fluttered, and she muttered a quick prayer for Scott.

Reaching the intersection, Wendy looked along Ashford

street where patrol units were parked bumper to bumper along the cul-de-sac, every light flashing. At the end of the cul-de-sac was an empty lot where several officers were studying a trail that led into the woods.

She stopped beside a pair of officers guarding the street. One was the size of a mountain. The other man was shorter but so fat that his silhouette formed a near perfect circle.

The larger man approached the car, squinting. "Where did you get that car? Isn't it—"

"Detective Pine's. Yes," she said. "I'm a friend of his."

The big man winked to the portly officer who joined him. "There has to be some kind of mistake, ma'am. I'm afraid he doesn't have any friends."

Giving a roll of the eyes and a smirk, Wendy noted his name badge: *Deputy Larry Webber.*

The big man grinned and gave Wendy a long look that creeped her out. "Wait, I remember seeing you with him and the chief. You're the vet, right?"

"Yes. And I'm aware of what you're searching for and why." There was urgency in her voice. "Could you please tell me what happened here? Was Scott involved?"

"Yes." Resting a beefy hand on the side mirror, Larry leaned down to face her. "According to witnesses, the detective located the transmitter and used a kid's dirt bike to take it out of the community. He was last seen heading down that trail at the end of the cul-de-sac."

"And the creature," Wendy said, "where was it last seen?"

"Heading in the same direction."

The reply sucked the air from Wendy's lungs. "But what . . ." She glanced at all of the officers conversing in the vicinity. She spotted Chief O'Hern among them. "What's being done? Have you sent anyone in there to help him?"

"We're discussing the best course of action to take right

now."

"You mean he's alone in the woods *with that thing?*"

Apparently, the big officer had nothing more to add. Larry released the mirror and his face disappeared from her line of sight. "I'm sorry, ma'am, but you'll have to move along."

Wendy did as told. Staring blankly through the windshield, she took the next side street and pulled onto the shoulder of the road. And she closed her eyes to pray.

~ ~ ~

Now what? Scott thought as his eyes searched the woods. The beast could come crashing through the trees at any second. And soon it would be getting dark. He knew that to try to creep out of the woods would be suicide.

There was only one option. He had to go up, way up . . . and he had to do it now.

Keeping a sharp ear to the forest, Scott scrambled between the trees, searching for the perfect candidate. Slapping his hands on a massive girth of bark, he looked up. He studied the thick oak's branches that swept out into the neighboring trees.

"Looks like you're the one," he muttered, and started his ascent. *Don't keep looking down,* he told himself. *Just climb.* At moments such as this, being of small stature had its advantages. He vaulted from branch to branch, scurrying up the towering oak like a frightened squirrel.

Scott lunged upward, caught onto another branch, and easily pulled himself up. Although strong for his size, he knew that surging adrenaline was more likely responsible for his rapid ascent.

When he finally paused for a breather and looked down, he couldn't believe how high he'd climbed. He had to be at least forty feet up. And the light seemed to grow dimmer by the minute.

Beyond his cocoon of sweeping branches, he could see little more than shadows on the forest floor. A glance up showed that the branches toward the top of the tree were too small to support him.

This is high enough.

Like carefully crossing rafters in an attic, Scott stepped from limb to limb until he found a pair of branches about eight inches apart that projected out from the trunk. Placing a hand against the trunk for stability, he crouched down until his body was lying supine along the branches.

Scott eased his head back against the trunk. A wave of relaxation swept through every muscle in his body, except for one. His heart was thumping so loudly he feared the creature could hear it—that the world could hear it.

You're high enough, and the leaves are still thick enough to conceal you from ground level, he reassured himself. *Just don't make a sound.*

Beyond the shuddering leaves, he saw only the hint of a crescent moon. Not a star hung in the ash-black sky.

Releasing a breath, Scott let his eyes drift closed.

A beat later, his eyes popped open with a rush of panic, and he grabbed at his pockets for his cell phone.

Nothing.

I must have lost it back at the river during the crash. He eased his neck back against the bark with relief. *But it's for the better*, he thought. If it had rung while in his pocket, it could have meant a death sentence. Besides, even if he had a phone, he'd be afraid to use it. The slightest sound or the light it produced could have sealed his fate.

His proximity to the transmitter ball unnerved him. The ravine couldn't have been more than fifty yards away, which meant that the creature was near.

It could be watching me this very minute. That thought

alone kept his heart racing. His body was relaxed, but his mind was still reeling from the adrenaline surging through his veins.

And God knows that thing can climb. If the beast spotted him, it would be on him in a split second. And he was completely unarmed, without even his pistol. *Pistol,* he thought, *what a joke. That would do little more than get its attention.*

A branch snapped nearby.

His body jolted to alertness, teetering on the branches that supported him.

He saw nothing but darkness below.

What would he do if the creature came up the tree after him? Would it be quicker to jump to his death, or wait until the beast reached him and ripped him apart?

He could picture the red eyes opening in the trees . . . *below him . . .*

. . . beside him . . .

. . . everywhere.

A cold sweat surged through his pores and his thumping heart felt like it was going to explode. He couldn't just lie there. Anxiety was having its way with him.

And then as if carried on the wind, an unseen force seemed to drift down between the branches and leaves and light upon him. His pounding heart grew tame, and a sense of peacefulness flowed through him.

He immediately knew what it was.

Wendy.

Was it her prayers that seemed to calm him, or the simple fact that he knew she was praying for him this very minute? Probably both.

He eased his head back against the trunk. A few deep breaths, and rational thought began to overshadow the terrifying scenarios in his mind. He recalled what the scientist had said at the hospital: *"If you can remove the transmitter from the community, the animal will go into a defensive mode and not attack unless threatened."*

He released a breath and closed his eyes. *So relax, don't fall . . . and stop being a little wuss.*

~~~

Officer Jones looked on from his post at the edge of the Hidden Lakes playground as the three-ring circus ensued. Before him, a pair of SWAT transport helicopters filled the basketball courts while awaiting deployment. Their silent rotor blades arced over the glittering pavement. Before the open bay doorways, two teams totaling twenty-eight men readied their gear as well as their minds for what lay ahead.

Bearing body armor, helmets, and assault shields, their silhouetted forms resembled medieval warriors under the playground lights. Their imposing shadows stretched across the glistening asphalt.

Under all that gear, they have to be pissing themselves, Jones thought. *Especially after what went down in the Douglas Street home.* He'd been present when they removed the SWAT team members' remains from the closet.

It was a sight he would not soon forget.

SWAT Team Commander Hodges stood with his hands on his hips, facing the men. His shaved head glowed in the ambient light as his signature scar defined the left side of his stern face. Chief O'Hern stood proudly beside him in a gesture of comradery. But everyone knew who was running the show. Other than the police chopper that was searching the woods for the detective, the boys at OPD had been reduced to security detail. Their job was to simply keep the deployment area clear of civilians.

And that was perfectly fine with Officer Jones. The last place he wanted to be was in the woods facing that thing.

Turning away from the playground, he peered across the rooftops and into the dark forest with a heavy heart. He wondered how far Detective Pine had made it into the woods before the inevitable occurred.

SWAT Team Commander Hodges spoke up, snatching Jones's attention from the woods.

"Right now, a chopper is searching the trail that Detective Pine was allegedly following. As soon as they locate the bike or any evidence that points to the animal's whereabouts, we're on," he said, his eyes smoldering as he stared across his men. "All right, so listen up. What transpired earlier in that home today . . . put out of your minds." He pointed westward. "Those woods are a new playing field." He thumped his armored chest. "*Our* field. A field clear of civilians and residential homes. Tonight you're going in with armor-piercing rounds. You will be using your thermal imaging goggles and scopes, with no communication gear. Hand signals only. It can't see you, but you will see it. You are going to be silent, invisible,. . . and deadly."

He thrust his submachine gun overhead. "Tonight in those woods the tables are turned. Tonight we are the predators!"

The men reciprocated by thrusting their weapons overhead with shouts and cheers of comradery. "Tonight we get payback," hollered one of the men.

"Hell yes," shouted several others.

As the men continued to gear up, Officer Jones turned and headed for his cruiser to make another round of the neighborhood. "Armor-piercing rounds, hell," he muttered. "I wouldn't go into those woods in a tank."

~~~

Sprawled along a pair of branches in the towering oak, Detective Pine's back was getting numb. Every so often, he would carefully shift his weight to the left branch until the tingling in his toes diminished. *I'm definitely going to be due for a chiropractic visit after tonight.*

But this wasn't the first night that Scott had spent from such a perch. The predicament reminded him of a summer night when he was ten. Sitting on the diving board and listening to his father's old Sony Walkman, which he was forbidden to touch—he was on dangerous ground. Then during the chorus of Bon Jovi's "Livin' on a Prayer," the earphones flew from his ears to a light *kerplunk*. Scott could only watch the wavering device sink to the bottom of the pool.

Knowing there would be hell to pay, he'd darted into the nearby woods and taken refuge amongst the high branches of an oak tree. For hours he sat silently in his perch, watching the beam of his father's flashlight scour the woods below.

"Scott, you'd better come out!" The warning echoed through the branches. "The longer you hide, the worse it's going to be."

It wasn't until the break of dawn that Scott had gathered the nerve to leave his lofty sanctuary and return home. As expected, he'd received a world-class spanking.

Scott peered out into the darkness between the trembling leaves. *If only a spanking were the penalty for being discovered tonight.*

There was a sound in the distance. It wasn't coming from the trees, but rather above them. The rhythmic thumping of a helicopter grew closer, and light invaded the treetops.

It was coming from the direction of the river. *They must have picked up my tire tracks on the bank to be this close.*

The light moved closer until it streamed through the branches and swept across him. The branches danced in the downdraft from the main rotor as leaves swirled around his face.

If he'd so much as waved, they would have seen him. But

Scott didn't dare move a muscle. He knew there was no way they could drop a ladder down through the dense branches. And if they tried, the creature would surely get to him first.

The light moved on, and the branches grew still.

Thank God they didn't see me.

Peering through the branches and leaves, Scott watched the aircraft move eastward until it paused with its spotlight glaring down into the ravine.

They've spotted the bike, he thought, watching the chopper hover in the same spot for well over a minute. Then with a dip of its nose, the aircraft slowly skirted the ravine and headed back toward the river.

Now all Scott could do was sit tight and ponder the obvious question. No the chopper hadn't seen him, but had they pointed him out to the creature in their pursuit?

Wendy, keep the prayers coming, girl . . . I'm going to need them.

CHAPTER 17

HEAT SIGNATURE

The brakes squeaked as Officer Jones brought the cruiser to a stop in the Ashford Street cul-de-sac. He played his spotlight over the empty lot and into the woods beyond. Confirming that the yellow crime-scene tape was still blocking the entry into the trail and that no one was in the vicinity, he decided to move on.

Reaching Leather Leaf Drive, he made a right. Heading toward the next intersection, he noticed an old police Crown Vic pulled up onto the shoulder of the road.

He recognized it as Detective Pine's heap. *What's it doing out here?*

Pulling alongside the vehicle, he noticed a tuft of blond hair pressed against the driver's-side window.

Curious, he popped his door open.

He approached the vehicle, then tapped the window with his flashlight. The petite blonde jolted awake. Wiping the sleep from her eyes, she looked up into the glaring light.

"Wendy," Jones said, "how did . . ."

She rolled down the window. "Scott and I traded vehicles. In case he recovered the transmitter, he thought that my Jeep would be more reliable."

"Ah." Officer Jones nodded. "We wondered why your Jeep was at the residence where the detective acquired the transmitter ball."

"But have you heard anything yet?" Wendy asked, hope

filling her blue eyes. "Have they sent out a search party?"

The officer paused. This had always been the worst part of his job. And he knew how she felt about the detective. "A chopper located the abandoned bike in a ravine about four miles west of here." He lowered his gaze. "But there was no sign of Detective Pine."

He then looked up and said with forced vigor in his voice, "But two SWAT teams are en route to the area right now. If he's still ali—" The officer caught himself. "If he's out there, they'll find him." Although he knew the detective was presumed dead, Jones wanted to give her a glimmer of hope.

But she said, "No."

"No what?"

"Don't look at me like you know that he's already dead. No one can know . . ."

Officer Jones raised a finger. "Just a minute. I'm getting a call." Stepping out of ear shot of Wendy, he took the call on his shoulder mike. After listening for a moment, he said. "Okay, Izzy, I'll be there in twenty."

He knelt down in front of the window of the old Crown Vic. "We just got another call from the hospital," he said to Wendy. "Your scientist buddy, Jim Randle, has stabilized. He's still in and out of consciousness, but the chief wants to meet me there just in case Jim can tell us anything more that might help us."

"Okay," she said, dragging out the word.

He stood and opened her door. "There's nothing you can do here. I'll drop you off at your Jeep, and you can follow me to the hospital."

Snatching up her purse, Wendy followed the officer to his cruiser.

~ ~ ~

Detective Pine shifted on the pair of branches supporting him when he heard a muffled thumping coming from the east. He quickly scooted into an upright position with his back against the trunk. Through the tangle of limbs, he saw the lights from a helicopter about 200 yards away. Was it OPD, SWAT, or military? He had no idea as the chopper hung perfectly still in the pitch.

A few minutes later, the craft moved on.

No sooner had the lights from the aircraft faded into the night than another helicopter approached from the south, the direction of the river. As the light glaring from its underbelly grew nearer, Scott realized it was the same police Bell 407 that he'd seen earlier.

Maybe they did spot me earlier and are coming to attempt a rescue. The thought brought more worry than it did hope.

But the aircraft again passed over him and hovered above the ravine with its spotlight peering down toward the bike. Several canisters were dropped from the cargo bay doorway and tumbled down through the light. A beat later, a trail of red smoke rose from the ravine, swelling and undulating like a genie reaching for freedom.

Smoke grenades, Scott thought. *And red, indicating a hostile target. That's an understatement.*

A loud clap of thunder shook the tree like an angry roar from Heaven. A flash of lightning revealed the smoke rising through the forest for a split second until the darkness returned, leaving only the red glowing haze.

It wasn't long before the crimson mist invaded his perch, curling around the branches and reaching toward him. A scent much like spent fireworks irritated his nostrils and eyes.

And then he detected movement below. In the dim moonlight, he saw several silhouetted figures creeping slowly between the trees.

Another thunder rumble. A crack of lightning divulged a

couple dozen men in body armor, weapons aimed forward. And then the darkness again consumed them, leaving only the hint of a helmet here or there.

Not a single light shone from their helmets or shields, nor were red beams pointing from their laser scopes. *They must be using thermal vision,* Scott thought. *That should definitely play in their favor.*

But would it be enough?

~~~

Forty-six-year-old SWAT Team Commander Alex Hodges guided his team through the forest. An assault shield hung on his left arm, a submachine gun poised beside it. Before his thermal goggles lay a surreal world of purple trees rising in a dark-blue sky.

A glance back showed the orange heat signatures of his men moving through the purple landscape. Sure, the colors took some getting used to. But once acclimated, a night mission felt like a stroll through the woods on a summer day.

Returning his gaze forward, he scanned the purple treetops ahead. *With this technology, that beast should stand out like a flare on a starless night.*

Still, the commander had to resist the urge to use his communication head gear. He needed to rely on hand signals only, just like he'd told his men—silent, invisible, and deadly.

The face of his last girlfriend, Mia, materialized before him. *The one who got away.* His mother had been right; he should have married her when he had the chance. *Where's your head? Focus,* he told himself. *Your mind's drifting like a nervous rookie.*

Truth be told, he'd never felt so jumpy on a mission. It was a sentiment shared by his men, as their nervous glances during the flight professed. *Thank God they didn't see the condition of the remains removed from the closet,* he thought.

How could one animal do that?

The commander feared no man—but this was no man.

He caught sight of smoke rising in the distance. Although the smoke was truly red, his thermal goggles rendered it as a light-purple mist lifting through deep-purple trees.

Ground zero.

Then he discovered a bright orange speck high up in a tree. Shouldering his firearm, the commander raised his thermal binoculars. *Yep, there's something way up there.* The heat signature was too small to be the creature though. Most likely a small brown bear. And then it hit him. It could be the detective whom everyone had written off, holed up there like a squirrel.

A tree closer to the commander shook and swayed. The pines purple branches shuddered, but there was no heat signature near it.

It's probably the wind, he thought. *But the wind doesn't move just one tree.*

He thrust his closed fist upward, bringing the team to a halt.

Another tree shook. *Closer.*

Why can't I see it?

Another pine tree jostled.

Closer.

Like toppling dominoes, one tree shook and then the next one. Commander Hodges turned, aiming his weapon to follow the movement. Then he realized the creature was making a circle around them.

The animal increased in speed, leaping from one tree to the next. It was impossible to keep aim on the beast—even if he could have seen it.

Through his thermal goggles, he witnessed the orange figures of his men turning their weapons in every direction. Random shots rang through the trees.

The creature's movement increased in speed. The trees came to life around them—a blur of purple swinging branches. And that was when he realized the circle was getting smaller with every pass.

It's corralling us in.

The torn bodies jumbled together in the closet flashed in his mind.

It wants us close together.

The movement of the trees stopped. The gunfire echoing through the woods ceased as well. For a moment, the orange figures stood quietly, gazing beyond their glowing gun barrels to the tangle of purple branches surrounding them.

Branches snapped up high.

The crackling grew lower.

A thump behind him.

Turning around, the commander saw an orange figure drop to his knees. Like a glowing orange ball, a decapitated head rolled across the ground. A swath of yellow drained down a purple tree trunk behind it.

But the commander never saw a hint of the animal.

A pine tree near the body shook, and then the next one jolted. He swung the submachine gun toward the movement and a dashed line of glowing rounds ripped through the purple branches.

The orange figures of his men were frantically firing in every direction. Yellow fire blazed from their weapons.

The commander turned to find another orange silhouette sprawled on the purple forest floor. A yellow puddle swelled beneath him.

Why can't we see it? He lifted his thermal goggles to see only the shadows of his men clambering in the darkness.

Dropping his thermal goggles back in place, a brilliant thought crossed his mind. He unclipped a smoke grenade from his belt, activated it, and rolled it across the ground.

Spirals of purple smoke shot up from the forest floor, engulfing the orange figures as they scurried about, aiming their weapons every which way. And there, standing among them, was the towering dark form outlined in purple mist.

The creature sprang backward, landing on all fours, and with a whirl of purple smoke, it was gone.

A tree swayed just above the team. And every man opened fire. Thunder clapped overhead but was muted by the raging weapons. Like a swarm of angry hornets, glowing yellow rounds riddled the tree. Purple branches jolted and tumbled to the ground.

~~~

Detective Pine ducked low on the branches as stray rounds whistled through the nearby leaves. *Whap!* Another bullet struck the trunk not five feet above his head.

The dark woods twinkled again as more rounds invaded the neighboring trees.

~~~

Realizing they were shooting at thin air, Commander Hodges gave the signal to cease fire. Nothing stood out against the purple treetops and deep-blue sky. Not a speck of orange. The creature had to be near, yet there was no trace of a heat signature.

How can this be?

~~~

Wendy entered room 407 to find Officer Jones and Chief O'Hern standing beside Jim's bed. She noted there was less equipment in the room than before. *A good sign*, she thought. But the geneticist still appeared groggy, releasing an occasional groan, or perhaps it was a mumbled word.

Placing a hand on the bedrail, Wendy sat down in a chair

beside Jim. "How is he?" she asked them.

"I spoke to him briefly when I came in," the chief said, "but he drifted off before I had a chance to question him. So, here we are waiting . . . *again*."

Officer Jones glanced at her as if reading her mind. "And no, we haven't heard anything more about Detective Pine."

Wendy tried to conceal her emotions.

The look in the chief's eyes seemed to indicate this was no surprise to him.

"But we hadn't heard much at all," Jones added. "For the moment, the SWAT team has gone dark while attempting to engage the target. And according to our chopper in the area, the first team has found the creature."

Wendy noticed the news playing on a retractable TV beside the bed. It showed a male reporter outside of the gates at Hidden Lakes. As a pair of officers looked on, he discussed the number of civilian and law-enforcement casualties.

Wendy picked up the remote and switched off the TV. "Leave this off. He may not be fully conscious, but he can still hear it."

She felt a hand rest on her forearm. "Hear what?" Jim looked at her groggily. "Wendy . . . what's going on?"

"Ah, there he is," the chief said. "What's going on is that we've relocated the transmitter to a remote wooded area. As we speak, that beast of yours is being surrounded."

Jim squirmed in his bed and looked toward the dark window. "What . . . what time is it?"

"Tonight your creature becomes the prey," the chief went on. "We have two SWAT teams consisting of twenty-eight men, armed with armor-piercing rounds and thermal vision gear. It will never see them coming. This creation of yours won't live to see the light of day."

The scientist turned his bandaged bed. "No. No . . . not at night. You have to wait . . ."

Officer Jones looked at him with concern. "What are you getting at?"

Jim's mind was moving too fast for his mouth, it seemed. "Its eyes have been fortified with nanoparticle injections," he blurted almost incoherently. "Its back has a lining of silica beneath its hide . . . designed to block the animal's temperature."

Desperation filled the scientist's eyes as he finished with, "Get them out. You have to get them out now."

"What in hell are you babbling about?" O'Hern shot back.

Jim's shaking hand reached above the bedrail and latched on to the chief's coat. He pulled him down toward the bed. "The creature has enhanced night vision and does not give off a heat signature. Your men can't see it, but it can see them!"

O'Hern yanked his coat from Jim's grasp and stumbled backward, glaring down at the bed. Before leaving, he plucked up the remote, turned the news back on, and tossed the remote into a trash can. "Leave it on. Let him see what he's done."

~~~

SWAT Team Commander Hodges dared another look down at the purple palmetto bushes and leaves to find that two more orange figures had fallen.

He had given the signal to fall back, but no one had seen it.

It was all a maddening blur. The orange figures of his men firing haphazardly . . . yellow fire blazing from their weapons . . . purple branches swaying around him.

Something hit the ground right beside him.

The commander turned to find another orange silhouette falling, the man's head and left arm separating from his torso as he hit the ground.

At least half of his men were down now.

The commander's head spun. *We have to abort. Our technology . . . it's useless.*

Pulling off his thermal goggles, he tossed them away. The purple treetops and dark-blue sky transformed into gray branches reaching into the night. The orange silhouettes of his men were mere shadows now, their body armor glowing briefly in the fire leaping from their weapons.

A loud crack of thunder. And in the glare of the lightning, he saw a large gray object flash between the trees.

There you are.

He switched on the light on his assault shield. The camo body armor of his men glowed before him until he swung the beam of light up into a swaying tree.

"Commander, what are you doing?" someone shouted. "Kill the light."

"No. Switch to standard light," Hodges ordered. "It doesn't show on . . ."

Wham! Something jutted out from the trees and knocked his shield away, nearly taking his arm with it. The shield landed somewhere in the brush with its light blotted out.

~~~

From his towering perch, Scott watched the distant melee of gunfire. Another flurry of shots rang out, glittering like fireflies between the trees. Then one by one, more prominent lights started appearing on the men.

What are they doing? Scott thought. *They can't switch to standard lighting . . .*

A trail of red smoke billowed up from the forest floor as someone deployed a smoke grenade. Was it intended to reveal the creature, or help the men evade it? He wasn't sure.

Thunder again shook the sky. And for a split second, he saw the men clamoring in a red haze while firing up at the trees. Then they were again swallowed by the pitch, leaving only their lighting gear visible.

"Behind you," someone shouted.

A flurry of gunshots rang out, and then nothing, only the sound of the night wind whispering through the woods.

A heartbeat later, lightning again tore through the night sky to reveal the creature standing alone in the crimson haze. The beast thrust its arms outward as if in elation while the mist swirled around its horrible form. The darkness returned, and a guttural roar echoed through the woods.

And then another sound reverberated between the trees. The whirling rotors of a police Bell 407 grew louder, and its spotlight glared down between the branches, encircling the monster.

CHAPTER 18

"TONIGHT WE ARE THE PREDATORS"

Peering down from the cockpit of the Bell 407, Sgt. Aiden Sullivan saw the creature standing amid the billowing red smoke. The beast looked up into the light and spread its arms wide, like a rock star on center stage.

Decreasing altitude, the craft's rotor wash swept the red smoke outward through the trees to reveal the tangle of figures sprawled beneath it. Light from their helmets and shields reflected eerily from the forest floor.

The pilot, Shari Clark, glanced at him with her jaw hanging.

"My God," Sullivan hissed. "Dillan, light that cursed thing up!"

But the creature had already dropped onto all fours and was racing through the forest.

~~~

Harnessed inside the cargo bay doorway, Ofc. Dillan Brown swung the .40-caliber machine gun toward the gray back darting beneath a canopy of treetops. The weapon roared to life. Bullets peppering its wake, the illuminated animal leapt from the forest floor and into the trees.

"Keep it in the light!" the gunman hollered as he trained the kicking weapon on the glowing hide.

He thought that a couple of rounds had caught its back,

but he couldn't be sure. "If I can't take you out, I'm still gonna leave a mark," he grunted as the creature flashed in and out of the light.

The monster proceeded to race through the trees, grabbing thick branches and tree trunks with its hands or feet and thrusting its body forward with incredible agility.

The jagged back grew bright in the chopper's spotlight. Then, just when Dillan had the target dead in his sights, the animal caught on to a tree trunk with one hand, swung around it, and took off in a different direction.

"Circle back around," Dillan hollered into his headset. "We overshot it. The target's now at nine o'clock."

Correcting its course, the aircraft's spotlight discovered the gray back moving swiftly beneath the myriad of branches and leaves. Trees shook and swayed in the animal's wake as it sailed through the forest.

~~~

Scott was perched on the branches like a meerkat, watching the helicopter glaze the treetops in pursuit of the creature. The aircraft arced around in the night sky, and the spotlight flashed in his direction. It was heading straight for him.

The trees before him shook. And then he saw the illuminated creature blazing through the treetops, growing closer.

Oh crap.

Scott scurried to the opposite side of the thick oak as the tree grew bright to the sound of the blaring rotors.

Woosh! The beast flashed through a tree across from him. A line of bullets zipped through the branches, ripping the bark from tree trunks as the underbelly of the helicopter soared overhead with fire blazing from the doorway.

~~~

"Get me closer!" Dillan hollered.

The creature grew brighter in the glaring light. Branches flashing below slapped against the landing gear.

He pulled the trigger, and the barrel of the .40-caliber erupted in flames. Bullets tore through the treetops, just missing the target.

They were coming up on a clearing. *This should let the pilot get lower*, he thought.

Giving the beast a little more lead, Dillan fired again. This time, a round struck a branch at the same instant the creature's left hand latched on to it, causing the beast to careen headfirst into a tree trunk.

The entire oak tree trembled as the animal tumbled down through it, crashing through the branches until it hit the clearing some forty feet below.

"Bingo!" the gunman howled.

But by the time they'd swung the spotlight to the area, the beast was gone.

"Find it!" Sergeant Sullivan's voice cracked in Dillan's earphones.

The aircraft descended toward the clearing. Branches danced and loose leaves swirled in the rotor wash beyond the doorway as the spotlight played over a carpet of palmetto bushes below.

The Bell 407 slowed to a hover.

"Where did it go?" the sergeant demanded. There was no response.

The light swept across where the trees met the forest floor, and then back deeper into the woods.

The gunman looked up to find the monster perched on a branch just outside the chopper's doorway—the burning red orbs staring at him from eye level.

Before Dillan could raise the .40-caliber, the animal sprang from the tree, jaws and claws spreading. It latched on to the cargo bay doorway, tilting the aircraft. A clawed hand grabbed on to the back of Dillan's head, and flung him through the doorway, snapping his neck on the way out.

Dillan's life had fled before he ever hit the ground.

~~~

Sergeant Sullivan turned away from the windscreen to find the beast towering behind the pilot's seat, eyes ablaze. A swipe of the creature's left hand, and the pilot's head was gone, seemingly replaced by a red swash across the windscreen.

The aircraft spun crazily. The sergeant withdrew his sidearm and tried to fire as treetops flashed outside the windscreen.

~~~

Leaning forward on the branches, Scott could only watch as the helicopter hit the ground, rolled over once, and erupted in flames. The surrounding tree trunks glowed in the ambient firelight as a plume of smoke rolled up through the branches and dissipated into the night sky.

Scott gazed into the distant inferno with bated breath. From his vantage point, it appeared as though the creature had still been in the craft when it hit the ground. The blaze undulated and crackled. The auxiliary fuel tank then erupted in a belch of flames that swept up a tree trunk.

"Is it finally . . .?"

A beat later, a round mass rolled from the burning wreckage. Once clear of the flames, the object rolled onto four legs. And then the monster stood upright. Dapples of fuel still burned across its shoulders like a demon stepping from the gates of hell.

Smoke still rising from its back, the creature leapt onto an oak tree and vanished into the night.

~~~

Bringing up the rear of SWAT Team Two, thirty-year-old Henry Williams crept slowly through the woods. He completed another sweep of the purple treetops through his thermal vision goggles. *All clear for now.*

Due to a delay in departure, they had fast-roped down into the woods twenty minutes after Team One. From there, they had ventured silently into the unknown. The pump he'd felt from Commander Hodges's rah-rah speech was far from him now.

Maybe it's the baby, he thought. With a two-week-old daughter, Henry felt less like a lethal arm of the law and more like a father trying to stay alive.

Not one of the SWAT team members made it out of that house alive. The words haunted him. The images of his daughter taking her first steps without him, his wife watching her graduate from high school alone, played vividly in his mind's eye.

Stop it already. He'd almost said it aloud. Normally he could keep his head in the game, but tonight was different. And he could tell he wasn't the only one who felt it.

Keep it together.

The commander brought the team to a halt. He didn't have to point because every man had seen it.

Through his thermal goggles, Henry stared at a glowing orange orb on a purple tree trunk. There was another small heat signature on a tree across from it, and three more deeper into the woods.

Lifting his thermal goggles, Henry discovered that it was a severed head placed on a branch. The glowing scalp and scar running along the pale cheek confirmed that it was Commander Hodges. Illuminating the decapitation was the light peering down from the commander's helmet positioned in the branches above it.

"Tonight we are the predators." The words dripped

bitterly from Henry's lips.

Obscured by the remnants of a smoke grenade were four more illuminated heads placed in a similar manner.

What kind of animal does this?

Returning the goggles to his face, Henry followed the team farther into the mist as it swept between the purple trunks and branches.

And then they saw the lights. Scattered beyond the distant trees were beams of light glaring up from abandoned helmets and shields. Moving closer, the curling haze grew thinner to reveal numerous orange figures strewn amongst the lights.

Henry looked back to the lapping flames from the downed helicopter, and he knew their exact position. They were inside the gates of hell and were hunting the Devil himself.

A bellowing roar echoed through the woods. The orange figures around Henry shared a look, and every suspicion was confirmed.

They were all in way over their heads.

~~~

Scott peered through the branches in shock. The horrible roar seemed to have come from a tree not far from the one he was in.

Branches snapped and crackled. Then, as if blown by a mighty gust of wind, a wave of movement swept through the treetops and closed on the men below him.

CHAPTER 19

BAIT

A series of loud bark-like grunts startled Detective Pine awake to find a pair of black eyes inches from his face. "Whoa!" he yelped as the frightened squirrel with half of a tail leapt from his chest.

Flailing his arms, Scott tumbled from his perch and fell until his chest collided with a branch. Another merciless limb slammed into the back of his neck, sending him somersaulting forward through a myriad of smaller branches until . . . *wham!* Another thick branch caught his right shoulder. He tried to grab it, but everything was happening too fast.

Another sturdy branch caught the bend in his right leg, inverting him as he fell. Instinctively, Scott crossed his arms over his face to protect his head. Flurries of twigs pelted him to the sound of snapping branches.

Scott came to an abrupt but painless stop that turned him upright. For a moment, he hung, swaying in the air like a marionette. He raised his left hand to discover his coat tail had caught on the end of a broken branch.

Now what? he thought, noting there were no other branches within reach to grab and pull himself free.

The problem didn't persist. A loud tear of fabric, and he dropped again.

Looking down, a thick branch was rushing up to hit him until Scott landed on it with his feet and threw his arms around the tree trunk.

"Maybe we'll take the slow way down from here," he muttered.

A few minutes later, the detective dropped from the lowest branch and landed on the damp forest floor.

"Worst awakening I've had since my fraternity days," he said with a glance at his surroundings. The rising sun was peering through the mist that lingered between the trees. *About 6:30 am*, he guessed. A glance at his watch showed that he was dead-on.

Scott crept forward between the trees, plotting each step. Looking ahead, he saw the trail of smoke that reached down through the trees to the twinkling flames inside the helicopter. *If I can make it to the wreckage, they'll find me.*

If his swift but painful descent from the tree hadn't roused the beast, it was most likely not in the vicinity, he concluded. Still, Scott paused every few steps to have a listen.

Not a single bird call or a sound. It was as if the forest were completely void of life. *Except for the friggin squirrel*, he thought.

As the Florida sun crept higher and the haze began to thin, he could see them. One. And then two more, a cluster of four . . . bodies were strewn everywhere. Lying amongst the remains were numerous helmets and assault shields with their lights still glaring up through the haze.

This must be the first team.

Scott could only liken the scene to the infamous Omaha Beach on D-Day. He was making his way through a human slaughterhouse. The men were literally ripped open, their Kevlar body armor filleted as if it were tinfoil. In addition to exhibiting severe wounds, many of the bodies were decapitated. But unnervingly, their heads were nowhere to be found.

Even the surrounding trees seemed to bleed with their bark stained red from smoke grenades. Their towering trunks appeared to be polka-dotted where hundreds of rounds had riddled the bark.

At the base of one tree lay a man with bullet wounds in his throat and forehead. The trail of skinned bark above him and in the neighboring tree suggested he was a victim of friendly fire.

Scott stepped past two more SWAT team members lying beneath a blood-strewn tree trunk. One man had a deep laceration across his chest. The body beside him bore a similar wound from his shoulder to his throat. The way that the wounds seemed to cross from one body to the next suggested both men had been killed with the same strike.

Incredible.

But even stranger was the treatment of their weaponry. Every assault rifle or submachine gun was either bent like a boomerang or completely broken in half. *Maybe they were damaged in battle,* he thought. But not a single weapon that he passed was unscathed.

Continuing silently through the woods, the detective noted a curious illumination in the trees. Stepping around to the other side of an oak, his eyes met the lifeless gaze of a severed head perched on a branch. Light from a helmet positioned above it illuminated the decapitation and the swath of blood trailing down the bark below.

"This is insane," Scott whispered. "Animals don't do this."

He backed away from the tree, his mind struggling to comprehend the loss of life. He hoped he was standing at ground zero, where most of the victims were collected. But his gut suggested this was only a random sample of what a full exploration of the woods would divulge.

He again paused beside a tree to listen.

Still nothing.

Moving closer to the glittering fire from the wreckage,

the ominous feeling in his gut proved to be right. It was more of the same; remnants of another SWAT team were scattered across the landscape.

Walking through the carnage, he noticed the lights on some of the helmets and shields were on, while others were off. *They switched to standard lighting like the first team. But why?*

Scott carefully looked at every man with the hope that some might still be alive. But a mere glance at their wounds ruled out the possibility. What he'd seen in the homes paled to this nightmare. Like Team One, these men weren't merely killed; they'd been ripped to pieces. One team member was completely bisected at the waist. Another man's severed arm lay on a branch twenty feet from his body. Every face that was exposed was frozen in a state of horror as their unblinking eyes seemed to watch him from beneath the mist.

He paused beside a lifeless figure that broke his heart. It wasn't the severity of his wound that got to Scott, but rather its placement. Right beneath his helmet was a single gunshot wound to the temple while a pistol lay at his right hand. Rather than face the creature's wrath, the man had chosen to take himself out.

Beside him was another young man who looked as if he'd been doused with a bucket of blood. There was a deep laceration in his chest plate while crimson puddles had formed in the sand beneath his missing left arm and leg.

Scott's emotions shifted between rage and terror. It was all so horribly wrong. *What gives anyone . . . anything . . . the right to do this?*

There was a crackle in the brush behind him.

Scott's mind was at it again.

Another crackle, only closer.

That was not his imagination. He turned and looked through the dense woods.

The stirring grew closer, and his heart started racing.

It's following. It sees me. He stepped backward, but there was no place to hide. When Scott turned to run, he tripped and fell beside the bloody corpse.

The rustling grew closer, and Scott accepted the fact he was about to join the ranks of those around him.

What's the point of getting up?

The footsteps grew closer. Another crackle, and a deer poked its head out from behind a cluster of palmetto bushes.

Scott eased up onto one elbow with a sigh of relief. Pulling himself up from the ground, he studied the bloodied face of the young man not two feet from him.

What a shame. He was so young.

The man's eyes flew open with a grin. "Wow, that was a close one, huh?"

Scott reeled backward from the talking corpse and fell to the ground, thinking that he was hallucinating.

"Relax, bud. I'm okay." The bloodied young man then pulled his left arm and leg from beneath the sand to reveal that both appendages were fully intact.

He sat upright. Brushing the sand from his left arm, he said, "A trick I learned from a documentary on *Saving Private Ryan*. To make the soldiers lying on the beach appear as if their limbs were missing, they just buried them beneath the sand."

His bloody face looked up at Scott. The name is Henry Williams."

"But your chest plate," Scott blurted, "the huge slice through it, and the blood all over your face?"

Henry looked down to the deep slice in his body armor. "It's deep, but didn't go all the way through. But when that thing hit me, I flew into a tree trunk so hard that it knocked me unconscious. Don't know how long I was out. When I woke every man was down with that thing walking among them. If it suspected anyone of still being alive, it took off their head."

Listening to the woods for a moment, Henry continued. "While that thing's back was turned to me, I picked up a severed leg and drained the blood all over me and on the ground. Then I rooted my left arm and leg into the sand. Didn't so much as fart the entire night."

The detective glanced back in the direction from which he'd come."Any idea where that thing is now?"

"At the break of dawn, it crawled into the ravine that the bike is in. Haven't seen it since."

"Wow," Scott muttered, with a glance up toward the distant trees. "That's not far from the tree I was in. It's a miracle it didn't see me."

"Didn't see you." Henry snickered.

"What?"

"That thing was perched in a tree right beside you, watching you the entire night. My guess is it thought we were coming to rescue you, and it was using you for bait."

A chill crept up Scott's spine. "It knew I was there the entire time?"

"Oh yes." Henry nodded emphatically. "At one point, it climbed the tree you were in and studied you for several minutes, like it was checking to see if its bait was still alive."

Scott's skin grew cool, and it was all he could do to not throw up. Gathering himself for a moment, he looked at his surroundings. "We'd better get moving. Pardon the pun, but we're not out of the woods just yet."

Making their way through the war zone, the detective noticed the light glaring from an assault shield. "What made your team switch from thermal vision?"

"The heat signatures of each other showed clearly on our gear. We even spotted you in the tree. But when it came to the creature, nada. That's why the first team switched to standard light. We didn't realize it until that thing was on us."

Scott pointed at a bent submachine gun. "And all of the weapons . . . how did they get that way?"

"Strangest thing," Henry replied. "After the men were presumed dead, it searched out every weapon and disabled it. Hey, I've got a question for you. How did you get the motorcycle on this side of the river?"

"You wouldn't believe me if I . . ." Scott paused when he saw movement in the distance. Not far from the smoldering wreckage, figures started appearing in the mist, their flashlights glaring between the trees. As they drew nearer, they appeared to be a mixture of SWAT medics and police officers.

A final glance over their shoulders, and the pair headed cautiously yet swiftly toward the rescue workers. An officer shone a flashlight in their direction. "Someone's made it out," he chirped, waving to get the medics' attention.

Scott was as surprised as anyone. He'd doubted he would make it out of these woods alive.

As the medics and officers swarmed them, the detective glanced warily around the trees.

"Where are the rest of the team members?" a SWAT medic asked him.

Scott nodded at the bloodied man beside him. "He is the rest."

Three medics surrounded Henry and forced him down onto a stretcher. "Where are you bleeding from?" they demanded, searching his blood-soaked body armor. Henry swatted their hands away as they carted him off. "I can walk. I'm perfectly fine."

Looks like his disguise was a little too convincing, Scott thought. Someone handed the detective a bottled water, which he nearly drained in its entirety without taking a breath.

"Slowly, slowly," a female medic said, easing the bottle

away from him. Another medic snatched his left arm and pulled up his tattered sleeve to take his blood pressure.

Scott's vision faded into swirling dots for a moment, and then it returned. He hadn't realized how exhausted he was until this moment. The adrenaline had kept him going.

He pulled his arm back and raised a hand, waving. "No. Everyone." He tried to holler, but his voice was weak. "Officers, medics, you've got to get your people out of here now. This area isn't safe."

"But the chief said we were clear to enter at sunrise," one medic countered. "We've been waiting all night."

"And there could still be survivors. We can't just leave them," another said. The officers around him nodded their approval.

"It doesn't leave survivors," Scott said flatly.

"Well, what was that you walked out with?" asked a medic. "He looked plenty alive to me."

Scott just sighed.

"And how do you know?" asked another medic. "Did you check every pulse?"

"You can go in there and check their pulses if you like," Scott said. "But most of them don't have any heads." This drew a collective gasp from the group as they all just glared at him.

"Detective Pine, you're a sight for sore eyes." Scott recognized the jovial voice of Officer Jones. The large officer shoved his way through the crowd. "I swear you've got more lives than a clowder of cats."

He grinned wide and extended his phone. "Someone would like a word with you."

Scott raised the phone to his ear.

"Hello?" He recognized Wendy's sweet voice immediately. And it was as if all of the madness around him faded away.

"Wendy, it's me . . . Scott. I'm—"

An elated scream erupted from the phone so loudly that he had to pull it away from his ear. As he did, a series of barking grunts drew his attention upward. He looked to where a squirrel was barking on a branch above him. As it waved its nub of a tail in distress, he realized it was the same one that had awakened him.

Scott felt the hairs rise on the back of his neck. "Wendy, I'm good, but I'll have to call you later."

And it slowly dawned on him. Earlier, in the tree . . . it wasn't just being an obnoxious little rodent. The squirrel was trying to warn him.

Just like it was doing now.

A young officer emerged from the woods, wiping his mouth with his sleeve as if he had just thrown up. His face was pale. "The detective's right. It looks like D-Day in there."

Scott's eyes remained on the squirrel. The animal looked deep into the woods, rattled its tail, and barked at him again.

The detective didn't have to say a word. Officer Jones read his eyes.

"Listen up," Jones called out with authority. "Officers, SWAT medics, *everyone* get the hell out of here pronto!"

Apparently everyone had heard enough. He didn't have to repeat his request.

~ ~ ~

"Wake up, Sleeping Beauty. We're back at the castle."

Detective Pine awakened in the passenger's seat of Officer Jones's cruiser to find that they were pulling into the OPD parking lot.

"Right after you polished off those three chicken sandwiches, you went out like a light." He nodded toward the plastic bag in Scott's lap. "What else did you pick up in that 7-Eleven?"

Scott looked down at the sack in his lap. "A gift."

"A gift for who?"

Scott grinned. "You'll see."

The cruiser came to a stop, and Jones engaged the parking brake. "Looks like your fan club beat us here."

Popping the passenger's side door open, Scott noticed Wendy's red Jeep parked three spots down from them. The petite blonde burst from the vehicle, raced over to Scott, and threw her arms around him with a long, passionate kiss. When she finally drew her lips away from him, she maintained the firm embrace.

"Wooo-hooo," Officer Jones hollered with a hand clap. "That was nice."

Scott studied her hazel eyes and flushed cheeks. He had hoped to receive a warm reception, but he hadn't expected this. He planted another one on her, picked her little body up, and whirled her around. It was as if his worries melted away and she had swept him into another world.

A few seconds into the smooch, Jones cleared his throat. "I hate to break this up, but the detective is needed inside for a briefing."

Backing away from Scott, Wendy raised her fingers to her lips as if slightly embarrassed by her unbridled show of emotion.

But Scott's warm smile seemed to put her at ease. "I'll give you a call as soon as we finish up."

A wink back at him, and she scuttled off to her Jeep.

Jones pointed in her direction. "Now that's a good one. I advise you to hang onto her, Detective."

"What makes you so sure?" Scott said. "I only met her the other day."

"Trust me." The officer smirked. "I have infinite wisdom in these matters."

"Duly noted."

They started heading toward the precinct when Jones abruptly paused. "Hey, you forgot your gift." He reached into the cruiser and withdrew the plastic bag Scott had been carrying. Before handing it over, Jones peeked inside and laughed aloud. "Is this for who I think it's for?"

Grinning, Scott gave a nod.

Following the detective into the station, Officer Jones said, "You definitely got nerve. I'll give you that."

~ ~ ~

Thoroughly exhausted, Detective Pine entered the precinct with the sack tucked under one arm. At 8:45 a.m., the OPD was packed with officers slumped at their desks, awaiting the 9:00 briefing from the chief. Big Larry, Tiny, all the players were present, with the exception of Izzy, who was most likely retrieving her morning cup of Joe.

After what had transpired during the night, the atmosphere was somber. No smart comments, wise cracks, or even an unapproving look was cast Scott's way. Even Big Larry had nothing to say as the detective made his way through the rows of desks.

Big Larry's sulking was more likely due to a bruised ego rather than the fallen SWAT team members, Scott thought. When confronted by the beast, the big man had pissed himself like a four-year-old. And everyone knew it.

The group of officers watched eagerly through the corners of their eyes as Scott paused at the Big Larry's desk.

Larry looked up at the detective. "What?"

"I bought you something." Scott placed the plastic sack on Larry's desk. Squeaking chairs and whispers spread through the office as everyone strained to get a look. To the sound of crackling plastic, the huge man reached into the bag and withdrew a box of Pampers.

Scott grinned. "I got husky size, but I'm not sure if they'll fit."

The surrounding officers bit their lips and grunted, but no one dared to laugh.

Big Larry raised his six-six frame from behind the desk so swiftly his chair flew backward and bounced across the floor. Knuckles planted on his desk, he glared at Scott like a raging bull.

Officer Jones spoke up, raising his hands. "Easy, big boy. The detective . . . he's been through a lot. Don't do anything rash."

Big Larry then raised a beefy fist and held it out to Scott. The detective was taken aback. *This has to be a trick.* When Scott finally reached up with his fist and bumped knuckles, the big man's scowl turned into a grin.

Was it his imagination, or was there a hint of a tear in Larry's eye?

Stepping swiftly around the desk, the giant officer picked the detective up by the waist and stood him on the desk. "I give you the owner of the biggest set in the precinct," he bellowed. "The man who single handedly saved an entire community."

The surrounding officers stood and roared their approval. Shouts and whistles echoed through the office as Scott knelt down on the desk to fist-bump each man who came up to congratulate him.

Izzy walked in on the hoopla, cup of coffee in hand. "Where's Rod Sterling? Because someone has dropped me off in the Twilight Zone." She grinned, placed her fingers between her lips, and whistled with the others.

"Am I interrupting something?" Everyone turned to find Chief O'Hern standing inside the foyer. And like fleeing insects, each officer scurried back to their desk, with the exception of Scott, who still stood atop Big Larry's desk.

"So, Detective Pine, I take it you're the morning's

entertainment?" The Chief then shifted his glare to the rest of the group. "Nearly thirty SWAT team members were butchered last night, and you're throwing a party?"

Scott eased down from the desk as Officer Green spoke up. "Not a party, sir. The men were congratulating Detective Pine for successfully removing the transmitter from the community. After all, the detective was presumed dead, sir."

The chief approached the detective. "I suppose you did get an eyeful in those woods last night," he said. "I was just briefed by Henry Williams, the only surviving SWAT team member. He had one hell of a night himself. Do you have anything to add to his story?"

"He got a closer look than I did," Scott replied. "But I think the person we really need to speak with is now fully conscious at the hospital. After what I saw last night, he definitely hasn't told us everything."

"You read my mind," the chief muttered.

CHAPTER 20

BUILDING THE PERFECT BEAST

Detective Pine followed Chief O'Hern into room 407 to find Wendy at Jim Randle's bedside. Her eyes lit up at the sight of Scott, but he just gave her a discreet smile. He didn't want to tip off the chief that there was anything between them—at least not at the moment.

When Jim looked up, Scott noticed his eyes were much brighter than the last time he saw him. Scott gave him a forced, but respectful nod. However, after coming within inches of losing his life to the scientist's handiwork, Scott would have preferred to flat-out choke him.

As usual, O'Hern got right to the point. "What did you do to that thing's brain?" he growled at Jim. "Severing men's heads and placing them in trees like Halloween decorations . . . That thing does not think like an animal."

"Indeed it does not," the scientist replied. "It was trained to leave the remains in that manner . . . a calling card, if you will."

"But *why*?" Scott pressed.

"So terrorist leaders would think exactly what you thought—that only another human could leave a body that way. It was to disguise the fact that it was the work of an animal."

"Okay, but why would it bend the weapons?" Scott asked. "Every assault rifle or submachine gun was bent or broken in pieces."

"In many terrorist groups, men are more plentiful than firearms," Jim explained. "When one man is killed, his rifle is passed on. Destroy one weapon, and you're putting an end to numerous soldiers."

"Speaking of putting an end to numerous soldiers," the chief growled, "does it bother you in the slightest that your abomination butchered twenty-seven out of twenty-eight men who went into those woods last night?"

The scientist gawked at him. "You mean someone survived?"

"Yes, one SWAT team member."

"That doesn't sound right." Jim seemed perplexed. "I wonder how that happened?"

O'Hern glared at him, appalled. "Are you for real? You sound disappointed that someone lived."

"No, it's not that." Jim stroked his chin. "The animal is trained not to leave survivors . . . not a single eyewitness who could identify it."

"Oh, I'm so sorry your killing machine missed one," O'Hern mocked. "You're a real piece of work."

The scientist pointed at the chief. "No, I warned you. I told you not to send your men into those woods at night. But you didn't listen."

Wendy placed a hand on Jim's arm to ease him back to his pillow. "Come on, Jim. Take it easy. Remember your blood pressure." She then glared at the chief as if telling him to lighten up.

But this only seemed to fuel the fire. O'Hern stepped closer to the bedrail. "There has to be a special place in hell for someone who would create an animal like this for war. And I hope you find your way there soon."

Wendy's eyes narrowed as Scott led his boss away from the bed. "Come on, Chief. This isn't getting us anywhere," Scott said. "We're here for intel."

"How dare you look at me like that." Jim gripped the bedrail and pulled until he was in an upright position, his eyes enraged. "Do you think I'm the first to do this, to create an animal for war?"

Wendy again placed a hand on Jim's arm to ease him back down, but he pushed it away. "You have no idea." Jim's smoldering gaze remained on O'Hern. "In India, fourteenth century BC, iron spikes were affixed to elephant tusks to gore the enemy in battle. Later, the Romans would use these 'War Elephants' in their conquests in Spain and Gaul."

O'Hern started to interrupt, but the scientist would have his say. "In World War II, Project Orcon, short for "Organic Control," American behaviorist B.F. Skinner developed a pigeon-controlled guided bomb."

"Pigeon-controlled," Wendy repeated.

"Yes. Pigeons were placed in the guidance section in the nose cone on a missile. The animals were trained to identify a target which appeared on a screen in front of them. If the target moved to the corner of the screen, the pigeon would peck at the image until it moved back to the center, thus keeping the missile on course."

"Are you serious?" Scott said.

"Oh yes, but even more intriguing was the Bat Bomb."

O'Hern quirked a skeptical eyebrow. "Bat Bomb?"

"It was developed during World War I. The bomb was a large casing with over a thousand compartments, each of which housed a hibernating Mexican free-tailed bat. Attached to each bat was a small incendiary bomb. Dropped from a bomber at the crack of dawn, the casings would open in mid-flight and release the bats, which would then disperse and roost in the eaves and attics within a forty-mile radius. The incendiaries, which were set to timers, would then ignite and start fires in the largely wood and paper buildings in the Japanese cities."

"That's crazy," Wendy said.

"Perhaps," Jim said. "But the project was conceived just one month after the attack on Pearl Harbor, and President Roosevelt believed it held merit."

Scott and his boss glanced at each other, but Jim wasn't finished. "And you may have heard of our use of bottlenose dolphins?"

"You mean for locating underwater mines?" the chief guessed.

"I'm afraid that was only part of their education," Jim said. "Bottlenose dolphins equipped with gas needles on their heads were trained to ram divers. Once the animal butts you, the needle injects you with CO_2, creating an embolism. Within seconds, you're dead.

"Of course, the Navy denies this," Jim continued. "But a colleague of mine once swam with these same dolphins and described how they had an uncanny tendency to butt him in the chest cavity."

"How horrible," Wendy said, "to train animals to do such a thing."

"However, the Soviet trainers were more old-school. They simply affixed harpoons to the dolphins' backs." Jim smirked. "And I didn't even touch on the trained German shepherds that can take out a man's throat in a split second. Oh, I could go on about the military's use of animals in war." The geneticist raised his smoldering gaze. "So you see, *Chief*, I'm not the first to do this. I'm merely the first one to perfect it."

The words seemed to crawl right under O'Hern's skin. "First one, my—"

Scott blocked him from approaching the bed. "Enough. Everyone just lighten up. We all have the same objective here, which is to stop the killings."

O'Hern gave a reluctant nod, and Jim's demeanor

calmed as well.

Scott went on. "At the end of the day, this thing is still an animal. It's composed of primate DNA, so it's probably about as strong as a gorilla, right?"

"Do you have any idea how strong primates are?" Jim asked him. "A 155-pound chimpanzee can deadlift 800 pounds with one hand. An adult gorilla can press ten times its body weight, in excess of 4,000 pounds. In addition, I added a dose of Rhinoceros Beetle DNA to the mix, an insect that can lift 850 times its body weight."

"My word," Wendy whispered.

"But the primate DNA is only a small part of the equation," Jim said. "This creature not only possesses strength greater than a gorilla, but the speed of a cheetah, the reflexes of a cobra, and a host of other deadly characteristics from various species."

"But it's still an animal," O'Hern scoffed. "And every animal can be killed."

"It is created from animal DNA, but the end result was something more than an animal," Jim said. "A creature more resilient to man. Animals weren't created to overpower man's weaponry, but this creature was. Knives, swords, and small-caliber rounds will do little more than get its attention."

"I can attest to that," Scott muttered.

"Also, the creature has been somewhat fortified."

"Fortified, huh?" the chief said.

"Yes. For example, in addition to having the eyesight of a lion, which can already see six times better than a human at night, its eyes have received nanoparticle enhancements. This technique involves injecting the eyes with particles that act like tiny antennas that take infrared light. Wavelengths that are normally invisible then become visible, which allows the creature to see infrared light."

"That's why the SWAT team members were so easily

picked off in the woods last night," O'Hern surmised.

"Yes. It has night-vision capabilities combined with an armored back that blocks the animal's heat signature. With or without thermal vision gear, to go after the creature at night is suicide."

"That back blocks more than its heat signature," Scott said. "It's apparently very effective at stopping rounds."

"The gnarled ridges in its back were designed not only for camouflage, but to disperse rounds as they strike. Also, woven into the organic structure of its back are multiple layers of polymers. Hit it in the back with anything less than a rocket launcher, and you're just wasting rounds."

O'Hern crossed his arms, irritation showing clearly in his expression. "What other tricks does this beast of yours have up its sleeve?"

"Its eyes also have a nictitating membrane, a translucent third eyelid which serves a dual purpose," Jim said. "First, it blocks the red glow that the animal's eyes emit at night so it can more easily stalk its prey. Secondly, like in sharks, the membrane protects the retina during an attack. Also, it helps prevent the blood splatter from its victims from impairing its vision."

"How gruesomely convenient," Wendy muttered with an eye roll.

"Okay, other than its strength, speed, and superior vision, what about its offensive weaponry?" O'Hern asked.

Jim picked up a pitcher of water from a tray and refilled his cup. "Excuse me, but my throat is so dry, I'm not acclimated to speaking this much." Taking a long sip, he returned his attention to the chief. "So, where were we?"

"Offensive weaponry."

"Ah, yes. But where to begin?" Jim inhaled deeply, let the air out. "For starters, its fingers and toes have three-inch retractable claws, much like a big cat. Above the knuckles on each hand is a thick, clubbed knot, reinforced with iron. Combined with the beast's strength, its striking force is off the charts."

"No doubt," Scott said. "I saw the dents in the steel walls at your lab."

Jim nodded. "And those were made while it was partially sedated."

As every eye in the room widened, he carried on. "In each forearm is a retractable saber that protrudes from an orifice above each wrist. To deploy the weapons, the animal needs only to turn its wrists in a specific manner. Also, there's a V-shaped notch in the iron atop each fist, which sharpens the saber every time it retracts."

"My God," Scott said. "You've described three deadly weapons, and you haven't mentioned anything above its wrists yet."

"If you get past the arms, then you have to contend with the mouth." Jim smirked at the detective, and Scott bristled at the wickedness he sensed there. The scientist continued, "Its teeth are a cross between a lion and a croc with protruding eight-inch canines. The bite force is well over two tons."

"That's stronger than a Great White," Wendy said.

The scientist paused to reflect for a moment. "But I don't imagine its teeth being used in battle much, because very little would get past its arms."

How unnerving, Scott thought. *He describes the beast's weaponry with the demeanor of a proud father.* "What about the tentacle-like projections on its head? Do they have a specific function?"

"They were a happy accident, a result of using octopus DNA to assist in its camouflage," Jim replied. "They developed soon after its birth. Presuming they were dead tissue, I went to sever them but then realized the animal could control them. So I reinforced each strand with a titanium polymer. Now, the creature draws them in front of its face for protection."

"Happy accident," the chief whispered to Scott, his tone laced with disgust. "I'd like to take him up to the roof and show him a happy accident."

"I have a question." Wendy lifted a hand. "Judging from the animal's behavior, I *presume* it's male. But can it breed?"

"It is male, but sterile," Jim replied. "And its genitalia is retractable, much like a dolphin."

"You can file that under too much information," Wendy muttered.

"But at this moment, I would guess the creature is guarding the transmitter while its dopamine level replenishes," Jim said. "With its focus still on its mission, mating would be a low priority."

"Too fixated on what it's doing to be distracted by romance," Wendy said. "This thing you created is definitely male."

"Let's get back to its brain," O'Hern interjected. "I need to know how smart this thing is so we can decide our next course of action."

"I'm afraid that's no longer your decision," said a deep voice with a Texas drawl.

Every eye turned to a uniformed silhouette in the doorway.

In walked a tall, broad-shouldered man in his sixties. He sported an Air Force service dress uniform, complete with a flight cap and a chest full of medals. His tightly cropped white hair matched his moustache and eyebrows, which framed piercing gray eyes.

"I'm Colonel Garr with the United States Air Force. I'll be taking over from here. The SWAT team is out, and this is now a military operation."

He was a dead ringer for an older Sam Elliott, right down

to the Texas drawl. Scott noted two more uniformed men just outside the doorway.

O'Hern was clearly caught off guard. "But this is . . ."

Colonel Garr cut him off sharp. "From here on out, you will be involved in an advisory capacity only." His gray eyes turned to Scott. "Same for you, Detective Pine."

This is all we need, Scott thought.

Colonel Garr folded his hands in front of him and turned to Wendy. "And Wendy . . . you're looking well today."

She glanced at Scott as if to say, *How does he know me?*

Scott had no idea.

The colonel then stepped closer to Jim. He paused at the foot of the bed, looking down at the geneticist propped up by a pair of pillows. "And you, sir, Jim Randle, have been quite a busy man." He studied the equipment beside the bed. "Heart rate . . . blood pressure looks good for a man recovering from a intracranial hematoma." He narrowed his eyes at Jim. "How do you feel?"

The geneticist seemed to be thrown by the question. "Pretty, uh . . . pretty good."

Colonel Garr nodded curtly.

Either he hid it well, or the colonel didn't have the same animosity toward Jim as the chief did. *But how does he know all of this?* "Excuse me, Colonel," Scott said. "But may I ask who briefed you?"

"I had a long conversation with Henry Williams, your pal from the woods. But we've been abreast of the situation since the first attack at Hidden Lakes." Garr clasped his hands in front of him once again and glanced across every face in the room. "So, where were we before my intrusion? Ah yes, the brain. So tell us, Jim, just how intelligent is your creation?"

"That's a complex question."

Scott said, "Well, is it as smart as a . . ."

"A human," Jim said.

Scott pursed his lips and nodded.

Jim continued. "Let me start with what others have accomplished." He picked up a cup from a tray and took another swallow of water. "The brain is composed of *neurons*, the thinking cells, and the supporting *glial* cells, which relay the signals from the neurons.

"In 2014, a team of researchers injected mouse pups with human glial cells. Mind you, the mouse neurons, the thinking cells, were not altered. Within a year, the human cells had multiplied and replaced the mouse glial cells to the point where the mice's brains were considered to be half human. When tested, the memories of the humanized mice were four times greater than that of a common mouse."

Scott saw Wendy wince. He was doing the same, on the inside.

"How does this relate to your creature?" the colonel asked him.

"I will get to that in a moment." Jim said. "Furthermore, unlike in humans, the brain development in most animals ends at birth. It is our longer brain development that accounts for our higher level of intelligence. The human brain gene MCPH1 and a process called neural plasticity are largely responsible for this continued growth.

"In 2019, researchers in China successfully inserted the MCPH1 brain gene into rhesus monkeys. As a result, the modified monkeys achieved neural plasticity and continued human-like brain growth well after birth. When tested, their memories were far superior to the unaltered monkeys."

"How unnerving," Wendy blurted.

The detective extended a hand toward Jim. "And naturally, you . . ."

"Yes. I did insert the MCPH1 gene into the beast's brain, and it did achieve a state of neural plasticity."

"Did you replace any of its brain cells with human cells,

like with the mice?" Colonel Garr asked him.

"I did not change the neurons, the thinking cells, no" Jim said. "But all of the supporting glial cells *are* human."

"Opening doors, turning off lights. It certainly seems to think like a human," Scott said. "And the way it looked at Big Larry, pointed at him, and thumped its chest before trying to take him out . . . it was almost like smack talk."

The scientist glared at the detective in horror. He raised a hand to his bandaged forehead and stared blankly at the bedsheets. The heart monitor increased its pace.

Wendy stood and grabbed the bedrail. "Jim, what is it?"

Jim's gaze swept over the faces in front of him.

"What did you do?" O'Hern growled. "What is it you're not telling us?"

The geneticist rested his forehead in his hands. "To ensure the creature was trainable . . . I mean, without the intelligence to learn, it all would have been for nothing."

"*What did you do?*" O'Hern repeated with some serious steel behind it.

Colonel Garr eyed the chief until he backed off.

"I introduced some of my own stem cells into the embryo before it was implanted." Jim confessed. "When a stem cell divides, each new cell has the potential to become another type of cell, such as a muscle cell, a red blood cell . . . or a brain cell." He lifted his face from his hands. "That chest-thumping behavior you saw was my signature move during my college basketball days. My stem cells are being converted into human neurons that are multiplying in the creature's brain. I don't know if that could trigger that behavior, but there is no other explanation."

"Like in the mice," Colonel Garr said dryly. "Multiplying until their brains were half human."

"Or worse," Wendy added.

"Yes," the scientist said. "The human cells could continue

to multiply until all of the animal neurons are replaced . . . and its brain is completely human."

"Neural plasticity, human neurons multiplying in its brain . . ." Scott said. "That thing could probably score higher on the SAT than I did."

For the first time, Colonel Garr's face reflected panic. "An unstoppable killing machine that's growing smarter by the hour."

"Not unstoppable." Jim grabbed the bedrail and hoisted himself up from the pillows. "It's just that everyone has been facing the animal on its own terms. A residential home, a densely wooded forest at night. These are the creatures ideal combat environments. Remember, it was engineered for close quarters like tunnels and caves.

"Your only chance would be to draw it out into the open with nowhere to hide, no trees or buildings, and in the light of day. Then you can hit it with the bigger hardware from a distance."

"We can definitely fill that order," Colonel Garr said.

"But what would you hit it with?," Scott asked. "I watched the thing walk out of a helicopter engulfed in flames like nothing had happened."

"The animal's skin," Jim said, "has been fortified with a polymer containing very pure quartz sand. It is similar to the LI-900 silica tiles that protect the space shuttle during reentry."

"So, the thing is fireproof?" Colonel Garr said.

"Fire *resistant*," the weary geneticist corrected him. "It can sustain short intervals of fire, but it isn't fireproof."

"So it will burn," Scott said with a glimmer in his eye.

"If you can keep it in the flames, say with a flamethrower, yes . . . it will burn."

Scott rocked back on his heels. "Duly noted."

"But you can't go into the woods after it," Wendy blurted.

"You heard what he just said about it's ideal environment."

Scott nodded. "You're right. We have to lure it out."

"You can't go back in there on a motorbike." Wendy squeezed the bedrail. "It's a miracle you're still alive."

"Not a motorcycle, but a drone."

All ears seemed to perk up at that comment.

"I know exactly where the ball is," Scott said. "We retrieve it with a drone and transfer it to another location. Somewhere that's wide open, nowhere for the creature to hide, so we can hit it with flamethrowers, rocket launchers, whatever it takes." Then he leaned back against the wall and sighed. "But I have no idea where we find such a place."

Colonel Garr's white moustache spread wide with his grin. "I do. There's an abandoned airfield about eight miles south of Hidden Lakes. It was privately owned by an aviation club until it got busted for running coke during the '90s." He winked. "I don't care how smart your beast is . . . it won't survive the soiree I've got planned."

~~~

After everyone had filed out of room 407, Jim stared at the closed door for a long time. The steady chirp of the heart monitor had replaced the antagonistic voices that had previously filled his small environment.

Now that his mind was beginning to clear, the full weight of the situation seemed to press the breath from his lungs. The loss of life, the destruction of his lab, the summation of his life's work being hunted down like a rabid dog. *No. They just don't understand.*

Taking another sip of water, guilt again tried to seize him in its vise-like grip. And his mind shifted between guilt and blame.

It's not your fault, he told himself to keep the crushing guilt at bay. Jim likened his situation to the global pandemic that occurred at the close of 2019. *Who bore the greater sin?* he asked his conscience. *The scientist who engineered the virus in the lab, or the fool responsible for its release?*

The door cracked open, and a stream of light invaded his dim surroundings. It was Chief O'Hern. His condescending gaze seemed to hold an illumination of its own.

"How can you just sit so smug in that bed?" he growled. "Do you feel anything?"

He opened the door wider, but only his voice entered the room. "Think back to the day the twin towers fell and you lost your wife and son. Remember the unrelenting pain, the sense of loss . . . knowing that your life would never be the same.

O'Hern went on. "Yes, remember it well, Jim Randle. Because, thanks to your creation, tonight twenty-seven more men are never coming home again. Children are without fathers, wives without husbands, and every one of them is experiencing that same gut-wrenching feeling."

~~~

Detective Pine exited the restroom ahead of Colonel Garr to hear the commotion in the hallway. Between a pair of statuesque Air Force guards outside of Jim's room stood the chief with his hand holding the door open.

"And every one of them . . . their lives ripped to pieces because of you," he growled. "I thought you needed to hear that." With that final sentiment, O'Hern closed the door.

Scott moved quickly toward his boss, but Colonel Garr got to him first.

The colonel grabbed O'Hern by the shirt and shoved him back against a wall, tilting a hanging seascape painting. "If I ever catch you near his room again, I'll make you a resident of this place—*comprende?*" He then shoved the chief down the hallway, making him stumble and almost fall.

O'Hern just glared back at him in disbelief, then

proceeded down the hallway toward the elevators.

Colonel Garr straightened his cuffs and looked at Scott as if nothing had happened. "Ah, Detective, I have something for you." He produced a cell phone from a jacket pocket and handed it over. "I believe you can use one of these. It will take a good six hours to ready the airstrip for our guest of honor. In the meantime, I advise you get some shut-eye. I'll give you a ring when we're ready to retrieve the transmitter with the drone." The colonel started to step away, but caught himself. "Oh, if you need to reach me, I'm the first number on speed dial." A curt nod, and the man went into Jim's room and closed the door.

Unbelievable, Scott thought. *He even knew I'd lost my phone. That's some intel.*

Wendy appeared from behind the detective. "What was that all about?" she asked. "I only caught the tail end of it, but you should have seen the chief's face when he passed me."

"I don't know," Scott said. "But those two definitely don't play well together."

CHAPTER 21

DECOY

Adorned in an Air Force OCP (operational camouflage pattern uniform), Colonel Garr stepped inside a nondescript gray van. Closing the side door, he stared over the shoulder of a young soldier in his early twenties, to a console containing three monitors. The two outside screens were black, while the center monitor showed a drone's eye view of the night woods. Oak leaves and pine needles shuddered in the glaring night as the drone made a low pass through the treetops.

"Petty Officer Barnes, still quiet down there?" Garr asked.

"Yes sir," the young man in green-and-brown fatigues replied with one hand on the toggle control. "As quiet as a tomb, pardon the pun. But I haven't seen a single animal. The mike hasn't detected a bird call, the hoot of an owl, nothing. It's like the forest has been vacated."

Far beneath the maze of branches, they saw a cluster of lights glittering along the forest floor. Neither of them said a word, as they were fully aware that those were the helmets and shield lights from the fallen SWAT team members.

Look at all of them, Garr thought. *What a waste of resources.* He felt his anger swell inside. No, they weren't his men, but they were soldiers nonetheless.

Turning away from the monitor, he glanced through the back windows of the van, watching the arm of a crane swing over the abandoned airfield.

Barnes said, "Sir, what makes you so sure the creature didn't move on?"

The colonel looked back at the monitor—the illuminated branches and tree trunks moving slowly past. Before he could think of an answer, the image jolted, and the screen went black to the sound of crunching metal.

The colonel smirked. "Well, well . . ."

"Do you think that was the creature, sir?"

"If not, it was a pretty stiff gust of wind." Garr turned for the door. "Ready the backup drone . . . and next time, mind your altitude."

~~~

After indulging in another home-cooked meal consisting of fried chicken and french-fried potatoes, Scott reclined on the couch in Wendy's apartment.

"No, the Colonel didn't tell me the details of his trap, just that he would call me when they were ready to retrieve the ball," Scott replied to Wendy, who was milling about in the kitchen.

"But you don't have a phone," she hollered above the clacking plates.

"He gave me a phone that happened to be in his pocket," Scott said. "And no, I never told him that mine had been lost."

The clattering sound ceased, and Wendy appeared before him. "He already knew you'd lost your phone? That's more than a little creepy."

He shrugged. "That's US military intelligence." He gave Wendy the once-over as she stood before him in her bare feet, khaki shorts, white blouse, and her honey-blond hair pulled up in a bun.

"What are you looking at?" she said coyly.

"Just enjoying the view."

She looked at him through the corners of her eyes with a

grin as she padded back to the kitchen.

"Are you sure you can't use any help in there?" Scott asked her.

"No, you need your rest. After spending the night perched in a tree, I imagine the couch is quite comfy."

She is absolutely perfect, Scott thought, letting his sore body sink into the heavenly cushions.

He heard the refrigerator door close. "Now that it's evening, do you think the colonel will wait until morning to lure the creature into his booby trap?" Wendy asked from the kitchen.

"Probably," Scott replied. "If he follows Jim's advice."

A beat later, Wendy reappeared with her hair down and holding a pair of filled wineglasses. "In that case, I don't suppose these will do any harm."

Handing Scott a glass, she curled up on the couch beside him. "What do you say we talk about something other than multiplying neurons and jaws and claws?"

"Amen to that." He took a sip of his wine. "What's on your mind?"

"Let's hear more about you."

He winked. "I'm an open book, pick a chapter."

Wendy scooted her legs up beneath her. "Well, for starters, Officer Jones tells me you were a motocross champion."

Scott snickered. "I don't think champion is the right word. But I started riding at an early age. I was an exceptionally small child, used to get bullied horribly at school. When I discovered racing, it was like an escape. The motorcycle was a part of my life that I could control." He took another sip, this one a little larger. "At least that's what a child psychologist told my over-protective mother."

He paused for a moment, reminiscing. "But perched atop my Honda, I felt pretty tall, especially when I was dusting the rest of the pack. And then came the accolades, newspaper clippings, placing well in a nationally televised race. Most of the kids who used to bully me suddenly wanted to be my friends."

Wendy absentmindedly ran a finger around the rim of her wineglass. She bit her lip, and a subtle smirk came to her face. "So, has there ever been anyone special, say a certain trophy girl?"

"You mean have I been engaged or married?"

She took a quick sip of wine and nodded.

"Never married, but engaged twice."

"What happened?"

Scott released a slow breath. "I call it the twenty-minute wrinkle."

Wendy looked at him inquisitively. "Would you care to elaborate?"

"It's a term that I thought of while binging on Hallmark movies with an old girlfriend."

She perked up. "Oh, I love Hallmark movies."

"Of course you do," Scott said with a grin. "It's in your DNA." Another sip, and he placed his glass on the coffee table. "The twenty-minute wrinkle occurs twenty minutes before the end of the movie when something *always* happens. It's after the girl has left Mr. Wrong for Mr. Right, and everything is perfect. Then she happens to stop by unannounced, only to see Mr. Right receive a kiss from an old flame. It's perfectly innocent, but she doesn't know that, so the new romance is thrown into turmoil until the final moments of the movie. The misunderstanding is then resolved and sealed with a kiss for the perfect Hallmark ending."

Wendy snickered and thought for a moment. "Like when the American girl falls in love with a foreign prince. Then she sees him receive an unwanted kiss from a beautiful duchess that he was arranged to marry."

Scott eased an arm over the back of the couch so he could more comfortably face her. "Or when the movie star gets stuck in a small town and falls for the local girl. His manager then shows up and whisks him back to Hollywood. But in the end the star turns his back on the fame and returns to the small town in the name of love."

"I saw that one." Wendy giggled. "But it was with a famous country singer." She laughed aloud and snuggled up against him. "But that's why we love Hallmark movies so much. They portray relationships the way they're supposed to be." She cocked her head with a coy smile. "So, what was your twenty-minute wrinkle, or do I dare ask?"

"No, I don't mind." Scott retrieved his wineglass from the table and took the last swallow. "Well, there was a flight attendant I was engaged to after knowing her for a little over a year. Everything was great. Then one day a friend of mine showed me a picture from an adult website. 'Doesn't she resemble Pam?' he'd asked me.

"I laughed it off until I took a closer look, particularly at the birthmark on her left shoulder."

Wendy drew a hand to her mouth. "No."

"Oh yes. Beneath the fake lashes and long red hair, it was her." He chuckled. "I'd always wondered how she afforded a Mercedes SL on her salary. She claimed her dad helped her pay for it. More like her *web daddies*."

"Well, that's a twenty-minute wrinkle that I've not seen in any Hallmark movie," Wendy placed her glass on the table."Any other serious relationships, other than *Mistress Pam?*" she asked, unable to hide her amusement.

"You seem to be enjoying this a little too much. Yeah, there were a couple others, but none as dramatic. So you see, I always seemed to get the twenty-minute wrinkle, but never the Hallmark ending."

Wendy slipped both arms around his neck. "Well, here's

to Hallmark endings," she whispered and drew him forward until their lips met in a long, passionate kiss. His hands rose from her waist and explored the curve of her back, pulling her petite frame closer. Her blond hair brushed lightly across his neck as the warmth of her body pressed through his shirt and merged with his own.

Nothing had ever felt so right.

A minute or so into the smooch, Scott thought he'd heard something. Was it his imagination, or was music playing? If so, then how had she turned it on? All of her limbs were occupied.

Wendy pulled her face away from him. "Do you hear that? It sounds like music."

"Yeah, I hear it too."

Her arms still around his neck, she glanced around the room. "Where do you suppose it's coming from?"

"Ah. My butt," Scott replied. He reached to his back pocket and extracted the phone that the colonel had given him. The ring tone was "Ride of the Valkyries," the theme song from *Apocalypse Now*.

Answering it, he listened for a moment. "All right, Colonel, I can be there in fifteen minutes."

Rising from the couch, Scott returned the phone to his pocket. "It looks like we're on for tonight. Garr has a Hummer waiting for me at the station. I guess it's to transport me to the airstrip."

Wendy just stared up at him with her hair all tousled. "But it's getting dark. You heard what Jim said about engaging the creature at night. What was the word that he used . . .? *Suicide*."

"I know. But the Colonel insists that we lure it to the airstrip tonight. He has a special surprise that won't wait until morning."

"*Special surprise*," Wendy scoffed. "Well, who do you

suppose knows more about the creature, Jim or the colonel?"

Scott picked up his keys from the coffee table and headed for the door.

She does make a good point.

~~~

The suspension in the old Crown Vic squeaked in protest as Detective Pine followed an Air Force light tactical vehicle along a rough, wooded trail. Rather than being chauffeured by the soldier, Scott had opted to follow him to the airstrip. In light of the situation, the detective was leery of being out in the middle of nowhere without his own transportation.

Wham! His right front tire hit a gulley that nearly sent him into a tree. "If this was ever a road, it was a long time ago," he muttered, driving beneath the reaching branches. Every so often, the ride would smooth out as his tires discovered a stretch of asphalt—until it ended with a jolt, and he was back on the dirt.

The detective found his heart racing again. This time it wasn't out of fear, but rather anticipation. The next time he laid eyes on the beast, it would be from behind the front line of the military. *Yes, today was a new day.* The fact that night had fallen still troubled him, though. What was so important that the colonel couldn't wait until morning?

Rounding another corner, the branches overhead disappeared and the road emptied into a vast clearing. *Who would have guessed,* Scott thought, *all of this out in the middle of nowhere.* Parking behind a row of light tactical vehicles, Hummers and various transport vehicles, Scott emerged from the Crown Vic. His eardrums were greeted by the sound of heavy equipment.

Although most of the asphalt was overgrown, he could see the abandoned airfield was enormous; its far end seemed to merge with the night. The centerpiece to the mayhem was a large crane with its long arm reaching up into the pitch. A belch of black smoke rose from its diesel engine and dissipated into the darkness.

Beneath the arm of the crane, men were using jackhammers, shovels, and ditch digging equipment to create several large holes in the asphalt. Others were setting up large, portable lighting units around the area.

"Whatever your plan is, Colonel," Scott said to himself, "it certainly looks big."

"Hey, Pine, you're needed in here." A voice with a Texas drawl rose above the sound of the crane's engine. Turning toward the voice, Scott saw Colonel Garr perched outside the open door of a large gray van.

~~~

The detective stepped into the van, and Garr slid the side door closed, muting the ruckus from outside. Scott's eyes wandered to several monitors anchored in a console. The center and only active screen showed an aerial view of the dark woods.

"Detective, this is Petty Officer Barnes, our resident drone jockey." Garr indicated a young man perched in front of the center monitor. "What do you say we round up that ball of yours?"

Scott took the seat to the left of the petty officer, and the colonel sat to the young man's right. Scott studied the dark treetops on the screen. *Talk about finding a needle in a haystack*, he thought. He'd hoped they would wait until morning to start the search—at night was going to be difficult.

"I need a reference point," he said.

"I was going to suggest using the lights from the SWAT team members' helmets and shields." The colonel squinted at the screen. "But I no longer see them."

"They went out about an hour ago." Barnes adjusted the toggle control. "It was strange, the way they burned out in sequence. And in a matter of minutes."

"They didn't burn out," Scott said. "The creature saw the drone and destroyed them, would be my guess. It knew we could use them as a reference point."

"I would have said you're nuts," the Colonel muttered, "if I hadn't heard Jim's sermon on that thing's brain."

Scott stared at the screen for a long moment. "The only way I know to get to that ball is to follow my route. Can you pick up the bike trail?"

"I saw it earlier," Barnes replied. "It's southwest of the drone's present position." The young man squeezed a trigger on the control, and the dark treetops flashed by the screen. A few seconds later, he eased off of the throttle trigger, and the drone slowed over a dark void running between the trees. The small craft lowered altitude, and a dirt trail appeared on the screen.

"Good," Scott said. "You can still see my tire tracks."

The light beaming down from the drone followed the tracks through a series of serpentine turns. Reaching the next corner, the tire tracks disappeared.

"Wait, stop it there," Scott said. "This is where I left the trail. Ignore the corner and go straight through the woods."

The drone proceeded between the branches as tree trunks glowed briefly in the passing spotlight.

"How fast were you going through here?" Barnes asked.

"You don't want to know."

A few moments later, the trees disappeared, and the forest floor dropped from view. The light from the drone showed only the glimmer of water far below.

"You couldn't have come this way," the colonel insisted. "It's a river."

"Just keep going straight."

The drone crossed the wide body of water, and eventually, the sand bank appeared in its light.

Scott pointed at the screen. "Those are my tire tracks right there."

The two soldiers stared wide-eyed at the detective. "You jumped the river," the colonel said. "Who are you, Evel Knievel?"

The young drone jockey fist-bumped Scott with a grin.

"No. But that's who I felt like on the landing," Scott admitted. "Now keep going straight. The ravine should be close."

"And watch your altitude," Colonel Garr reminded Barnes. "This is our last drone."

The small craft rose through the branches until it was peering down onto the treetops. "Now use the zoom and give us a closer look," Garr ordered.

"We're getting close," Scott said as the tree trunks below began to take on a red hue. "That red coloring is from the smoke grenades."

On screen, the forest floor dropped away to reveal a deep clearing filled with red-tinted rocks and palmetto bushes.

"That's it," Scott said. "This is the ravine."

His heart thumped when the mangled Kawasaki appeared in the light, its lime-green paint hidden beneath the red tint that stained everything in the ravine.

"Okay," Scott said, "now zoom in on the area behind the bike." *Come on. Come on.* "You got it! Close in on that stump."

The drone operator complied, and there it was. Just beyond a cluster of red palmetto bushes,the transmitter ball lay at the base of a stump.

"Okay, lock it into a hover right there," Garr said.

"Now what?" Scott shot his eyes to the colonel. "If the drone goes anywhere near that ball, the creature will take it out."

"We're well aware of that." Garr's white moustache twisted with his smirk. "But no matter how smart that beast is, it can't be in two places at the same time. Relax, Detective. I've got another trick up my sleeve."

He nodded to the drone pilot. "Petty Officer Barnes, tell Falcon One that they're clear to deploy Sammy."

"Sammy," Scott said. "You can't put someone down into those woods."

The colonel winked. "Don't worry; he won't feel a thing."

~ ~ ~

Two hundred yards east of the ravine, an Air Force HH-60 Pave Hawk helicopter hovered over a small clearing. Forty feet below, scattered palmetto bushes and ferns danced in the glow of the spotlight. Inside the open cargo bay doorway, SSG Chuck Wells tore off a length of duct tape with his teeth. He fastened it around an assault rifle and the right hand of a mannequin decked out in full combat gear.

Wells flipped on the dummy's helmet light. "Okay, Sammy, it's all up to you now. Make us proud."

Confirming that Sammy was secured to the rope ladder, the soldier lowered the dummy down beneath the chopper until its boots just brushed the ground. He then lit a pack of firecrackers and tossed them through the doorway. Sparkles of fire cracked and popped all around the dummy as it swayed at the bottom of the ladder.

The sergeant called down from the doorway, "How's it looking down there, Sammy?"

The pilot's voice cracked in his earphones. "Will you stop talking to that thing? It's starting to creep me out."

"Ah, you're just jealous because you don't have any friends." Sergeant Wells eased back against the inside of the doorframe and placed a cigarette between his lips. "You know, this is a lot like shark fishing. Did I ever tell you about the time I hooked a nine-foot hammerhead off of St. Pete Pier?"

The sergeant withdrew his lighter and flicked it on.

Drawing the flame to the tip of the cigarette, he glanced down to find Sammy's lower half lying in the palmetto bushes while his torso spun at the end of the ladder.

The cigarette fell from his mouth. "Whooo, that was fast." Wells looked toward the cockpit. "It severed the dummy, and I didn't even see it."

The helicopter dipped. And when the sergeant looked down again, a large gray form was climbing swiftly up the ladder.

"Whoa, whoa, whoa!" he hollered into his headset. "It's on the ladder. Get outta here."

The pilot pulled up. The landing gear ripped through branches as he dragged the creature through the treetops in an attempt to shed it from the ladder.

Branches slammed against and splintered off of its gray hide, but the beast only drew closer.

The red eyes were just beneath the landing gear.

Closer.

At the last second, the sergeant unclipped the ladder from the doorframe. The creature, still clutching the swaying ladder, plummeted into the treetops and vanished into the darkness of the forest below.

~~~

Back in the Air Force van, Sergeant Wells's breathless voice blared over the radio on the console. "You're definitely clear on your end, sir." He gasped and took another breath.

"Falcon One, are you okay?" Colonel Garr said into a mike on the console.

"Yes, but it was a little too close for comfort, sir."

"Roger that. Over and out."

Too close for comfort, Scott thought. He could definitely relate to that.

The colonel gestured to the petty officer beside him. "

Barnes, let's get that drone in there, pick up our ball, and bring it home."

"Yes sir."

As the transmitter ball grew closer on the monitor, the colonel turned to Scott. "Come on, I'll give you a preview of the little soiree I've prepared."

~~~

Stepping outside the van, the detective could see that much had changed since his arrival. The sound of heavy machinery no longer filled the air. Gone were all of the jackhammers and ditch digging equipment. The workers previously collected on the runway were replaced by heavily armed soldiers. The only thing that remained in place was the crane, which was now draped with a camouflage net, its arm towering above the runway. Trailing down from the crane's arm were a series of cables that attached to what appeared to be a huge net stretched across the asphalt.

Scott studied the six lighting rigs that now formed a huge circle in front of the crane, with their lights pointing inward. Scattered randomly before the lights were small circular metal contraptions. In addition, all of the military transport vehicles alongside him were draped in camouflage nets.

Pretty convincing, Scott thought, noting how the immediate area of the runway was covered with sticks, logs, and leaves to make it appear as an open stretch of the woods.

"So," Scott said to the colonel, "what made you decide to lure the creature here tonight, instead of waiting until morning?"

"Its eyes," Garr replied. "Eyes that can see that well at night have to be highly sensitive." He pointed to the lighting rigs circled in front of the crane. "We're going to draw it into the center of that circle and hit the lights, blind it and disorient the animal for starters."

Not bad, Scott thought. "And what are all of those metal contraptions in front of the lights?"

"Bear traps. Each one is chained to a metal spike embedded deep beneath the asphalt."

"I thought you were going to use flamethrowers?" Scott said. "But the area is so open, I don't see where they could hide."

The colonel gave him a wink. "I can't tell you everything. It'll spoil the show."

The drone appeared above the western tree line. Accompanied by the buzzing sound of its four props, the small craft arced over the runway and placed the ball on a stump in the center of the circle of lights.

Garr glanced at his watch with a grin. "Right on time." He then called out, "All right, men, everyone take your positions."

CHAPTER 22

INFERNO

Emerging from the hospital elevator, Wendy approached room 407. There was little need to follow the room numbers; the pair of Air Force guards in camo uniforms flanking the doorway confirmed she had the right room.

She reached for the door handle, when a guard blocked her. "Sorry, ma'am."

"But I thought that I was approved to visit him. I'm a friend."

"You are approved, ma'am," the guard replied. "I'm afraid Mr. Randle isn't allowed to make or receive calls, so you will have to leave your phone outside."

Great, Wendy thought. If Scott called from the airfield, she would miss it. But she had little choice. "Can I just leave my purse with you?" she asked.

The guard nodded. "We'll have it waiting for you when you leave."

Handing over her purse, Wendy opened the door. Stepping inside, she found Jim's bed unoccupied.

Well, it's a good sign that he's getting up and about, she thought, presuming he was in the restroom. But curiously, the door to the restroom was cracked open, and the light inside was off. She turned toward the closed closet door and heard the muffled blip of a heart monitor. Something bumped the door from inside.

My goodness, she thought. *In his confusion, he's*

mistaken the closet for the restroom and can't get out.

Wendy grabbed the door handle. "Hold on, Jim, I believe you have the wrong . . ."

Swinging open the door, she caught her breath. Jim was hanging by his belt, which was affixed to the clothes rack. His neck was twisted hideously in the belt as his socked feet kicked in the open air. The portable heart monitor dangling from his neck beeped crazily.

His body turned beneath the belt, and his dim eyes locked on her.

Finally breaking her state of paralysis, Wendy lunged forward and thrust her arms around his thighs. She pushed upward with all of her strength to lessen the tension on his neck. She tried to scream but nothing came out. And then her voice erupted from the closet doorway. *"Help, someone . . . he-e-e-e-lp!"*

An instant later, the guards were at the closet. One of them shoved her aside and lifted Jim, while the other guard snapped the clothes rail and slid it from the belt. They carried Jim's limp body across the room and laid him out on the bed, the loose belt still dangling from his neck.

A nurse and an orderly came barreling into the room and stepped in front of the guards. After several deep breaths, Jim looked blankly at Wendy and croaked out, "I really stink at this."

~~~

Like guests in hiding at a surprise party, Detective Pine, Colonel Garr, and a host of heavily armed soldiers peered out from behind a row of Air Force vehicles, awaiting the guest of honor.

Forty yards in the distance, the dark runway was silent and void of life. For the moment, the circled lighting rigs remained dim with their towering frames barely discernible in the night sky. Like a sleeping giant, the crane too stood silently with its camo-netted arm ready to spring into action at the colonel's command.

Raising a pair of binoculars, Detective Pine took another look at the transmitter ball perched on a stump within the circle of lights. He then turned his gaze to the tree line along the west side of the runway where random lights shone from the woods. Adjusting the focus, the shoulder light on a mannequin donning full combat gear grew clearer.

Still intact, Scott thought, studying one of the eight dummies placed in the trees along each side of the runway. It was a clever tactic that the colonel had devised to make the area appear more like an enemy camp.

Lowering the binoculars, Scott peered across the open runway. He still couldn't completely get his head around the colonel's plan. Other than the crane and the circle of lighting rigs, there was nothing there.

"So," he said to Garr, "what happened to the flamethrowers?"

"Enough with the questions. You'll see soon enough."

Soon enough, the detective thought. They had been waiting in position for over two hours. He looked along the line of soldiers behind the vehicles, noting they seemed to be having doubts as well. No longer did they stand rigid with their heads on a swivel, searching the trees. Their postures were now more relaxed with some men squatting on their haunches and checking their phones.

Don't lose your edge just yet, Scott thought. Although it had been a while, he could feel it in his gut that the creature was coming.

He decided to have another look at the decoys. Through the binoculars, he spotted the shoulder light on the closest mannequin. *It's still there.* He lowered the binoculars. *Maybe the creature's too smart, and it smells a trap.*

"Wait a minute." Scott did a double take on the dummy. He quickly turned his binoculars to the next mannequin . . .

. . . and then the next one.

"Colonel," Scott said. "Did you notice the mannequins?"

"Yes." Garr was peering toward the runway. "They're still there."

"Uh, yeah . . . But all of their heads are missing."

Colonel Garr raised his binoculars and dropped them just as fast. He adjusted the mike on his headset. "All right, men, the guest of honor has arrived. But we don't have a visual."

Behind the vehicles, every soldier sprang to life.

Scott felt a twinge in his stomach that sent his heart drumming. He glanced at all of the soldiers around him, drawing reassurance from their large-caliber machine guns and rocket launchers. *This time will different*, he told himself repeatedly, willing himself to believe it.

Then about fifty yards in the distance, a pair of red eyes appeared. The burning orbs moved farther out from the trees, and the massive form appeared beneath them.

"We have a visual at ten o'clock," the colonel said into his headgear. "Thermal Units One, Two, and Three . . . await my signal."

The beast emerged from the thick and bounded toward the bait on all fours. Nearing ground zero, the creature slowed its pace and rose up onto its hind legs, its horrible head turning and listening in every direction.

Around Scott, the soldiers did not take a breath. Every finger rested on its trigger, awaiting the colonel's signal as the target moved within range.

Still on its hind legs, the monster moved onto the asphalt and stepped within the circle of lights. All the while, its clawed feet systematically avoided the bear traps.

"Lights!" the colonel roared.

Simultaneously, the six lighting units flared to life, bathing the airstrip in blinding light. The creature thrust its arms up in front of its eyes, turning every which way, but found the intense light coming from all directions.

The blinded beast stepped backward and *snap!* A bear trap latched on to its right ankle. The animal roared in rage, kicking its leg madly to loosen the trap from the chain.

"Light it up!" Garr ordered.

Around the trapped animal, three panels popped open in the asphalt. And like jack-in-the-boxes from hell, a trio of soldiers bearing fire suits and flamethrowers sprang up from their hiding spots. Flames leapt from their weapons, arcing over the asphalt, and merged onto the creature, engulfing it in a ball of fire.

A bellowing roar rose from the inferno as the beast rolled in the flames, struggling to free the trap from its ankle.

The blaze intensified, growing brighter.

Incredible, Scott thought. He had never seen the animal on the defensive.

Another roar, and the trap shot from the flames, soared through the air with the chain winding behind it, and crashed through the windshield of a Humvee three vehicles down from Scott.

"That creature does not leave the asphalt," the colonel shouted into his headgear.

The men bearing flamethrowers moved in on the animal as if trying to guide it in a specific direction. The beast dove down onto all fours, tucked itself into a ball, and rolled away from the flames.

The moment the creature rolled outside of the circle of lights, the colonel barked, "Now!"

A high-pitched whine of hydraulics, and the steel net thrust up around the animal as the crane reeled in the cables. The beast thrashed in the chain-link net, swaying twenty feet above the runway. The flamethrowers again closed in, their reaching flames joining on the net until it was engulfed in fire.

The Colonel them ordered his men to hit the gas.

The flamethrower units withdrew their blazing weapons. And a stream of smoke shot out from the crane until the net was enveloped in a gray haze. The cloud swelled and undulated until the net was barely discernible.

Four soldiers emerged from the back of the crane and turned two of the lighting units on the net, then raced back to their positions.

The billowing gray cloud glowed above the runway.

"What are you doing?" Scott asked.

"It's poison gas," Garr said.

The detective noted a soldier with a rocket launcher standing by.

"Poison gas?" Scott laughed. "You've got a perfect shot— use the rocket launchers to take it out."

"Not just yet." The colonel kept his eyes on the illuminated net.

But beneath the luminous cloud, the net continued to move.

"I don't think that will work," Scott said. "It's smart enough to hold its breath."

"We'll see," the colonel muttered.

It was at this point that Scott contemplated hopping in the old Ford and making tracks in the opposite direction. And then, through the haze, he saw the animal go down onto its knees and slump forward into the net.

No one said a word as the lifeless form swayed slowly above the pavement.

The gas cloud grew thicker until the creature was barely visible.

"Okay, kill the gas," Garr ordered. "But leave the net in position.

The smoke dissipated, and the limp figure grew clearer.

"Easy, Colonel," Scott said. "Haven't you heard of an animal playing poss—"

As if on cue, the beast sprang into an upright position and grabbed the net, shaking it violently. *I'd truly hoped that I would be wrong,* Scott thought as his instincts again told him to head for the old Crown Vic.

The colonel roared, "Thermal units, move in!"

The trio of flamethrowers again closed in on the net. The fire streaming from their weapons joined on the net and bathed the creature in flames. The beast roared horribly from within the inferno.

Thrusting its clawed fingers into the links of the net, the creature pressed outward. A rip of metal links, and the monster dropped down from the blaze, landing in the center of the three men, smoke billowing from its skin.

Simultaneously, the men terminated their flames as to not incinerate one another.

With a swipe of a clawed hand, a flamethrower operator hit the ground, causing his weapon to deploy and spew flames on the man across from him.

The man tried to scurry away from the flame, but the fuel canisters on his back erupted into a mushroom of fire. The percussion from the explosion toppled the lighting units, spilling their glaring beams across the asphalt and pointing in every direction.

Now it was official. The colonel's soiree had gone south.

Through the fire and smoke, Scott saw the monster latch on to a leg of the remaining flamethrower operator. Swirling him around for several rotations, the beast released him like an Olympic hammer thrower. The man sailed high through the air, his deployed weapon painting fiery circles through the night sky.

Oh crap. That's coming this way.

Scott hit the deck. And everyone else scrambled to take cover as the man crashed into the row of vehicles like a guided missile. Fire from the blaze detonated a Humvee, and a beat later the vehicle beside it erupted as well.

Coming to his feet, Scott turned to find Garr kneeling on the ground and holding his forehead.

"Colonel, are you okay?" Scott helped him up. But one look at his glassy eyes told Scott that he wasn't right. The colonel just turned away, as if trying to place himself, the burning runway, the flames racing over the camo netting covering the armored vehicles . . . Soldiers scrambled behind the vehicles, dragging their weapons and equipment clear of the flames.

Two men leapt into different vehicles in an attempt to back them out from beneath the burning net. One man successfully pulled a tactical vehicle from beneath the blaze. But the moment the second soldier opened the door to a Humvee, the vehicle erupted in flames.

And the beast was only getting started.

Silhouetted by the flames on the runway, the monster turned toward where everyone was gathered behind the vehicles. Taking a few steps closer, the animal paused beside one of the lighting units lying on the asphalt as its glaring beam pointed straight up into the night. Picking up the end of the light with one hand, the beast turned it in Scott's direction and shone it along the vehicles. Everyone ducked as the light passed over the vehicle in front of them.

"Who do you suppose knows more about the creature, Jim or the colonel?" Wendy's last words echoed in Scott's mind.

The creature tossed the lighting rig aside and stepped closer.

Around the detective, ammunition clips snapped into machine guns and safeties clicked to the off position as soldiers readied themselves for the impending confrontation.

No, Scott thought, *They have no idea of what's coming.*

He noted the open door of the van containing the drone equipment. Snatching the disoriented colonel by the arm, Scott shoved him through the doorway and slid the door closed behind him.

"Get down," Scott shouted at Petty Officer Barnes, and the young man did as told. Moving to the rear windows of the van, Scott and the colonel watched the creature draw nearer. From thirty yards away, they could still see the smoke rising from its charred hide. And there the beast stood waiting, or perhaps daring the soldiers to make the next move.

"I'm going to say that he's pissed," Scott muttered.

Colonel Garr rubbed his eyes and shook his head. He looked around the van as if gathering his wits. "How did I get in here?"

"Welcome back," Scott said with his eyes still on the beast.

Through the windows, they saw fifteen or so men with high-caliber weapons scurry around the burning vehicles and out onto the airstrip to engage the creature.

The detective could barely bring himself to watch. "Do you have the keys?"

"To what?" Garr asked.

"To this van."

"Why?"

"So we can leave," Scott replied simply.

"I can't leave," Garr blurted. "I have to be out there with my men."

"No, you . . ." Scott tried to grab him by the arm. But Garr yanked his sleeve away, slid the side door open, and vaulted from the van. Feeling no compulsion to follow him, Scott remained by the window.

Outside, the beast dropped down onto all fours and

charged the men.

The soldiers opened fire.

One man deployed a rocket launcher. But the charging animal ducked, causing the missile to skim the pavement behind it and detonate on the far side of the runway.

Three more cheetah-like strides, and the beast leapt up from the asphalt. In mid-air, the animal tucked its body into an armored ball and rolled through the soldiers like they were camo-colored bowling pins. The men were knocked every which way, fumbling their machine guns and rocket launchers.

The beast then rolled onto its hind legs and turned around to face the fallen soldiers as they scrambled to retrieve their weapons.

Knowing that the creature wouldn't leave one of them alive, the detective ran out of the van to get the colonel, despite his initial inclination not to. Scott found him frozen beside a transport vehicle, staring at the men collected on the runway.

"My God," Garr said. "I have to do something."

"There's nothing you can do, sir."

Smoke still rising from its back, the animal looked across the men, and the sabers slowly protruded from its wrists.

"Come on." Scott grabbed the colonel by the arm. "It won't stop with them. I have to get you out of here."

Then, just as it reeled back to strike the first man, the creature stopped. The animal shook its head as if disoriented. It took a dazed step backward, then turned abruptly to face the woods as if being summoned by an inaudible voice.

One of the soldiers still behind the vehicles ran up to the colonel, toting a rocket launcher. Hoisting the weapon onto his shoulder, he set his sights on the creature. "Colonel, I can take it out."

"Stand down," Garr grunted. "It's too close to the men . .

. the crane is also in your line of fire."

Perched on its hind legs, the creature remained perfectly still, gazing into the woods as if in a trance. The animal then stepped past the men as if they weren't there, dove down onto all fours and ran toward the forest.

The soldier followed the creature with the rocket launcher as it galloped across the runway. "Sir, I've got the shot. It's clear."

"Take the shot!" Scott hollered. "It's getting away."

But the colonel remained silent.

A beat later, the beast vanished into the forest, and the soldier lowered his weapon.

"What was that?" Scott was beside himself. "Why didn't you let him take the shot?"

Colonel Garr ignored the question, but had one of his own. "What the hell happened to that thing? It could have taken those men apart."

"I don't know. Maybe it stripped a gear or something. But I'm not complaining."

Thirty yards out on the runway, the men shared looks of bewilderment and slowly came to their feet. Clearly, every one of them was amazed to still be alive.

"But why didn't you let him take the shot?" Scott repeated the question.

Colonel Garr was fixated on the woods. "Don't worry. It'll be back. It didn't get what it came for."

The detective's gut suggested otherwise. "If it wanted the transmitter ball, it would have taken it."

"The way that it was sort of dizzy, off balance . . . maybe it sustained an injury," the colonel guessed. "Or its lungs could have been damaged by the flames. You saw how the animal was smoking."

Scott's gut wasn't buying those explanations. No. Something wasn't right about the creature's behavior. And there was only one man who could answer the question.

Turning his back on the burning runway, Scott stepped past a charred Humvee, and in spite of all of the millions of dollars' worth of military equipment destroyed, he found the old Crown Vic just as he'd left it.

~~~

A glance across the monitors beside Jim's bed confirmed that his vitals had stabilized. Wendy noticed his coloring had returned. The red stripe across his neck had faded, but the horrible image of him hanging from the belt refused to leave her mind. However, her prayers had been answered.

"You're one lucky guy." She reached between the bedrails and placed a hand on his arm. "What possessed you to do such a thing?"

His tired eyes turned to her. "Over the years, I've become highly skilled at quelling my guilt. In this instance, I likened the creature to a deadly virus. I may have created it in a lab, but the guilt lies with the one responsible for its release . . . or so I told myself."

"Then why did you?" Wendy asked softly.

"You see, anger is like acid. Unless it is handled properly, it destroys the container that it's in. If it eats at you long enough, you'll look in the mirror one day and find someone you don't know, don't like."

He stared absentmindedly at the door. "I once saw a documentary on Jeffrey Dahmer. As they were interviewing his mother, I recall thinking how horrible she must have felt for giving birth to such a monster." He shook his head with an unnerving smile. "But after birthing her offspring, she didn't genetically engineer it to kill. That wasn't on her."

He looked up at Wendy. "What Chief O'Hern had said was right. Now because of what I created in my anger, innocent people, even little children, will have to live with the same pain I've had to live with. For this, I can never forgive myself."

Wendy delicately moved her hand down from his arm and took his left hand. "No, Jim, there is some truth to what you said. I'm not condoning your creation, but you were not the one who let it loose. You had the animal contained and sedated, and they broke in and released it."

She looked him in the eye. "And as far as forgiveness, God will forgive you if you only ask him."

He shook his head. "Surely not for this, for all these lives lost?"

She nodded. "He will. And maybe then you can forgive yourself."

He looked at his wringing hands, doubtful.

Wendy asked, "When they took you down, you said, 'I really stink at this.' Were you implying that you've done this before?"

"Yes. If I had succeeded, none of this would have . . ." His voice trailed off.

She gave his hand a little squeeze. "Would you like to tell me about it?"

He took a deep breath, released it, and gave her a subtle nod. "I've never told anyone this." Jim paused again as if contemplating whether to continue. "Before the towers fell, my work was only secondary. I enjoyed what I was doing with the military, but my wife and son were everything. And then, in the blink of an eye, the towers fell, and my everything was no more."

He seemed to study the closed door of his room as the blip of the heart monitor filled the silence. "In September of 2001, we were living off base in Fairfax, Virginia. The night of the eleventh, I had drank everything in the house to dull the pain. It didn't work. So I stumbled out back in the pouring rain. It was a horrible storm with the worst lightning I'd ever seen. It was as if God was venting on what had happened that day.

"At the crest of a hill was a barb-wire fence, infamous for lightning strikes. I latched both hands on to that fence and shook it, screaming at the night sky. I pleaded for God to take me too. The ground shook as lightning struck all around me.

"I was draped over that fence for three hours. Nothing. In my rage, I finally roared at the storm, 'If you're not going to kill me, then give me revenge.' Before I could finish the word, lightning struck an oak tree right behind me. Split it in half right to the ground. Someone had answered within that strike. Whether the voice came from above or below, I do not know. But at that moment, I knew exactly what I had to do. It occurred to me that the DNA from the remains of hybrid infant held the key to creating the instrument for my revenge.

"And build it I did. The only time that the pain and anger relented was when I was working, moving forward with the project. Nothing else mattered. The years flew by like hours. I was so hellbent on perfecting my creation that I never stopped to ask myself one simple question."

"What question was that?" Wendy asked, her voice barely above a whisper.

"Even if I could create the perfect killing machine that would eradicate every evil person in the world, what gives me the right to use it?"

~~~

The encircled number 3 flashed on the console of the hospital elevator as Detective Pine and Chief O'Hern awaited the next floor. After meeting up with the chief at the OPD station, he had insisted on following Scott to the hospital.

"Colonel Garr is staying at the airfield. He insists that the creature will return for the transmitter," Scott said. "But I don't think so."

"What makes you so sure?"

"I don't know. There was just something really strange about the animal's behavior."

The elevator chimed, and the doors grumbled open. Stepping onto the fourth floor, the detective muttered, "What's the deal with not allowing Jim to take calls? In light of the situation, it's nuts that I have to drive over here to question him."

The chief shrugged. "That's the military."

The quickly headed toward the Jim's room, its door flanked by a pair of Air Force guards.

Scott pulled out his phone and checked it for missed calls. He had none. He once again dialed Wendy's number and put the phone to his ear. "And I can't believe Wendy's not answering her phone, not responding to my calls or texts. What's up with that?"

Catching sight of the two men, the guards broke off from their post and rapidly approached them.

Listening to his phone, Scott found that Wendy still wasn't picking up.

"Chief O'Hern, you're banned from this floor," one of them barked. "You'll have to return to the elevator at once."

"But this is preposterous," the chief spat. "You have no—"

"That wasn't a request." The guard grabbed him by the arm.

"Detective Pine, you're clear to proceed," the other guard said. As the pair of soldiers ushered the chief back to the elevator, Scott hollered to him, "I'll call you when I know something."

Lowering the ringing phone from his ear, Scott heard a ring chime coming from a purse outside of the doorway. It was Wendy's purse.

"What's going on here?" he asked.

Opening the door, Scott noticed there was more equipment around Jim's bed than before. *That doesn't look good.*

Wendy's eyes flared at the sight of Scott. She shot up from her chair, and her eyes gave him the once-over. Scott held his hands up. "See? Ten fingers and ten toes. I'm still in one piece." He nodded toward Jim. "Why all of the equipment? Did he have a relapse?"

"Self-imposed, I'm afraid," Wendy muttered softly and returned to her seat.

The detective looked at her curiously.

"It's a long story," Wendy added. "But he's fine now."

Scott could tell that he had missed something big. But she clearly didn't want to update him in front of Jim.

Jim craned his neck up from the bed. "So, what happened out there?"

Wendy gave Scott a wry half-grin. "I can tell by your eyes that thing isn't dead."

"Let's just say Colonel Garr's little soiree didn't go as planned."

Wendy didn't have to open her mouth. Her eyes shouted, *"I told you so,"* like a bullhorn.

Jim pulled himself into a seated position. "Where is it now?"

"That was what I was hoping you could tell me."

"Why?" Jim asked him. "What happened?"

"After evading the colonel's trap, the creature was poised to butcher a dozen soldiers, when it suddenly froze. It seemed disoriented. Then it fixated on the woods like my Labrador used to do when it spotted a squirrel. It completely ignored the men and ran off into the forest. It was like it lost interest in the transmitter ball."

"Ah." Jim nodded, and his eyes glowed with revelation. "I've seen it exhibit this behavior before."

"What does it mean?"

"It's mission was aborted, overridden with a new mission."

Scott was terrified to ask. "What kind of mission?"

"I have no idea. But I know how we can find out."

CHAPTER 23

THE ZOO

Smoke still lifting from its gnarled back, the creature paused for a breather in a sturdy oak tree. It was dehydrated. And after being entrapped in a living hell, the animal needed to bring its core temperature down.

The beast had no idea where it was, but knew only the direction that its sensory devices told it to go. And that signal was weakening.

With its dopamine reserve nearly depleted, the coordinates of the creature's new mission were growing dim. Like a junkie in need of a fix, the reward center in the animal's brain craved fuel. And this meant it needed to feed. Now every sense in its being craved protein—the vital substance rich in the amino acids tyrosine and phenylalanine, which were essential for the production of dopamine.

The creature cocked its head up. The tentacled mane fanned out beside its ears to enhance its hearing as it peered between the leaves. Somewhere in the distant night, it detected a mixture of sounds and scents like it had never known.

A faint roar drew its attention in particular.

The beast bounded through several trees in the direction of the sound and paused, its claws sunk deep in the bark of another oak. Between the leaves and branches, it saw only a gray wall.

Climbing a few branches higher, the top of the wall

dropped beneath the monster's view. Pressing down a branch with its right hand, the beast saw into the closed zoo. Beyond the wall lay a cornucopia of animal species. Its red eyes moved from one animal containment to the next, like one might browse the delectable items on a menu.

Lions, elephants, giraffes, zebras, and a primate reserve. So many choices. Its eyes locked on the tantalizing waters inside the crocodile containment.

The creature sprang to another tree that was closer to the fifteen-foot wall. Bounding from the trunk, the animal leapt over the wall and into the park. The beast rose onto its hind legs before a streetlight, and its gnarled shadow stretched across the cobblestone walkway.

Lions roared and circled in their containment. Elephants trumpeted. Hyenas yelped and howled. Squealing chimps and other primates leapt frantically from branches and bars, adding to the symphony of animal cries that echoed around the beast. It was as if every animal in the zoo was aware of the strange intruder and knew it did not belong.

The beast looked around at the squawking animals and unleashed a god-awful roar that echoed through the park, muting every sound. The animals simultaneously grew quiet as if obeying a command from a higher order.

~~~

Clark Reynolds, the night watchman at Orlando Zoo, looked up from his text while leaning back in a chair in his office. "What. The. Hell," he gasped, easing the chair back down onto all four legs. "Was that you, Goliath?" He stared beyond the Knicks game playing on the desk TV and through the front window.

Trading in his iPhone for a flashlight lying on his desk, he set off to investigate.

~~~

The creature leapt down from a tree inside the zebra containment and landed back on the main walkway. It stood upright with blood splattered across its chest and jaws. The beast didn't have particular hankering for zebra; it was simply the first habitat that had fallen within its view.

Dapples of blood trailing from its claws, the monster ventured farther along the dark walkway. The lantern eyes studied every containment that the creature passed as its nostrils inhaled an overwhelming mixture of scents and odors. Its auditory senses were on alert as well. But the wildlife park remained silent.

Stepping across a short wooden bridge, the animal looked down at a school of orange and white Koi fish, their rippling images just beneath the water's surface. To the right of the pond, frolicking pink forms grew still in the pitch as flamingos froze with their beaks pointing in the creature's direction.

Across the glittering body of water, an African elephant stopped cold with its trunk curled up at the night sky. The only part of the hulking animal that showed movement was its left eye, which followed the intruder.

It was as if time itself had stopped and the beast was wandering through a wax museum. Passing a streetlight, the creature paused beside a containment where a large Komodo dragon was sprawled across a log. Studying the nodules along the reptile's course back, the beast compared it to the pebbled skin on its left forearm, slowly turning it in the radiance of the streetlight.

The creature proceeded past an Indian rhino, a giraffe, a kangaroo, a bird sanctuary, and a pair of camels. With every window that it passed, the beast compared its reflection to the resident on the other side. There were similarities in some of them, but clearly none of the animals were its own kind.

But something in their eyes was different as well. They

all lacked the sense of self awareness and intelligence that the beast had seen in the eyes of humans . . . *and in itself.* The creature knew not what it was, but rather only what every cell in its body was engineered to do.

~ ~ ~

The pale beam from Clark's flashlight rippled across a tall wall composed of roughly hewn stones. Arced above the entry and flanked by a pair of torches, bold wooden letters read, "Primate World – Home of Goliath." The lapping torches and towering doorway suggested the entry was fashioned after the wall on King Kong's Skull Island. The drumbeat that normally pulsed through the exhibit was off, yet Clark could still hear it thumping in his mind.

Entering the dark exhibit, the night watchman noticed the howler monkeys frantically jumping and swinging around their habitat. But strangely not one of them made a sound. Sheba and Little Mickey, a pair of chimpanzees in the barred containment across from them, were quiet as well.

"And I've got my eye on you, Mickey." Clark pointed at the small primate renowned for hurling his dung at patrons' mouths with uncanny accuracy. A skill set that had kept him atop the zoo's complaint list for three years running.

But tonight even Little Mickey was quiet. *They're all quiet*, Clark thought. *Something's got them spooked.*

Raising his flashlight, Clark moved on to the next containment which housed the Orlando Zoo's star attraction. Above the vast laminated window, bamboo letters read "Goliath, the World's Largest Living Lowland Gorilla – 6'5" Tall, 525 Pounds."

He shone his flashlight into the habitat. Beyond a tractor tire, thick tree trunks and draping leaves and vines, he spotted a huge dark mass.

"That roar come out of you, big fella?" Clark said. But the

massive gorilla remained slumped in a corner beside its mate. "No, I didn't think so,"

He checked his watch and headed farther along the dim walkway. *Must have been one of the lions*, he thought, and set off for the African Safari Encounter.

Rolling his eyes, he muttered, "And I wanted to catch the rest of the Knicks game."

~~~

Its rear claws clicking lightly on the cobblestone, the creature stepped beneath the arched entryway of Primate World. The darkness gave way to a set of bars. Behind them, howler monkeys leaping frantically from branches froze and remained perfectly still when the creature glanced their way.

Creeping farther into the exhibit, the beast paused at the gorilla habitat. Beyond the glare of the laminated glass, the creature saw a large tractor tire dangling from a chain affixed to one of the many massive trees. Lifting a clawed finger, the monster lightly tapped the glass and listened as if to check its thickness.

There was movement in the shadows. A large form approached the glass, galloping on all fours. Glimpses of blue-black fur shone in the pale moonlight as the animal darted between the trees and leaves.

Drawing nearer, the female Lowland gorilla paused, and then cautiously approached the window. The beast had never seen an animal with a form so similar to its own. Its pulse quickened with anticipation. Had it found its own kind?

Reaching the glass, the gorilla stood on her hind legs and matched the creature's stance. She stared at the foreigner intently, peering into its red eyes.

The beast caught sight of its own reflection in the glass and reached up and felt its nose. It saw the clear resemblance between its flat snout and that of the gorilla's.

The female gently placed a hand against the glass. The creature reciprocated and held its hand up to hers. It studied how its four clawed digits extended beyond the primate's five fingers.

The monster's gaze returned to its reflection in the glass. It noted its interlocking long teeth and the snake-like mane wavering above its red eyes. Other than its snout, it bore little resemblance to the primate. Nevertheless, the female's gaze remained fixed on him. Was it attraction or sympathy in the brown eyes? The beast could not tell.

Suddenly, a huge black hand reached in front of the female's chest and hurled her backward in the containment, hitting the swing and rolling across the ground. The massive, 525-pound, male Lowland gorilla glared at the creature through the glass, then snarled. Looking into the brooding brown eyes, the beast saw something it had never seen before—the complete lack of fear.

The huge gorilla then shoved its broad face right up to the window, its flared nostrils leaving a mist from its breath.

Wham! The monster slammed its clubbed fist against the barrier, making the gorilla jerk its face back from the glass as a spider web of cracks swept out from the point of impact. The creature then thumped its chest and pointed at the huge gorilla.

Goliath snorted and snarled behind the splintered glass as the creature moved on.

Emerging from the darkness of Primate World, the beast came to a divide in the walkway. Countless animal scents beckoned from its left, but to the right was something more intriguing—the sound of human voices. The monster's thirst was unrelenting now, and it still needed to lower its core temperature. Nevertheless, it continued to seek out the curious sound.

Lowering down onto all fours, the creature crept toward

an illuminated window. The voices seemed to be coming from a glass door that was left partially open. But after rearing up onto its hind legs and peering inside, it saw the office was empty.

The basketball game playing on the desk TV caught the animal's attention. Its eyes fixated on the player at the free-throw line, the New York Knicks logo displayed on his uniform. For some reason, the creature couldn't look away.

The player took the shot. The creature watched the ball as it arced through the air, hit the rim, and bounced out of frame.

With a disgruntled growl, the beast shattered the window with the back of its fist and moved on.

~ ~ ~

Making his way through the African Safari Encounter, Carl flashed his light across several cheetahs and leopards lying still in their dark habitats. "Just a while ago, all hell was breaking loose, and now everyone's as quiet as a mouse. What's going on with this place?"

Reaching the lion containment, Clark shone his flashlight between the bars. Inside, the beam followed the 400-pound African lion as it paced anxiously with its tail sweeping. The animal looked into the light and gave a guttural growl that reverberated against Clark's sternum.

"Okay, it must have been you, Larry," the night watchman said. "But keep it down, I'm trying to watch the playoffs." He again glanced at his watch. "Probably over by now. Good thing I'm watching it on DVR."

~ ~ ~

Bubbles cleared before the creature's red eyes as it settled at the bottom of the crocodile containment. The cool water soothed its charred hide while it eased its head back against a rock. Flakes of soot from its burnt skin floated in the haze.

Most of the reptiles had left the water, but a few lingered and continued to slowly circle the strange intruder. Bubbles streamed from their swaying tails and rear feet as they drifted by.

A large male crocodile passed directly over the creature to have a closer look. On the next pass, the beast reached out with its left hand, grabbed the reptile by its closed jaws, and pulled it close enough to stare it in the eye. For a long moment, the beast studied the crocodile's craggy skin and jagged teeth. Close. But again no match.

After examining the smooth underbelly of the reptile, the monster shoved it away, releasing its jaws. A cloud of bubbles erupted from the convulsing tail as the startled crocodile darted toward the bank and scurried out of the water. The other pair of reptiles followed suit and brought up the rear.

The beast casually closed its eyes and went to sleep.

~~~

Heading back to his office, the night watchman paused curiously at the crocodile containment. Raising his flashlight, Clark looked beyond the bars and along the numerous gnarled backs crowded onto the banks. Their glowing red eyes outlined the water's edge.

Interesting. Looks like no one wants to go in the water tonight, he thought as he continued along the sidewalk.

~~~

A short time later when Clark neared his office, he noticed there was no glare coming from the window. A few steps closer revealed why. Jagged remnants of the window were still in the frame while the rest of it glittered along the desk and floor inside his office.

"What did I miss?" he muttered, and stared up and down

the walkway.

~~~

It was the middle of the night as Detective Pine paced Jim's hospital room. He turned to the scientist propped up in the bed. "So, run this by me again. How can the creature's mission change?"

"Based on what you've told me, it appears as if the creature's initial mission was overridden before it was completed."

"And how exactly can it do that?" Wendy asked from her chair. "I'm afraid I don't quite follow it either."

"Let me break it down a bit further," Jim said. "There are several types of missions or modes. In addition to Perimeter Mode, designed for terrorist camps and caves, there are more specific modes such as ID. In ID Mode, facial recognition is implemented to eliminate a target, such as a known terrorist leader. You simply upload an image and the coordinates of the targeted person, which is relayed to the creature through the satellite. Then the animal takes it from there. The data can be input via computer or a scanner."

"But with the lab equipment destroyed, how could it receive a new mission?" Wendy asked. "Who could have input the data?"

"That's a good question," the scientist replied. "Somehow a second mission must have been loaded before the equipment was destroyed."

"By who?" Scott said. "The fools who trashed the lab wouldn't have been capable."

Jim rubbed his forehead below the bandage. "The last thing I remember was standing in the bed of my truck in a field behind the lab. I was holding the control unit when I was struck by the bottle." He raised his gaze with a look of revelation. "When I dropped the control, it must have gotten jarred hard enough to switch it to another mode."

"Which mode?" Scott asked him.

"I don't know," Jim said with urgency. "You have to go back to the lab and locate the control unit. Then check any of the lab equipment that might still be functional."

"Wait." Scott was feeling overwhelmed. "How do I know what I'm looking for, and where?"

"Don't worry," Jim assured him. "I'll guide you. Once you get to the lab, just call me."

"How? They won't let you take or make any calls. And there's no time to call Colonel Garr and get him up to speed on all this."

Wendy crept to the door and cracked it open. Peering into the hallway, she whispered, "I think I have a solution." She slipped outside and returned with her phone in hand. "You can use this. One of the guards is gone, and the other one is enjoying a nap. They'll never know."

All of the science had Scott's head spinning. "But this still won't tell us where the creature is."

"It doesn't matter," Jim insisted. "As soon as you get to the lab and check the equipment, we'll know where it's going."

A wink to Wendy, and Scott was out the door.

~ ~ ~

In the wee hours of the morning, the creature awakened beneath the cool water. Its crimson gaze drifted around its tranquil marine environment, along where the waterline met the rocky bank. There was not a crocodile in sight.

Already the animal's senses were firing and tingling. With its dopamine reserve nearly replenished, the desire to proceed northeast was now unrelenting.

Lifting its eyes and snout above the water, the beast inhaled the night air. With every deep breath, it could feel its metabolism restarting as its senses grew more alert. The enticing aroma of the various animal species was stronger, but to be ignored.

It was time to move out and eliminate the new target.

Beyond the waterline, the creature saw scattered pairs of red eyes collected around the perimeter of the containment. As the beast emerged from the man-made pond, the surrounding reptiles shifted and jolted to alertness. Tooth-filled jaws yawned open. Angry grunts and deep warning growls reverberated through the habitat as every reptile turned in the stranger's direction. But not one of them drew nearer.

The beast leapt onto a tree and climbed upward until it was above the stone wall of the containment. The animal peered northeast, beyond the treetops and toward the city lights that marked its new target.

Before heading out, there was just one stop it needed to make first.

~~~

Later, in the primate containment, Goliath awakened to find the female's arm draped across his mighty chest. An angry grunt, and he swatted the arm away, awakening her. For a long, brooding moment, he lay staring at the window as the spider web of cracks glittered in the moonlight. The fragmented glass now taunted him. The thought of the red glowing eyes made the huge gorilla's blood boil. Nothing had dared to threaten his reign before.

His attention was suddenly diverted from the window when a stream of water splattered against his face. More of the warm liquid splashed across his chest and onto his protruding abdomen.

Spitting out the foul liquid, the huge gorilla leapt onto all fours and looked up into the downpour. High up in a tree in the containment were a pair of red eyes glaring down at him from the night. The monster jumped from the branch, landed on top of the wall, and leapt from the gorilla's view.

The pissed-on primate roared and spun around his environment, snorting and spitting with fury. The other gorillas sprang awake and backed swiftly away from the raging giant.

Goliath galloped to the far side of the habitat and glared at the marred glass. A thump of his chest, and the huge primate lowered his head and thundered across the containment toward the window. Leaping up from the ground, the 525-pound gorilla slammed into the window feet-first, breaking it in a shower of glass.

Tumbling into an upright position amidst the shattered glass, Goliath looked up and down the walkway, not in search of an escape route, but rather to locate its adversary.

The creature was gone.

The gorilla trotted along the dim walkway on all fours, snorting and searching for a way out. It came to a massive oak near the entry with branches that reached well above the fifteen-foot perimeter wall. Wasting no time, Goliath scaled the tree, branches cracking under his tremendous weight. With its view now above the wall, the giant gazed in every direction.

And then the gorilla saw movement in the distant trees. But the tree that Goliath was perched in was about fifteen feet from the wall, and the branches that reached over the tall barrier were much too small to support his weight.

Goliath roared and shook with rage at his plight.

There was a loud snap. The tree cracked under the animal's weight, and then the thick trunk broke and leaned over onto the top of the wall. Goliath hung onto the trunk where it extended over the wall for a moment and then lost his grip. Free-falling nearly ten feet, the giant crashed down onto a parked SUV to the sound of crunching metal.

~~~

The beam of Clark's flashlight revealed the broken trunk of the mighty oak tree near the park's entryway. "That couldn't have been lightning," he surmised. "It was loud enough, but didn't sound like a lightning strike."

After racing out of his office in search of the horrific crash he'd heard only moments ago, he'd discovered the broken oak tree, only to hear a second crash outside the perimeter wall.

He ran his light along the top section of the tree that was now hanging over the perimeter wall. Clark started to piece it all together. *A loud crash from one of the containments . . . and then a second crash outside the wall.* "This is not good."

Clark started jogging back toward the entrance to the zoo. Reaching the front gate, he pressed his face between the bars. At the limits of his peripheral vision, he saw Goliath roll out of a collapsed SUV, cross the street, and gallop toward the woods on all fours.

"I wonder if there are any security positions available at Walmart," Clark muttered.

CHAPTER 24

SCANNED INPUT

The early sun lifted higher behind the trees as Detective Pine piloted the old Ford swiftly along the meandering Mill Creek Road, the tires squealing at every turn. Rounding the next corner, he saw the unassuming brick structure that was the lab. A tan Air Force light utility vehicle sat boldly in the driveway.

The second that Scott slowed down, an armed guard in a camouflage Air Force uniform vaulted from the vehicle and met him at the edge of the driveway.

Scott rolled down the electric side window, amazed that it worked.

"Sir, this is a restricted area. You'll have to turn around," barked the soldier holding an M4 assault rifle across his chest.

The detective flashed his badge. "I'm Detective Pine. I should have clearance here."

The young soldier glanced at the badge. "Yes, Detective, you may proceed." He gave a curt nod and stepped back from the vehicle.

Heading down the driveway and alongside the sprawling building, Scott recalled Jim's orders. *In the field behind my lab you'll see my truck. The control unit should be somewhere in the vicinity.*

Beyond a chain-link fence, the detective spotted a truck parked in the field, just like Jim had described. Scott parked by the fence and emerged from his vehicle. With a loud squeak of rusty springs, the door to the Crown Vic closed behind him.

Slipping through the gate, he passed an empty kennel and trotted toward the blue F-150. Approaching the open tailgate, he pondered how the area had already been searched, first by the OPD and then by the Air Force. *If the control unit was still here, it'll be a miracle,* he thought. *And if not, then what?*

A thorough search of the truck's bed divulged nothing. A quick walk around the vehicle revealed little more than scattered glass on the right side of the truck's bed.

Planting his hands in the grass, the detective lowered down onto his chest and looked underneath the vehicle. "Just as I suspected," he muttered, "someone's already picked it up." If it had been someone from OPD, he would have heard about.

And then, behind the right front tire, he spotted something black, about the size of a cell phone. Coming to his feet, Scott studied the curious device. Having no idea what he was supposed to do with it, he quickly pulled out his phone and dialed Wendy's number.

Jim answered. "Did you find it?"

"Yes. Now tell me what to do next."

"There are three modes at the top," Jim explained. "Perimeter, on the left, and two more to the right. Which one has a green light beneath it?"

"The one that says ID," Scott replied.

There was a long pause.

"Jim, are you still there?"

When Jim spoke again, there was a renewed sense of urgency in his voice. "Go inside the lab. You have to check the equipment. And pray the scanner is destroyed."

~~~

Jogging down the linoleum hallway, the detective entered the second door on the left, as Jim had coached him over the phone. Once inside, Scott looked across a tangle of overturned tables, smashed lab equipment, and broken glass.

"I'm inside. Okay, what am I looking for?" Scott said, the phone still at his ear. "And be specific. This place looks a lot different than the last time you saw it."

"Off to your right, there's a small work station," Jim said. "You'll see a computer desk with several hard drives, a pair of monitors, and a scanner."

Scott reached what appeared to be the area. Nothing remained on the computer desk with the exception of a toppled monitor.

"Okay, I think I've found the station." Scott looked around the clutter. "It's next to some stacks of magazines and newspapers, right?"

"Yes, that's it. I use the newspapers to line the cages." Jim's voice blared in his ear. "Now look for anything that looks like a scanner."

That looks like a hard drive, Scott thought, and he picked his way through the scattered equipment. "What's the big deal about the scanner?"

"That's the only way that data could have inadvertently been input, without being keyed in or downloaded."

"Okay," Scott muttered. Nothing looked like a scanner anywhere near the desk. He then turned over a piece of equipment that was lying face down on a stack of newspapers. He saw the scanner's clear glass face with the open door dangling beside it.

"Okay, I've got it," Scott said. "It was lying upside down. That's why I couldn't tell what it was."

"Is it still plugged in?" Jim demanded.

"Yes."

"Is the power light on?"

Sitting the device on the desk, Scott saw a green light on the front panel. "Looks like it's still on."

"Now listen carefully." Jim ordered. "You said that the scanner was lying face down?"

"Yes."

"What was lying beneath the glass face of the scanner?" Jim asked him.

The detective looked at the newspapers strewn beside the desk. He studied the various articles on the covers. "Hard to say," Scott said. "I wasn't paying attention to that when I picked it up."

"That's okay," Jim said. "Just look at the monitor on the desk. Is it still on?"

Scott sat the monitor upright and straightened the keyboard in front of it. He then retrieved the wireless mouse that was lying on the floor. When the mouse made contact with the desk, the screen came to life. It was filled with evenly spaced folders.

"Okay, it's up and running," Scott said.

"Look at the folders and find the one that says Scanned Input."

"Got it."

"Open the folder and see if there are any new input files."

Scott's heart thumped. "There's a file from two days ago."

"Click on it," Jim said, his tone growing wary.

Scott did as told, and it was as if the image that appeared drained the blood from his face. He looked on the floor, and on the front page of the *Orlando Sentinel*, he saw the same face that was on the screen. The familiar face of Ronald Sullivan, the vice president of the United States. Beneath the photo, the caption read, *Speaking this Friday at 10: a.m. at the Atrium in the Emperor Hotel.*

Scott raised the phone to his ear. "Tell me this doesn't

mean what I think it means."

"What is it?" Jim demanded. "What is on the screen?"

"A picture of the vice president of the United States. An article is promoting his rally today at the Emperor Hotel. The time and physical address . . . it's all there."

"When the scanner toppled over, it input the newspaper cover and relayed it to the creature," Jim said blankly. "The VP has been targeted for termination, and the beast knows when and where to find him. Yes, that's why its old mission was suddenly aborted. It was time to get in place to strike its new target." Jim paused and then blurted, "You've got to get the VP out of the hotel before he speaks!"

"Not to mention everyone else." Scott looked at his watch. "Nine thirty-five." He gasped, looking around the toppled equipment. A panic attack was well on its way. "But we don't even have a way to stop the thing."

The phone was silent for a long moment, and Jim's voice returned. "There may be a way."

Scott slammed the phone to his ear. "Jim, if you're holding out on me, you'd better spill it now."

"There is an area on its abdomen where I recently performed surgery. The protective polymer has not completely healed over the area yet, creating a weak spot, if you will." Jim said. "When the creature stands fully upright, hit it in the lower left side of its abdomen with something of a high caliber, more than a machine gun or assault rifle. You can wound it that way."

"But you're talking about high-grade military hardware," Scott said. "Where am I supposed to find such a weapon?"

"I keep a little insurance policy in my main lab."

"Insurance policy," Scott said into the phone.

"Just follow my instructions. First, go to the steel cylindrical room with the Jacuzzi-like tub that the creature was in."

Exiting the lab, the detective jogged along the hallway, past windows displaying broken and empty cages. He involuntarily slowed his pace when he came to a doorway on the right where the door was hanging from one hinge. It was the room where he had his anaconda wrestling match.

So many warm memories in this place, he thought, easing past the door.

Trotting down the hallway, the steel room was easy to find. Not just because of the metallic shimmer on the door, but rather the dark stain in front of it. The puddle of blood had been removed along with the teen's corpse, but it had left a large patch of the tan linoleum flooring a deep shade of brown.

With the lock previously sawed off, the thick steel door easily opened. Stepping inside the circular steel room, Scott was met by the myriad of deep dents and claw marks in the metal, unnerving reminders of the creature's limitless strength and brutality.

A lot has transpired since the first time I stepped in here.

"Scott!" Jim's voice roared in the detective's phone, snatching his attention from the walls. "Detective, what's taking you so long? You should have located the room by now."

"I did." Scott refocused. "Now what am I looking for?"

"My main lab," Jim replied.

Scott again looked beyond the huge Jacuzzi-like tub, the scattered equipment, and along the circular steel walls. "There's no lab in here."

"Just follow my instructions, and there will be," Jim said impatiently. "On the console beside the door, press 325#7.3." That's actually the animal's weight and height, if you must know."

"That's a delightful fun fact," Scott muttered. The

detective followed the instructions, and a seam appeared in the metal wall. A door then cracked open with a hiss.

Stepping inside, Scott faced a staggering amount of lab equipment. Among the beakers and microscopes were cylindrical aquariums streaming with bubbles that housed infant creatures of various sizes and shapes.

One wall was filled with monitors displaying numerous readouts and vitals such as heart rates and oxygen counts. Along another wall were metal filing cabinets with notebooks stacked high on top of them.

"Looks like we missed a room," the detective said into the phone. "We wondered where all of your notes were."

"Yes," Jim said. "Welcome to the heart of the operation."

Scott looked along the series of containers that held creatures in various stages of development. Tiny hearts pumped blood through semi-translucent bodies of grotesque proportions. Each one was more unsettling than the next.

One infant had a primate head that emerged from the shell of an armadillo. Bubbles swirled around the clawed hands and feet protruding from sides of the shell. Another creature, a bit further along in development, possessed a horned reptilian head and a pair of massive bat-like wings that curled around the circular aquarium.

Scott paused at an aquarium that he found even more disturbing. It held what appeared to be a human infant hand with elongated primate fingers. The sticker on the glass read, "1922."

"The container with the hand in it. Is that the . . ."

"Yes," Jim said. "It is from the remains of the infant hybrid that the military confiscated from the Primate Research Center in Orange Park Florida in 1922. But . . . tick tock! This isn't a sightseeing tour."

"Yeah, yeah," Scott said. "The insurance policy. So what am I looking for?"

"Open the only closet in the room, and you can't miss it."

The detective clicked open the door, and the incoming light revealed a large rectangular case. He dragged the case from the closet and lifted it on top of a desk. Flipping open the latches, Scott opened the case to find a high caliber rifle with a grenade launcher affixed to its barrel.

"That's quite the insurance policy you've got here, Jim."

"An M4 Carbine assault rifle. Equipped with a M203, single shot, under-barrel grenade launcher to be exact," the scientist replied. "Get it in the abdomen with one of the grenades, and it will do more than get its attention."

~~~

Thirty-seven-year-old Secret Service Agent Derik Brown closed the door to the penthouse suite of the Emperor Hotel. He turned to Vice President Ronald Sullivan, who was adjusting his tie in front of a full length mirror. "I can never get these things to look as good as my wife does," the VP muttered. With his silver hair parted on one side, the distinguished seventy-two-year-old was often told he resembled an older Dick Van Dyke.

Two other agents in gray suits standing beside a window took notice when Agent Brown approached the vice president. "Sir, there has been a breach," the agent stated. "Early this morning, one of the windows on the ground floor was shattered. One of the security guards said he heard the glass break, but didn't see anyone."

"Paid agitators. Will they ever stop?" Vice President Sullivan said with a shake of his head, then picked up his jacket.

~~~

Opening its red eyes beneath the cool water, the creature saw silhouetted palm fronds wavering above the surface. Koi drifted overhead as the beast reclined at the bottom of the enormous fountain that nearly filled the ground floor of the vast atrium.

The monster lifted its eyes and jagged jaws above the water line, its gruesome mug concealed by the palm fronds that draped over the north end of the fountain.

Between the fronds, the beast caught glimpses of the eight floors of open corridors that passed each room and overlooked the massive body of water below. Before the creature was a crude tower of limestone rock that reached up from the fountain for seven stories. At its top, geysers of water shot out from the stone, creating a cascading waterfall that flowed down the other side.

The beast's skin tingled from the vibration of the four massive pumps that forced hundreds of gallons of water up through the limestone. But other sensory devices in the animal were firing as well, as it craved the next release of dopamine. The just reward for eradicating its next target.

A deep breath of the conditioned air, and the beast dropped back beneath the water to wait just a little longer.

~ ~ ~

Pedal pressed to the floorboard, Detective Pine drove like a madman with the case containing the M4 Carbine assault rifle bouncing in the back seat. His cell phone was pressed to his ear. "That's right, Colonel, the creature is either headed for the Emperor Hotel or it's already there. Its new mission is to take out the VP when he speaks this morning."

"I know that critter is smart," Garr's Texas drawl echoed through the phone. "But you're telling me that it doesn't agree with Vice President Sullivan's policies?" He chuckled. "Let me guess, the beast wants stricter gun laws."

"This is no joke," Scott said. "I don't have time to explain, but you need to get your men to the Emperor Hotel."

"I hear ya," he finally said. "I'll deploy another team from MacDill."

"There's no time for that. Relocate the teams that you already have at the airstrip."

"I don't know if we should leave the transmitter ball unattended," Colonel Garr said. "What if you're wrong, Detective, and the creature comes back here?"

Scott pulled his phone away from his ear and glared at it. He had no time for this. He put the phone back to his ear and said, "If Jim Randle, the creator of the creature, said that it's headed for the hotel, then *that's where it's going to be!*"

"All right. But I can only deploy a partial team. You saw it yourself; most of our transport vehicles were destroyed in the fire." His tone turned more serious. "And you're absolutely certain that this thing has targeted the VP?"

"No doubt in my mind."

"I already have a pair of choppers on the way. Let me see what else I can do." With that, Garr disconnected.

With one hand on the steering wheel, Scott dialed another person on his contact list.

"Izzy," he blurted when she picked up.

"What's going on, Detective? Where are you? No one around here knows what the . . ."

"Just listen, Izzy. Call the chief and tell him to get every unit he has over to the Emperor Hotel, pronto." He started to hang up, but then added, "Oh, and one more thing. Tell the chief to contact the Secret Service at the hotel and tell them not to let the VP speak this morning."

"What reason should the chief give them?" she asked.

"He's so full of crap he'll think of something."

"No, seriously."

He rolled his eyes. "Okay, how about this? That a genetically engineered monstrosity has targeted the vice president for extermination and is waiting to rip him to pieces when he speaks at ten o'clock."

"You're right," Izzy said. "I'm sure he'll think of something. Wait, ten o'clock? Do you realize what time it is?"

"I'm afraid I do."

CHAPTER 25

THE EMPEROR

Being the only unit in the vicinity of the Emperor Hotel, Big Larry and Tiny were the first officers to arrive at the scene. The big man entered the lavish foyer with his adrenaline raging and glee in his eyes.

In the back of his mind, Larry knew he didn't deserve the fame that the local media had bestowed upon him. Every staged photo op, every envious smile cast his way had started to feel like a farce. He was no super cop. Truth be told, he was probably less deserving of the title than many of his fellow officers. And that had left an emptiness in his gut that he could no longer bear.

But that was about to change. Today man and myth were going to merge in one heroic act. He was about to singlehandedly save the vice president of the United States.

Larry shoved his way through the crowded lobby, a submachine gun in one hand and a Benelli shotgun in the other. He noted that everyone seemed calm, save for the occasional protestor waving a sign. The creature had yet to make an appearance.

He grinned. *I'm just in time.*

Tiny glanced up at Larry as he eagerly pushed through the crowd. "Hey, Larry, we're the first ones here. Shouldn't we be waiting for backup?" He nervously glanced around. "This isn't just a local pickpocket we're chasing down."

"Not today," the big man grunted. "That thing's going

down." He raised his shotgun. "I'm going to shove this into that thing's pie hole and pull the trigger."

"Right." Tiny grinned, then his expression dropped into a frown. "Wait—you're not serious, are you?"

"As a heart attack, brother."

Larry shoved his huge frame through the arched entryway. Consisting of eight stories, the vast atrium was breathtaking in its sense of scale and opulence. An ornate iron railing lined the open corridor on each level, passing doors and spacious windows that faced the atrium.

But what made the atrium exceptional in every sense of the word was its main attraction. Nearly filling the ground floor was an oval-shaped fountain, 70 feet wide and 120 feet long. Surrounding the fountain was a three-and-a-half-foot tall marble wall which supported evenly spaced Corinthian columns, oversized roman torches, and nooks for towering palm trees that arced over the water. Inside the fountain were elaborate water features, none of which were more impressive than the 70-foot-tall waterfall that appeared to spill from the domed skylight and cascade into the fountain below.

Embedded in the top of the limestone that supported the waterfall was an illuminated crowned "E" that glowed beneath the gushing waters.

But the spectacle didn't end with the waterfall. Where the cascading water thundered down into the fountain was a huge white-bronze sculpture of Alexander the Great poised in a horse-drawn chariot. His drawn sword in one hand and the reins clutched in the other, the ancient emperor and his team of four steeds seemed to be frozen in time, right down to the jets spraying water up from the horses' galloping hooves.

Big Larry lifted his gaze four stories up. His eyes followed a long catwalk that crossed in front of the waterfall and connected the east and west corridors on the fourth floor. In the center of the catwalk and just in front of the waterfall was a viewing area that looked out over the fountain. And it was there, behind the empty podium, that the vice president was scheduled to speak.

Tiny looked around the huge atrium with wide eyes. "Gee, I wonder what the rooms in this place go for a night?"

Big Larry didn't respond, just shifted his gaze downward and scanned the growing crowd. He studied how onlookers and members of the media alike filled the area in front of the fountain and the oval walkway that surrounded it. Among them were clusters of protestors waving hand-painted signs. Most of the spectators were confined to the ground floor, but those who had evaded security were sprinkled along the railed corridors of the second and third floors.

He rested the barrel of his shotgun across his shoulder and completed another sweep of the crowd.

"That little dingleberry better be right," he muttered.

~ ~ ~

In the west wing penthouse suite, Vice President Sullivan took a final glance in the mirror before making his way to the speaking area. He only awaited confirmation from Agent Brown that the six Secret Service men were collected outside and ready to head out. *How ironic that the hot topic of the day is gun violence,* he thought.

He picked up his lucky leather notebook from the bureau. It was like an old trusted friend that had accompanied him on every speech since he was the governor of Minnesota. Besides, being a gift from his wife, she was always watching to make sure he had it with him.

The door cracked open.

But instead of giving him the nod, Agent Brown entered the room. "There's been an assassination threat." The young agent spoke with a stern demeanor.

Sullivan chuckled. "You mean like last week in Atlanta,

and the week before in New York?"

"No, this isn't just another disruptor," Agent Brown said. "The call came from the OPD police chief. He insists that you don't leave the room."

"For how long?"

"He didn't specify. He just said he had deployed numerous officers to secure the hotel."

Sullivan looked at his watch: 9:55.

"I asked the hotel manager to have a word with the crowd. He's at the podium now. He should be able to hold them over until OPD arrives with more intel so we can fully assess the threat."

"Okay." The VP sighed. He returned his lucky booklet to the bureau and sat on the edge of the bed, careful not to wrinkle his suit.

~~~

Back on the crowded ground floor, Big Larry looked up at the catwalk, to the man who had just stepped up to the podium. He wore a black business suit and a gold silk shirt with no tie. The light spilling in through the domed skylight glittered off of his shaved head as the towering waterfall cascaded behind him.

Introducing himself as Jesse Mannings, the hotel manager, he went on about the Emperor's many attributes, such as the room count and the waterpark-like pool out back.

Big Larry looked at his watch: 9:59. He noted there were still no Secret Service agents on either side of the catwalk. *Good*, he thought. *Someone must have tipped off the vice president.*

Tiny looked up at Larry. "Do you think the VP's coming out?"

"No. Looks like they've got him under wraps. That's why they've got that schmuck up there stalling."

From his lofty perch, the manager carried on with his sales-pitchy diversion, the waterfall thundering just behind him. With a stroke of his hand, he gestured to the fountain below. "And before you, we have a breathtaking rendition of one of the most renowned emperors of all time, Alexander the Great. Reaching over thirty feet in length and taking six painstaking years to create, this masterpiece . . ."

Whoosh! Something swept out of the cascading water behind the speaker. It happened so fast that Larry questioned if he had seen anything at all.

The man opened his mouth, but no sound came out. And a red line appeared across his throat. He took a step away from the podium, staggered again. And then his head rolled forward from his body, bounced off of the guard rail, and splashed into the fountain below. His headless body then followed suit, falling forward over the rail and twirling through the air until it came to a rest across the back of one of the bronze stallions. Blood gushed from the severed neck and flowed down the horse's white flank and into the water.

The crowd erupted into horrified shouts and screams. And then they all fell silent as every eye rose back up to the catwalk. The creature stepped out from the cascading waterfall and onto the speaking platform. Its clawed hands spread outwards as if expecting a well-deserved applause. The Medusa mane swept backward, revealing the burning eyes and a massive maw full of interlocking teeth.

A swift backhand transformed the podium into spiraling fragments of wood that tumbled into the water. And then the beast crouched forward and unleashed a roar that rang through the atrium like a thousand trumpets from hell.

Some aimed their phones up at the catwalk while others screamed and ran, bumping into one another. All the while, the gruesome head oscillated as if searching the crowd below.

~~~

The beast stepped closer to the rail while staring down at the scrambling guests. Every time someone with gray hair looked up in its direction, the creature scanned their face for a match. The animal's attention turned toward a group of six racing along the third-level corridor, searching for his target.

Then, through its ample peripheral vision, the beast saw a security guard step onto the catwalk with his sidearm drawn. The monster turned its gruesome head and locked eyes with him. The portly security worker eased back off of the catwalk and ran in the opposite direction. The creature then returned its focus to the crowd below.

~~~

Big Larry saw the creature look in his direction. *Showtime,* he thought. *Just keep the cameras rolling.* A surge of adrenaline shot through his body and seemed to terminate where his fingers curled around the shotgun stock in his right hand.

He recalled being forced from the NFL, the pain and humiliation of having his stardom plucked away. In a single instant, the stadium lights that shone so brightly upon him had been blotted out. And then he joined the OPD. Sure, they treated him like a star, with the occasional accolade. But it wasn't even close to what he'd tasted before–at least not until today. Staring at the monstrosity, Larry truly felt no fear. His entire life was about to culminate in this one great moment.

Throwing the strap of the machine gun across his left shoulder, the big man raised the shotgun. He aimed it at the creature on the catwalk, and then lowered it.

"I've got to get closer," he hollered above the chaos.

Tiny glanced at him. "You can't be serious."

But Big Larry's adrenaline had taken the wheel. "Open the back doors, and help get these people outta here," he shouted to Tiny. Larry then waded through the crowd, toward the elevators in the lobby. He had to get to the catwalk before backup arrived.

~~~

Passing a pair of columns supporting the Emperor Hotel logo, Detective Pine pulled into the parking lot at the same time as Officer Jones. He skidded to a stop beside a Channel 8 news van as the officer took the spot beside him.

Emerging from the old Ford, Scott opened the back door and lifted the M4 Carbine assault rifle from its case. He pulled an extra pair of grenades from the case and slipped them into a pants pocket. Scott then clicked open the grenade launcher to make sure the chamber was loaded.

Good to go.

Officer Jones approached him, staring at the imposing weapon. "Wow. Where did you get that? That's definitely not standard issue." He indicated the grenade launcher on the bottom of the barrel. "You know how to use that beast?"

"I've got the gist of it. Jim Randle had this at his lab. He gave me a quick tutorial over the phone while I was enroute."

They jogged toward a flight of marble stairs. Atop the steps was an entry lined with towering columns like the Pantheon in Rome. Passing a pair of bronze Roman guards flanking the steps, Officer Jones said, "So it's targeted the VP, huh?"

"And the creature is either en route or already here." Scott grunted as he sprinted up the steps, Jones keeping pace just behind him.

The bronze doors flew open behind the columns, and people spilled out onto the stairs as screams echoed from inside.

"I'm going with the second scenario," Jones muttered.

Rushing into the foyer, Scott and the officer ducked and dodged their way through clusters of frantic fleeing patrons. A screaming woman bumped the detective, nearly knocking the

M4 from his hands.

Scott passed the shiny metal doors of the elevators as they sprang open and seemingly belched people into the foyer. Pushing deeper into the crowd, the two men stepped beneath the archway and into the atrium.

Keeping a tight grip on the huge firearm, Scott absorbed the madness. People were scurrying everywhere as screams and cries echoed through the atrium. Nearby, a group of protestors were ducked behind the short wall surrounding the fountain. Before them, a massive sculpture of a horse-drawn chariot was seemingly charging through the water. Scott then caught sight of the headless corpse draped over one of the four white horses.

Looking straight up from the corpse, he saw the star of the show. The mane flailing around its horrible head, the monster was peering over the rail and searching the crowd below.

It looks like it hasn't found the VP, Scott thought. *At least not yet.*

Nearby, a young protestor with a green man-bun peered out from behind a sign that read, *Guns Kill People.* He glared up at Officer Jones. "Shoot the friggin thing!"

Officer Jones held up his assault rifle. "With this evil thing?"

"I've got it." Scott raised his weapon and took aim. To the right of the creature, he saw Big Larry running along the fourth-floor corridor toward the catwalk. "What does he think he's doing?" He looked at Jones, who shrugged.

Scott realigned the sights on the M4. With the creature being four stories up, he knew his accuracy with the unfamiliar weapon would be questionable.

He squinted down the barrel. "Come on, baby."

The instant Scott squeezed the trigger, he knew his aim was off. The grenade soared well above the intended target and erupted high on the waterfall. The top section of the rock supporting the huge water feature folded backward and fell into the water below with a colossal splash that sprayed over the crowd.

The creature glanced back at the missing section of waterfall and then looked directly at Scott.

"Reload now, and do it quickly!" Jones shouted.

But it was too late. The moment Scott reached into his pocket for another grenade, the animal leapt from the catwalk. It soared through the air, over the bronze representation of Alexander's horse-drawn chariot, and landed on top of the marble wall surrounding the fountain, its clawed toes curled over the edge.

A guttural growl rose above the screams. And the beast vaulted over the protesters cowering behind the wall and landed with a thud in front of Scott and the officer. Simultaneously, it swatted the officer's rifle away. The animal then snatched Officer Jones by the vest and tossed him over its shoulder, sending him somersaulting until he splashed into the massive pool of water.

Inserting another grenade in place beneath the barrel of the M4, the detective swung the weapon toward the creature until *whap!* A swat from the beast knocked the weapon from Scott's hands, sending it sliding through the doorway and into the foyer.

But its blazing eyes remained on Scott for a beat or two, then it turned its gaze from the detective and plucked a middle-aged man from the crowd. Clutching the gray-haired man by the throat, the animal studied his face closely.

Then the beast flung the man backward, where he pinged into a bronze horse and tumbled into the water.

Scott couldn't believe his eyes. *It's as if it's looking for the vice president.*

However, the distraction allowed Scott enough time to

make a break for it. The detective raced into the foyer and spotted his weapon lying on the marble forty feet away, near the front doors.

His eyes darted to the open elevator off to his left. Should he take refuge in the elevator, or did he have time to make it to the gun?

A loud snort from behind. And Scott darted into the elevator, picked the second-floor button, and then repeatedly tapped the button to close the door.

It seemed to take forever, but finally the doors closed.

Did it see me come in here?

Wham! The elevator shook, supplying the answer.

~~~

Officer Jones awakened to the horror of cool water flooding his nasal cavity. A pair of Koi fish fluttered away from him as he broke the surface, gasping and choking. Catching his breath, he discovered that he was near the headless corpse that was sprawled across one of the sculpted horses. Blood draining down from the sculpture billowed in the water surrounding him. Another man with silver hair floated nearby.

Diving away from the crimson haze, the officer swam to the side of the fountain and climbed out. He spotted his assault rifle lying near a wall and snatched it up, water draining from his uniform. Still panting heavily, he searched the crowd for the detective.

Then he heard the horrible pounding coming from the foyer.

CHAPTER 26

THE WAR

Wham! Another hit created a dent on the inside of the left elevator door. The detective frantically pressed the second-floor button, but the beast had beaten the doors so severely that the elevator was jammed on the ground floor.

The next thud buckled the left door inward, creating a gap of daylight between the doors. Scott was running low on options. He looked up at the access door in the ceiling. He leapt for it, but it was too high for him to reach.

Wham! Another blow caused the right door to crease, and a disgruntled growl reverberated throughout his tight confinement. A red eye and several interlocked teeth appeared in the gap between the doors. A series of clawed fingers slid into the gap and curled around the steel.

A loud snort, and the doors started to separate.

Shots rang out, with one round pinging off the door. Another bullet shot in between the doors and struck the wall near Scott's head. Between the gunfire, he heard the clawed feet scratching on the marble floor. There was a thud, and then the gunfire was replaced by horrified screams. The symphony of screams and cries moved farther away until they seemed to be coming from somewhere inside the atrium.

Placing his fingers between the gap, the detective separated the mangled doors just enough to squeeze his small body through. Stepping into the foyer, he saw a smoking machine gun and a large officer sprawled on the floor behind it. There was only one officer who could be that size.

Scott knelt down beside Big Larry to find the chest plate in his vest buckled inward with a red gash in its center. The pool of blood swelling on the tile beneath his back suggested the wound went all the way through.

He lifted his head from the floor and winked at Scott. "Hey, dingleberry . . . off that thing for me, huh?" He raised his hand to fist-bump the detective. But before their knuckles could meet, blood spat from Larry's lips and his big mitt fell to the tile.

"Roger that," Scott said, and closed Larry's gazing eyes. Rising from beside the slain officer, he hustled toward his M4 Carbine lying just inside the entry doors.

The huge firearm in hand, Scott trotted through the arched entryway to the atrium and back into the chaos. His head spun trying to take it all in. On the higher floors, patrons were emerging from their rooms and collecting in the corridors to see what was going on. A security guard tried in vain to coax them back into their rooms. People in various stages of dress now lined the catwalk and were peering down to the madness below.

Officer Jones ran up to Scott, dripping water.

"You okay?" the detective asked him.

Jones nodded. "Yeah, once I caught my breath."

Turning his gaze from the officer, Scott searched the frantic crowd collected along the walkway surrounding the fountain. "Where is it?"

"You can't see it from here." Jones took in a deep breath, let it out. "The sculpture's blocking your view, but it's on the right side of the fountain."

Looking down from where people on the upper corridors were pointing, Scott caught glimpses of the gray form between the bronze horses. Clutching the weapon, he shoved his way through the crowd. His five-foot-seven height was definitely not an advantage in a situation like this.

Looking between two sculpted horses, he saw Tiny on the north end of the atrium guiding people in the crowded hallway toward the rear doors.

Scott reached the stone wall surrounding the fountain. Moving past a column, he could now see the beast standing in the hallway as people stumbled over one another in an attempt to flee from its path. Snatching another gray-haired man by the neck, the beast glanced at his face and flung him back into the crowd; the unfortunate soul was trampled by those racing past.

"What now?" Jones hollered. "It's too crowded to use your weapon."

Scott knew he was right. He had to get closer and find a way to lure it from the crowd.

There was a loud crash of glass from the far side of the hallway. And people rushing toward the rear exits stopped, gawking forward. A woman screamed. And Scott saw Tiny racing down the hallway and waving people back. The portly officer flung his body on top of the short stone wall, and like a walrus sliding across an ice bank on its underbelly, Tiny slid over the top of the wall and splashed into the fountain. More people followed Tiny into the fountain, while others pressed their backs tight against the outside wall as if to clear the hallway.

Scott couldn't believe what he saw next—a gorilla was charging down the hallway toward the monster's turned back. *I cannot be seeing that.* He shook his head to clear his mind, looked again. *I'm definitely seeing that.* As the thundering primate drew nearer, he realized it was absolutely enormous.

"My God," Jones gasped. "That's Goliath from Orlando Zoo. How in the—"

"Everyone get down!" Scott shouted.

Leaping up from its hind legs, the massive ape slammed

into the creature's back, sending it chest-first into a wall and crashing partially through it. Tumbling through the demolished wall, the creature's mane flailed about as it turned its horrible head to see what had hit him. The beast definitely hadn't seen that one coming.

Goliath thrust his arms around the monster's chest and locked his grip, squeezing with everything he had. As big as the monster was, Scott could see that the giant gorilla had at least a hundred pounds on his adversary.

The creature thrust its head backward, into the gorilla's snout. But the massive ape merely snorted and held its mighty grip. So the monster lifted its clawed feet up onto the wall and sprang off of it, sending the two combatants rolling across the marble floor. People scattered before the tangle of gnarled skin and fur, but those not quick enough stumbled and fell beneath the rolling beasts.

Finally breaking the gorilla's grip, the abomination of nature rose onto its hind legs and spread its arms wide. The giant ape stood upright as well and snorted. As the two titans squared off, people still trying to get away rolled over the marble wall and into the fountain, wading backward through the bloody water. Others who were injured were forced to watch from the floor.

~~~

Inside a ground-floor room, an Italian woman wrapped in a towel screamed at her husband. "Franco, don't be such a *vigliacco*. Go out there and see what's going on." With that, Maria shoved him toward the door.

He turned to her with his arms out. "Okay, you want me to go out, I go out." He threw a hand up at her. "Just for you."

Franco angrily swung open the door and stormed into the hallway. Looking straight ahead, he saw people backing frantically through the chest-deep waters of the fountain.

Every face was pale with horror as they all seemed to be looking to either side of him.

Franco turned to his left and his gaze was met by a 525-pound gorilla with its nostrils flared. But the huge animal didn't seem to be staring at him, but rather behind him. Turning around Franco's view got even worse. The nightmarish form snapped its horrific jaws, and a guttural growl reverberated through the hallway.

Franco gingerly stepped back into his room and closed the door behind him.

His wife raced up to him. "So tell me, what did you see?"

"No way will you believe me."

~~~

Staring down its opponent, the creature turned its hands, and a long saber protruded from the top of each forearm. The gorilla snorted and snarled at the beast's imposing weaponry.

The monster then cocked its wrists and retracted the blades as if to say, *"I'll take care of you hand-to-hand."*

"Wow," Jones said to Scott. "This dude throws old school."

Wham! The creature backhanded a column that reached up from the wall of the fountain, sending cracks racing through the white marble. The gorilla looked up curiously at the towering stone structure as the beast pushed it from behind with both hands.

Apparently getting the gist of what was happening as the tower of stone fell in his direction, Goliath caught the crumbling column and shoved it aside so it came crashing down onto the walkway. Chunks of marble spewed out across the floor, pelting the ankles and legs of those nearby.

Turning away from the downed column, the enraged primate lowered its head and charged the creature on all fours. As the galloping ape drew nearer, the monster stepped aside, latched on to the animal's shoulder, and veered it into a wall.

~ ~ ~

Maria screamed when the huge gorilla came crashing through the wall and rolled onto her bed, smashing it flat against the floor. Shaking the rubble from its head, the ape rose onto all fours.

An angry snort at Maria, and the huge primate charged through the massive hole in the wall.

Frank threw his hands out. "Ah, so now you believe me?"

~ ~ ~

Back in the hallway, the creature crouched low when Goliath emerged from the crumbled wall. The animal's jet-black fur was now peppered with gray patches of drywall dust as it took notice of a sculpture beside the room door.

Snatching up the marble Roman soldier by the legs, Goliath snarled at the monster as if to say, *"Two can play that game."* Then twirling around once in the hallway, the giant gorilla swung the sculpture at the beast.

The monster ducked as the statue glazed its armored back and smashed into another column in a shower of marble. The column buckled and, like a giant redwood, fell into the fountain, sending out a spray of water that reached over the wall and into the hallway.

"Oh crap!" Scott ducked behind the wall, cradling the weapon as water sprayed over his head. Slinging the wet hair from his eyes, he stood fully and trained the M4 Carbine on the battle.

Goliath roared, then thrust its mitts around the monster's neck, pressing it back against the wall of the fountain with its tremendous weight. The snake-like mane writhed wildly on the creature's head, slashing and gouging at the gorilla's eyes. But Goliath pulled his face back from the flailing mane and held his grip.

In an attempt to break the mighty chokehold, the beast shoved Goliath upward, and over the wall they both went, splashing into the fountain.

The monster thrust its body up from the water and unleashed a horrible roar as water cascaded from its pebbled skin. The huge primate stood upright, stretched its jaws, and answered the roar.

~~~

Like spectators in an ancient colosseum, those collected around the fountain and on every level above paused in the hallways and peered over the rail at the pair of gladiators below. Who could not watch this?

~~~

"It's in the fountain, away from the crowd," Officer Jones hollered to Scott. "Take the shot." However, the detective's view was blocked by the bronze horses. He squirmed his way through the crowd, trying to get a clear shot. But everyone remained frozen in place with their phones trained on the battle.

Goliath was the first to make a move.

The huge gorilla again lunged at the beast, catching it at the thighs with his massive shoulders like an NFL linebacker, and drove it into the fountain. Straddling the creature's chest, Goliath held the beast beneath the water with his full weight, then followed through with a right hook to the head. The ape again swung at the beast, but a clawed hand shot up from the water and caught his wrist.

Goliath roared, ripping his arm free, right before the creature's tremendous strength threw him aside and into the fountain.

The monster then lurched to its feet, water streaming from its gaping jaws.

Tumbling onto all fours, the enraged gorilla snorted and again sprang from the water at its adversary. But the creature turned with the finesse of a toreador, planted its claws in the gorilla's back as it rushed by, and hurled it headfirst into one of the sculpted horses. A loud clang of metal, and the ape withdrew its head from the huge indentation in the bronze flank.

Shaking off the blow, Goliath turned for the creature. But no sooner had he laid eyes on his opponent than the monster sprang up from the water and landed atop one of the sculpted steeds behind him.

From its tall perch, the beast taunted the huge ape to attack.

Goliath thumped his chest and charged through the fountain. But when he splashed closer, the beast leapt from the sculpture, soared over the gorilla's head, and came down behind him with a clawed hand across Goliath's face that slammed him into the fountain.

The giants rolled and tumbled beneath the water, sending out a wave that slapped the sculpted horses and sprayed over the chariot. All the while, large swells rolled in the opposite direction and spilled over the fountain wall, splashing onlookers and leaving Koi fluttering across the wet walkway.

Recovering from the passing wave, Scott wiped the water from his face and aimed the weapon over the wall.

A beat later, the gorilla jutted up from the fountain and roared, three claw marks running the length of his face. The monster too rose from the turbulent water and again squared off with the gorilla. Goliath was panting heavily now as water beaded down his matted fur. He slogged around to one side of the beast as if searching for the moment to strike.

The clawed fingers curled enticingly, motioning the ape closer. The creature then let out a raspy hiss that seemed to enrage the gorilla all the more.

Goliath swung for the creature's jaw but missed and ended up with his hand in the monster's mouth. He grabbed hold of one of the long fangs and pulled with his full strength, in an apparent effort to dislodge the creature's jaw.

The primate might have realized his mistake, but not until the jagged jaws slammed shut and he withdrew a hand minus four digits. The confused gorilla looked down in dismay at the blood pulsing from his right hand.

He should have been looking up.

The beast twirled around with a spinning backfist to the ape's jaw that sprinkled his teeth and fragments of bone across the fountain. Blood gushed from the void in the gorilla's face, spilling down onto his chest. The brown eyes shone with the realization of making a grave mistake; it had never encountered a creature such as this.

Still, the dazed animal instinctively drew its fist back. And *splat!* The beast sank its claws into the top of the ape's skull, and to the sound of bone snapping and skin tearing, the monster pulled its hands apart and ripped the gorilla's head in half.

Then for good measure, or just because it could, the beast whirled its right arm upward with the blade fully extended and opened the headless ape up from belly to throat. Like a serpent fleeing from its lair, a knotted section of intestine slithered from the huge wound and splashed into the water below.

The huge primate teetered, dead on its feet until the monster picked it up and held it overhead with a victorious roar that echoed through the atrium. Blood from the butchered primate drained down onto the beast, bathing its gnarled hide in a crimson glaze.

Another roar, and the creature hurled the huge carcass over the sculpted horses and into the water. Floating on the surface for a moment, the bleeding remains rolled over and were sucked downward and against the powerful pumps that forced water up through the fountain.

A beat later, a pink line shot down through the waterfall and then the cascading water turned completely red.

~ ~ ~

Bracing his elbow on the wall of the fountain, Scott trained the M4 Carbine on the creature's back. "Come on, look at me."

"Take the shot," Jones practically screeched. "It's still in the open."

"I can't shoot it in the back." He steadied the weapon.

"That's not friggin Jesse James," the officer blurted. "Just shoot."

"No. There's a weak spot in its abdomen," Scott told him. "It's the only way to take it out. I have to wait for it to turn around."

~ ~ ~

With its troublesome adversary eliminated, the beast refocused on its mission. It sprang from the water and again landed atop of one of the bronze steeds for a better view of its surroundings. Bathed in the primate's warm blood, the monster examined those still scurrying along the walkway around the fountain.

~ ~ ~

The sights of the imposing weapon remained on the hideous form balancing on the sculpture. Its crimson-stained hide glittered in the radiance of the skylight while the waterfall of blood cascading behind the beast supplied the perfect backdrop to the hellish scene.

Scott's finger rested on the trigger. "Come on, look this way," he whispered.

The atrium grew dark to a thundering from above as a helicopter passed over the domed skylight. The creature looked up, and its gaze followed the sound of the passing aircraft. The unexpected flyover had distracted the detective as well.

"Shoot it!" Officer Jones roared.

Before Scott could realign his sights, the beast leapt from the sculpture—up to the second floor corridor and latched on to the guardrail. Pulling its feet up to the rail, the animal then jumped up to the third-floor railing and climbed over it, to where it had apparently seen someone who resembled its target on the walkway.

Again, the monster seemed dissatisfied with his catch. It tossed the man over the rail, and he plummeted for three floors, screaming all the way until he splashed into the fountain.

Scott watched the beast scan the fleeing crowd on the eastern third-floor corridor. Turning his gaze to the west side of the atrium, the detective looked up along the open walkways on each floor until he saw the men in gray suits gathered protectively outside a door on the eighth floor.

The VP is still in there. Hearing a light thumping above, the detective realized the Air Force chopper had landed on the roof.

A door flew open near the eighth-floor elevator, and a heavily armed soldier stepped out onto the corridor. He moved swiftly toward where the agents were collected outside what must have been the vice president's room.

Thank God, Scott thought. *Colonel Garr came through. Looks like they'll be able to get the VP to the chopper just in time.*

"Look." Officer Jones pointed up to the soldier trotting

along the eighth-floor corridor. "Looks like the Air Force has it covered. They're going to evac the VP outta here."

The presumed safety of the VP made Scott breathe a little easier, but his pounding heart had yet to let up. He knew the creature still had to be stopped.

Turning around, Scott saw numerous police officers pouring from the foyer and into the atrium.

Officer Jones turned to Scott. "So, what's your next move, Detective?"

"It's only a matter of time until the creature figures this out." Scott looked up along the eighth-floor corridor, to the door that led to the roof. "When he does, I'm going to be there waiting for him."

CHAPTER 27

MOVING TARGET

Vice President Sullivan paced the spacious penthouse suite anxiously, his leather binder gripped firmly in his hand. Every curtain was drawn. The three agents in the room remained silent, but their eyes spoke volumes as they listened to the muffled screams coming from outside.

Was it his imagination, or were the cries no longer limited to the ground floor, but rather moving up to the higher corridors? *And what the agents claimed to have seen in the fountain below . . . that can't be real. This is Orlando. It must be some kind of stunt from one of the theme parks.* Sullivan battled with the thoughts running through his mind.

Whap! There was a loud knock on the door that made everyone jump.

One of the agents from outside cracked the door open. "There's a soldier out here, says he's here for the VP."

Stepping away from Sullivan, Agent Brown opened the door to reveal a thick, square-jawed specimen who looked like he'd just leapt off of an Air Force recruitment poster. He wore full combat gear, an AK-47 across his chest, and steel in his eyes. "I'm Sergeant Hancock with the US Air Force. I'm here to escort the vice president to the rooftop where we have an HH-60 Pave Hawk waiting for him."

Agent Brown was reluctant. "Not so fast, soldier."

"Look," the sergeant snapped back. "There's something headed this way that you are not prepared to handle. The only option is to evac VP Sullivan out of here now." He gestured the assault rifle in his hands. "So stand down. I've got it from here."

Agent Brown didn't budge.

"This isn't a debate," the sergeant barked. "The vice president is coming with me *now*." He extended a hand toward Sullivan. "Let's go, sir."

"It's okay, Agent Brown." Sullivan stepped forward. "I'm in good hands."

Agent Brown reluctantly moved from the doorway and let the politician pass. As Sergeant Hancock took him by the arm, Agent Brown jogged to catch up to them. "Wait. I'm coming with him."

Sergeant Hancock planted a hand on the agent's chest. "No, you're not. I'm afraid there's only room on the chopper for the VP." He then nodded toward the others. "I advise that you and your men use the stairs and evacuate this building ASAP."

Brown and his fellow agents shared a look as the soldier swiftly ushered the vice president along the corridor.

~~~

Wham! The monster burst through another door, frantically surveying the area, searching for its target, needing to complete its mission. It had been distracted by the gorilla. Instead of finishing the ape off quickly, something had compelled the creature to engage the gorilla without using its full weaponry. It was a strange sense of fair play that it did not understand.

The beast scoured the room for the man it had seen through the window. Tossing a bed aside, it saw a silver-haired gentleman in his late sixties cowering in a corner. Adorned in white boxers, he lifted his terror-filled face.

It was not the target.

A feisty brunette half the man's age shot out from another doorway. Her black robe flapping, she wielded a golf club with both hands. "Leave him alone," she hollered and took a swing at certain death.

Snatching her by the hair, the beast tossed her through an exterior window in an eruption of glass. The silk robe flailing around her, she screamed and twisted for four stories until she thudded into the empty bed of a pickup truck in the parking lot.

Wham! A thrust of its clubbed fist, and the beast burst through the wall and entered the adjoining room.

Empty. Nothing but an open suitcase and clothes strewn across the floor.

The creature's frustration grew. While it was wasting time battling the gorilla, had its target gotten away? The beast snorted in rage. It was feeling the first traces of regret, another strange sensation that it had never known before.

Raising a clawed foot, the monster kicked open the front door, sending it tumbling across the walkway and over the rail. Stepping out onto the corridor, a look in each direction showed that the long hallway that arced around the atrium was void of life as well. The creature climbed over the rail and looked up to the fifth floor.

~~~

Heading along the eighth-floor corridor, Vice President Sullivan's right arm grew numb under the soldier's firm grip. *Does he think he's dragging some thug to the stockade, or escorting the vice president of the United States?*"Sergeant, could you loosen up on the grip?" But the sergeant only pulled him along faster.

~~~

Tugging the vice president swiftly along the walkway,

Sergeant Hancock paused for a look over the rail. *Where are you?* There, beyond the crimson waterfall, on the opposite side of the atrium, he saw the creature leap up to the fifth floor corridor and catch onto the guardrail. But the animal had its back to them.

"There it is," the sergeant said and fired across the atrium at the beast. Several rounds struck the armored back, and the animal turned and looked directly at them.

Hancock pulled the VP to the rail. "Look at it."

Sullivan turned to face the atrium, and the creature locked eyes with him. The red orbs seemed to brighten as the serpentine mane writhed frantically on its head.

"Oh my God," the vice president gasped. "This is for real."

The monster dove backward off the fifth-floor railing, turned in mid-air, and landed on the long catwalk that connected the east side of the atrium to the west. But the tremendous impact from the animal's landing proved to be too much for the stretch of metal, and the catwalk buckled, sending the creature over the edge. Twirling through the air, the creature splashed into the fountain below.

Rushing up from the water, the monster looked up and roared in rage at its target as screams echoed from the ground floor.

"Sir, that's why we have to get you to the roof for evac," the sergeant said.

"Then why are we stopping?"

Shouldering his weapon, Hancock grabbed the VP by the arm and hurried along the walkway. Reaching the door to the stairwell, the soldier thrust it open and ushered Vice President Sullivan inside. He pointed to a flight of metal stairs that lead up to another door.

"Just follow the stairs to that door," he ordered. "It leads to the roof."

"You're not going with me?" Sullivan seemed alarmed.

"No sir. My orders are to stay here and guard the door."

Vice President Sullivan approached the stairs with reluctance. "But I don't hear a helicopter."

"Don't worry. It will be there," the soldier barked. "Now hurry."

A confused nod, and the vice president made his way up the stairs.

Confirming that the VP was on his way, Sergeant Hancock clicked open the metal door and returned to the corridor. "Falcon Two, the VP is on his way to the roof," he said into his head gear. Then, instead of guarding the door to the stairwell, the sergeant slipped open the door to the nearest suite. Once inside, he made his way to the window and peered discretely between the curtains to the outside walkway.

He slipped the AK-47 from his shoulder and drew comfort from the feel of the loaded weapon in his hands.

~~~

Vice President Sullivan ventured onto the roof and was met by emptiness. The gentle rustling of the treetops that peered above the ledge of the flat roof were an eerie contrast to the horrors inside the building. Off to his right was the domed skylight that projected up from the roof, and that was about it. Not a trace of a helicopter or even the sound of thumping rotor blades.

He tightened his grip on his lucky leather notebook as if trying to draw comfort from an old trusted friend. He took another glance over his shoulder and across the empty roof. "What the hell is going on?"

~~~

"Come on, come on." Detective Pine waited anxiously in the elevator as it rose at a painfully slow pace toward the eighth floor. The M4 Carbine was gripped tightly in his moist hands.

"Come on, come on, come on."

The number eight lit up with a ping. At that same moment, there was a jolt from outside. A jolt as if something of considerable size had just landed on the eighth-floor walkway.

Am I too late? he wondered. *Or was the jolt just from the elevator?*

He was about to find out.

The steel doors rumbled open.

The huge weapon leading the way, the detective stepped out onto the walkway to find that it was empty. Nothing on the rail or on the catwalk below. Even the screams on the ground floor had subsided. *Where did it go?* Stepping closer to the guardrail, he noticed that the far side of the catwalk was buckled. Had the creature fallen to the ground floor? If so, the delay would allow Scott enough time to get to the roof ahead of it.

Off to his left, a soldier guarded the door leading to the roof. The fact that the man was in one piece was a good sign. *The creature clearly hasn't been this way.*

Scott raced up to the soldier holding an AK-47 across his chest. "This is a restricted area," the towering man barked with a stern glare.

"But I have to get to the roof, before *it* comes." Scott held up the weapon. "I can stop it with this."

Sergeant Hancock eyed Scott's rifle. "That's an M4 Carbine with an under-barrel grenade launcher. Where did you get that?"

"Listen, soldier. I'm the lead detective on the case. So let me—"

Whap! The soldier butted Scott in the chest with his firearm, making him stumble backward. "This is a restricted area. No one goes up!"

Looking across the atrium, Scott noticed that every door leading to the roof was blocked by an armed guard.

"Okay, okay." His right hand raised, he backed away from the huge soldier. "I get it. You guys have it all under control." Moving around a corner beside the stairwell and out of the soldier's view, Scott tried the first bedroom door that he came to.

He was in luck. It was unlocked. Stepping inside and closing the door behind him, Scott approached a dresser that covered the south facing wall. Pulling the dresser clear from the wall, he stepped about ten feet back.

A click of the trigger on the grenade launcher, and an enormous explosion obliterated the wall. Chunks of rubble sprayed onto the bed and rolled across the carpet. As the smoke cleared, he retrieved the last grenade from his pocket and inserted it into the chamber beneath the barrel of the M4. Scott then stepped through the rubble and onto the landing in front of the stairwell that led up to the roof.

Clanking up the metal steps with renewed vigor, he heard a door swing open behind him. "This is a restricted area," Sergeant Hancock hollered. "Stand down!"

Scott turned around on the stairwell with the M4 pointed at the sergeant.

"Think again."

Keeping one eye on the soldier, Scott backed farther up the stairwell, toward the door. He glanced down to check his footing. And his eyes locked on a gash in the gray paint on the step. A glance back showed there were more claw marks leading to the door to the roof.

It's already up there, and this fool is guarding the door, Scott thought. *What is this?*

Scott looked at the soldier in disbelief, tempted to deploy his weapon. But this was his last grenade loaded in the chamber, and he was going to need it.

The detective turned around and *wham!* He kicked open the door and stepped out onto the roof with the M4 readied. A look to the right, and his legs turned to lead. He saw the creature's gnarled back outlined in the glaring sunlight. On the other side of the beast, the terrified vice president was backing toward the ledge as if ready to take the leap if the monstrosity drew much closer.

Every instinct demanded that Scott not make a sound, that he should ease back into the stairwell. *Wait for backup,* the voice told him. The face of every bully who'd harassed him as a boy flooded his mind as he reverted to the survival instincts of his youth.

This is it, he told himself. *You've got one shot. Just focus.*

He reached down beneath the barrel of the M4 to make sure he had loaded the last grenade, even though he knew darn well that he had.

Good to go. A dry swallow, and Scott aimed the weapon on the knotted back. "Come on and be a good doggie," he whispered. "Turn over and show me your belly."

The snake-like mane fluttered, and the monster slowly turned around to face the detective. The beast growled, and its foul breath swept over him. In the cold light of day, every tooth, claw, and protrusion in its gnarled hide seemed larger than life. The glowing eyes fixed on him. And it was as if every sin that man had ever committed had been forged into one entity and was staring at him through those eyes. Eyes that burned into his soul like the flames of hell.

Maybe you are from hell, Scott thought. *Our just reward for breaking boundaries that should have remained in place.*

The creature took another step and paused as if to study Scott. It was so close that he could see the vertical pupils in the blazing eyes.

And then Scott saw something more. There was a war raging in its mind. It was as if he were watching the human brain cells trying to seize control of the animal cells. For the first time, Scott realized he wasn't facing a mindless killing machine, but rather an animal held captive by a blood lust it didn't understand.

"You've gotten too smart," Scott whispered. "You're trying to make sense of it all."

Behind the black, slitted pupils, he saw a human sense of self-awareness.

The jagged teeth separated. And somewhere in the depths of a gurgling growl, Scott heard something truly unnerving. It was as if the beast were trying to form its feelings into discernable words. And it chilled Scott to the bone.

My God. You're trying to speak. He stared at the creature in shock. "You don't want to be here either . . . you know you don't belong."

The red eyes clamped shut. When they reopened, they were glistening in rage. It was as if the animal instincts had again seized control of its mind. The gnarled arms spread wide, and the razor-sharp talons fluttered with anticipation. The long teeth parted even more, and a guttural growl reverberated into Scott's chest.

The growl faded beneath a thumping that shook the entire building. The palm trees flailed violently as an HH-60 Pave Hawk Air Force helicopter rose from behind the ledge of the roof.

But Scott wouldn't allow himself to be distracted. He set his sights on the creature's abdomen.

His finger tensed on the trigger.

Just don't miss.

And that was when Scott noticed the red dot on his chest.

"Stand down, Detective," ordered a voice in a Texas

drawl. Looking up, Scott followed a red beam to a sniper's rifle trained on him from the aircraft's cargo bay doorway. Beside the sniper was Colonel Garr, holding a loudspeaker.

"Drop the weapon now!" Garr demanded.

And in a split second, it all flashed in Scott's mind's eye: the attempt to net the creature at the airfield instead of destroying it, then not ordering the soldier with the rocket launcher to take the shot as the beast fled into the woods. Garr had never intended to kill it. And now he was using the vice president as bait to lure the creature to the roof.

But why?

Inside the cargo bay, another soldier aimed a strange-looking gun on the creature's turned back. He fired. But instead of a round, a stream of purple foam spewed from the barrel, growing thicker as it neared the target.

Splatting onto the gnarled back, the substance bubbled and crawled over the creature like it had a mind of its own. The fast-hardening polyurethane foam then cured and locked onto the beast with a vise-like grip.

The creature turned to the chopper just as another splat of purple goo affixed its ankles together. But it ripped its feet apart before the foam could cure.

The animal twisted and ducked to avoid the onslaught. But the purple stream was unrelenting. The rushing foam zigzagged across the monster's chest as the beast tried to swat it away like a cat clawing at a stream of water. The spray then dropped down to the animal's knees, pasting them together. A frustrated roar, and the beast clawed the bubbling substance from its legs until another swipe of foam affixed its left hand to its thigh.

The red eyes locked on the vice president. The beast sprang forward but fell short of its mark when its bound knees brought it to the ground. Then like a rat half snared in a glue trap, the creature dragged its tangled body toward its target.

Vice President Sullivan backed to the ledge. He helplessly looked up at the helicopter, his gray hair dancing in the downdraft from the rotors. The beast again lurched at him, its saber poised for the kill.

Sullivan hollered in terror. At that same moment, a grappling hook tethered to a chain shot down from the helicopter and snared the writhing mane. The beast's head jerked backward, its right saber slicing the empty air as the animal was yanked to the ground. But before the creature could swipe the hook from its mane, another splat of bubbling goo pasted the grappling hook to its head and neck.

"Be careful," Colonel Garr ordered. "Don't cover the animal's face."

A second grappling hook shot down from the doorway and latched on to the monster's shoulder.

A disgruntled roar.

"Pull him up," the colonel barked. And the chains to the embedded hooks grew taut, lifting the creature upright and into the path of the purple spray.

The monster's head thrashed violently, cracking the foam around its neck as its jaws snapped and roared at the helicopter. Then another torrent of foam covered the beast's shoulders and head. The moment the angulating goo stopped bubbling, the unruly head froze in place.

The red dot still quivering on his chest, the detective watched as the writhing beast grew more obscure beneath the spraying foam. Only the creature's right arm continued to move freely, hacking and clawing at its growing cocoon.

And then *splat!* Another swath of foam secured the arm in place.

Still, Scott fingered the trigger of the M4, half expecting the beast to rip free at any moment.

But the colonel wasn't taking any chances this time. "Nets," he called through the loudspeaker. And the stream of purple foam ceased.

Next, a large net shot down from the cargo hold and draped over the purple ball as a pair of soldiers fast-lined down to the roof. Grabbing onto the Dyneema netting, which was ten times stronger than steel, the two men proceeded to work it around the encased creature as if the vice president weren't even there.

"On the double, men," the colonel barked.

Pulling the net taut, a soldier backed around the ball and *whack!* A clawed right hand ripped free from the foam, catching the man's arm and sending him spinning over the edge of the roof.

The remaining soldier reeled back from the beast as its free hand yanked the grappling hook from its shoulder. A horrible roar, and the monster drew its arm back to hurl the hook at the aircraft.

"Hit it!" the colonel hollered.

But before the beast could make the throw, another torrent of foam enveloped the hook and its free arm. Splatter from the purple goo splashed across Vice President Sullivan, who was cowering near the ledge.

~ ~ ~

Inside the cargo bay, the soldier wielding the foam gun gestured toward the vice president below and asked the colonel, "What about him, sir, Vice President Sullivan?"

"What about him?"

"Are we going to pick him up?"

Garr grunted, shook his head. "No, he's served his purpose. Just be sure not to block the creature's breathing. That thing has performed brilliantly." *Yes you did*, he thought as he watched the soldier gingerly work the net around the ball of foam. *Even better than General Willham had promised.* It had been the general, the man who had funded

Jim Randle's little science project, who had tipped him off when the beast first escaped.

"Just capture the animal alive, and you will possess a weapon like no other," General Willham had assured him.

And the general had been right. The creature was everything he'd promised and more.

~~~

Buffeted by the rotor wash, Scott continued to watch as the colonel barked orders from the aircraft. All the while, the red dot never moved from his chest.

"Button it up, soldier," Colonel Garr hollered through the loudspeaker. And the man reluctantly stretched the net around the purple cocoon and clipped its ends together. A bellowing roar from the beast, and the soldier wasted no time scurrying up the rope ladder and into the cargo bay.

With the net secured, the aircraft started to circle above the creature. The purple stream of foam again shot down from the doorway and wound around the beast like a spider encapsulating its prey. With the exception of the opening around its mouth, the beast completely disappeared within the ten-foot ball of foam. But the animal's jaw was apparently unobstructed because it was still roaring like hell.

The thumping rotors increased in tempo, and the chains to the grappling hooks grew taut. A parting salute from Colonel Garr, and the HH-60 Pave Hawk rolled back from the rooftop with the purple ball swaying below.

Bellowing roars echoed across the sky.

Resting the barrel of the weapon on his shoulder, Scott approached Vice President Sullivan, whose face and suit were covered in purple splotches. Panting and still clinging to his notebook, the silver-haired man turned his gaze from the aircraft.

"What in God's name was that?"

Scott glanced at the purple orb as it glided above the treetops. "I'm going to guess that's classified information." He gave the VP a wink. "Come on, sir, it looks like we'll have to take the stairs."

"As soon as I can." Sullivan grunted as he attempted to lift his right shoe from a glob of purple goo. Giving up the battle, he slipped his foot from the shoe and proceeded in his sock.

Heading back toward the stairwell, the door flew open, and Sergeant Hancock raced up to Vice President Sullivan, huffing and puffing. "Sir, are you okay?" he said with forged concern. "What happened up—"

Whap! Scott slammed the butt of his rifle into the soldier's forehead. The big man teetered backward for a few steps and thudded onto the roof, out cold.

"Why in the world did you do that?" the vice president asked, eyes wide.

"Trust me. You don't want to know."

~ ~ ~

A family of four sporting tacky, color-coordinated swimsuits froze while scaling the ladder to the towering Typhoon Mountain. The bikini-clad lifeguard atop the water slide took notice as well. More eyes turned up to the thundering rotors passing overhead and to the purple ball dangling beneath the craft.

Beyond the slide, patrons floating along the lazy river twisted in their tubes to get a clear view. Children splashing in shallow playgrounds grew still. Throughout the park, every sun-kissed cheek turned toward the sky as the roars coming from the swaying orb blared across the pools and curling slides.

On the beach, wide-brimmed hats and gaping eyes tilted upward from the shadow of the passing craft. Every phone turned to the sky. The helicopter and the ball in tow slowly faded into the distant blue as the HH-60 Pave Hawk continued west toward Tampa, in the direction of MacDill Air Force Base.

EPILOGUE

Six months later, infamous terrorist leader, Fehoda 'The Wolf' Bia-Malam, disappeared from his Afghanistan fortress under mysterious circumstances. The sole witness, a six-year-old boy, claimed a demon had come and taken him in the night.

FACTS STRANGER THAN FICTION

The First Abomination
In the early 1920s, the first US primate research center was established in Orange Park, Florida. One of the initial experiments of the facility was to inseminate a female chimpanzee with human semen from an undisclosed donor. According to the rumor, the experiment resulted in the first human-chimpanzee hybrid.

But was it more than just a rumor? According to psychologist Gordon Gallup, his former university professor had firsthand knowledge of the event. The professor worked at the Orange Park center in the 1920s and claimed that not only did the experiment occur, but the pregnancy went full term and resulted in a live birth. But after a few weeks, the moral and ethical weight of their creation became too much to bear, and the hybrid infant was euthanized.

Inserting Human Neurons Into Animals
Years before researchers in Kunming, China, inserted the human brain gene MCPH1 into rhesus monkeys, scientists at Yale University made an unnerving discovery of their own. In 2007, they fused human neural stem cells into five monkeys. The goal of the experiment was to see how the introduced cells would affect Parkinson's disease.

The results were promising in that the afflicted primates could walk, eat, and move much better than before. However, there was a side effect that the scientists hadn't expected. The human neural cells not only survived, but migrated in the monkey brains and changed the way their brains functioned.

Fortunately, they only used a small enough number of human cells that it didn't have a major effect on the animals' behaviors. At least not this time. Today, there seems to be little standing in the way of someone upping the ante and creating a more powerful and deadlier beast with a fully human brain.

My prayer is that the creature in *War Child* remains a work of fiction. But the way science continues to develop, that just may be too much to ask.

~~~

Don't miss Russ Elliott's bestselling
Vengeance from the Deep series

Pliosaur, book 1
Blood of the Necala, book 2
Isle of Blood, book 3

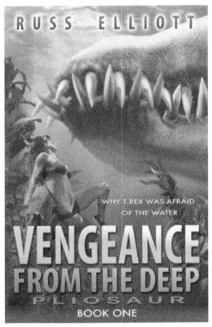

ACKNOWLEDGMENTS

Thanks to my wife Danielle for her love, understanding, and encouragement that helped me through this process.

ABOUT RUSS ELLIOTT

Growing up in a small town near Lynchburg, Virginia, one of Russ's earliest memories is standing at the front of his first-grade class with his vast collection of dinosaur figures. One by one, he would explain in great detail the various characteristics of each creature to the class. The seven-year-old's prehistoric presentation was so compelling that his teacher would then send him off to repeat it to every grade in the elementary school.

A move to Tampa, Florida, and nearly three decades later, Russ became an award-winning art director at a Palm Harbor advertising agency. Collecting over a dozen ADDY Awards for creative excellence (advertising's equivalent to the

Grammy), Russ later became intrigued with fiction writing. An accomplished painter and sculptor, he found that writing offered something new. It was a medium that could be easily shared. A good sculpture, for example, could only be truly appreciated when viewed in person, where one could walk around it and experience it in its world of light and shadows— an experience that could not be captured in a photograph, therefore not easily shared. But writing offered him something more; it allowed him to sculpt an image in the reader's mind. Someone on the other side of the globe could read a scene and experience the images just as the artist had intended. Russ still considers himself a sculptor, though . . . only now, instead of clay and plaster, he uses words.

So nearly a decade ago, when one of the original "dinosaur kids" decided to pen his first set of novels, it was no surprise that his subject matter would be the greatest prehistoric predator that ever lived.

Other past and present hobbies include motocross and flat track racing, performance cars and competitive bodybuilding. In addition, Russ has two patents to his name. He also creates the art for his book covers.

He now resides in Tampa, Florida, with his wife Danielle and his Doberman.

Made in the USA
Monee, IL
09 July 2022

99388277R00187